Best Wishes

Martine Lillycrop

Martine Lillycrop

High Tide in the City

First published in 2013
Published by Rite Stuff UK

Copyright © 2013 by Martine Lillycrop

All rights reserved. This book is sold subject to the condition that it shall not, by way of trade or otherwise, be lent, re-sold, hired out, or otherwise circulated, including electronically, without the publisher's prior consent. Any person who does any unauthorised act in relation to this publication may be liable to criminal prosecution and civil claims for damages

High Tide in the City

By
Martine Lillycrop

Martine Lillycrop

1

Always knew there was a chance I'd kill someone. It was bound to come down to it one day: me killing someone, someone killing me. When it finally happened, the penny came down in my favour. Can't say I'm sorry, though there's those who might wonder why, given this is me. There's some who've seen and done the things I've seen and done and come through it feeling nothing any more. So I always hoped I'd feel something, taking my first life.

As it happened, I did.

Couldn't have been happier deleting the fucker's ass.

*

Seem to remember it starting out on a night pretty much like any other. But back then, for me, most nights tended to be pretty much like any other. This one adopted the standard format - it was busy and it was raining.

Most cases are easy. Some, not so.

I already knew this wasn't one of the simple ones. I knew because when I swung my hydro-job into the car-port, the ambulances were already there but the sense of urgency wasn't.

This was my third call tonight - one rapist, one joy-riding senior citizen and now this. Which brings me to my job. What I do.

There's this Native American saying.

'Don't judge a man till you've walked a mile in his moccasins.'

These days that mile can get a person arrested. But it doesn't stop them. If you've never tried it, you might wonder why. You might wonder what makes someone want a digi-chemical cocktail injected straight into their brain.

They say it's for the experience - taking on a new persona, becoming someone else. Escaping themselves for a while. To an extent it's true, but often it's just for the needle. The cold, sharp stab at the base of the skull which gets colder and sharper as it goes deeper. Until your brain fills with stars like the universe has just been born inside your head and the endorphin rush hits, making you feel invincible. It fades as the squirt comes on. But some people do it, all of it, for those few seconds of feeling like God.

For others it's the surrender. Because you have to, to get it in you. It's impossible to upload a squirt yourself, get the needle just right so it goes in at the right angle, the right depth. Get it wrong, you're blind or a vegetable. Or dead. So someone else has to do it. Usually the same someone who just sold you your black-market fix.

Handing your life over to a stranger, a criminal - letting them do something to you a qualified doctor would baulk at - it demands something of you. Gets to be a thrill, that total surrender, that flirting with death or coma.

Just so you can *'Walk a mile in someone else's shoes'*.

That was the tagline, back when it all started. Everyone wanted it then and everyone did it. Until it was found to be addictive, caused brain tumours, then suddenly doing it was illegal.

Then the trouble started for real, and black-market squirts aren't clean - you can never be sure what you're getting. Dirty squirt. The users mostly come off badly and their victims, worse.

Rain greyed out the street lamps like vertical smoke, but it hadn't deterred the onlookers huddled outside the address. The night flickered white as two dozen data-cams strobed across me. Looked like someone had cashed in with a call to the Media Desk.

Media. I could almost read their minds: *Photo opportunity - some guy stepping out of a car.* They didn't know who I was, why I was there, but they had to have me. Just in case there was a tasty morsel waiting there to be plucked over.

I might even make it onto the morning download again.

At least I'd shaved. Mind, eight hours later is long enough to make it look like I hadn't bothered, but even so. Plus I always seem to miss that bit, just under the jaw - the bit the other guy never misses when he's throwing punches at it.

Fuck 'em, anyway. Wasn't like I had to keep Public Relations sweet these days. With any luck the black stubble and sour face'll keep me off the splash page. Ugly don't sell.

I heeled the door of my converted Ford shut, blinking at the after-image scored across my retinas. Turned my collar up against the downpour and glanced round for whoever was in charge.

They saw me first.

'Oh, for Christ's sake!'

The voice came from behind - what I call clean British, not the cut-glass type, just clean. Barely any accent. The whip-crack tone made me wince.

'Nixon. I forgot you worked nights.'

Yeah. Course you did.

I didn't need to see the face to know who was standing there. My shoulders tensed anyway. I breathed it out before turning.

Rain had given her panda eyes. It dripped off the bun she'd pulled her hair into, turned escaped strands into slick dark lace which clung to her cheeks. The coat she wore fell to just below her calves and a stream ran off the bottom like a Japanese waterfall.

'Need an umbrella?' I asked.

She rolled her eyes. 'My night's already turned to shit. And now they send you? Who did I piss off this time?'

I managed a grin. 'You look fantastic, by the way. Done something with your hair?'

She gave a sneer, but her bracer jangled before she could add anything. She flipped back the sleeve of her coat, turned away so the front fell open, showing me a tantalising glimpse of curvy figure beneath the fitted suit she wore. She twisted her wrist, so the screen lit her face, and gave the facia a brutal stabbing.

I sucked my teeth, feigning indifference while she answered.

Maybe I should explain. This was Lian. Detective Inspector Morrison. We used to be partners. Friends. More than friends. Before I got hooked. Before I got fired. Nothing like getting kicked off the Force for squirt addiction to turn a girl against you. But we'd been a team once. A good team.

Yeah, okay. Her approach and mine had always been different. Psychological profiling was her special skill, her strength. All very well for regular crims, but once we'd been assigned to the sparkling new Persona Task Force, all that extra schooling was pretty much redundant. Not according to her, though. I never understood why she didn't get it. How can you profile someone who's playing out a fantasy through another persona? Soon as the squirt dies off, they're different people - model citizens.

Me, I'd always gone for the suppliers. The sack-of-shit hard-asses who sold the squirts in the first place, after downloading them from some sad fuck arrogant enough to think other people wanted to be like them. So I went undercover. I entered that world. Did my best to turn it upside down.

I walked a lot of miles in that time, wore out a lot of different shoes. Closed down a few shoe-shops, too. Before it got out of hand.

I'd always known there was a price to pay - there usually is. But it was more than I'd counted on. Wasn't the first time I'd heard that excuse from a user.

Pretty pathetic when I heard it from me.

Lian finished her call and turned towards the taped-off apartment block. Colour washed over her, radiating down from an infrared hover-cam passing overhead. It warmed the pinched features for a second, brightened the street enough for me to pick out the vertical lines on her forehead, the ones which always appeared when she scowled.

I didn't need to ask what she was thinking. The crowd were still there, waiting in morbid anticipation.

Lian looked me up and down, disapproving. 'Got your kit?'

'Always.'

I strolled to the back of my car, opened the trunk and pulled out the aluminium briefcase holding my magic cap.

Cerebral Anomaly Projector. The CAP. Probably still warm from the last skull I'd put it on.

That familiar smell was drifting up from the exhaust. The smell you always got with these hydro-jobs, like wood-smoke. How the hell do you get the smell of wood-smoke from an engine which hadn't seen a carbon atom since Tokyo pancaked? Made you wonder what they put in the tap-water these days.

'So,' I said. 'Got a scenario yet?'

I slammed the trunk shut and headed for the doorway, but Lian snatched my sleeve, turned me back.

'You're not a policeman any more - remember? All you have to do is get a reading, work out what he's had. That's it.'

'I need to know what I'm looking for, don't I?'

'You're looking for evidence of an upload. That's it. Stay in your little box, Nix. We don't pay you to think.'

Shit. Can't you play nice, just for once?

I sighed. 'Okay. Where am I going?'

'Second floor. And get a move on. The squirt's probably wearing off by now.'

'You're not coming with?'

'In the unlikely event I even wanted to, nope.'

'But you're SOCO, aren't you?'

'Yep. Which makes it my job to talk to the press.'

'My. You get all the plum gigs. Must be your sunny and carefree disposition.'

That earned me another scowl. She turned and started towards the building. I shrugged, followed.

Lian halted when we reached the waiting bystanders, leaving me to shoulder through them alone. There were a few curious residents milling about, but most of the crowd appeared to be journalists. One or two had recognised me by now, jostled in my direction shouting questions. A data-cam was pushed under my nose. I shoved it aside, fixed my gaze harder on the doors ahead.

There wasn't much I liked about my job. Getting into the news was one of the things I hated about it. I broke through, flashed my bracer at the fractious uniform barring the building's entrance. He checked the data which then appeared on his own forearm and let me in, just as Lian Morrison announced behind me that an official press release would be issued in ten minutes. The door whispered shut, cutting off the feeding-frenzy which followed.

I took a second. Tugged the impregnated cloth from my jacket pocket and stooped to dab it over the rich leather covering my feet, wiping rain off before it soaked in. I had a thing about my shoes. Reckon it came from Mom. She always said you can judge a person by their shoes. That's why I wear Italian ones. Imported. Cost half a month's wages but they were boss as hell. I straightened, tucked the cloth away.

The foyer felt ice-box chill after the humidity outside, the lighting so fashionably low I had to stand there, scanning the walls for the elevator. I finally spotted it, tucked round the left-hand side of an empty concierge station.

Hell of a place. Scrupulously clean, emphasis on luxury. The scent of flowers and musk from the air-con blended with the smell of new carpet - the reek of expense and privilege. Money. That's what I could smell.

Figures that I then spent a full minute stabbing the elevator button in increasing frustration.

Activity from my right, next to the courtesy bathroom. A couple of forensic specialists pushed a door open and ambled into the foyer. They didn't notice me as they headed across the expanse of deep pile, mumbling between themselves. Just before the door swung shut behind them I caught a glimpse of railings, going up. More deep-pile carpet and low-level lighting. Reminded me of the movie theatre I went to as a kid. But it didn't fool me. Stairwell.

That confirmed it. Forensics. Stairs. Cosmic Paradox. The lift must be out. Probably a local brownout, courtesy of power rationing. Here we were in a city which produced more power per head than the rest of the West Country put together and energy was rationed. Go figure.

So, instead of it being tastefully subdued like I first thought, I'd take a guess the lighting in here was running at quarter capacity. The fact the air-con was still spewing frigid air told me the residents preferred comfort to safety, even if it meant using the stairs.

Fire exit guidance seeds lit my shoes as I took them two at a time. Rashly as it turns out, since I forgot... In this god-forsaken country, second floor means third level up.

*

Constable Jasper stood outside the apartment. He was one of the two 'artificials' the South West Constabulary were always boasting about. Half a billion dollars each. All that taxpayer's money and here he was, guarding a door.

Jasper grinned when I leaned an arm on the wall and wheezed at him. The plates under his skin produced cracks around his mouth when they moved apart, telling the world he was an older model. I heard they fixed that thing with the skin now. They reckon it's hard to distinguish the newer ones from humans - realistic skin, body language. Everything.

Jasper unzipped the forensic seal locking the area beyond.

'Morning, Nixon.'

I nodded breathlessly, stepped past him. 'Only just.'

Half past midnight - this was just the beginning of the night's activities and people were calling it morning for Christ's sake!

Through a door to my left a spider-shaped robot was crawling up the far wall, a blade of light arcing from its back, slicing the room into countless digital segments for AI analysis. In the backwash of the laser, the room's pale décor appeared splashed with black. Pools, spirals and whorls. Blood. It had travelled a long way. Seemed the killer had found an artery. A woman's naked leg hung off the side of the bed, bare foot displaying toenails painted an even darker colour than the blood dribbling off it onto the snowy carpet.

I flinched as the robot took a series of holo images, its flash strobing the room. There would be people back at forensics that'd spend the next forty-eight hours checking those pictures for every scrap of evidence. Even if my part in this turned up a positive, the police would ensure their case was sewn up tighter than a politician's ass before they took it to court.

The suspected user was under guard, sitting on the living room couch with his head lowered, his cuffed wrists dangling limply between his knees. He was somewhere between middle-age and retirement. Pot belly, good haircut. A salesman, maybe. He wore only boxers and his arms and chest were coated with blood, which a forensic detective was busy datagraphing.

I spotted the tremor in his fingers and tapped the detective on her shoulder.

'Nearly finished?'

She gave me a *'who the hell are you'* look, but unclipped the media wafer from behind her camera lens, slotted it into her bracer. It took a second for the two devices to synchronise, then came the blink-blink sound of data transmitting.

'That a good idea?' I asked. The whole point of media wafers was they couldn't get hacked, so what was she doing sending it electronically? 'There's two dozen news-leeches outside, all waiting for just that kind of traffic.'

'It's encrypted.'

By now she'd noticed my accent.

You get to know that look. Most don't mind, but some Brits resent ex-pats. Don't get me wrong, I understood. But, Christ, we had to go somewhere! Guess I could have tried losing the accent, made things easier for myself, but there's this streak in me I could never lose either -

the one entitled '*Stubborn Bastard*'. So, when some snooty, self-inflated, over-educated squint looks at me like that, it tends to generate something of an attitude malfunction.

By now the detective had wiped the displeasure off her face. She looked me up and down, spotted the steel briefcase. 'You must be Nixon.'

I offered my most sickly grin. 'My reputation obviously precedes me.'

'Yeah, it does. Morrison warned me you were an arrogant bastard.'

The woman waddled off, plastic overalls crackling, while the prisoner's guard - a uniformed standing to one side with his hands behind his back - chuckled quietly.

'Shut up, Stevens,' I growled. 'I have a self-delusion to maintain.'

I bent over the prisoner and took a look into his eyes, which he had a problem with, so I caught his chin, made him look back. One end of my pencil, 'borrowed' from another crime scene, had a light on it. His pupils were wide, shivered when I shone the torch into them. I pulled one of the man's lower eyelids down with my thumb. It was purple in there. Classic signs of a squirt in progress. The tremors in his fingers, and now his knees, suggested it was dying,, though.

Glancing over my shoulder, I caught PC Stevens' eye.

'They finished in the kitchen?' I asked.

He nodded. 'You want him in there?'

'Sometime this year would be good.'

He shrugged, hauled the prisoner up onto unsteady feet and steered him through the narrow doorway before bundling him into a kitchen chair. The guy didn't resist, just obeyed, trance-like. I waited for Stevens to leave then laid my briefcase down on the marble work-top and unlocked it.

'Can you tell me what you had uploaded?' I asked.

The man glanced up quickly, eyes widening at the rubber cap I held. He shook his head, cast his gaze down again.

'Okay. You can at least tell me your name, can't you?'

'You already know my name. I'm sick of telling you people!'

Unfortunately, Lian had been too busy sniping at me to bother passing it on. I dragged the job details onto my screen.

'John Fielding.'

'It wasn't me,' he said. 'I didn't do it!'

'I'm not here about that.'

Fielding's fingers twitched again. The uploaded persona was dying in there and it didn't like it. It was fighting back. It was also sufficient evidence for the guy's human rights to count for nothing.

I dabbed conductive gel onto the pads, stuck one to his chest, the other to his neck. Fielding flinched, angry.

'Why are you doing this? Why's everyone blaming me?'

'I'm just here to find out about the squirt.'

I slid the cap, with its retracted needles and wiggling tubes, over the expensive haircut. He didn't resist, but then, maybe he didn't know what he was in for. I secured it under his chin. Left him sitting there with a tangle of rubber pasta on his head.

'I tried to stop.' he said. 'I tried to stop the bleeding.' He lifted the handcuffs and examined the cracked red stains coating his hands. 'I just came home and found her, I swear! She was bleeding. She was bleeding so much. I tried to stop it, but... She was bleeding so much.'

'I'm really not interested.' Plus, I hadn't been given details. Not my job any more. For a brief second, I was glad.

I placed the projector on the table in front of him, opened it flat and switched it on. The matt grey surface glowed, began to bubble - multi-coloured like witches' brew - fizzing and frothing across every sector on the grid. That was the guy's base reading. General cerebral activity. Evident already were larger domes and troughs which indicated anxiety. No sign of trauma or grief.

Too early, maybe. What he's done hasn't sunk in yet.

Fairly common, that lack of reaction, but something to be noted - just in case it turned out he fully intended to murder his wife all along, using the squirt as an alibi. That scenario was highly unlikely, to be fair, and a squirt is completely unreliable as murder weapons go, but there are the few stupid ones who try.

Otherwise, everything looked normal. Once the cap got to work, I had no doubt those bubbles would become spikes. I'd get hits across the range, concentrated in some regions, weak in others. The pattern would tell me exactly what was going on in the guy's head. Mind reading, in effect. And I'd be able to tell if there were two personalities inside John Fielding.

It was what the police had called me here for. To prove their prisoner was squirting. It was what my job as a civilian consultant entailed. That and interpret the readings to work out what was in the squirt to make him do what he'd done.

The cap's needles are micro-thin, but they feel like hot knives when they go in. Believe me, I know. The prisoner flinched as they engaged, pricked his scalp. He shifted uneasily in his chair.

'Jesus! Stop this, now! Plea... I-I want my lawyer.'

He reached up to snatch the cap from his head but I was ready. Caught his wrist, took a grip on the cuffs and pushed his hands down to the table. Held them there.

The process hurts. A lot. But painkillers are out of the question. There were already enough chemicals in this guy's brain, adding more would only confuse the issue. He handled it better than a lot of them. Kept it down to a whimper, a few tears. Seen men a lot harder, a lot tougher, beg and plead, cry for mercy during this part.

I knew the cycle had moved to phase two when Fielding relaxed. His eyelids flickered as the cap fed a flash-speed range of sounds, images and scenes direct to his audiovisual cortex. His reaction to them was assessed by my equipment, recorded for the courts. I glanced at the display dancing beside me. There were already multiple hits.

From all those spikes, I had to figure out what, among the jumble of synapses and chemistry I was looking at, had turned him into a killer?

'You've got to believe me, I didn't do it.' Fielding's voice was quiet now, calm.

I sighed. 'I'm not the one you need to talk to.'

'I'd never...hurt anyone. I just...' He frowned, blinked lazily. 'Snowflake...elephant...'

I let go the cuffs and lifted my thumb, chewed a ragged corner off the nail. Fielding was out of it. He sat there unseeing while the cap, coupled with the come-down, caused his nervous system to spasm occasionally in protest. He wouldn't say anything worth hearing now, not until he was himself again. I had what the police wanted anyway.

I waited a few more seconds. Long enough to double check for signatures pointing to this being a Synapware persona. There weren't many left on the street now - Synapware had hunted most of their rogues down. Rounded up all the hijacked equipment which allowed dealers to download anyone they liked. But the factory-made personas still turned up, once in a while. Synapware squirts. And when they did, I was there, waiting.

Today, I was out of luck. No branded spikes on the readout. John Fielding had gone and found himself a home-baked mess to deal with. Not that he'd have known the difference. Guy didn't look to be a regular user.

I took out the scanning wand and rose to my feet. Part of the routine. It was vital to check if the squirt was administered by force. Easier to do it while he was hypnostatic. It was unlikely, but I had to cancel it out or the case was over.

The needle-mark at the base of his skull was easy to find. Let's face it, big enough needle. No anomalous bruising, visible or invisible. Medics at Chedminster would check for any other chems or trauma. Again, routine. The guy hadn't pled assault. First thing you do if you've been assaulted, right?

Satisfied, I downloaded the cap's data to my bracer and mentated my report into the same folder. The Constabulary would need it as evidence in John Fielding's trial. Stupidly, this was the most difficult part of the whole process. Along with the data itself, my interpretation of it could see the man in front of me face execution.

2

The rain was still there but the ambulances, and the crowd, were gone when I got back to the street. In their place was a black van. Meat-wagon. The body was being brought out on a robot gurney, tagging along behind one suitably-sombre coroner's assistant.

John Fielding, dressed in yellow paper overalls, was also being led from the building. He looked dazed and frightened now he'd had the persona wiped from his system by police drugs. The thin coverings he wore were soon saturated and the underlying blood soaked through, turning his torso red. Fielding was made to stand there while they brought the car over. He watched blankly as the robot and its black-shrouded burdens trundled past. The gurney rolled up the ramp into the back of the van then Fielding sagged, weeping, as the doors slid shut.

My forearm tingled, gave a warble to make sure I noticed. I flipped my sleeve back, actioned the bracer's screen.

'Yeah, Nix.'

The caller's image nodded at me - John Gage from CID. His team covered Redfield. Well, someone had to.

'We've got one for you,' Gage said. 'Don't stop for breakfast on your way over.'

Breakfast? I was beginning to think my watch was wrong.

*

The car's GPS took me to an automated brewery on the western side of Redfield. Three police cars were converged in a fan-shape outside the facility and a blue custody van stood near the wrought-iron gates, the security bars on the back slotted down into place.

I pulled up near the van, leaned across and wiped condensation from the inside of my car window. No sign of life in the van, but the lights were on in the building and the tall sliding doors stood open.

Good job Gage hadn't told me where he wanted me or what to expect. Deliberate, probably. Last time I'd been out here, people had lost their breakfast the second they walked inside. The feeling this was going to be just as bad had already hit me.

Talk about Déjà vu.

I got my kit out the back, scanned the area for the chief source of activity. Seemed to be coming from inside the main building so I crunched over the gravel towards it. Hunched my shoulders, even though the rain had stopped. As I reached the open doors I had to step aside for two uniformed who were leaving. The tallest guy knew my face.

'Hey, Nix!' He jerked a thumb behind him as he passed me. 'They can advertise this batch with extra body, right?'

The wan grin the second officer gave in response, before stuffing an anti-vomit pad to his nose, told me this was no joking matter. Then the smell hit my nose, too. Brewer's mash, overlaid with something you only baulk at when you realise it's human.

I paused, the uniformed's glib comment echoing in my skull, and gave a groan.

Jesus. Not again!

Trouble is, in my line of business - my *former* line of business - you get to know. No matter how foul, how inhuman, how demonic someone's actions are, there's always some bastard ready to top it. Or repeat it.

So I already had a good idea what I was likely to find inside and John Gage was right about needing an empty stomach. I found him standing by a group of forensic experts who were crouched over, carefully prodding something that wanted to fall apart.

I halted behind him, looked past his right shoulder so I couldn't see the body. 'Got an ID?'

The policeman didn't look round, shook his head. 'We've blipped a tissue sample over to Central. We're expecting...'

My voice filtered through whatever train of thought he was lost in and he turned in recognition. He looked me up and down, let his eyes come to rest on my face. When you've worked as closely together as Gage and I once did, in the line of work we once both had, a greeting was unnecessary. Especially under these circumstances.

He grunted, dug a wad of gauze from the bag he was holding and passed it to me with a wry twitch of his lips. I pressed it to my face and my eyes watered from the fumes - a mix of peppermint and other oils intended to suppress the urge to vomit.

'Unless she's in the UK illegally,' he finally went on, tipping his head towards the body. 'We're expecting a hit in the next few minutes.'

I risked a brief glimpse. What was lying on the floor was only discernable as female because of her clothing. My stomach rippled, despite the peppermint, and I took a deep breath.

Was a time I used to be a better cop than John Gage. I say that without conceit or rancour because it was the truth, back then. But the world turns and so had our roles. I could tell because this time he stayed outwardly untouched, unaffected. Yet he'd been there too, that first time, and he'd crumbled. Not today, though. While he'd gotten hardened to it all, I'd gone soft.

I turned side-on to the body so I didn't have to look at it. 'What's her bracer say?'

The policeman shrugged. 'Probably quite a lot, but until we find it, we have to do things the old fashioned way.'

'Well, I'm here. Means you think this is down to personality abuse.'

The broadest of the forensics stood up, ripped sticky gloves off his hands.

'The temperature wasn't enough to kill her straight away,' he said. 'And he lowered her in slowly, feet-first. It took her a long while to die. Time of death? I'd say four hours, for the body to reach this state.'

Four hours? Bullshit!

'What am I doing here, John? I thought this was a persona case? Since when did an upload last four hours?'

'You're the consultant, you tell me.'

I sighed. They always threw that one at me. Always. Cops hate experts. Fact. Still, I'm always free to throw it back.

'Never, in my *expert* opinion. I take it you have this "squirter", then? This guy who miraculously managed to get his overlay to last that long. And there's the other thing. You're saying he lowered her in there then sat for four hours and watched while she cooked?'

'Remind you of anything?'

So that was why I was here. I stabbed a finger at the girl on the floor, heard my voice rise, couldn't help it.

'I don't *do* this shit any more! I don't do bodies! I'm a consultant. I do personality abuse. Seriously, John, why'd you call me here?'

Gage grabbed my sleeve and tugged me away from the jellied mass and its cluster of busy professionals. People, most everyone in the room, who had stopped to watch my outburst, turned back to their business. He planted me in a new spot. When he spoke, it was soft - for my ears only.

'The guy's squirting, Matt. I'd stake my life on it.'

'I don't do this shit any more,' I repeated. I'd gotten my voice under control, but I heard it crack, cleared my throat.

Gage gestured back at the corpse in frustration. 'I'm not the only one who recognises this, am I?'

'He's *dead,* Gage. We both saw it happen.'

'Yes. But this is just too similar–'

'There's differences.' I heard the defensive tone in my voice, the denial. 'Not everything matches the MO.'

'Oh, get real! You're a *consultant*! You know about this shit. If Dietrich was downloaded–'

'Dietrich was on death row six years. Isolated. No black-market dealer got anywhere near him.'

'*Before* that! What if he sold his personality to someone before he was caught?'

'And they waited six years - waited till he's dead - before they used it?'

'Well, stranger things have happened. And oddly enough, I have a squirter. Sitting right over there in my custody van.' He gave a bitter laugh. 'Can't wait for you to meet him.'

Yeah. Meet the man who boiled a woman to death and sat there watching. I already met someone like that once. Always hoped it was a one-off event. That about tells it where my luck's concerned.

But Gage was right about one thing. If there was a chance Dietrich, or any other serial killer, had been downloaded by a black-market persona ring it was bad, bad news.

'And talking of squirts,' Gage said. 'Something's not right with this one. I think the upload might have been forcible.'

I wasn't listening. I was still on the subject closest to my hatred.

'No dealer would touch Dietrich in the first place. Psychotic overlays are a bad business proposition. No market for it. Think about it. Why would anyone in their right mind want to upload a murderer into their own head?'

Gage sighed. 'Like I said, I think it was forcible. It explains why he called this in.'

'Forcible uploads are rare. A buyer wants to kill with a persona, ninety seven times out of a hundred it's the vic they squirt, not themselves. That's official. Self-destructive stuff, usually. Safer that way. Less chance of becoming the victim themselves, plus they can have themselves an unbreakable alibi and there's no evidence at the scene pointing to them.'

'Anyway.' Gage looked unimpressed. 'The punter has contusions to the back of his neck consistent with needle trauma. And, as you said, squirts don't live forever. We need recordings before the damned thing dies inside him.'

Gage headed towards the exit, gestured for me to follow.

'So. This "punter",' I said, catching up. 'He said anything about how he ended up here?'

'He doesn't remember.'

'That's original.'

'His memory might come back later, once we've Wiped the squirt.'

'Either that or his nose'll grow longer.'

*

The killer wore a dark-grey suit - one of those air-conditioned ones which clean themselves, order coffee for you - you know the sort of thing. In any event, not your standard squirter's wardrobe. He sat in the back of the van on a pull-down chair - suit immaculate, hair in disarray, hands cuffed behind his back. Their chain was looped through the restraint bar behind him.

Second I looked at him, I knew Gage was right. The man was squirting.

When you've done this stuff as long as I have, when you've been around so many folk who upload, when you've seen egos fighting their subjugation despite the fact the false persona was put there voluntarily, you get to know the signs. The slightly 'off' skew in the expression, the subtle discrepancy between stimulus and reaction, the facial tics. Those without my experience tend to feel creeped out when they meet a squirter, get the feeling something's not quite right there. Me, that feeling's how I know. It's how I spot them, even before the twitch of a come-down begins and it's there for all to see.

Guy in front of me was not only setting off my internal squirt detector, he was already twitching hard, allaying all doubt that there were three people inside the wagon, rather than the two I could see, and telling me I had to work fast.

I laid my briefcase on the steel table bolted to the floor and reached into my pocket.

'What's inside you?' I asked, leaning forward.

The prisoner flinched at the light I shone in his eyes but didn't answer, just glared through the beam at me like he wanted his hands round my neck. I tugged the lower lid of his left eye down then darted back and swallowed convulsively. I hadn't expected the jerk of his head, the low snarl, the snick of white teeth.

I hid my shaking hands by putting the torch away, unclipping my briefcase. I waited for my heart-beat to calm, the adrenaline to rush fade. Used the time to reassess what I was looking at.

Yeah, you get all sorts and, yeah, it was disturbing, that behaviour, but it wasn't what bothered me.

If forensics were right, this man - or whoever he'd put inside himself - had started torturing the vic at least four hours ago. That didn't account for the time he must have spent locating her, getting her here, subduing her, putting her in the vat. By now this persona should be long dead, the prisoner back to his normal self. Given the outward symptoms, what I was seeing here wasn't this guy's normal self. The squirt was still in him, even after all this time. Evidently dying, but still there and still going strong.

Given the twitching, the sweats, he should be feeling sorry for himself by now. He should have started realising how deep the pile of shit was he'd just squirted himself into. Most especially, he should be much more submissive. Not tensed up, snarling and snapping at me.

If I didn't know better, I'd say a there was a full-on persona overlay still in progress. That was a new one to me. With the apparent level of deterioration, the overlay should be in the background of this guy's psyche, not the forefront. Not only that, I couldn't recall ever coming across one so blatantly hostile. Looking at him, the hate-filled glare, the rage-spittle at the corners of his mouth, I was glad the guy was in cuffs.

Why the hell would anyone put that *inside himself?*

So maybe Gage was right about the other thing, too. Maybe this upload had been forcible.

'Okay,' I said, laying my kit on the table in front of him. 'How about you tell me your name? You can do that, can't you?'

Part of me expected insults. The other expected something worse. Instead, the man's features contorted into a leer. His voice was flat, mocking.

'You can call me Mephistopheles.'

I stopped what I was doing, glad I'd at least gotten a human response.

'This isn't a game,' I said. 'You've killed someone. A young woman. Soon as your DNA results come through, the cops'll know who you are.'

The killer shook his head, stretched his lips back over perfect teeth. 'They'll know who *he* is, Nix. But I'm leaving. You'll see me again though, Squirt Man. Count on it.'

I stared at him, unnerved, wondering where the hell he'd picked up my name. I'd never seen the squirter before. Never met him. Unlikely the guy would know me or remember me from the downloads. But that wasn't the problem.

I'd seen so many people with personality overlays I couldn't start to count them. In all that time I'd never come across a self-aware persona. The squirt changed the brain's chemistry, altered behaviours. It had no neurons, didn't affect the host's, so it couldn't be self-aware. So why did I have the feeling I was talking to the upload right now?

I grimaced, annoyed for even thinking it. *You can read people better than that, Nix. And you let this sad sack fool you?*

Whatever the case, whether this guy was some sick copy-cat killer who'd uploaded something nasty to give him the balls to do it, or if he'd been squirted by force, I wanted what was in him known about and targeted so it never got inside anyone, ever again.

But I had to be careful. Instead of pleading temporary insanity, this guy could be acting it out. All this, the snarling, the teeth, the weird look in his eyes... It could all be an act. The cap would tell me, of course. Which made it critical I did this right, or the courts would give any insanity plea more credence.

I avoided further eye contact while I set up my gear, but I felt his gaze. Knew he kept it on me, on every move I made.

The CAP needles barely had a chance to go in.

The guy's head went back without warning, tendons straining on his neck like they were trying to burst loose, shoulders warring against the cuffs. He grunted - a guttural, agonised sound - stared at the roof of the truck through bulging eyes, then threw himself forward. I was lucky to react in time, lucky to get my forearm across his chest and pin him back before he smashed his own face in on the edge of the table.

He shuddered against my weight, eyes rolled up inside his head like marbles, white spittle spraying from his mouth. He rocked back again, threw himself forward with all his strength.

'Jesus Christ, Mister! The fuck is your problem?'

I couldn't tell if it was the upload, him or the cap causing this, but this man was trying his damnedest to bash his own brains out.

'Gage!' I yelled at the door behind me, but I already knew no one would hear.

I risked a brief a glimpse at the 3D projection on the table. The cap, still on his head, looked to be working normally, and I'd had enough practice to pick out some weird spikes on the read-out.

'What the hell have you got in you?'

I dedicated an elbow to pinning his back against the truck wall, put my weight behind it and used my free hand to twist the bracer, where it was wedged against his chest. I keyed in Gage's number and a second later the detective's image appeared on the screen.

'Get a medic in here,' I told him. 'Now!'

The prisoner's breath was hot against my neck, panting. 'Let me talk to him. I want to confess.'

I passed the message on through my throat mic while Gage gestured to someone out of view. He gave a nod.

'The medic's on her way. Okay, Nix I'll talk to him.'

Thumbing 'record' I switched my bracer to its external mic. Ramped up the pick-up rather than put the bracer any nearer to those snap-happy teeth.

Martine Lillycrop

First warning I got was the sly grin the bastard slid at me. Then his lips stretched wide and he let out a lung-wrenching, ululating screech. It reached a pitch I'd never have believed could come from a human being and it reverberated in the confines of the van until my ears rang with the force of it. For a second I was frozen, shocked, unable to react while my whole being flinched under the assault. Seemed an age before I managed to stagger back and press my hands over my ears.

The scream must have lasted until his air gave out but it seemed to go on a lot longer. I couldn't take my eyes off his face, fascinated by the wide-mouthed shriek, the joyful, elated expression. It was no howl of pain. It was something deliberate and sinister. When he was done, the prisoner slumped forward as if everything else gave out, along with his breath.

3

'Joseph Samuels, research consultant.'

I turned at the voice in time to see Gage wave distractedly at the ambulance.

The paramedic tightened the last strap then stood back as his gurney trundled into the back of the ambulance. The killer had been woozy when he came round - confused, complaining of a headache and nausea. But the judders had gone, along with all evidence of an uploaded persona. There was a twenty-second recording on my equipment of whatever was inside him, then the readings vanished, just like that. Faster than Wipe and far more effectively. Like whatever had been in there just stood up and walked out. Except that was impossible.

'His bracer was password protected. Harper just got access.'

'You okay?'

Gage didn't look it and I wasn't surprised. Bad enough standing next to Samuels - and my ears still rang - but the scream had gone directly from my bracer's mic into his aural implant.

The policeman gave a wan smile. 'Got a bastard of a headache and I'll probably be deaf that side for the rest of my life.'

He stuck a finger into the offending body-part and waggled. But the sound hadn't touched his ear. Samuels' scream had gone straight to Gage's aural nerve without even air waves to get in its way. And covering his ears wouldn't have stopped it.

'Listen,' he said. 'I have to ask. When did your equipment go for its last LOM check?'

'The CAP? April.'

Yeah. A LOM check. It was their damned equipment, but I'd had to pay to get it overhauled and calibrated. The alternative was to hand it back to them and find another job.

'Well, the medics found some weird burns beside his right ear. I need to know what they are.'

That got me defensive, naturally. Nothing worse to the Constabulary than having to take the blame for something one of their employees has done. So if those burns were anything to do with me...

'What the hell are you saying? The nodes don't even touch the ear, let alone carry enough juice to burn someone!'

I would have gone on, but Gage held up his hand.

'I know. I had to ask, that's all. Did you check for forcible?'

'Well, I did–'

'*But?*'

'I found the contusions you said to look for, but no evidence of an upload. At all. Not even forcible.'

Gage already looked like shit but his face managed to go a couple of shades paler.

'You're kidding me! Fuck it, Nix! What the hell do we pay you for? That man was a squirter. I'd stake–'

'No needle marks. Nothing. Unless someone's worked out how to get it in him without squirting it. And.' I braced myself. 'I didn't get a long-enough recording for persona abuse to stick.'

I'd expected a minor thermonuclear detonation, but Gage just sagged. He glanced round to where the victim's body was packed up ready for transfer to the morgue.

'Well, at least Erin Smart's family get the satisfaction of seeing him on death row.'

I followed his gaze. 'Erin Smart. That the vic's name?'

'Yeah. The DNA test came back.'

'So, like you say, you can get him on a straight murder charge. It's better than manslaughter, right? And, look, if it had been forcible, he'd have walked. You know that. Can't prosecute a smoking pistol.'

Problem is, I agreed with Gage. Samuels had been squirting. I just couldn't, for the life of me, figure out how.

*

My landlady was not so elderly she couldn't give me a true ear-roasting if I woke her. Given the fiery temper, I suspected those native Welsh dragons of hers existed somewhere in her genetic history and they were best avoided. So, with the first glimmer of sunrise scratching the horizon, I did a ninja-sneak up the creaky stairs, the ones laid with carpet older than I was, and slid into my apartment.

The building stood on a cliff overlooking the old railway line, meaning my bay window took in the entire city sprawl and the estuary beyond. It was a view. One I paid for. But these days it wasn't a pretty one. Even so, I found it perversely soothing, watching silt-grey water churn through Bristol's drowned history, eroding the city's roots.

The once-prime real estate standing between me and the ancient docks had long-ago lost its value, since most of the buildings were now just broken shells poking from the water. From up here you could see the new extent of the tidal river, the new course it took through the submerged geology. They'd said it couldn't happen - the sea levels would never rise that high, overflow the Floating Harbour, drown the entire city.

They hadn't counted on the Pennine Fault.

I'd been a kid still living in the States when it happened. Because Mom was a UK citizen, in spirit as well as by birth, we'd paid attention to news of the aftermath. Watched the death toll rise, looked out for people she knew, for anything about Bath where she'd grown up. It had been too abstract, too distant for a ten-year-old to understand. Then, four years later, I got dumped in it.

The first real earthquake to hit the UK for thousands - maybe millions - of years had dropped the west of England and the whole of Wales by two metres. With Beijing and Rome also happening the same year, people began saying something sinister was causing it. End-of-the-worlders made their pitch on chat shows and seminars, made a fortune from those who wanted saving. Legitimate scientists got in on the act. Blamed global warming, sun spots, the moon's orbit, the Earth's magnetic field. Anything but the raw fact that Mother Earth was always apt to get pissy now and then.

Rising global sea levels had only added to the problem the Brits now faced. Bristol had survived being drowned completely, but, with its massive tidal range, when the sea came in to fill the river basins, the city became a series of islands joined by bridges, suspended roads or accessible only by boat.

Looking out my window, though, it was still a hell of a view. And, usually, looking at it helped.

One thing years of policing had taught me - at the end of the day, throw it off. Wasn't too hard most of the time since, despite still being involved in the shit going on out there, I was only a consultant. My job - my involvement - was finite. Get a recording, make my report, get paid. I didn't have to do all the follow-up, the footwork, the hours in cyberspace tracking down alibis or watching camera footage. I still had to deal with the stuff I saw, like Erin Smart's body, but I had this. A place I could go to and forget it all, shut it out. At least until I went back out there.

My apartment door was normally the release trigger. The tension would fizzle out once it closed behind me and the lock snicked shut. This morning that didn't happen.

Lack of closure, I told myself, biting down on annoyance when I realised I was still thinking about Joseph Samuels and his 'Mephistopheles' persona. Putting aside what he'd done to Erin Smart, the duplication of a murder seven years old - the psychological aftermath of which, I knew, would follow me to sleep - this one didn't fit into any of my boxes. I didn't like that.

The persona had been there, I knew it. Despite its vanishing act and the sore lack of evidence, there'd been two personalities inside Samuels. And one of them was a psycho. Problem was, aside from a few inconclusive spikes on an abortive recording, I had nothing. Not enough to convince anyone else, anyway. The only thing I had was my gut feeling and an apparent lack of motive. And the latter could disappear any minute if the police found a connection between Samuels and Erin Smart.

Even so, I should've been able to just switch off. I wasn't a cop any more, so why the hell should I give a shit? Maybe it was professional pride. Squirts don't usually get away from me, not if they're still twitching when I get my cap on the head they're in. But this one... This one had escaped.

It wasn't the only thing irked me about it, though it was bad enough. Part paranoia, part curiosity, but how the hell had Samuels known my name? Yeah, I'd made a few morning downloads, but you'd have to be paying extra attention to notice, let alone remember. So there had to be a reason. I didn't know the guy, I'd never seen him before. I was sure of it. So how did he know me?

High Tide in the City

On top of that I couldn't shake off the creepy feeling it was the persona I'd been talking to, not Samuels at all. Right. Like I had no idea how crazy that notion was. Didn't matter how much experience and logic I threw at it, though, the feeling stayed with me.

By far the most disturbing thing was the hatred. The black, poisonous look he'd speared at me when he'd first laid eyes on.

I moved to the kitchen, placed the back of my hand on the table and unhooked the catches holding my bracer in place. It came off in one piece - the casing with all its hidden magic parts; the screen, a little scratched these days; the thumb-and-finger loops which stretched the web of kinetic bands across the back of my hand, charging the device with every minute movement of my fingers.

Was a time the things were nothing more than a phone and a smart card. Now they were you. Everything about you. Lose it, you lose your cydentity - your electronic existence which, these days, bled over into everything else you ever did, do or will do from now until the day you die. Social security, DNA registration (under which also count blood-type, retina and fingerprint pre-scans for access to god-knows how many facilities), bank account, insurance, passport and infinite other documentation most of us have never even heard of. Let alone everyone you ever knew and how to get hold of them. It kept you in touch with everything going on in the world, brought you TV and cyberspace, provided GPS, data-bots, personal health and fitness monitoring. A million apps, for anything you could think of. All in one little device.

Word was the next gen bracers were scheduled to fit inside your head. There were companies already working on it, rumours they'd already cracked it. If you've ever seen a bracer short out, you'll understand why I never intend to get me one of those.

'Mephistopheles,' I told mine.

Its bio-matrix thrummed against the table, making it buzz, and I switched the kettle on while the search-bot went hunting in cyberspace. The cohesive package was back an instant later and I glanced in dismay at the mass of data it had returned with.

I made coffee - the liquid stuff the Brits had to put up with and all I could get hold of - while I browsed the first few entries. Mephistopheles. An evil spirit. Fictional - as if a demon could be anything else. And someone called Faust had sold him his soul.

Disturbingly, taking an upload did feel something like that. Like selling your soul. Selling it to acquire something experience had erased from you so you didn't get into that kind of trouble again.

Flashback of something, barely recognisable as a woman, lying in a pool of brewer's mash. Drowned or cooked to death. They still weren't sure yet. I slurped coffee, blinking hard. Burnt my mouth.

I was still looking through the sub-texts when the doorbell rang. I answered with the coffee still in my hand - almost dropped it when a blow across the cheek knocked my head sideways.

'You bastard!'

I backed up, stunned.

'Lian? What the hell was that for?'

'For being a stupid fucking bastard!'

I'd recovered from the shock now, but my cheek had begun to sting - joined the burnt mouth in painful solidarity against me.

'As far as you're concerned, that's old news,' I said. 'Out of interest, what form of stupidity am I a "fucking bastard" for today?'

'I know you're a guy,' Lian said. 'And you need to get it every now and again. But screwing a street whore?'

'The hell? I've never–'

'Erin Smart was not even registered. She wasn't with an agency. How could you be so stupid?'

'*Erin Smart?*' I shook my head, bewildered. 'Erin Smart was found dead last night, I... Wait, she was a tom?'

Come to think of it, Gage had referred to Samuels as a punter. That one had slipped past me. Maybe something to do with seeing Smart's body - swollen, red mush. Enough to smear anyone's lens.

'The fact you had to pay might have given you a clue.'

'What are you talking about?'

'You should have mentioned you knew her to DI Gage.'

I snorted, still more puzzled than annoyed, but I was getting there.

'Oh, real funny. For your sanctimonious information, I never heard of Erin Smart, alive or dead, before last night, so–'

'So why does she have tax receipts from you lodged on her bracer's transaction summary?'

I stared incredulously, wondering if Lian had gone nuts overnight. '*What?*'

'They found her bracer. At the bottom of a beer vat and barely functional, but they got what they could off the matrix. You paid to have sex with her. She had the receipts, so don't deny it.'

'Lian, I've never paid for sex with anyone, ever! Plus I never even met the woman. In fact, I can prove it.'

I really did. Think I could prove it. Except when I went to fetch it off the kitchen table, hunted down my transaction account, my bracer proved different.

'Oh.'

I was staring at my financial details for the past two months. And there she was. Three times. Erin Smart. Her cydentity widget glowed beside a sexy emoticon which stooped forward, revealing cleavage every couple of seconds.

'You're allowed to pay for sex.' Lian moved closer, until she had to tilt her head back to look into my face. 'But as a police consultant you're expected to show discretion. You're expected to use registered establishments and submit to regular health checks. You're not supposed to take some whore you happen to meet down one of those sleazy Redfield alleys and fuck her against a wall! Especially not when she winds up dead. And Samuels? What the hell did you do to him? How's this going to look, Nix? You're going to get shit-canned, you know that? You'll be crucified.'

I waggled my bracer at her so the finger loops rattled against the casing. 'This? On here? This is bullshit. I never met Erin Smart. I have no idea what's going on here, but I swear... Lian, I swear to God, I never touched her. I never paid her any money and I never... Samuels?'

'He's in a coma. From what I hear he was fine right up until you put your "magic cap" on him.'

*

Cilla was unusual. Unlike a lot of voluntary hermaphrodites, who generally enjoy men, she preferred women. Though I imagine she was happy to service either gender, as long as she got paid. She was one of the girls you couldn't easily miss if you passed through this neighbourhood. She stood out. Probably would have stood out even if she'd tried blending in, which she didn't. Whether it helped in her line of work, I couldn't say. Made her easy to find, though.

Tonight she was working on the corner of Ashdown Road, touting to drunks on the far side of the street and head-popping to the overspill of music from a nearby nightclub.

Her dress should have come with a warning. Enough to give someone a seizure. The array of holographic cells sewn onto the fabric displayed a knot of alien tentacles squirming over naked hentai flesh. Wasn't subtle. Wasn't illegal either, however indecent, since it wasn't *her* naked flesh the tentacles were caressing.

I blipped my bracer at hers, getting her attention, then asked her to switch the animation off. Cilla grinned, reached inside the neckline for what I assumed were the controls, flashed an artificial tit at me instead.

'Yeah I remember Erin,' she said - somewhat sourly, once I'd established my actual interest. 'Course I remember. Stuck up little cow!'

The husky tone gave it away, reminding me what lay beneath the improbable curves her dress was showing me.

'Did she ever mention me?'

Cilla stopped popping and perched a hand on her hip, arched an eyebrow as she looked me up and down.

'Now why the fuck would she do that?'

I shook my head. 'Doesn't matter.'

'None of us gives a shit who the others do.'

'Anyway... About Erin. She get many punters?'

Cilla flicked pink hair behind her shoulder, applied a disapproving pout to silvered lips.

'Sure, she got a shit-load of interest. But like I said, she was stuck up. Like she could afford to turn down business. With *that* nose-job? Anyway, me and the other girls, we got fed up with it. You know, the ten percent kitty? The all of us missing out on hard cash if you don't pull your weight kitty? We all got bills to pay and business is forever up and down.' She laughed at her own joke. 'It's the only regular income some of us get. So in the end we made sure she took the ride when it came along, know what I mean? And we made sure we saw the cash afterwards.'

'You made her get into cars with men?'

'We just had a word with her. Nothing heavy. No one forced her.' Cilla turned away from me, dropped the strap off her shoulder as a car rattled past. She sent an obscene gesture after it when it didn't stop.

'Male anyway.' she said dismissively. Turned back to me. 'But that's why us girls're here, isn't it? To pick up punters. You're either on the street or you're on the road, sweetheart.'

'What about last night?' I asked. 'Did anyone make her get into a car then?'

Cilla's face lost its camp affectation. Her voice grew quieter. 'She'd got the hang of it by then. Didn't need the extra encouragement. And that's your hundred. Want any more, it'll cost more.'

I couldn't afford it - prostitutes aren't the only ones with bills to pay - but I had my bracer waiting on the page, ready. Flashed it at hers and waited for the transaction to confirm. I frowned, noticing the name the payment went to.

'Simon Reece?'

Cilla drew herself up to her full six and a half feet, heels included. 'I didn't choose to be born in this body,' she pointed out. 'What's it to you, anyway?'

I shook my head. 'No, it's not that. I just... Did Erin use an alias out here, too?'

'Well duh! We all do.'

'So, what did she call herself?'

Cilla touched a long fingernail to her bottom lip like she was thinking. Hard. I gave her a warning look. I'd just paid her as much as she'd normally earn on a good night. She could go home now if she wanted.

'Kate,' she said, once she got the message.

I had to grin. Yeah. I didn't know the name Erin Smart, but I remembered Kate. Lian was right, I *had* paid her money, but it wasn't for sex. I'd paid her for the same thing I was paying Cilla for. Information. Now all I had to do was remember what the information was.

'Now, about the night Erin died.'

'Yeah, there was a car,' Cilla said.

She was irritable now, uncomfortable. I got it. She wanted me to leave, now I'd paid her all I was going to. Never a popular move, talking to the police. Or their consultants. But I wasn't going anywhere till I'd got my money's worth.

'I've seen it around before - or something similar. Hydro-engine. Circled the district a few times that night. Dark saloon, expensive but not flashy.'

Something to pass on to Gage, if he hadn't already checked.

'And it picked up Erin - Kate?'

'Eventually. I'll tell you one thing, though. That driver stops beside me, he can take a hike!'

'He's in custody,' I told her. *Of a kind.* 'Think he was looking for Erin in particular?'

'Fuck should I know?'

'Can you describe him?'

Cilla shook her head. 'She got in the back. With the passenger.'

*

Took some fancy footwork, a 'borrowed' white coat and a few white lies to get past the police guard outside the room, but I wanted a look at Samuels for myself. If Lian believed what had happened to him was my fault then others would think so too and I didn't like that. Could get a man arrested.

I found Samuels unconscious in a private room down a corridor announcing itself as 'Transmittable Pathology'. I shut the door on the guard, avoiding eye-contact with the nurse marching past, and waited for my chest to stop banging. I didn't know where the cam would be, but it would be there, so I kept my head lowered as I moved to the bed.

Fact he was in this ward at all meant he was benefiting from an expensive insurance package while languishing here. Plus, he was getting the VIP treatment - hair combed, face epilated, duvet tucked neatly under limp arms that were multi-ethnic in colouring. He was getting the best care possible. Given his condition right now, though, it didn't look to be enough.

Peeling back the tape behind Samuels' right ear I took a peek under the bandage and grimaced. The suppurating wound was raw, the skin around it inflamed. I had to agree with Gage - it looked like a burn. Rows of tiny blisters radiated from a larger focal point, forming a crooked starburst. Wasn't hard to figure out what could have made that kind of burn. Rubbing the same spot behind my own right ear, my fingers found the cyst-like bud - my audio receiver - clamped to the bone back there, just under the skin. So, something to do with my bracer while it had been next to his face? Feedback or something? But why would it burn out the guy's implant like that? No wonder he'd screamed so loud.

I stuck the tape back down and straightened up.

Much as I didn't like it, I couldn't rule out the chance my equipment had caused Samuels' burn. Still, it didn't explain the coma, whichever way you looked at it. That was down to something else.

Since my magic cap was on his head when he'd lost consciousness, I guess it was understandable people were blaming me for Samuels' condition. But the CAP was working perfectly. I knew it was. I'd attended another incident later that same night and the squirter I'd used it on was fine.

I shook my head. Instead of feeling reassured, I'd just ended up confused and not entirely convinced I wouldn't get shit-canned, just like Lian warned.

I flashed my bracer at the status screen above Samuels' bed, linked in and downloaded the medical notes. They were adumbrated - I didn't have hospital clearance - but I got the gist of what the doctors thought was wrong with him.

'Meningitis?'

Even the doctors considered it odd. They'd ordered a lumbar puncture, scheduled for that afternoon, to sample his spinal fluid, see if they could identify which meningococcal strain was responsible. Or, if I was reading it right, if they could find any meningococcal strain at all.

And that was as far as it went because Friday night meant the cockroaches were more active than usual. Thirty minutes later I was watching my latest squirter being wheeled away on a stretcher. Fortunately, this time, I could prove the CAP wasn't responsible.

I growled at the blues on the scene, told them to shut up - not that they had any reason to listen and I couldn't blame them for sniggering. Their crime report would say it was an attempted burglary gone wrong. My squirt report would say the user was a moron. Only explanation for being dumb enough to try putting a brick through an unbreakable glass window. My magic cap had stayed in the briefcase this time - the user's head injuries too severe to consider using it.

Guess it proves bricks bounce.

I rubbed my palm across the stubble on my jaw as the bracer tingled again. Hooray for the weekend! Let's all do an upload.

*

I'd always thought River Division had it easy. Cruising up and down the estuary checking fishing licenses, chasing tourists speeding along in their hire-boats at six miles an hour. Bit of excitement when illegals tried entering the country via the coast. Crackdown on smugglers once or twice a year. Sounded pretty idyllic.

At least until Port Town appeared.

It was River Division's territory, so they got to police it and it was the toughest beat in the city.

Port Town was nasty. From Clifton it was easy to forget the misery happening down there, right now. Easy to forget it was the permanent and only home to over a thousand families, each forced to live on the floating slum with little hope of ever escaping it. Cholera, malaria and dysentery were becoming a popular pastime, now the bugs which brought them had a climate to breed in. Muggings, burglary and alcohol-related violence were standard entertainment out there on those slimy pontoons. No one employed a Port Towner - for those reasons and more. End up down there, you might as well forget there was anything worth striving for.

Port Town's population were once regular, law-abiding families who'd survived The Pennine Quake and its aftermath. Those who still had them had gradually been flooded out of their homes by the ensuing inundations, abandoned by their insurance companies, swamped by rising mortgages, their equity evaporating before their eyes. Seemed ironic they ended up here, on a floating cess-pit, shoved together with no social or demographic filter. People who'd once led respectable lives had become homeless low-lifes through no fault of their own. Now they lived in a ghetto, surviving on benefits and charity and whatever they could scavenge. Little wonder so many turned to crime.

High tide in the city. It took an hour to get to the police launch, another half for it to get me to the jumble of lashed-together boats, rafts and barges, all strewn with detritus and soggy laundry.

The sky already showed an expectation of dawn.

A uniformed police sergeant stood on a steel-grill jetty, holding out her arm. '*Dickens*', I read on her breast pocket. She was slim, bordering on skinny, her waist cinched in by a police-issue belt. I had one just like it - a left-over from my time on the Force. Difference was, the holster on hers carried a smoker - a real firearm which shot one of the types of smart bullets legal only to the army and police. Only certain arms of the

Constabulary got issued with those. Reminded me where I was.

I grabbed her sleeve to steady myself, hopped off the launch and onto the floating mass.

'You took long enough,' she said.

I swayed unsteadily, took a deep breath to disperse the motion-sickness the ghetto's rolling was already evoking and expelled it fast when the smell hit.

I tried to keep the grimace off my face. 'You the one who blipped me?'

Dickens nodded, pointed out a low-slung cable as she started forward.

I ducked under it, falling into step behind her. 'Get the squirter?'

'Sort of.' She hopped to the next bobbing island, setting it tilting. 'He asked for you.'

I followed more cautiously. 'He have a name?'

'Oh, you'll know him.'

Dickens halted, waited for me to catch up. She pointed to a vessel ahead - a cargo ship from the twentieth, or had been once. Now it stood above the rest of Port Town, silhouetted against the pre-dawn sky. The ship's outline was long and flat - a hundred times bigger than anything else the Port Town structure possessed. The ship had been stripped of everything but its steel carcass, including the wheelhouse, and was rusting in-situ - a hulk living out its last days in ignominy.

I'd seen it before - hard to miss it - on every one of the few trips I'd had to make out here. But I'd never had the chance, or inclination, to ask. Since it appeared we were heading there, though.

'What's that place?'

'The storage area. Everyone gets to keep their stuff there, till they find a new home, either for it or themselves.'

Took several minutes to pick our way across the floating landscape and by then the side of the wreck was towering over us like a cliff. Dickens climbed the ladder running up the rusting hull and jumped over onto the decking. I followed, cursing. My shoes were slippery on the metal rungs and I could barely see where I was going in the half light. I clambered over the rail in time to see her enter a hatchway to my right. I trailed after, ducking my head to avoid the low lintel. Dickens led me down a metal stairwell.

Rotten seaweed, rat shit and corrosion. The ambience was overwhelming. There was a corridor at the bottom, plastered with so much luminous graffiti it had merged into one colourful shade of barf and glowed enough to make lamps unnecessary, even this far down.

Dickens entered a code into the keypad at the far end and put her eye to the scanner. The hatch beside her clunked and she shoved it open. We stepped through into a massive vault lit by isolated kinetic lamps, evidently powered by the tilt and yaw of the ship. They glowed dimly - pools of pale against a sea of dark. I hit my bracer light, shone it around. Picked out my own breath and very little else. The smell was different in here but it was still rank. Rot and rust and old engine grease. I glanced back as the heavy door swung shut behind us. Heard the lock reset.

'How did a squirter get in here, anyway?'

'You'll see.'

She led me along a narrow gap between a canyon of formless shadows. My bracer light didn't penetrate far enough to make out what the objects were, but it caught the glint of water between the planking beneath us. The shallow, oily lake sloshed as the draw from a passing ferry set the ship tilting.

There was more light further ahead. As we approached I made out the shadows I'd seen earlier. Wooden crates covered with tarpaulins stacked to each side - belongings and furniture which creaked as the ship's motion shifted each ponderous, towering weight on its Schaefer gimbals. The remnant of peoples' dreams, packed away in the hope of a better future. Since we'd now arrived I could tell there were a couple of families who wouldn't be in a hurry to get their stuff back.

Forensics were here already. They'd cut the body down. Lit it up. That and the stains it had left on the sickly-green sheeting.

'Jesus.' I stared in dismay.

Crucifixion, of a sort. The victim had been lashed between two of the storage stacks and left to dangle. But the gimbals those towers rested on were independent, each constantly striving to keep their individual burdens as upright as possible on the unstable swell. That hadn't done the victim any good at all. Right now I couldn't tell if the guy had been crushed to death or torn apart.

'Nasty, huh?' But Dickens wasn't looking in that direction. Maybe she'd already seen it and wasn't in a hurry to repeat the experience. She craned her neck, flicked her gaze over the gantry above us, glanced back at me.

'You want to meet the squirter? See if you can talk him down?'

'Talk him down? What else is he on besides an upload for Christ's sake?'

Dickens gave me an exasperated look and shook her head. 'Not on. Up.'

She lifted her finger and jabbed it skywards. I looked to where she was pointing, but the gesture had been random. There was nothing up there.

'*Hey, Squirt Man!*'

The voice drew my attention. Off to one side, thirty feet above the tallest packing crate, crouching on a black beam and holding on one-handed. Gage leaned out, relying on his grip to stop himself falling.

'Told you I'd be back.'

'Jesus Christ! Gage?'

'Wrong guess, asshole.'

I turned to Dickens. 'You're sure he's the doer?'

She shrugged. 'He's confessed. Now all we need is for him to come down so we can arrest him.'

'And you're sure he's squirting?'

'No, but he asked for you. So I called.'

I looked up at Gage again - stunned that a sane, intelligent policeman, one of those I actually respected, was hanging from the rafters like a chimpanzee. Moreover, he'd apparently strung a young security guard between two moving weights just so he would watch him die horribly.

'Are you crazy?' I shouted at him. 'What the fuck you doing up there?'

'Do you think I should come down?'

'Yeah. I really think you should.'

'Well. If you're sure...'

Gage turned his back, shuffled left along the girder. The spotlight a uniformed officer was pointing at him wavered, followed.

Beside me, Dickens craned her head forward. 'What's he...? Is he making a call?'

'What?'

I peered harder, just in time to flinch at the ululating scream as it came. The fact it was Gage up there screaming wide-mouthed, just as Samuels had done, opened a hollow pit in my gut, made the back of my neck prickle. Distance diluted its power, but I knew. I recognised that scream. The realisation came a little late, but like he said, he was back. *Mephistopheles*. And somehow he'd gotten inside Gage.

Gage's breath ran out. I heard him moan, anguished, saw him stagger to his knees. The guys up there with him had kept back, given him space in case he was suicidal. Meant there was no one close enough to save him, nothing anyone could do when he lost his grip. Still moaning, the policeman tipped head-first off his narrow perch, plunged through the air. Beside me, Dickens shrieked. Off to my right someone among the forensics yelled in alarm. Can't honestly remember if I joined in.

Gage's body arced, turned gracefully in the air. The sound of it exploding through stacked crates echoed around the hold. It was followed by absolute, stunned silence.

It was Dickens who found the courage to move first, to go look in the unlikely event he'd survived. I caught up in time to see her turn away from the tangle of wrecked crates, furniture and broken human flesh. She hunched over, braced her arm against an adjacent stack and heaved her guts up. I reached out, squeezed her shoulder while she tried to get her stomach under control.

There wasn't much blood, considering. First thing I noticed, though, was the small burn, just behind his ear. Like a little crooked starburst.

4

Saturday morning, so in theory I should be sleeping. Except I couldn't. Far too many questions rattling round my head. Instead, I took a trip over to Parson Street, see if I could do some digging.

Saturday also meant Carbon Neutral Day. Pain in the ass. Aside from cars like mine - built with or converted to solar or hydro-fusion - powered vehicles were banned. Instead, the roads were swarming with bikes and scooters, all weaving round each other - stopping, starting and dinging in frustration. Since I didn't feel like crawling through it all in my Ford, I took a tram.

The one I picked wasn't on the Parson Street circuit so I stepped off it ten minutes later at Black Boy Lane, at the wrought-iron gates leading into the city's last surviving public park. Sweat prickled between my shoulder-blades, uncomfortable where the t-shirt clung to my back.

Two solid weeks of relentless rain and then, for this morning at least, out came the sun.

Saturday and sunshine meant the park was busy - dog-walkers, kids playing ball, joggers, skaters - all of them brilliant in reflective clothing or hidden beneath shimmering umbrellas. I hadn't remembered my own UV-protection. Goes to show. I was joining the ranks of the undead. Too many nights chasing squirters, not enough days living among the human race.

An automated mower terrorised the amenity, throwing a green bow-wave to either side as it criss-crossed the playing field on its pre-programmed, fuel-saving route. The cut-grass smell cleared my head, lifted my mood a little. I gave the mower a wide berth, took a short-cut across the park to Parson Street Police Station.

The Duty Sergeant knew my face, so he didn't call me back when I ignored the booking-in desk and headed up the central staircase. The upstairs offices were quiet - typical for a Saturday morning, but that wouldn't last. Even so, tension deadened the air.

I could guess why. It would still be on the grapevine, but I'd give it an hour before the news was official. Gage hadn't been based at Parson Street, but the shock would still be felt here. I saw it on their faces, overheard a female PC ask if he'd be okay. If he'd make it.

You'd think cops get used to it - losing their colleagues - but they don't. It hits hard, every time. Because whenever you get news like that, it's always there - out of the subconscious so quick you can't lock it down. And on the heels of it, guilt for even thinking it. Guilt which lasts a lot longer than the 'thank God it wasn't me' that sets it off. Takes a while to get round to the other stuff, like loathing. Like anger. Like sympathy for the loved ones.

A couple of the looks I got told me some of them knew I'd been at the scene when Gage died. I didn't meet their eyes, didn't want to answer their questions.

Sgt Virginia Plummer was too immersed in her virtual world to have been touched by the news yet. She hunched behind her desk, the wraparound heads-up making her look vaguely mutant. She spotted me through her filter, went immediately into Rottweiler mode.

'Listen, Nixon. I don't have time for you. Not today.'

'I just need–'

'I got a core server down, anti-Port Town demonstration to coordinate and five warm bodies off sick.'

'Well, can I talk to Harris?'

Plummer tugged the heads-up goggles forward and peered over them.

'What did I just say? He's off sick.'

'Then can I use the database?'

'Do I look like I need to get fired?'

'Um... You might like the time off. You look stressed. Hey, how about a massage?'

She held up a warning finger when I reached over to rub her shoulders.

'Make another move and I put you in hospital.'

I shrugged and backed off. 'Just trying to help.'

Plummer gave a sigh and pointed at a machine in the corner.

'Use that. And if anyone asks what you're doing there, you sneaked in and overpowered me.'

'This'll be good karma for you. You know that, don't you?'

'It'll be a murder charge if you don't get out of my face. And stay clear of the AI. It knows you're not on the Force any more and it's my neck on the block, you know.'

'And such a lovely neck, too.' I gave her my sleaziest grin.

'Perv.' She shoved the goggles back up and returned to her work.

The terminal was ancient, but it was fully integrated and, hell, as long as it worked, right? Plummer wasn't kidding about the AI, so I logged on using Lian's password. Only a matter of time before she found out I was still doing that and I wasn't looking forward to when she did, but meanwhile...

I found the file, got up to speed on it before fitting the headset so the goggles and earpieces were snug, and adjusted the mic so it brushed my top lip. The old machine took forever to synchronise with the Chedminster server. My fingers drummed impatiently while I waited.

Still had trouble equating that jellied mass in the brewery with the girl I'd known as Kate, but once I found out the alias she'd gone by, it hadn't taken long to remember what I'd paid Erin Smart for. It was because of her I'd known where to look and who to talk to. Knew where to send Vice when they finally got round to pulling his mean little ass off the street.

Just because Greg Davies was in custody, though, didn't mean he had nothing to do with her murder. Didn't mean he couldn't have ordered it - he had enough friends on the outside. It was unlikely she'd have been called to testify, but it didn't mean he didn't still want her dead and he had buddies out there with access to some downright nasty squirts.

Three minutes later, I was sitting in a virtual holding cell, staring at the man Kate had sold to me a month ago. Greg Davies - persona supplier running the Redfield district. A man who'd gotten the street girls over there pissed at him for downloading personas from them - whether they wanted him to or not.

One night he'd dosed Kate with K9, a Ketamine variant, and downloaded her persona while she was under his control. She was non-specific as to what she'd endured during those two hours in his company but hell hath no fury like a hooker who's been mind-fucked. Especially when she don't get paid. She wanted to get even. Sold him out.

Given her current condition, I'd say vengeance has its price.

Davies was in Chedminster Holding Facility. By the look on his face when he plugged in at his end, he'd assumed it was his lawyer calling, working overtime for him. When he saw my face instead, his expression went from hope to disappointment to outright hatred in the space of a second.

'Hi, Greg.'

'What d'you want, shit'ead?'

It's difficult to make a Welsh accent sound harsh, but this guy managed it, no problem.

'I want to talk about Kate.'

'Yeah. I heard. She's dead. So fuckin' what?'

'So the only person I know who wanted to see her dead. Is you.'

Davies sat back in his chair, cocked his head, raised his eyebrows.

'Not guilty.' He lifted his hands and gestured at his virtual cell. 'I got an alibi, see?'

'You got friends, too. Any of them go by the name Samuels?'

Davies offered me a wide grin. 'This is harassment, that's what this is. I can get compensation for this, you know.'

I leaned forward. 'Bit of co-operation goes a long way, Davies. Thought you'd have figured that out by now.'

'Right. Like you can pull strings for me in here, Squirt Man.'

'Funny.' I said. 'Samuels called me "Squirt Man", too.'

'Everyone calls you Squirt Man, shit'ead. Coz that's what you are. Ex-user, ex-cop turned fuckin' squirt-buster. Fuckin' loser, that's what you are.'

Was a time a comment like that would have got to me. I'd have felt the pressure rise under my collar, heat creep over my scalp. My fingers would have itched for his throat. Not these days, though. These days I figured it just wasn't worth the effort. Plus, real as he looked through the goggles, what I was seeing wasn't actual. Just an image sent from a scanner miles away in Chedminster Prison.

I gave a thin smile. 'So tell me about Kate's killer.'

'Way I heard it he was a punter.'

'So you *do* know him, then?'

'Don't be an arse'ole.'

'I'm not hearing a "no" here.'

Davies gave a sneer. 'Like I'd tell you. You're all fuckin' bullshit. If this goes down, I'm in here till I'm sixty. So why the fuck should I care if she's dead? Or who did it. She deserved everythin' she got.'

That time I *did* feel the heat rise, clamped it down. Kept my voice soft.

'You know what he did to her, then?'

'Like I fuckin' care. Not going to change anything, is it? With this fucked-up penal system, I'd be out quicker if I'd killed the slack cunt myself, instead of just downloadin' her. She got what was coming far as I care. And you got the doer. So now I'm wonderin' why you're here and why I'm botherin' answerin' your stupid fuckin' questions.'

'You got something more interesting scheduled, Davies? Like your morning shower with your buddies? Must be fun for you in there - good looking boy like you.'

Davies dropped the sneer and his expression darkened. He sat back, glowering.

Well now. Maybe I'd just hit a raw spot. Seemed Davies had buttons which could be pushed, too. I waited, half-expecting him to kill the feed. Eventually, he leaned forward, rested his forearms on the desk, closer to the scanner's lens.

'If I'd ordered that bitch killed, I'd've had her squirted with something Japanese, wouldn't I? I'd've had it videoed so I could watch it while I'm stuck in here. It'd be all over the net by now - spilling her own guts on the floor while one of my mates fucked her up the arse. Except she wasn't at the top of my list, was she? *Squirt Man.*'

'That a threat, Davies?'

He just chuckled.

I sat back, folded my arms. 'While I'm here, I might as well ask. What's the deal with this new stuff I heard about?'

Davies snorted. 'Don't fuckin' start. That shit don't work with me, see?'

'Just thinking of all the mullah Danny Brooks'll be raking in, now he doesn't have to share. And a whole new market to play with.'

Davies' eyes narrowed. 'Danny's all right, shit-'ead. We're solid. Don't even go there.'

I shrugged. 'Way things're going, though - even if you walk - time you're out of here, Danny'll be way ahead on this new stuff. Hope you like playing catch-up.'

Davies snorted, but a flicker of doubt crossed his face. 'What you on, mon? What new stuff?'

'New personas.'

Davies laughed, relieved. 'You know as well as me, there's as many new personas out there as people to download 'em from.'

I shook my head. 'I'm talking about something else. Something different. Something which doesn't need a needle. I'm talking about something that can get up and leave whenever it wants to.'

'You're talkin' shit, that's what you're talkin'. Squirts want to survive. They don't up an' "leave", even if they could. They want to live. And anyway, why would I want anythin' to do with a squirt that can't be squirted. Puts me right out of a job, doesn't it?'

*

Forget the turban, the Asian music, wispy beard and joss sticks, where he lived said more about Sitaroo Man than his appearance. His next-door neighbour was the council's high-level housing project - a giant scraper-complex built on stilts, like some hip urban oil-rig. Port Town aside, the building's vast underbelly, during the dry season, was responsible for more crime per metre than any other part of the city. Just living here, right next to it, was good reason to call Sitaroo's sanity into question.

Mini-whirlwinds chased litter under the concrete overpass, scraped and rattled it across the rough asphalt. I steered clear of the handrail as I took the steps to ground level. Still had a scar at the base of my thumb, where I'd once been caught by the razorblades someone had chem-welded to a handrail as a 'joke'. Yeah, great fun. Laughed my ass off.

Stepping into the shadows should have been a relief but it always put me on edge, walking past the stilts. Because you know they're in there, watching.

I took off my sunglasses and was rewarded with a face-full of dust -

dried silt left behind by the last Spring Tide, whipped up by wind eddies into powder so fine it wasn't even gritty in my mouth. My eyes were more sensitive, though, and I blinked, tried to clear them before any ganglanders lurking down here could take advantage.

Ganglanders. They've been around longer, they're more organised than Port Town scum and more dangerous because of it. Like all the city's night-life, they prefer dark places. Like under the stilts, where no one could see the punishments they dished out, the vengeance killings or the plain, old-fashioned hits. And while they can see you walking past, it's much harder for you to see them lurking in the darkness.

I bluffed it. Moved deeper under the tower's shade.

Feet disturbing gravel and low, muttered comments filtered from way back under the concrete supports. I resisted all but the briefest glance - chemical torches and half-seen figures huddled together. Or maybe glowing graffiti and piled-up rubbish. Hard to tell. There was crime afoot in there, in the urine-drenched gloom, but you don't walk into Hades with only a Sandman for company. Even the gun-jockeys with their automatic rifles, their Kevlar and their AI back-up know better than to venture in there, except in large numbers.

Christ knows why anyone would want to live right next to it. And if that wasn't enough, Sitaroo Man had to live in a basement. In a part of the city where, with the lower-level geology and the monsoon weather we got these days, even stilts couldn't guarantee to keep you dry.

His house was a survivor of the Victorian era, its steam-age façade vying with the multi-legged monstrosity stealing all its daylight. Cast-iron spikes cordoned off a stairwell separating the basement entrance from the street. Sandbags were piled against two rows of hexibricks surrounding the railings - their old-fashioned pragmatism shoring up the flood defences where high-tech had obviously failed.

My shoes crunched grit as I took the steps leading down. Flakes of paint came away with my hand when I hammered on the warped door with the side of my fist. I brushed them off, listening for sounds of movement coming from inside until it cracked open and a miasma of garlic, curry and sandalwood flooded out.

Sitaroo opened the door wide. He grinned, flashing the gap in his mouth where his missing incisor should have been.

'Hey, Paydirt! Perfect timing, man. Landlord's due Monday.'

'You know, you could let me in before you mug me,' I said.

'You're a harsh man, Nix. I only ever take what's due, you know that.'

He wasn't wearing his turban. Let loose, his hair reached his waist. Baby blond, but the peach-fuzz beard gave that away first time I ever met him. Just because he had no ethnic links to India, though, didn't stop him living like he was born and bred in Delhi. And he could cook a mean phal, which was authentic enough for me.

'You could pretend to be less mercenary.' I stepped over another row of sandbags and into the apartment. 'Puts me in a better mood.'

'You pay me for dirt, man. Paydirt. I just call it like it is.'

'Not today. I'm not here for information.'

Sitaroo muttered something under his breath and the door rattled shut behind me. He shouldered past and I followed him to his inner sanctum.

A single window was set high on the left-hand wall. Grime and a security grille fixed to the outside blocked most of the light coming through it. The insipid beams highlighted the wisps of sandalwood smoke creeping across the room. The incense tumbled through holes in the church-style censor, which hung alongside the H-projector in the ceiling, and entirely failed to mask the pervading smell of damp.

Indian musical instruments hung on the walls, festooned with cables and optical wiring, and a dancing figurine of Ganesh stood on an antique sideboard littered with circuit boards and casings. Saris and psychedelic silks were draped over a couple of benches that, I knew from previous visits, contained the hardware pertaining to Sitaroo's latest current project.

My reason for this visit.

He was always telling me how great the damned thing was. Now was his chance to prove it.

He'd built the Turing-grade Dakka-Hoddern rig from spare parts filched from god-knows where and it was his long-term obsession. It lurked in the far corner, humming darkly to itself, clearly impressed by its own, autistic brilliance.

Sitaroo seated himself cross-legged on a shabby moonchair and rested the backs of his hands on his knees, yoga-style.

'So what do you want? If you're not here to give me money, make it quick. Gotta hungry habit to feed.'

He gestured at the rig with his chin, as if I'd forgotten he rarely talked of anything else. I glanced at the crate-sized black box and pulled a face.

'Ever think it might be cheaper to take an Einstein squirt on a daily basis? Then you could just act like an eccentric genius instead of being one.'

'Ah,' Sitaroo basked shamelessly in the compliment. 'Did I just hear you encourage me to engage in a heinous, degrading and illegal activity, ex-Detective Nixon? What's up? Been short of victims lately?'

When I didn't bite, Sitaroo shrugged.

'Okay, so supporting her costs for now. But I got plans, my man. I got a top lawyer working on it so she gets declared a sentient being. Then I can claim benefits.'

'You gotta be kidding me.'

'Hey, she's my bitch. About time she earned her own keep.'

I sighed. 'In the meantime, maybe *it* can earn its keep today.'

I crossed to the black cabinet inside which, so Sitaroo claimed, sat the three semi-sentient stem-cell arrays which had brought me here. The Dakka-Hoddern's tone changed pitch as I approached. I put it down to the room's acoustics.

'She's alive, you know.' Sitaroo was watching me through half-closed lids. 'Takes lots of attention, keeping her happy. And cash. Lots of cash.'

I shot him an annoyed look. Just stepping through Sitaroo's front door cost lots of cash. I didn't need reminding.

'Alive? So what does she... What does *it* feed on?'

Sitaroo's eyes took on a keen glitter. 'The blood of my enemies.'

I snorted, despite myself, perched my rump on the black cabinet and folded my arms. Got the satisfaction of seeing the city's best, if wackiest, computer nerd visibly flinch.

'Don't do that,' he said. 'She won't like it.'

I shook my head. 'You're creepy sometimes, you know that?'

'Come on, Nix, I mean it, get off! What do you want, anyway?'

I stood up, slid the bracer out from under my faux leather sleeve and flashed it at him like he might be able to see the problem from there.

'I want you to take a look at this for me.'

Sitaroo lifted a skinny-fingered hand, pointed at the door. 'Repair shop. Downtown.'

I dropped the sleeve again. 'It may have fried someone's implants out a couple of days ago, but I can't figure out how. Plus it's been acting up since then. On top of that, I found something on it I want you to get your bitch here to check out.'

Sitaroo gave a sour grunt. He rolled his eyes, closed them and exhaled slowly, deliberately. Wasn't the first time I'd seen him do this and experience had taught me not to interrupt. Not if I hoped to get what I wanted. I waited for him to *'re-focus his chi'*, while fatigue tore shreds off my patience.

I'd often wondered if he had a reservoir of something relaxing tucked away sub-dermal. Easy enough to get installed these days. Easy enough to trigger with a preset mental image. Or maybe meditation really works. Whatever it was, when he opened his eyes his voice was chilled and his expression mellow.

'So what are we talking about? A virus?'

I stared at him blankly. While he'd been seeking his focus, I'd gone and lost mine. I massaged my stubble, irritated. Sleep. I needed sleep.

'Don't think so. A deep-root system check should find out if it's faulty, but the thing I want your love-bot here to look at...' I waved at the Dakka-Hoddern. 'Is just a file.'

'Well, cash is everything where files are concerned. How big a file?'

I took a deep breath. This was starting to sound like it could be an expensive visit.

'Six petabytes.'

Sitaroo didn't actually sit back, mainly because he was already as far back in the chair as he could be. But the expression on his face told me if he could have, he would have.

'Six petas? You've got a six petabite file sitting on your bracer.'

Sounded a lot like he didn't believe me.

'Slowing my systems down like a son-of-a-bitch.'

'No kidding. What have you got in there, a couple of AI's and their 2.3 kids?'

I shrugged. 'You tell me.'

High Tide in the City

I unclipped the device, slid it off my arm and passed it to his outstretched hand. He flipped the lobster-scale plating over his left hand and began shuffling through the menus like the damned thing belonged to him.

See, that's the reason I come to Sitaroo Man for stuff like this. No chance in hell I'd trust my bracer to some High Street hacker. Handing your bracer over to someone, that takes trust. The kind of trust which comes from knowing your fixer not only has the biggest brain in the city, but would also happily sell his own mother for the briefest chance to play with technology, especially if it didn't belong to him.

He was an addict of a very different sort. Digital coding was his particular drug, but it wasn't all he was hooked on. He could programme an AI in a week, strip a VR system to its core components in one hour and construct a self-repairing robot from spare parts and glue. He knew his way around bracers like most people know their way around the inside of their nose.

'This it?' Sitaroo looked disappointed. 'But it's just an audio file.' His brow puckered. 'Wait a sec. Twelve seconds?'

'Huh?'

'A twelve second audio snip is taking up six petas of space in there? No, no, no. It's not an IUM file, it's a–'

'Yeah it is.'

Samuels' scream. It had taken until yesterday to remember flicking that record button. Six petabytes, give or take, for a thirteen-second recording of a man screaming.

'No, it's not just audio, man. There's something else hiding behind it.'

'*Hiding*? Like what?'

Sitaroo unfolded his legs and pushed off with his feet sending him, and the moonchair, rolling towards the Dakka-Hoddern. He used his palms to brake himself against the cabinet then flicked a switch somewhere towards the back and the man-chine interface slid out of its recess.

I took a step back.

Should have figured. This was Sitaroo Man. So he insisted on using a keyboard? Fair enough. But God forbid he'd use a regular one. Even so, I'd have expected tits and fannys. Lips. Something on those lines. Not the shallow cavity arrayed with ribs, tongues, tubes and orifices, all with teeth. What dark fantasy had inspired Sitaroo to install that nightmare I didn't want to guess.

'Jesus! You really do feed it blood!' Wouldn't be the first time I'd wondered what my magic cap could tell me about what went on in the guy's head.

Sitaroo replied with a gap-toothed, evil grin. 'Wanna stroke it?'

'Thanks, but I'm straight.'

'Remember what's in there next time you're looking for a chair.'

While the computer was powering up, he unravelled a cable from one of the cabinet's shelves and slotted the loose end into my bracer's linkup. Struck me as too low-tech for him, until I realised it was for the rig's protection. Hard bottleneck, just in case there was something in my bracer's storage bin which might quite like a new home.

For all its bizarre appearance, the interface was still just a keyboard. Plus it was further proof of Sitaroo's eccentricity, considering he lived in a world where text could be mentated - created, manipulated and disseminated by thinking the words in your head. Evidence, also, that he was as paranoid as he was brilliant. The man refused to put hardware inside his head which, theoretically, might be controlled by external agencies. In that regard he was even more Neanderthal than me.

I recognised my own home page when the Dakka-Hoddern's screen finally lit up. Sitaroo began prodding the mini monstrosities in front of him, navigating deeper into my bracer's system, looking for what he'd seen earlier.

'So, what's on the file if it's not just audio?'

He paused to glance at me and I could see him trying to figure out if I was serious. Problem with nerds - they kind of assume what they know, you know.

'Looks like machine code,' he said eventually.

'*Machine* code? Come on! That's a recording of a man screaming. It can't–'

'Lots of machine code.'

'No.' I shook my head. 'That's impossible. The sound came from a man's mouth.'

'Not impossible. As long as the carrier wave is gonna to be digitised, it's totally possible. Been doing it for decades, right? Radio? TV? Digital info over an EM frequency. Only difference is wetware versus hardware. The key is the codec. The sound waves act as a bridge, see? Get the right frequency, when the codec on any kind of data manager processes it - a bracer's a perfect example - it translates it into something it thinks makes sense. If there are enough cohesive sound packets on the signal, they're processed together and, crunch, you got machine code. The clever part is getting the right frequency. That's more tricky, natch.'

'Natch. So what kind of machine code we talking about?'

'If you'll stop yakking for two nanosecs I'll try and find out!'

Trouble was, my mind was now spinning and I always think better out loud.

'How the hell did whatever it is get inside Samuels so he could transmit it in the first place?'

Sitaroo gave me a bug-eyed look. 'I don't do people stuff, Paydirt. You know that.'

'Hang on.' I leaned over, tapped the screen. 'That's changed.'

Sitaroo slapped my hand away, irritated. 'What's changed?'

'I found thirteen seconds of audio earlier. You just said there were twelve. Now it's saying there's eleven-point-nine seconds in the storage bin.'

Sitaroo picked up my bracer again, took another look at the file.

'And five-point-nine-three petas. It's erasing itself.'

'*What?*'

'You know what, Nix? I'm starting to get a really bad feeling about this file.'

*

Four hours sleep and I'd barely crawled out of bed. Made for a bad-tempered Nix. I was still shaving when the loaner bracer sprang awake. Saturday. It always starts early on a Saturday evening. Even so, they could at least let me get dressed.

I grimaced into the age-dappled mirror, not really seeing the too-pale complexion, the hollows under the cheek-bones. I saw the eyes, though. Barely recognised them. The dark rings I put down to waking up slick with sweat, listening to my ill-considered words echo back at me in answer to Gage's question.

Should have played it different was my wake-up Mantra and it accompanied a gut-deep knowledge that it wouldn't have changed a thing. *Still should have played it different. Because you never know.*

I scowled again.

Sitaroo had wanted to decipher the stuff he was sifting from the IUM, but flat refused to download it into his precious Dakka-Hoddern. So I let him keep my bracer - an act of faith if ever there was one - little realising how much I'd miss it in the meanwhile. He'd fixed a shunt-receiver to one of his outmoded models and loaned it to me. It meant I still got my calls, but it felt like I was missing one of my arms and both feet. Sitaroo's cast-off didn't have the nice, soothing chime mine did, it didn't give the customary buzz which warned of an incoming call, it simply blared noise, unannounced - something between a constipated duck and a fog-horn.

The device farted again. I wiped epilating gel off my cheek with the corner of a towel. The stuff hadn't finished working yet and the fabric snagged on half-dissolved stubble, left a streak of fluff behind.

'Fuck it!'

I padded into the living room, leaving wet footprints on the carpet, hit the wall-bud. The window shimmered, lost its opacity, let the last dregs of daylight into the room so it could highlight the peeling wallpaper. I reached over, snatched the bracer off the table before the landlady took to thumping the ceiling with her broom-handle.

I checked the caller's ID and stifled a groan, made a conscious effort to shrug away the tension already manifesting between my shoulder-blades. I was wearing a towel and had gunk slathered across my face, so I selected audio only.

'Lian! How nice to hear from you.'

'I know.'

Despite myself, I grinned. She hadn't missed a beat.

'What's up with your bracer?' she said. 'Lost the will to live? You sound like shit by the way.'

'Yeah?' I scratched my jaw, came away with beard-remover under my fingernails. 'Then I sound just how I feel.'

The towel around my hips was only just holding on, but I scraped the gunk off on it, rather than have my fingernails dissolve.

'So. This an official call, or you asking me out on a date?'

I heard a snort. 'You requested to see DI Harris.'

An image came back to me. Plummer's skinny finger hooking VR goggles forward, cynical eyes peering over them.

'Sergeant Plummer is *way* too efficient.'

'That's why she does what she does. Harris is off sick. What do you want?'

I managed to suppress a sigh, but only just. 'I assumed he'd be taking on Gage's case-load. You ended up with it, instead, huh?'

'I got Gage's case, too. Lucky me.'

'Told you, you get all the plum gigs.'

'Yeah. Listen, Nix. It's Saturday night and I just got on duty. I've got three times my normal workload and a pile of cases to come up to speed on so let's get this over with so I can do some real work, okay? What do you want?'

'I want a look at John Gage's bracer.'

'Not a chance.'

'Why not?'

'For one thing, it's still being examined. For another, this is a simple murder-suicide, it has nothing to do with you.'

'A *simple* murder-suicide? And it has plenty to do with me. They called me out there. Gage was squirting.'

'No, they called you out because he asked for you.'

'Listen, we're talking about a policeman here. A policeman who, only days ago, was perfectly sane. Why would he–'

'In your expert opinion,' she sneered. 'The AI's examining his behaviour over the last month to see just what state of mind he was in prior to the event.'

'The *AI*?'

There was a pause as she waited for me to continue. In my opinion, I'd said it all. Her breath buzzed in my aural nerve as she sighed.

'It's not happening, Nix. Forget it.'

'Samuels' bracer, then.'

'It's in Evidence.'

'Your point being?'

'Viewing evidence is the prerogative of the police or someone with similar legal rights. You have neither.'

'Aw, come on, Lian. This is part of my ongoing on the Erin Smart murder.'

'According to the file, you didn't get enough evidence to prove it was a squirt-job. There *is* no ongoing. Your expertise is no longer required on that case. Sorry.'

Strange how someone can make a word sound the exact opposite of what it means. I twitched my face, the burning sensation reminding me that what was left of the beard-cream ought to be coming off about now.

'You're right, I didn't get the evidence, but I found something anyway. Something else. Something new.'

'Like what?'

'Like a squirt, but...not.'

The silence on the other end was not encouraging. She broke it, eventually, by clearing her throat.

'You're pissing me off. Take heed.'

'Lian, I'm serious. I think there's something new out there. Something got into Samuels, made him kill that girl. Then it left him and went straight into Gage. Whatever the AI comes up with, we both knew him. You and me. We both know John wouldn't do something like that - not to his victim, not to himself. Not it in a million. You're a good police officer. You must be wondering what made him do it.'

I waited for her to comment. When all I got was silence, I soldiered on.

'I think whatever was in Samuels got into Gage through my bracer signal. Whatever the hell it is, it made Gage do that security guard. And then himself.'

She laughed. 'So you're delusional these days as well as being a complete scumbag. You got a glitch on your bracer and now there's some weird tech out there trying to kill everyone? Listen, Nix. Gage's case is nothing to do with you. Leave it alone.'

'He asked for me, Lian. He *asked* for *me*. That makes me–'

'Forensics did a routine check. No evidence of needle marks.'

'This is needle marks on the head they scraped off the floor of that storage hold you're talking about? Good luck finding those. Lian, aren't you listening? I just said. Whatever it was went through my bracer, not a needle!'

'What are you looking for, anyway? What's on these bracers you're so interested in?'

I growled, frustrated. Hadn't I just explained? I made an effort to keep my tone even.

'Just a file. An audio file.'

'Listen, I need you over at Naleigh Cemetery asap. Suspected persona incident. Details on your job screen.' She breathed out, reluctant. 'I'll clear you to take a look at Samuels' data manager. But that's it. No more favours.'

5

Chedminster Holding does one job. It stores stuff. Prisoners, contraband, that sort of stuff. And because the authorities didn't want the stuff they stored getting out again, they'd made the place tough to get to, to get into and, most especially, to get out of again.

To get there by road, I had to drive to Chedwell, take a left off Selworth Lane and head north for about a mile. The hill was enough that I had to switch my car to bio-fuel to get me up it and the engine grumbled all the way.

The headlights picked out Chedminster Monastery through the trees on my right - nothing but ancient ruins. I dragged the car round another stiff bend and the deciduous woodland parted, making way for a massive wall a hundred yards ahead of me.

Chedminster Holding's facade was not designed with aesthetics in mind. Tall, smooth and angled inward, the wall was blank save for the bridge-lock gate system glowing green at its base. The surface gave off a metallic glimmer as hover-cams moved over it, their lights criss-crossing as the automated machines patrolled the featureless expanse.

The metallic sheen was deceptive. The structure wasn't metal, but it had the same hue and texture as brushed steel. Silicrete hexibricks, like those used in the city's failed sea defences. I could just pick out the low-relief outlines - scale-like at this distance, like reptile skin. The uber-tough tri-hex shapes - designed to slot together with hermetic precision - ensured the only way someone could get through that wall would be to unslot it again, brick-by-brick.

Or, like me, use the gate.

Spotlights snapped on, already focused on my car. My tyres slid on gravel as I pulled to a halt, blinded, and way too fast. The spots came from both facing corner turrets and tracked just slow enough to suggest there was a human on the other end. I figured the guys were just letting me know they were there - the AI sensor net would have had me minutes ago. If they were really worried about me, I'd have been stopped before the monastery.

'Good Morning, sir. How might we help you?'

The voice came over the link fitted to my car media system and was, annoyingly, much too bright and cheerful for this time of day. I flipped the sun-visor down, cutting off some of the glare from the spots, hit the button for the pick-up and shielded my eyes with the flat of my hand. The guy on the screen wore lancer glasses. Possibly for enhancement, maybe for night-vision, but more likely just to look cool.

'Yeah. Morning. I'm DI... I'm Matt Nixon. You're expecting me.'

The connection cut dead, without the guy making further comment. The following delay was long enough I started worrying that Lian had forgotten to issue the authority she'd promised. Or worse, just plain not bothered to do it. She'd get off thinking of me sitting here with half a dozen lethal-class weapons trained on me, but I told myself she wouldn't go that far. Even though she hated me, she wouldn't go that far. I hoped.

After leaving me to sweat a couple of minutes, the spots died and a figure appeared at the gate. I blinked through the afterimage, saw the man push the business end of his rifle down and around his hip, sliding the weapon onto his back. Then he lifted a black-gloved hand and waved me forward.

It took an hour to get through their security, which included a physical search where my Sandman, with its clip of darts, was confiscated for the duration. Then there were retinal, DNA and skeletal scans, followed by a list of mandatory security questions.

'I'm not asking for the fucking Crown Jewels,' I growled eventually. 'I just want to examine a suspect's bracer. Jesus!'

'It's routine, sir. Security.'

'Yeah. I'm glad you cleared that up. I'd have missed it otherwise.'

Eventually I found myself in Evidence, sitting in a privacy booth opposite a constable whose calloused temples suggested she spent a hell of a lot of time in VR.

The evidence bag she'd brought was bulkier than I'd expected. It had also seen a lot of use in its short lifespan. Folds, wrinkles and creases had left a lacy white pattern on the translucent material, obscuring the contents further. The self-seal zipple was also broken.

The bag crackled as the woman lifted it by a corner and its contents sagged towards the table, swaying gently.

I frowned. 'That's a bracer?'

The object inside looked to be the same size and shape as a magazine for those old riot disks they let us practice with in training. She dropped the object into the tray in front of me and sat back. Seemed she wasn't the talkative type.

I shifted my attention to her nametag, reached for the bag.

'I assume you guys got everything you want from it, PC Warren? Wouldn't want to be accused of tampering with evidence.'

'Just don't try to leave with it.'

I sighed. The guys on the gate were already starting to look friendlier in comparison. I tipped the bag up and the bracer dropped onto the table with a solid clunk.

'You're kidding me.'

'Do I look like I have a sense of humour, Mr Nixon?'

A reply sprang to mind. I found a question instead.

'You're telling me this is Joseph Samuel's bracer?'

Warren's eyes were angel blue and she levelled them at me, loaded with true evil. She retrieved the evidence bag, smoothed it out on the table with long-fingered hands then ran a nail along the writing at the top.

'Joseph Samuels, Case Number five one sev–'

'Yeah, but this bag's unsealed, it could–'

'Mr Nixon. This is Joseph Samuels' bracer. Trust me.'

'Even so.'

Even so, the object lying on the desk like a hunk of ancient battle armour was three to five years older than the antique on my arm. I hadn't seen it, back in the custody van. Samuels' hands had been cuffed behind him. Give you some idea - what was a web of kinetic bands on modern devices was a membrane of resistant wiring on this one. The self-charge feature had then been stuffed inside a solid plate, which attached to the back of the hand by a single knuckle piece. Uncomfortable and awkward to use. At least my loaner, dumb as it was, had flex-plates.

I turned Samuels' monstrosity over, slid the screen cover - an actual screen cover - back out the way. The device stayed dead, either switched off or out of charge. No obvious upgrades on the facia, no add-ons. No slots for add-ons in the first place.

'You're telling me a man who dresses in a smart suit and wears a tie worth a thousand Euros, uses a bracer that went out of date before you left school?'

Warren didn't react to the jibe about her age. 'It's to do with his job.'

'Software consultant, right?' I dropped the bracer onto the smoothed-out bag and sat back, folded my arms. 'I'd've thought someone with his background would be wearing something flashier.'

'He works for Synapware,' Warren said. Like that explained it.

'He does?'

She managed to hold back on the next comment, but it was there, behind her eyes. Just a guess, but I read it as, *"Well, duh!"*

I was obviously missing something. But if a little light really could switch on inside someone's head when they make a connection, I doubt there was a better opportunity for it to happen to me.

'Are we talking about the same Synapware that developed chemical personas?'

The same personas, now illegal, whose mess I go out each night and help clean up. Warren flicked her eyebrows up, all sardonic.

'Unless you know any other companies going by that name. They've already "been here, done this", by the way. That's why the baggie's open.'

I ignored her twist on the wording - her wry adaptation of Synapware's motto. Gave an inward groan instead.

'Tell me you people downloaded everything off it before they got to it?'

Warren shrugged. 'There was nothing relevant there. The AI checked personally.'

'The AI.' Great.

So that meant no. If there had ever been anything useful sitting on the bracer, it was gone now. But maybe this was more interesting.

'Okay. So Samuels is a Synapware consultant?'

'Nope.'

I eyed her, annoyed. I'd met her type before. Low self-esteem - compensates by being a total asshole. Well, at this rate, she wouldn't be getting my number.

'So, what then?'

Warren gave a shrug. 'He's in Creative Acquisitions. Industry speak for research and development.'

'So I'm guessing the guy's not a technophobe.' I gestured at Samuels' bracer again, my question obvious.

PC Warren cracked her rigid features for the first time, delighted by my stupidity.

'It's to stop employees stealing research. Synapware's paranoid. Intellectual theft, industrial espionage.' It was her turn to gesture at the offending item. 'He could get himself fired for owning anything with higher specs than a GK Ramrod. Sounds like legalised torture to me, but there you go.'

I dragged a corner of the evidence bag towards me and hooked the bracer up in my paw again. It explained why Mephistopheles had waited for something racier, like mine, before he did his disappearing act. Yeah, made sense. Erin Smart's had ended up at the bottom of the brewer's vat, and Samuels' device had nowhere near the power to transmit what Sitaroo had found in that IUM.

'Anything else you can tell me about this thing?'

I ran my fingers over the bracer's casing, hunting for the 'on' switch.

'Nope.'

I paused my fiddling, looked back at her. 'Synapware have a problem, d'you think? They've maybe lost something?'

Warren sat forward, leaned her arms on the table. 'How should I know?'

'Hmmm. By the way, you got a number?' I asked. When she pulled a face I gave her my most innocuous stare. 'For Synapware.'

Dummy.

*

By shoving my nose against the door and cupping my hands around my eyes, I could just about see through the mirrored glass. Enough, at least, to make out the boredom-weary guard heaving himself up from behind a backlit, polished black desk. The man unhooked the stun-stick from his belt and sauntered towards me. I gave him a cheery wave while he leaned a forearm against an access panel and thumbed a button. I stood back, thinking he was opening the door, but it was just the intercom.

'It's Sunday morning, sir.' The drawl came from above my head. 'We're shut. Why don't you come back tomorrow?'

I grinned into the overhead camera, noted the mini-turret sitting next to it. Wouldn't be loaded with anything lethal - too extreme even for today's social climate - but it would be carrying darts heavy enough to put me out a couple of hours. Made it hard to keep the smile in place, but I managed it. I'm a trooper.

'I probably will,' I said. 'This is Synapware, right?'

Mini-turret aside, I'd been expecting something more. More what, I wasn't sure, but the block of glass and marble towering over me wasn't it. Considering what Synapware did for a living, this place should hover or something.

They claimed cutting edge was what their competitors handled. Synapware had already been to the edge and redesigned it. Whatever the latest thing was on the market, Synapware had already 'Been There, Done That', just like PC Warren said. Being the original developers of persona overlays back in the 60s hadn't hurt their business interests, either. Probably driven their 'cool' notch higher. Word was they also handled most of the country's weapons development.

Now there's a scary thought.

First glance, the building entrance looked low-tech - three wide steps leading to a rank of six push-me/pull-me doors of long-chain carbon glass, standard scanning arches over each and a welcome placard set into the tiles underfoot.

That was first glance. Second glance picked up a row of small holes, also set into the tiles, each ringed with copper and running parallel to the doors and up the marble pillars to either side of the entrance. Some kind of EM grid or stun field. Closer look at the scanning arches suggested they were capable of giving someone a jolt, too.

At present it seemed the doors, and the presence of the mini-turret, were considered enough to handle one nosy guy turning up on a Sunday morning. Or I'd be waking up with a headache pretty soon.

'I was hoping to have a word with Geoff Tyler.' I leaned towards the pickup, heard the turret tracking me. 'I don't s'pose he's around? Doing overtime maybe?'

'No, sir. I don't s'pose he is.' I heard the guard sigh, but he had enough courtesy to switch on the external monitor so I could see who I was talking to. 'I can give you an out-of-hours code if you want to leave a message.'

'It'll go straight to him, personally?'

'It'll go through the filter system, like everything else.'

Yeah. Which meant the chance of any message getting through to Geoff Tyler - the name PC Warren had given me - without monitoring or editing was zero.

'Maybe I'll call back tomorrow.'

'Good idea.'

I made as if to turn away, paused. 'Is this a good gig?'

'Huh?'

'Working here. Any good?'

The man's features relaxed. 'It's okay,' he said. 'The hours stink, but the job's easy.'

'Yeah. Bet they treat you better than my employer treats me.'

On screen, the guard's mouth quirked upwards. 'Who do you work for, then?'

I laughed. 'Me.'

He looked puzzled a second, then gave a chuckle. 'You ought to give yourself a break. Fucking Sunday morning? Most sane souls are still in bed.'

'No argument there. That's a Wolf Line uniform, right? You agency?'

The guard shrugged. 'Yeah, but I'm on a permanent contract. You have to be to work here. At Synapware, I mean. I had to go through all these special clearance checks and stuff. A right pain in the arse, but I wanted the gig. That crap's mandatory to get in here.'

'That'll be down to the MOD contracts they have, I guess.'

No reply. I waited till it started feeling awkward.

'And all you have to do is sit at a desk and tell people they can't come in? I'm in the wrong line of work. What they pay you - forty, fifty a year?'

The guy gave a splutter of laughter. 'I wish! No security gig pays that much! But it's not just watching monitors. Sometimes we're out at the Island or on security shakedowns - they can be...interesting.' He gave another chuckle. 'The best gig is driver detail, though. Now *that's* cushy. You should apply to Wolf Line. They'd take you on, I bet. You look the sort.'

'Driver detail? What, vans and trucks?'

'Yeah, sometimes, when they got something they want moving. But mainly it's just driving. Courtesy stuff, like a chauffeur. You know - driving people around.'

'People like executives?'

'Sometimes.'

'You hear about that security guard who was murdered over in Port Town on Friday? He was Wolf Line, right?'

The guard looked away from the cam for a second, looked back.

'Yeah, he was.' He shifted closer to the pickup. 'I knew him, too. He was a good bloke. Bloody nutters! Everywhere these days! Nowhere's bloody safe any more.'

'So how come you knew him? He work at Synapware, like you?'

On screen the guard's expression froze. Then hardened.

'Are you a reporter?' he demanded. 'You work for yourself, yeah? All these questions? Freelance journalist or fucking PI, that's what you are! Shit!'

'Neither,' I told him. 'Relax, buddy. You haven't told me anything I didn't know already. And I'm going to ask Geoff Tyler tomorrow anyway, so don't worry about it. It's cool.'

He shook his head. 'No, it's not cool—'

'Just one more thing.' I struggled to remember the name of the security guard Gage had killed in Port Town. Failed and gave a wince of self-reproach. Victims deserve more respect than that. 'Did your friend drive people around? You know, like you were telling me? Did he ever drive Joseph Samuels?'

The guard switched off the screen and his voice over the intercom was no longer friendly.

'Sir. The security grid will be activated in five seconds. I strongly suggest you step back, right now.'

'You're doing what? Why?'

Nevertheless I backed up a safe distance. Safe enough to be down the steps and standing on the pavement.

The guard's voice continued over the intercom. 'If you return outside office hours, I'll have you arrested.'

I gave a sigh. Scratched the stubble on my cheek. 'Well, I guess that's me leaving, then.'

And I fully intended to.

Except just then tyres rasped the kerb behind me and a vehicle scraped to a halt. Its riot skirt caught my ankle, knocked it out from under me. I was still off-balance when my hand was grabbed and my wrist joint-locked. Hard.

Momentum twisted me round and I was slammed onto a car hood - the same car which had almost mown me down. One arm was wrestled behind me, then the other. Then I noticed the stun mesh digging into my cheek.

Only one type of car wore that on its bonnet. The guys riding in it were assholes, obviously.

'What the hell are you doing?'

The first cuff clicked shut.

'Sir, if you resist, you'll be rendered immobile. Do you understand?'

I tried to get a look at the uniform leaning his weight on my shoulders but I was pinned down too hard to move. All I could see in my limited field of view was the Synapware building with its mirrored entrance doors and, standing at one of the windows above it, guy in a suit peering down at the activity below.

Embarrassing as hell.

'Why am I being arrested? Loitering with intent to hold a conversation?'

'Weapon!' A second voice gave a warning cry and the Sandman was snatched from its holster for the second time that morning.

'I have a license. Look, guys... I just asked a few questions. Next you'll be arresting people for ordering coffee!'

'You'll have a chance to make a statement back at the station, Mr Nixon. Do we need to read you your rights?'

High Tide in the City

*

She coughed twice more and then she was gone.

I woke up sweating. The bench I lay on was grey plastic, etched with a thousand disgruntled messages - a permanent legacy of the cell's string of temporary guests. The place was scrubbed daily but all that did was overlay the smell of pee with disinfectant.

Mom's deathbed, the sanatorium where she'd spent her last weeks... The sounds and smell in here had dredged them up from my memory, caught me off-guard while I slept. Those last two coughs. And she let go my hand. Trying to hold on to it had made me break out in a sweat, but it was knowing what followed that woke me.

She'd left me alone in the country that raised me but saw me as a foreigner because she hadn't been able to get either of us naturalised. In a devolving United States where space, resources and welfare were sparse to non-existent, a fourteen year-old kid had no business being either alone, or a foreigner.

Military enforcers, queues of rough-looking families, state-funded lawyers, deportation camps, bureaucratic fast-tracking. All I owned I carried with me in a bin bag, shuffled from place to place, sleeping in a different bed each night. I'd lie there with my eyes screwed shut, clutching the covers and listening to strangers moving past the fold-out bunk I lay on, too afraid to sleep. Too sad to sleep.

I still had wishes then. Mine was Mom. I wished she'd come get me. I was almost grown, yet every single night I still wished for that. Even though I knew she wouldn't. Couldn't.

Uncle Sam finally disowned me and Auntie Sam was my new family. My only living relative. She was widowed, no kids, owned her own house. The US authorities couldn't wait to be rid of me and Aunt Samantha was obliged to take me in. Always had the feeling it was more to gain the approval of others than from any sense of familial duty. Aunt Sam's dissatisfaction with her new burden was appeased by the weekly payments she got on my behalf, but only just. I spent the next couple of years hearing what an ingrate I was, how lucky I was to have a roof to sleep under, food in my belly.

She was right, I guess. Hell, if my luck had been different, I might have been related to a millionaire.

I joined the Constabulary the second I became a full adult citizen. That's right. Get abandoned by one system only to embrace another, first chance I got. At least the police paid decent wages. Offered digs for recruits in their section house and - bonus - forbade its employees to work in the town where they grew up. In my case, that meant where I had family, so I moved away from Bath, away from Aunt Sam. Haven't seen her since.

*

'You're sick. You know that, don't you?'

Lian grinned, tossed chestnut curls back over her shoulder and leant her elbows on the table. She was ready to go off duty and her hair was down. Guess I was her last loose end of the night and she was here to tie it off - with scissors if she had anything to do with it.

'You're right,' she said. 'I was sick of you two years ago.'

Two years and she was still mad at me. Well. Guess some people are just like that.

'Okay. So you want to explain what I'm doing here? Kidnap's illegal, you know.'

I got one raised eyebrow and a pair of pursed lips.

'Kidnap? Don't be a tosser, Nix. You're here to assist with my enquiries. You booked the appointment yourself.'

I sat back in my chair, arms behind my head, stretched my legs out. She shifted when my feet brushed hers under the table. Truthfully, I was surprised she'd opted to interview me herself, given her current disposition regarding me. More to the point, I still wasn't sure why I was here at all.

'I know you'll explain,' I said. 'Because I know you know you won't get anything out of me until you do.'

I'd straightened out the Erin Smart thing with her yesterday via bracer-interface - no direct comms, just the way she liked it. So that wasn't why I was here. The visit to Synapware wasn't illegal, either, however early it had been on a Sunday morning. The Chedminster visit she'd authorised herself so...

'Impersonating a doctor.'

'Ah.' I dropped the act.

'You downloaded Samuels' medical records - that's a data protection issue. And if that doesn't make your visit to the Memorial illegal, you already have a history with him.'

'I do?'

'You're the last person to speak to him. The last coherent moment he spent was in your company, before your scanner went on his head. Someone suspicious - like me - might think you went to the hospital to tidy up a mess you made. You'd better pray he pulls through or this is going to get a lot more serious.'

I shook my head. 'Hospitals have cams. I imagine you've checked, so you already know. I took a look at the burn, took a look at his records. Nothing else. Why am I really here?'

'So I could spend time in your sparkling company, of course. Why else would I add more hours to an endless shift when what I really need is breakfast, a shower and ten hours sleep?'

'Hey, good plan! I take my eggs scrambled. But you know that already... Ow!'

Not much warning. A glint as her eyes widened. Outrage and anger. And humiliation. Brought a flush to her cheeks, too. Beautiful.

But why do women's shoes have to be pointy?

She shifted in her chair - uneasy, just at the suggestion.

'Don't start!' she warned. 'Just don't.'

Yeah, I could call police brutality here, but I guess I deserved that kick. I leaned forward, rubbed the new bruise on my shin. Just above the one I got from the police car's crash skirt.

'As a point of interest,' I said. 'I didn't "start" this. You're the one who arranged to put cuffs on me.'

Lian pushed hair out of her eyes, leaned back in the chair.

'All right, fuck it,' she said. 'I don't have the energy and I can't be bothered to run round in circles with you. The hospital's shut me down so I need to see the data you downloaded.'

It was close, but I managed to keep the grin off my face. I leaned back again, sucking my teeth instead.

'I rather think,' I told her. 'You've overstepped your boundaries, Detective Inspector Morrison. Unlike Samuels, I'm not a murder suspect, so you don't have the right to access my bracer. You have no just cause, so I don't have to let you see anything.'

'That's why I'm asking.'

'Ask nicer.'

'Please.'

'Can't help you.'

She rolled her eyes.

'Seriously, I can't. My bracer's in the shop. I got a loaner. What you looking for on there, anyway? More prostitutes? Someone suspicious - like me - might think you were jealous.'

Lian didn't dignify that with a reaction. She stared at me for a long time. Long enough to make me shift in my seat, draw my legs in and hunch forward, elbows on the table, mirroring her.

'I have the autopsy report,' she said at last. 'Gage had an elliptical burn behind his right ear, right over his internal link. The technical report said his aug burnt out completely. What we didn't know is that his throat mike did exactly the same thing. It's too similar to Samuels' to be coincidence, so I want to see what else the Memorial has to say about him.'

'And you couldn't just ask them? You *are* the lead investigator on this one now. Right?'

It was Lian's turn to sit back in her chair. 'Right,' she agreed.

The bulge in one side of her cheek told me she was grinding her teeth. Poor girl. A long night, three caseloads and a dead colleague. Oh, plus me. The pressure must be really piling up.

'Right,' I said. 'But instead you come to me. Wait, no. You didn't. You had me arrested, forcibly and in public. You had my gun taken, my rights read to me. You had me locked up in the drunk tank and had me wait until you got around to asking me what a bunch of doctors could tell you in five seconds flat.'

'Except Synapware have found themselves enough legal clout to get their employee "mummified",' Lian said bitterly. 'I can't get near him. He's off-limits, murder suspect or no. I can't get anyone over there to even talk about him. Samuels might as well *be* a mummy, the amount of information I can dig up on him.'

'Nice choice of words.'

She picked at a gouge in the tabletop, feigning nonchalance. 'Come on, Nix, I have a murdered whore, a murdered security guard, a dead policeman and a lot of unanswered questions. I did you a favour, now you help me out. What did you find out at the Memorial?'

'How about we trade?'

Lian lifted her gaze, looked through her fringe at me. The hair shifted when she blinked.

'Trade? Trade what?'

'I tell you what I found out at the hospital. You let me look at Gage's bracer.'

She shook her head, but it wasn't a refusal, it was disgust.

'You're a seedy bastard.'

'I'm looking for the same file on Gage's bracer I was looking for on Samuels's. More importantly, I think this "Mephistopheles", whatever it is, is jumping through bracer signals. It jumped from Joseph Samuels to John Gage through mine. I'm guessing it then jumped from Gage when he made that call just before he fell. I'd like to know who he called.'

'So did you find it?'

'What?'

'On Samuels' bracer. The file you were looking for.'

'Nope. Synapware got there first. The entire bracer was blank. Wiped.'

*

Truthfully, I was surprised she let me see John Gage's bracer. Might have been because she was madder at Synapware than me at that precise moment. Small shred of time in which I wasn't Lian Morrison's number one enemy. So she'd been magnanimous.

It also gave her an excuse to leave.

DI Gage had a device equal to or cleverer than mine. Lot cleverer than the one weighing my arm down now and a star-ship compared to Samuels's bi-wing. It was one of the soft ones with a claytronic gel casing. The self-moulding sheath you wore instead of regular, solid plates was supposed to be more comfortable - like part of your own arm. Plus it made you look less like a cyborg. Soft bracers were way more expensive than the solid type but, truth is, they were crap. Data kept corrupting and the trylon screens wore out too fast.

Gage's was no different. It was cracked along three natural folds on the screen's surface layer and fibres were poking through like frayed netting. Crashing through packing crates and hitting steel decking had split the claytronic sheath in three places. The thumb loop was all but torn off. I unclipped the closures and smoothed the bracer out flat on the table in front of me. Say this for it, the screen lit up first time, nice as you like.

The file I was hoping to find on it wasn't there. I was surprised enough to check three times until it occurred to me. Ancient habit had made me flick the record button on my bracer when I'd put Samuels through to Gage. In case he said something incriminating. Something that might help in court.

Gage's case was different. For one thing, there had been no intermediary. No one there except Gage to hit 'record'. Besides, even if Gage had been himself enough to think of it, even though he was a cop, why record himself screaming? I was looking for a file which didn't exist.

Looking for one on Samuels' bracer had been little more than cross-checking. I already knew Mephistopheles hadn't exited him through *his* device before I ever went out to Chedminster. The rogue squirt had waited for me. For *my* bracer. Hadn't known at the time his couldn't handle it but, anyway, looking for the IUM there was an excuse. A long shot until some other clue showed up to get me pointed in the right direction, such as a list of callers. A list of suspects. An inventory of possibles who might have sent Mephistopheles into Samuels so he could carry out the random murder of a street-class call girl.

With a list of possibles, I might be able to find a motive. Might find the real killer. But Synapware had stepped in, deleted the list. Pretty sure they shouldn't be able to do that, legally, but Lian had looked pissed off enough to make me think they could.

Gage's bracer, on the other hand... Even though there was no audio file the size of the Euro Building in there, it had a complete list of all his calls, received and made. I flicked through till I found the last number called, checked it for date and time, pulled up the contact details.

'Shit!'

6

DI Harris was one of those cops you tend not to think of, until you need something done right. He was a plodder. Not one of those uber-fit, Kevlar-wearing gun jockeys they like to highlight on TV. Mid-forties, overweight, hair getting thin and a little snowy. He didn't make the news. He didn't make waves. But if you needed someone dependable, someone who wouldn't fuck up and leave you with your ass exposed, Harris was your guy. He was the only one whose evening barbecues I ever attended. He'd missed his calling in that regard - should have worked at a crematorium. But he threw a mean party.

He was the only one, when I was awaiting trial for persona abuse, who'd come out to Chedminster in *person* to see me. Asked me how I was doing. If I needed anything.

He always said he'd die for his wife. From the moment I saw them together, I believed it, too. It wasn't like they shoved it in your face, but you could see it. A shared glance over a joke, casual touch as they passed each other in a crowded room. They'd had kids late, or met late, because the sprogs were still at school. Still young enough to be cute. Harris swore he'd die for them, too.

The door, when I got there, was open. Wasn't unusual these days - now air conditioning was taxed. Easier to let a draft blow through the house on a hot day like this. So I heard the cartoons before I got inside and for a short moment that was a relief. Sunday morning, why wouldn't the kids be watching cartoons?

Sunday morning, now it was getting towards midday, though, I also expected to smell cooking. Sunday Roast. Still a tradition, even if the beef came from a bean these days. Instead, all I smelt was the bowl of flower oils on the table by the door. I stabbed the button, heard the doorbell toll somewhere inside the house.

'Harris?'

No reply. Maybe the TV volume was enough to cover my voice. And the doorbell. I gave another shout, louder, and pushed the door. It swung back, showing me carpeted hall, cream walls, no pictures. The door at the end stood half-open and colours were flickering in the darkened room beyond. I took a step over the threshold. Waited another second for a reply.

When it still didn't come, I reached back under the faux leather, flicked the clip on my holster and pulled out Mr Sandman. Didn't like drawing my weapon in a policeman's house, but half an hour after Gage had fallen to his death, Harris had called in sick. Three guesses where Gage's Last Number Dialled had led me.

Didn't matter how much I believed it. Lian was off duty by now and no one else would listen to a disgraced detective who'd used up all his favours three weeks after he turned freelance. So here I was with no back up. And if Mephistopheles was inside Harris then there was a wife and two kids in the persona's way and so far it hadn't needed an obvious motive to kill.

It had taken around twenty-four hours before the psychotic overlay had driven Gage to commit murder. That was my hope. That Harris had spent yesterday feeling like shit and Mephistopheles had stayed dormant. If I was right and there was a squirt involved here at all, then it should follow a pattern. It meant I had time. Time to get to him before it touched the family. Time to subdue Harris, flush it out of him and stop this shit spreading any further.

The room at the end of the hall was the Harris Den and it was alive with movement. The long French window was opaqued to dark, the projector focused towards the back wall. The holographic movie playing on it filled half the room with light and colour, sound and movement. Full-size characters leapt and shrieked around me as I moved in, covering with the Sandman.

I slid into the room slow, trying to look past the light show. Trying to pick out what was real, what was projection against the chaos of speed and noise. A demon-headed character two feet taller than me materialised a foot from my face, making me flinch. It turned, stomped towards then through me and out my back so it could hack a creature part-angel, part fish into a dozen pieces. The room turned red with blood.

I let out a breath. Kids' movies. Go figure.

To my left my peripheral vision caught something - something more solid than the projected light around me. When I looked properly it was gone. I adjusted my grip, the Sandman slick in my palm.

In a situation like this, sometimes it's easier to see what's real when you look for what's *not* moving. Seizure-inducing colours flickered over the couch, across the coffee table, highlighted the toys scattered on the floor.

'Harris?'

My voice hardly carried over the audio from the system's four speakers. I crossed the room, reached out with my left hand and shoved the only other door in here, let it swing open.

Four years ago Harris had paid nearly twenty thousand for that kitchen. Polished silicrete worktops, self-cleaning sink, high-end cooker. Still groan inside when I remember how he'd go on about the whole episode: how they'd picked out every last gadget and recess, the loan he'd had to take to afford it, the stress of getting it fitted. It was apparently still his wife's most precious possession beyond the kids - the place was immaculate. No sign a meal had ever been produced from it. That was Eileen. A touch OCD, if you ask me, but she loved her home, always kept it clean and tidy.

I glanced back, frowning. So why were the toys left out? And why was the TV left on with no one watching?

Stairs led directly from the living room. Looked like the only way onward was upward. Two bedrooms and a bathroom. Not much space for a family of four, but that wasn't unusual - especially not these days - so it didn't take long to check. Not a living soul. All three were gone. And none of them had gone painlessly.

Natural to wonder who he made live longest. Eileen probably, so she could hear her babies crying before she went herself - heard them scream while they died slowly and in terror. In agony. I found her in the bathtub tied up and pinned to the bottom by a mock-deco iron stool while water dripped onto her submerged face, rippling the surface. Tiny bubbles clung to her skin and hair like a scatter of seed pearls. Her lips were parted, gasping for the air she'd finally been unable to reach. The kids had died worse.

I had to head downstairs before the temptation to get Paulie down overwhelmed me. Aside from checking there were no life signs, I had to leave the place as I found it, so forensics could do their job. But it was tough leaving the little four-year-old to hang from the doorframe by the nails driven through his forearms.

It took me until I was back downstairs. Until I'd opened the link to Emergency Services and was waiting for it to connect. Then a megaton of rage detonated somewhere south of my chest.

'You fucking *bastard*!'

'Hey, Squirt Man.'

I spun round automatically, the Sandman already lifting as I sensed him there, stepping from behind the kitchen door. Glimpsed glittering, crazed eyes and thin, snowy hair turned green by a splash of colour. The golf club's shaft gleamed purple, turned red as it bounced. My head bounced the other way and I staggered back. My legs disconnected, crumpled, but I got off one dart as I hit the ground, which spat, useless, into the stair post beside Harris. My arm came up, warding off the next blow, but he wasn't aiming for my face. The jacket absorbed some of it, but the clout shook my entire body. Left a band of lava scored across my ribs. The next time he hit me I heard him laugh. It was the last blow. The last I remember, anyhow.

*

Harris spoke low and quiet into my ear, but I didn't catch what he said. Too busy trying to work out where I was and too surprised I'd woken up at all. Harris - Mephistopheles - was a psychopath. If he'd used a golf club on me it was because he couldn't find a knife - he wouldn't put it down until I was pulp. Or so I'd thought.

I was lying face-down on the ground, my head pillowed by my left forearm. That's how I knew Harris had removed the loaner bracer I'd been wearing. Made sense, since I'd opened an implant link to the police, which he couldn't close. Safer to dump the bracer than risk them tracking me and, by extension, him. My jacket was missing, too, and the sun was boiling through the shoulders of my Tee. A breeze stirred my hair, cooled the sweat pooling in the creases of my neck. That much I could tell without opening my eyes. It added up to me being somewhere outside, meaning he'd moved me from the house.

I wondered if the neighbours - midday on a Sunday in that quiet cul-de-sac - had noticed Harris loading a body into his car. In his current state, he probably didn't care. Besides, it wasn't Harris I was dealing with and when - *if* - he was ever himself again he'd have to come to terms with a lot more than the murder of some sleazy ex-cop.

Should have thought it through sooner. Maybe I'd've gotten there before the overlay did the things it had done to the family Harris loved.

Or maybe I'd be dead, too. Maybe I'd've joined them in their long, slow deaths. Listened to their wails, watched their pain as their lives ebbed away. Which brought me back to why I was still alive.

I finally opened my eyes, found one of them wouldn't. Perspiration dribbled under the swelling, stung like hell. I had to twist to look upwards and that hurt, too. Warned me there might be a cracked rib. The act took extra effort because my hands were clamped together and held down so hard I couldn't shift them. Not an inch. But Harris was hunched next to me, waiting for me to look at him and there was one thing I knew. If the overlay inside him intended to kill me, which was a given, I'd make him look me in the eye when he did it. And I didn't care if it added to his pleasure or not.

'So, here we are, Squirt Man.'

I licked my lips, spat blood onto the hot metal slab under me.

'Why'd you hurt the kids? Eileen...'

'Why not?'

'Who are you? Where the hell did they get you from?'

Overlay or not, Mephistopheles must have come from someone. A serial killer some bastard had downloaded so he could sell it to someone as a weekend kick. Only the dealer wasn't making money on this squirt. This squirt was body-hopping at will and having a great time doing it.

Harris shrugged. 'Details aren't going to matter to you, not any more, Nixon.'

When I glared at him through my one good eye, the guy leaned closer, growled in my ear.

'Knew you wouldn't let it go, shithead!'

I blinked hard, cleared my vision. Tried to ignore the feeling the thing I was talking to knew me personally.

'Okay then. *What* are you?'

'I'm your worst nightmare. In case you hadn't noticed.'

I had noticed, to be honest. I'd noticed something else, too. Mephistopheles was failing inside Harris. Man's fingers were twitching, his eyelids flickering whenever he moved his head. His expression - the satanic grin I'd last seen on Samuels' face - was still there, though. The fiend dwelling inside a man I'd worked with, respected, wasn't about to go sane any time soon. I'd love a look inside Harris's head right now.

Another chance to record this phenomenon, figure out exactly what made Mephistopheles tick. And I'd make sure I got a *good* recording this time. Right now, though, the odds I'd ever get to do that looked bleak. Besides, the magic cap was in my trunk and my car was... God knows. Wasn't even sure where *I* was.

'So how come I'm still breathing? You could have killed me already.'

'Actually, I already did.'

Harris stood up and I shifted warily. If he was about to make his move, I didn't plan on just lying there. But the service-issue cuffs on my wrists had other ideas. They'd been trying to flatten themselves against the ground all this time, but flesh and bone - my flesh and bone - was in their way. When I moved, they dug in harder, locked my wrists tighter against the sidewalk.

No. I looked closer. This wasn't a sidewalk. It wasn't even a road. It was smooth, clean and so hot in the baking sun it shimmered like a river, further down the line.

A long strip of steel three feet wide and so hungry for metal it would snap my wrists sooner than let go the cuffs.

'Crap!'

Tugging did nothing but scrape the top layer off my skin. The cuffs didn't budge.

'You gotta be shitting me.'

Harris just grunted and stepped away.

'This is stupid!' I said. And felt it. Stupid, embarrassed, horrified that I was going to die like this, right in front of him. I pulled on the cuffs harder, loosened more skin.

I craned my neck, focussed my good eye on him while he stared behind me into the distance, sun glinting on white hair, which fluttered in the breeze. Finally Harris looked down and smiled like some cheesy super-villain.

'I think you'll enjoy Cornwall,' he said. 'The bits of you that get there.'

*

My hands were slick with blood, but the cuffs were too tight to slip off, no matter how hard I pulled, even if they'd been at an angle to let me do it. The steel was trying its damndest to lie flat against the rail and might as well be molecule-welded to it. I got my knees, my legs under me, raised myself until the metal hoop cut in too hard, threatened to snap bone. I had to sink back, rethink.

I expected him to stay. To watch. The thing inside Harris. Why else go to all this trouble? Why not just pound my head to mush with that club, back at the house? Maybe it meant to, but then it started dying. Harris fighting back. Once that started, it didn't have a whole lot of time to hang around.

I was too busy wrestling the cuffs to watch him leave. He stepped off the magway, slid on his heels down the raised embankment to the waste ground beyond. I hoped he wouldn't look back, just keep walking. Back to his car, somewhere out of sight in the dip beyond the scrub.

He was right, though. He'd already killed me.

People died like this all the time on the magway. By accident or on purpose - their own design or someone else's. Around eighteen people a month, according to statistics. Next month one of those statistics would be me.

So this was how I was going to die. A magway train up my ass. Talk about trite. Mephistopheles was laughing *his* ass off now, just thinking about it. Had to be. I could almost hear him in the distance, cackling to himself.

A thousand tonnes of metal travelling at the speed of a meteor. I probably wouldn't even feel it. But I'd feel enough terror, seeing the magtrain flashing towards me with no chance of stopping. Probably shit myself waiting for the final, helpless instant.

Truth is, I was no pat hero. There were no super-ninja moves in my repertoire. There was no shred of genius tucked away inside my head, either. So there would be no clever escapes, no flash of inspiration to save my neck. All I had was dumb luck and I knew how that one usually played out.

The magtrain never touched the rail. Common knowledge. It rode friction-free and essentially silent. Made it more efficient. There was no engine to speak of - the string of pod-like carriages were repelled by the rail, meaning the whole thing hovered, drawn along by polarised magnetic pulses travelling down the rail at supersonic speed. Meant there was a small gap between the train's underbelly and the magrail. Within a tolerance of three mils, though, the gap was seven centimetres. No good to me. Even sucking in the gut I'd been cultivating for the past year, the next train passing by would spread my corpse out in a long streak from here to Plymouth.

Something under the metal *tocked*. The cuffs relaxed for a fraction of a second then moved. Slid. Their idea. Like a supernatural force took hold - pulled them down the line - dragging me with them, five feet along the magway.

'Shit!' It was a pulse. A distant one, but it meant one thing. A train was coming.

I already knew it was fruitless, but I took issue with the cuffs again, got on my knees and tussled. With them, with the rail. Pretty stupid, huh? Expecting my pathetic efforts to overcome a force which held a giga-ton of steel to the rail, but it was instinct mixed with a good measure of panic. And, besides, whether I was going to feel it or not, I didn't want to die.

When the tock under the rail came again, the pulse dragged me further, pulling on the popped rib hard enough to make my eyes water. Pulling me far enough for friction to warm my thighs through the fabric of my jeans. I glanced behind, fearing sight of a train at the limit of my view. It wasn't there, though, not yet. But that was no comfort. The pulses told me it was coming, sure as shit. Besides, the speed these things went, seeing it would give me just long enough to say...

'Son-of-a-bitch!'

I'd noticed it twice now. That brief second - less than a second - when the rail switched polarity. It was the heart of the pulse, the eye. The hook the magtrain rode on as it passed along the rail. A short moment when the polarised metal repelled the cuffs. It was barely long enough to lift them. Not enough time to escape. But...

My leather soles scrabbled on smooth metal until I got my feet up, as far under me as I could get them and round to the right. I stood there bent over, hands jammed against the rail. Next time the pulse came I was ready for it, leaning my weight back, braced for the sweet-spot. *Tock*. My legs went out from under me as the pulse came and went in a flash. It came quicker this time and the pulse dragged me fifteen, twenty feet. Far enough for the thin shirt I wore to snag on grit and tear. The drag wrenched my shoulders and the grit left my skin raw, but there was no time to care. I was already picking myself up. I angled over to the right again, bracing my weight against the cuffs, ready for the next pulse, ready to pull when I heard the next 'tock'. Couldn't be sure I'd achieved anything at all that first time, but maybe the cuffs were a little more off-centre now. Or had they been off-centre to start with? For a blind moment, I couldn't remember.

The next pulse lifted the cuffs clear of the rail, but it didn't let go. I came down hard on my right shoulder and yelled when my ribs hit metal. I slewed sideways, helpless as the cuffs travelled south, drawn along on the pulse.

In the distance something blared. I looked round, knowing what it was, though I still couldn't see it.

By law it had to sound its siren whenever it exited a tunnel. Nailmarsh, probably. Be nice to know where I was in relation to that. Nice to know how many more seconds I had left to live. But the cuffs were closer to the edge now. This time I could tell for sure.

Problem was, the pulses were coming faster and stronger and it took longer to get to my feet since I was coming down harder, being dragged further. I was barely off my knees before the next one flipped the cuffs up, caught me on the jaw.

I twisted anyway, found myself caught in a weird somersault as the magnetic force got tangled round me. I came down on my back, caught a glimpse of something long and shiny, like a shower hose, streaking across the sunburnt flood-plain, a mile from me and closing. Almost impossible to turn onto my front again and the cuffs were like a vice clamping both wrists. My good eye was dimming with pain by the time I'd crossed my hands, pulled myself up.

The magtrain was filling the landscape behind me, blocking out the rest of the world with its bulk. It arced around, leaning into the solitary curve between it and me, without troubling to slow. The damned thing ran silent, but I could hear it punching through air hard enough to leave sonic booms trailing behind it - not that I could hear those yet. If I ever would.

Whoever was responsible for making the fucker stop and start had spotted me. The siren blared again.

'Yeah, yeah. I can *see* you!'

It was on me as the pulse came again, spiralled me round. This time I used the momentum to spin, pulled the cuffs in an arc over my body. The sky blanked out as the train rushed past. The massive wall of air travelling ahead of it picked me up then threw me off to one side. I landed on gravel, rolled hard down the raised bank, tearing more holes in the Tee. Felt my ribs crunch again as I came to a halt tasting grit. Chalk settled while I waited for the sonic booms which told me the magtrain was gone.

*

Seeing the car tripped my alarm circuits, set my heart thudding. It stood two hundred yards from where I finally got the energy to heave myself to my feet and take a look around. Spotted it straight away. He was in there. Had to be. I knew because the car parked alongside the old canal was mine. Mephistopheles had used it instead of Harris's. Meant he'd hung around to watch my exit. Meant he knew I'd survived. Now he'd need to finish the job and I was in no state to fight him.

Maybe it was because I felt so much like shit I didn't high-tail it in the opposite direction. I waited instead. See what he was going to do. After more than a minute and no sign of movement, I began to wonder if he'd just abandoned the car and walked away.

If I'd been too exhausted to run at the sight of my car, the idea of hiking Christ-knows how many miles back to civilisation was even less appealing. I needed transport. A couple more minutes just staring at it, looking for signs of activity, then I started forward. Halted when I was close enough to pick out the figure sat in the driver's seat.

Harris's face was like a slab of lard - pale and waxy, his eyes staring. His head was lolled back, propped up by the headrest behind it. For a second I thought he was dead, then his forehead creased in pain, relaxed. Then I realised. Harris had been coming down too hard for Mephistopheles to stay and watch me die. He'd had to jump. Find a new host.

I'd been too busy saving my ass to hear the scream.

I staggered into a run. Broken ribs don't like it when you run. I found that out about then. The cuffs had absorbed some magnetic charge from the rail. They got in the way as I fumbled for the handle. The central locking was off. I yanked the door open.

The burn was there alright, just behind his right ear. Mephistopheles was gone.

'Harris?'

Looking at him it was no surprise I'd thought he was dead. But not only was Harris still alive, he was conscious. He frowned, kept focussed straight ahead.

'Nix.' It was a whisper. His lips were pale and dry as paper. 'Don't feel too good.'

'I know. Take it easy. I'll get help.'

I moved around the car, scooched onto the passenger seat, hunted in the glove-box for some cuff keys. The cuffs came off reluctantly, twisted and scratched, and the key jammed in their lock. Once off, I tossed them. Resisted inspecting the damage to my wrists.

Instead, I flicked the in-car media panel to emergency services. Once I knew police and ambulances were heading to both the car's transponder and Harris's home address, I turned back to Harris.

His wrists were bare, but I knew Mephistopheles had jumped and he'd needed a bracer to do it with. So where the hell was it?

'Harris? You still with me? Stay awake, pal. They're coming.'

His eyes flickered and he blinked hard. 'Bad nightmare.'

'Yeah.'

Guy had the biggest headache ever invented. He was in no state for me to tell him the nightmare was real.

'Harris, listen. Can you focus a second? I need your bracer. Where is it?'

I'd started hunting the second I saw it was missing. Looked in the glove compartment again - as if I'd have missed it when I'd looked for the keys. It wasn't in either foot-well, or on the back seat.

I leaned forward, checking underneath, suppressed a groan as the change in position compressed my ribs and sent a rush of blood to my swollen eye.

'Threw it.' Barely a croak.

I straightened. 'Say again.'

'I threw it.'

I turned to look at his face, then past him to the strip of murky water lying only feet beyond the car. Not in there. Please, not in there.

'Why?'

'He told me to.'

Mephistopheles. Bastard!

'Where? Harris, this is important. Is it in the scrub? On the wasteland somewhere? I need to know. He's moved on to someone else. I need to find them, fast.'

'River. He said throw it in the river.'

7

'We'll be keeping you in overnight, Mr Nixon.'

The nurse straightened my gurney, stepped on the pedal that applied the brake. The trolley jerked and dropped an inch, making me wince.

Made me talk through my teeth. 'Not if I have anything to do with it.'

The guy - Tony, according to his name badge - bent over me again, checked the chem-weld sealing the gash over my eye.

'Those were very strong painkillers they gave you downstairs. You won't be in any state to–'

'How's DI Harris?'

'I've no news on that but he's in good hands, just–'

'Have you contacted Lian Morrison like I said?'

'Not yet.'

I sighed. 'Just contact her, it's vital I speak to her. Right now.'

'No, what's vital is that you get a good night's rest. The arnical needs time to get the bruising and swelling under control and we need to make absolutely sure you don't have a concussion.'

'I've had a concussion before, this isn't it.'

Tony showed me a tight smile.

'Thanks for the diagnosis. You need to rest, so if it'll keep you from walking out of here... Detective Inspector Morrison is still off duty, but she's been made aware of the situation and has passed your "lead" to her "oppo" at Parson Street.'

I wondered who that would be. My 'lead' was for her to track down Harris's bracer so I - we - could identify Mephistopheles' next host. Last

High Tide in the City

I heard the warm bodies needed to drag the canal for it were currently monitoring an anti-Port Town demonstration at Broadmeads. Stop it turning into a riot. Hell, the Port Towners had a point, but in my opinion their timing sucked.

Grinding my teeth hurt my eye for some reason. Wouldn't change anything anyway, so I stopped doing it.

Tony was still complaining. 'Detective Inspector Harris is comfortable and under observation. *You*, on the other hand, are a wreck.'

'Just a couple of scrapes, I'm fine.'

'Abrasions, multiple contusions, bone damage to both of your wrists and your ribs, split eyelid - lucky you have an eye left in there and we're still not sure if your vision will be permanently impaired - and a gash on your scalp requiring eight stitches.'

'Your point being?'

'It's thanks to that abnormally thick skull of yours you're here and not in the morgue.'

To be honest, I wasn't sure if that last was an insult or a compliment, but the guy hadn't finished.

'Hospital policy states that if there's any doubt a patient might not live till morning, we keep them overnight. So one way or another you're here till tomorrow. If I have to sedate you, I will.'

'Sedate me? When you think I might have a concussion?'

'Just lie there and shut up!'

No doubt about it. Man had a lousy bedside manner. It said something about my run of luck lately that I'd ended up with a churlish male nurse instead of the pretty female one from the emergency room. She'd been chatty, too. Meant I didn't have to do too much of the work, and the way I'd been feeling at the time, that was a bonus.

I'm always the same. I'll do anything when they're patching me up, except pay attention to what they're doing. Sitting upright on the same gurney I now lay on, only downstairs in A and E, I'd spotted a download printout pinned to the notice board opposite. Headline: 'Redfield Prostitute Murdered'. I'd asked the cute nurse with the needle and thread why that? With all the bad news out there, why had the news clipping of Erin Smart's murder been picked out for special attention?

'We used to know her,' the nurse - Angela, I think - said back.

'We? She worked here? At the Memorial?'

'She was a paramedic. One of the motorcycle ones. She used to bring cakes in when it was quiet.'

'So she went from leather jockey to skin jockey? Weird career path. Ow!'

Okay, not my most tactful moment, but she didn't have to get vindictive. When I blinked, my eyes were watering.

Okay, so when I'd known her she was a street prostitute called Kate. Didn't mean she'd always favoured that lifestyle.

'Was she nice, Erin Smart? A good person?'

'She was a good paramedic, too.' Angela put the tweezers down and dabbed at my skull. 'She just wanted to get out of Port Town.'

That made me reassess Kate all over again. She'd lived out there? No wonder she sold people, including herself. People do anything to escape that pit. There's evidence on the streets daily.

'So what happened?'

'She stole drugs from the pharmacy. Got caught. Sacked.'

'Then murdered,' I said quietly.

Angela had stopped then, to stare at the clipping. 'I still can't believe it. They won't even say what he did to her.'

'Maybe it's best not to know,' I'd said, and she'd gone back to stitching me up.

Tell the truth, even I knew I wasn't fit enough to walk out of the overnight ward. Not that I'd admit it. But I wasn't convinced the male nurse didn't sedate me anyway. It wasn't long after he walked out the room I was asleep. Lost count of how many times the bastards then woke me up again, checking I hadn't gone into a coma or something.

When I woke up for real, it was to the rattle of the breakfast trolley entering the overnight ward. Attracted by the aroma of toast and coffee, I rolled off my good side onto my back. Change in position reminded me why I'd been lying on my good side. The pain relief must have worn off because my ribs felt ready to burst. The stitches in my scalp tightened when I turned my head. I daren't wince. That hurt my eye.

Nix, that nurse was right, you're a mess.

I was still in my clothes, which were fast graduating from torn and dirty to rank and disgusting, but my shoes were missing. The overnight ward usually catered for a certain sort. A sort I didn't want helping themselves to my shoes, whatever state they were in after yesterday's activities. Right now, though, I couldn't summon what I needed to track them down. Guess that said something about the way I felt.

I helped myself to two cups of coffee and a pastry, which I wolfed down. The coffee was tepid and the soya milk curdled, but I was thirsty. I drank it with barely a shudder, looked round for seconds.

The trolley was down the far end of the ward by then, but before I'd found the energy to prise myself upright and follow it, I spotted two suits entering the ward, led by my pal from last night. Tony halted, said something to the shortest of the men and pointed in my direction. The man nodded thanks to him. Turned to look directly at me.

Wasn't a look I'd consider friendly.

I winced, continued getting off the gurney, but instead of the breakfast trolley, I headed for the other exit. My entire body was sore. Slowed me down.

'Mr Nixon?'

I wasn't in any state to make a real dash for anywhere, so I halted at the sound of my name, bare feet slapping the polished floor. I pointed at the *male* icon embossed on the door ahead.

'Gotta go. Urgent.'

The suit apparently didn't care.

'This is urgent, too. I'd rather appreciate your co-operation.'

*

We got to sit in a consultant's office. Took a lot of money, or a lot of power, to throw a consultant out of his own office. Told me these guys were bad news. The shorter guy took the role of consultant - lounging in the leather chair opposite me, elbows on the desk, fiddling with a pen he'd taken from his own pocket. The taller guy - muscle, no question - took the role of standing by my left shoulder, ready to add to my discomfort if I didn't act exactly like I was supposed to. Which, given this was me, was another reason why these guys were bad news.

The guy behind the desk slid his fingers along the shaft of his pen, rolled it between them. It looked solid, expensive. He took his eyes off it, laid them on me.

'So you're Matt Nixon.'

'Last I checked.' Glib, I know, and more related to a growl than the polite reply my circumstances maybe warranted. Well, I wasn't in the best of moods this morning and shrugging hurt. 'Who might you be?'

'You left a message for me at my offices yesterday.'

'I did?'

Blunt fingers. Soft. Manicured. Neat white cuff sliding out under a dark-grey sleeve more intelligent than me. Yeah. It was the guy behind me got his hands dirty. Guy doing the talking stayed clean, with nominal assistance from his Mensa-rated suit. I wondered what shoes Mr Soft-Hands wore. Russian, maybe. Looked like he could afford it. And probably wouldn't care if they were made of human skin.

'Geoff Tyler, Synapware,' he said.

The same sleazeball who'd emptied Samuels' bracer.

I stared at the hand, reluctant to take it - and not just because of the damage to my wrists - but I did, eventually. Once I sensed the muscle breathe harder down my neck.

Tyler's handshake was short, perfunctory. The way he took his hand back again suggested he was now in the market for sanitising gel. He did his best not to wipe the offending appendage on his nice suit. Took hold of the pen again instead. Unclicked the lid. Clicked it on again.

'I don't recall leaving my name,' I said. 'Kinda strange, that.'

Tyler smiled. The way the skin round his eyes responded, or rather didn't, suggested he'd been in his mid-thirties for a couple of decades at least. They were brown, had an intense look to them, but if they'd ever laughed it was probably one of those events they give out silver coins to the nation for. This smile was calculated, measured to the millimetre.

'You're well known to us, Mr Nixon. I think, last count, it was three court cases you managed to instigate against us?'

More like five, but hey.

'It was your product. Those people were victims. Someone has to stand up to Synapware.'

'And you did. Bravo.'

Hard to glare at someone when your left eye feels ready to fall out. I remembered not to wince. Still, I've never been one to pass up the opportunity to ask an awkward question.

'You mind if I ask what project Joseph Samuels was working on before he ended up in here?'

Tyler smiled again. 'Good. We're on the same page.' He turned to the tough, who'd come to stand on my left and who shifted slightly, like he was coming to attention.

'Mr Beck,' he said. 'Do we have that paperwork?'

Understandably, the peripheral vision out my left eye wasn't too good so I twisted to watch Mr Beck twitch his jacket open. He did it nice and deliberate, so I got a good look.

And I was right.

Shoulder holster.

But that wasn't a Sandman he was packing. The thick handgrip poking out under his armpit was all metal. Copper-ceramic, if the green colouration was anything to go by. Moscow Special. Not the kind of thing you'd want your kids to play with.

The gun wasn't what got my attention, though. Couldn't help noticing the hand Beck reached inside his jacket. Normal assumption - it was flesh and blood hidden under a glove - shiny black leather, no seams. But the fingers were too slender for his build, which made me check out his left hand, the one holding the jacket open. No glove there and the fingers were broad, tanned, capable. Folding round a stippled handgrip would be second nature to them. Except he wore the holster on his left. Made him right-handed. Or whatever you call it, when you have no right hand at all.

I'd put money on that too-small hand, and maybe the whole arm, being a prosthetic. And he used it for shooting with. Made sense, I guess. Probably gave him assisted aim, no limit on weight or recoil. Even so, not what I'd expect an exec's hired hand - no pun intended - to need in his repertoire.

I flicked a glance at the guy's face, ran my eyes over the web of scars running down the right side, forehead to cheek. Same side as his false hand. The scars were red, rimmed with pink. Meant they were a year old, maybe two. Guy had been through something nasty not so long ago.

Being me, I had to check out his footwear. Didn't like what I saw. Jesus Creepers. High grip, low noise soles. Guy liked to move quick and silent. Suggested he was worse than just a thug. He was a trained thug.

The fingers which were potentially capable of crushing that copper-ceramic smoker to dust without even noticing slid inside the jacket's inner pocket and extracted a long envelope. The paper was smooth, expensive.

Tyler took the envelope, flicked the stiff flap open with a white-rimmed thumbnail. There were several loose pages inside, folded precisely. He smoothed the sheets out on the consultant's blotter.

The pen lid clicked again. 'Have you ever signed Special States Secrets, Mr Nixon?'

'When I joined, same as anyone.'

The brown eyes pretended to smile again. 'I said the *Special* States Secrets. Besides, what you signed when you joined the Constabulary lapsed when you were...invited to leave.'

I managed to blink at him, dead-pan, before replying.

'Oh. "*Special*" States Secret? How'd I miss that? That the one spies have to sign?'

'Yes it is.'

'Then I guess I didn't.'

'Now's your chance.'

Tyler turned the opened-out document so I could read it. I noticed the Royal Seal embossed onto the paper.

'Read it thoroughly, so you know exactly what you're signing, Mr Nixon. I'd hate to see you executed for treason.'

'I'm sure you would.'

Sad, but maybe he thought I'd be intimidated by stupid threats. At least, I assumed it was a stupid threat. I'd gotten half way through the document before I asked myself what the hell I was doing. Placed my finger down on the paragraph I'd been reading. Looked up at Tyler.

'Is this for real?'

Tyler twitched a smile. 'Indeed.'

I glanced back at the page, the paragraph telling me I could be beheaded for giving privileged information to enemies of Great Britain and the European States. Okay, so, maybe the execution comment hadn't been a threat, at least not as such. But treason? Beheading? Did they still do that to people in this fucked-up country? I looked up at Tyler again.

'What's this about, anyway?'

Tyler had settled back in the chair while he waited.

'Keep reading,' he said, nodding encouragement. 'I'm unable to divulge further information without your signature.'

I spared a glance at Beck, looked back at Tyler.

'Oh, I get it now. Should have seen this coming. Oh, wait, I did!' I pushed the paper back across the desk. 'You're trying to gag me. Something bad's going down and you're scared I might actually find out what. Well, guess what? I don't *care* if it looks bad for you guys. People are getting hurt here and I aim to put a stop to it.'

Give him his due, if Tyler was upset, he didn't show it. He just repositioned the document on the desk, facing me again.

'Do you honestly think that's not what we want, too?'

'Honestly? Honestly, I don't think you give a fuck, as long as the company profits are up.'

Tyler pursed his lips. 'Okay, I sense some bridge-building may be in order. Suppose I'm willing to open up certain files to you as an act of good faith? Files which, I trust, will allay the negative image you seem to have of us. How does that sound?'

I grinned, as widely as my bruises let me. 'Sounds to me like Synapware's in a lot of trouble, Tyler. Much as that pleases me, I've a nasty feeling you're looking for a scapegoat right now.'

'By that you mean you, I presume? First we're trying to gag you, then we're trying to set you up. Isn't that somewhat melodramatic?'

'Paranoid even.' Beck chose this moment to chip in.

I gave him a look that said what I thought of that.

'You guys. You crack me up.'

Tyler suppressed the best part of a sigh. 'I understand your reticence. You've had a couple of run-ins with us and now you think everything we do is bad.'

'Yeah. Really. You're not like that at all.'

'We're actually trying to help people. Make life better for everyone, whoever they are. If people are getting hurt by one of our products, then we aim to stop it. We take our responsibility in that regard very seriously indeed.'

'Yeah. It costs you money if you don't.'

Beck leaned past me. I heard the suit fabric strain across his shoulders as he stretched out his arm. He laid a shiny black fingertip on the paragraph two below the one I was paused on.

'Sub-clause three beholdens you to act in the best interests of the common man and to uphold their right to justice and liberty.'

This time he said enough to show off his accent. I took another look at him, surprised. He was like me - a dispossessed Yank. Kicked out of the US for having the wrong paperwork. Or something more serious. I shoved the affinity I instinctively felt aside. He was a Synapware heavy. We weren't brothers.

'If you find we're doing anything illegal or dangerous,' Beck added. 'It'd be your duty to report it. How can that be gagging you?'

'Dunno. But this is fishy.'

'If you want answers, Mr Nixon,' Tyler said. 'If you want the information you need. Then first you have to sign.'

'We *are* talking about Mephistopheles, aren't we?'

The flicker of surprise on Tyler's face said he'd considered me less well-informed. Or maybe it was his way of answering the question without opening his mouth. Either way it confirmed it. Unfortunately. Because it meant if I wanted to know what was really going on here, I'd have to sign my life over to king and country. Wasn't convinced I liked the king, this country, or the European States enough to do that. I knew for sure I didn't like Synapware. But I did want to find out about Mephistopheles.

I read on. Three pages of it. When I finished I had to read a paragraph out loud, swearing loyalty to the States of the European Union, loyalty to Great Britain and loyalty, in particular, to King Thomas, who I was now prepared to give my life for. Even though he was currently holidaying in Switzerland and had been for the last two years.

Tyler handed me the pen. An even nicer pen close up than it had looked while he'd been playing with it. It was a power tool alright. So powerful, I smudged my name when I wrote it. In my defence, I'd never written anything in real ink before. How was I supposed to know the stuff was wet? My education continued when Tyler took the paper, and pen, from me. Went about drying said smudged moniker. And there I was thinking desk blotters were just for drawing doodles on.

'Thank you, Mr Nixon.' Tyler inspected the signature again, folded the pages and slotted them back in the envelope. 'I must confess I thought we'd have more trouble with you.'

'There's still time.'

Tyler handed the envelope to Beck, sat back in the plush chair. 'And now the legalities are concluded, I'm authorised to offer you a basic four point contract.'

My eyebrows were up before I remembered why I should be cautious about that. I prodded the foam-like dressing, blinking hard.

'You want me to work for you? For Synapware? You are joking, right?'

'Consulting for the Constabulary doesn't pay particularly well, does it, Mr Nixon? A regular stipend would bolster your earnings, make sure the rent's paid and so forth.'

I was already shaking my head. 'Would also present a conflict of interests. Your company *created* personas!'

'That's a good point,' Tyler admitted. 'I'll look into it - smooth over any difficulties with the Constabulary.'

But I wasn't finished. 'I ruined my career - my life - trying to get those monsters off the streets. Bust my guts each night still trying. Now you want me to work for you?'

'It's exactly *why* I want you to work for me! Mr Nixon, my job is to protect Synapware from negative publicity. That invariably involves tracking down...problems? ...that might come to light from one of our products. For whatever reason, you've taken it upon yourself to do the same thing. Where squirts are concerned, at least. You've proven yourself adept at spotting when a Synapware schema is present, and you're single-minded in your pursuit of punishment.'

'Yeah. Because there wouldn't *be* any squirts if your company hadn't–'

'It's that desire to catch Synapware with its hand in the cookie jar - is that the expression? - that makes you an ideal candidate for my department. I *want* you to find this rogue persona, Mr Nixon, and I'm not interested in your motives. I don't care if you like us or hate us. I just want Mephistopheles stopped.'

'The police would never allow–'

'Let me worry about them.'

I sat back in my chair and let out a long sigh.

Synapware had clout. I'd known that for years. Hell, they'd proved it only days ago, by putting a legal clamp-down on Samuels so hard even the investigating officer couldn't get near him. So maybe it was true. Maybe Tyler could fix it so the Constabulary would let me work on a Synapware case? More to the point, Tyler seemed sincere. Okay, maybe it was just because his job was on the line, but I'd take that over indifference any day. Plus I'd get insider info on what the hell that Mephistopheles thing was and how to stop it before it killed again.

*

'Paydirt! Bout fuckin' time, man.' Sitaroo pushed his turban past me, out the door. Looked up at the railings above us then ducked back in. He laid a hand on my arm and gave a sincere stare. 'You, my friend, are a hero. You're about to save my life. Feels good, doesn't it? All that karma?'

I frowned, puzzled, and he flashed a grin.

'Landlord's due.'

'And there I was thinking you were just glad to see me.'

Sitaroo noticed the state of my face for the first time. 'What happened to you? Fighting with Lian again?'

'Ha Ha. Cute.' I let him usher me inside. 'As it happens I came in over par with a nine iron.'

I was already following the back of his white turban as he headed down the hallway. He swivelled to glance at me again.

'Bloody contact sports.'

Before letting me leave their tender care, the Memorial had applied a round of needles to put long-acting pain killers into all my injuries. They then injected bone-knit into my ribs, injected more to shore up the cracks in my carpals and more arnical into my eyelid to bring down the swelling. When I asked why I had stitches in my scalp instead of chemweld, they said something about the density of head-hair follicles and how they tended to get permanently deformed by the glue. But they'd put a gel dressing on it in compensation. Plastered down one side of my hair, left the rest spiky. Class.

Sitaroo's inner sanctum reeked of frankincense today, rather than sandalwood. Reminded me of the church back in Philly where I said goodbye to Mom. Not a moment I liked to dwell on.

By the time my eyes adjusted to the gloom Sitaroo was already wedged in his moonchair, jeans straining to accommodate the lotus position he'd adopted.

'I hope you're feeling flush,' he said, settling back and closing his eyes. 'Coz I spent a lot of time and resources on your bracer.'

Innocent creature that I am, I ploughed on in there. 'I got bad news about yours, by the way.'

'Don't worry about it.' Sitaroo's eyes stayed closed. 'A man like you can afford it.'

He grinned at the groan that produced. Instead of arguing, though, I moved over to where the Dakka-Hoddern was ticking quietly to itself. My bracer sat on top - a welcome sight.

As if on cue, Sitaroo opened one eye, glinted it at me.

'It's a mystery, that file. Couldn't stop the fucker erasing itself, but I managed to save a few algorithms, before I lost it altogether.'

'Get rid of them.'

Sitaroo gave a sigh, opened both eyes.

If I wasn't in the mood to argue about paying for his crap bracer I sure as hell wasn't going to argue about this.

'I mean it,' I told him. 'Everything. Every loop and variable. I want it all deleted.'

Sitaroo unfolded from his pose and sat forward. He jutted his chin at the black cabinet where, presumably, he'd now isolated whatever he'd managed to save of the corrupted audio file.

'That's my new project in there,' he said. 'I'm betting it turns out to be something *very* interesting. Military AI maybe. Even if it's not, anything new's priceless and I got a hungry habit. Needless to say, deleting it is not high on my list of development criteria.'

I shook my head. 'Not any more. Whatever that thing was on my bracer, it's dangerous. Its parent's already responsible for one suicide, five deaths and two more possibles lying in the hospital. Plus this is a Synapware baby and they're aiming to retrieve it. You don't wanna get caught up the kind of shit-storm they can generate.'

Sitaroo stared owlishly for a second then gave a long, slow whistle through the gap in his teeth. He shook his head. What he said next made me flinch.

'They got to you, man.'

Hearing it from someone else didn't make it taste any better but I'd known it the moment I'd signed that paper. They'd got to me. They hadn't had to try too hard, either. Didn't like how that part made me feel.

'Delete it!'

Sitaroo's eyes widened at my tone, but it wasn't him I was angry with. He kept on staring, stayed inside his calm. Unlike me.

'Whatever Mephistopheles turns out to be, I don't want any of it turned loose out there! You fucking delete it, understand?'

The turban tilted - part shrug, part curiosity. 'If it's so *very* dangerous, how come it got out of Synapware in the first place?'

I got a handle on my temper, let out a slow breath. 'Far as I can make out, their employee, Joseph Samuels, stole it.' *The stupid fuck!*

Sitaroo blinked. 'Man, that's slick. How'd he get it past their security?'

Another exhale. 'By uploading it into his own skull.'

'And it leaked?'

I shook my head. 'Synapware employees aren't allowed implants. The product's designed for wetware so he uploaded it straight into his own brain. Walked out with it undetected.'

'Man! All that code inside a human brain? And it didn't kill him?'

'It tried. Hard. Still trying.' Although, according to Tyler, now Synapware were advising them, the Memorial's doctors were making progress treating both Samuels and Harris.

'Clever,' Sitaroo said. 'A digital product you can upload into your own skull. *Man,* that's clever.'

'It's not that simple.'

But the details about Mephistopheles - as I should have figured out before I signed the Secrets Act, let alone Tyler's four point contract - would be divulged later. I always had a tendency to dive in with my eyes closed. Had a criminal record to prove it and it seemed I was still suffering from the same malady. But since when was being a slow study a crime? Besides, Tyler was smooth, no question. Gave me just enough to make his pen twitch in my fingers of its own accord. I gave Sitaroo as much as I'd been given and to hell with their Secrets Act.

'To stay stable, this persona needed something Samuels wasn't able to supply. I don't know what yet, but its other hosts so far couldn't meet the criterion either. Maybe that's why it goes insane.'

'Yeah,' Sitaroo said softly. 'I forgot. The killing people part. Not cool.'

'Yeah.'

I picked up my bracer and slid it over my wrist.

'One Gee,' Sitaroo said before I could fasten the clips.

'One *what*? I could *buy* a new bracer for that!'

'You could buy two. But think of the hassle. Getting it registered... Listing passport, social security... All those files to transfer...'

'You're blackmailing me for my bracer?'

'Just pay up, Nix. You make that much in one night.'

'I do? Which particular universe do you live in? One where Matt Nixon earns a decent wage, obviously.'

'You see? You *can* afford it. It's all a case of entering the right state of mind.'

Sitaroo pushed off against the floor and his chair rolled towards me. He gestured and I slid the bracer off my wrist again, let him take it from my fingers. Watching him interrogate it was like watching another man make love to my soul mate. Twice, my fingers twitched in his direction until I clenched my fists.

'Take a look,' he said eventually, handing it to me and rattling his chair back to where it had started. He folded his legs again, went back into his lotus to align his chakra once more.

I stared at my screen. The page he'd put me on showed a single icon, blinking green. It was a new programme. Something I'd never heard of before, let alone owned.

'What's this?'

'That,' Sitaroo said. 'Is *The Rooinator*.'

'The what?'

'Rooinator. "Roo". As in Kanger - and Sitaroo, come to think of it. "Inator", as in...something...inator. Basic bounceback containment programme with a sprinkle of Sitaroo Man's ineffable charm, plus a good dose of whammage.'

'In other words, it's custom and it's illegal.'

'Stop whining, man. You're getting it for free.'

'Right. So you didn't add the cost of this to the thousand you're trying to stiff me with?'

Sitaroo beamed. 'Exactly.'

'Real generous.'

'You'll thank me one day.'

'So what does it do?'

'It's for protection. You gotta set up a code for it soon as poss. Once you've done that, any sus calls you get, you enter the code and the Rooinator blocks the incoming signal, sends it straight to a data dump, where it'll stay till you're ready to deal with it.'

'This is in case Mephistopheles tries to jump inside me?'

'Exactly. Be terrible if it ended up in *your* skull. That'd be digital cruelty.'

'Abusing an AI? Yeah. Love to add *that* to my list of sins.'

'So what we doing, then, Paydirt? You gonna pay up or do I get to keep your bracer? Sell it on to someone more worthy.'

'Muslims go in for haggling, right?' I asked him.

'Yeah. They do. Part of their culture. Problem is, I'm a Sikh. Totally different. Pay up.'

The transaction made a nasty dent in what Synapware had briefly made the best financial position I'd enjoyed for some time. But I liked the Rooinator. Then, of course, Sitaroo had known I would.

Making my way up the stairs outside, I stepped aside for a kid coming down. The swagger told it. If anyone didn't get that, the gang tattoos on his face and the initiation scars on his forearms made certain they knew for sure. The scars were old. The kid was ten, max. We took a look at each other. If he hadn't been on a mission, maybe I'd have regretted holding his stare. But the kid was busy. He had rent to collect.

8

Maybe I just hadn't stopped to think about it or maybe my head hadn't been clear enough. Maybe both. For whatever reason, it took a long shower and the time sitting still, waiting for the shaving gel to work, for me to appreciate how close I'd come to death yesterday. Twice. Surviving an old-fashioned bludgeoning was a minor miracle, but I'd never heard of anyone survive being mag-welded to a rail before. With hindsight, if I'd remembered that at the time, maybe I'd be dead by now. Maybe I'd've just lay down and waited for the inevitable. Then again it wasn't my style. Came from being a stubborn bastard, like I said.

I washed the beard gel off and leaned toward the mirror to inspect my scalp. Guess I can thank the pain-relief, because I'd forgotten there were stitches up there and gone and shampooed the dressing off in the shower. Finding the wound in the mirror was awkward - it was a little behind my left ear and the stitches blended in with my dark, matted hair, but when I finally did, I saw the cut was 'V' shaped, like a flap of skin had been gouged loose. I sighed. Pity someone hadn't invented virtual golf clubs. Lot safer for someone like me.

A knock on the door had me swearing.

I don't get many visitors but when I do, they usually pick moments like this. When they're least welcome and I'm therefore less welcoming. It had crossed my mind once or twice that it might explain why I didn't get many visitors. In any case, isolation suited me. Went with the vampire hours I kept and my decreasing desire for social company.

Hadn't time to hunt for a shirt, but I found a clean pair of jeans and was still buttoning them when I opened the door.

Lian was standing there - my missing jacket hooked on the forefinger of one hand, my Sandman resting in the palm of the other. She was partway through inhaling, ready to deliver some cutting remark. What she saw stopped her short.

She ran her eyes over me; the white circle around my ribs where bone-knit was drawing blood towards the damage, the dark bruise around it; bigger bruise, but less dark on my shoulder and down my arm where I'd hit the rail; wrists rubbed raw by the cuffs, also dotted white where the bone-knit had gone in; thick lip, split and still apt to bleed if I wasn't careful, earned from a blow I didn't remember receiving. *Christ, I read like a shopping list!* Finally, the eye. I'd just seen it in the mirror. I knew it looked bad.

Whatever she'd been getting ready to say must have fled her mind the second she saw me.

'Jesus, Matt!'

I summoned a grin. 'Hey, you found my stuff!'

Lian blinked through a hank of hair and closed her mouth. Her eyes looked sore - like she'd been crying, or staring at a screen for hours, or spending way too long without sleep - and her face was pale. Hair was pulled up into the bun she liked, but the hours had tugged most of it down again so it hung in soft curls round her neck.

'You look like shit,' I told her.

'Thanks,' she said. 'I'd like to say the same about you, but I'm beginning to think it's an improvement.'

I grinned. 'Go ahead and bitch at me. The painkillers they gave me are beasts. Can't feel a thing.'

'You started it.'

Yeah. I guess I did at that.

She lowered her hands, stepped inside, passing close enough for me to get a whiff of perfume in need of refreshing, faint trace of stale sweat. Been a long time since we'd been here - me half-naked and her walking in all skanky and without an invite.

'Come on in,' I said.

'They were at Harris's.' She ignored the wry comment and dumped my jacket on the back of the worn out recliner. My Sandman she balanced on top. She fished into her jacket, tossed the tranq clip onto the seat and followed it up with Sitaroo's old bracer, which was now mine.

'The fingerprints at the residence were all from the family, except on your stuff. Bloodstains downstairs are consistent with the injuries you say you got at the scene. The angle of the dart we found shows it was fired from the floor. No contradictions. The AI's confident your story matches the evidence so, unless something else shows up later, there'll be no follow-up. You're not under suspicion.'

'Good.' Guess Mephistopheles was too busy trying to kill me to bother trying to frame me. I took a closer look at her face. 'You okay?'

The line between her eyebrows made a brief appearance and she turned away.

'They were just kids, Matt. And Eileen... He made her die listening to them screaming. For God's sake, how could anyone...?'

The catch in her voice made me wince. Lian had been as close to the Harris family as me. I laid a hand on her shoulder.

'It wasn't Harris's fault. He was being controlled, like I told you. Did they find his bracer?'

She whirled, outraged, shrugged my hand off. '*Fuck* his bracer! Have you opted so completely out of the human race you don't give a shit about anything but catching your crim anymore?'

'No. Lian, listen. Mephistopheles has moved on. We need Harris's bracer to find out where he went. We have to stop him or he's going to kill again.'

Her eyes were still blazing, fury so hot she couldn't speak.

'Lian...'

'They're *looking* for it! Fuck!'

When she lashed out, it was at herself. Slapped her fist against her forehead, hard. Took till then for me to see her cheeks were wet. Told me the depth of her shock - Lian Morrison never cried. At least not in all the days I'd ever known her and we'd been through some shit, her and me. Not just at work, but together, as friends, as lovers. Most surprising thing was my reaction on seeing it. Was a time even the suggestion of a tear would have me scooping her into my arms, trying to make it okay. Today I just stood there, empty.

'Why do I have to be such a stupid bitch?' Her face twisted so another flood could pour down it.

'You're asking me?'

She looked aghast at the glib comment but there was no scathing retort. The come-back I was bracing for never came. Instead she just shook her head.

'Look at you! You nearly died!'

I snorted. 'Yeah, it did occur to me.'

'Those things he did to Jake and Paulie? To Eileen? It's all down to me, Nix. It was my fault.'

That pulled me up. 'Hang on. Where did *that* come from?'

'I always have to get in your way, don't I? Slow you down, make you pay.'

'How did that make you a mass murderer?'

'If I'd listened to you... If I'd just trusted you... I told them to give you a hard time out at Chedminster, to hold you up, just to piss you off. I made you wait in the cells while I did my paperwork. If I'd–'

'Jesus, Lian! Were you SOCO on this? You were out there?'

She shook her head, wiped tears away with her jacket sleeve, but she had to suppress a sob. Her voice was soft now, but still shaky.

'Fox is SOCO. I just... I had to go round there. I had to make sure I'd heard it properly. That it wasn't some stupid mistake.'

'Is there a time of death yet?'

She shrugged. 'All different. They all took different times to die.' Her face twisted again. 'Paulie longest of all. He was so little, Matt, and his daddy nailed him to a door frame! And the fucking neighbours didn't hear him screaming because the TV was on so loud. I mean, for Christ's sake! Why didn't someone call in a complaint? Bang on the door? *Something*!'

Yeah, as if. These are Brits we're talking about. Always so tolerant. So polite. Especially the ones they call the upper working class, the ones who live in quiet little cul-de-sacs like the one the Harris's had lived in. God forbid they'd be seen making a fuss. If Mephistopheles had tried the same thing in Redfield, the neighbours would have broken the door down to shut that damned TV off, interrupted his sadistic game. Guess he'd chosen his playing field just right.

Lian took a deep breath and blew it out again.

'They think Eileen went first,' she said. 'Drowned as the bath filled up.'

'I know.'

'About ten yesterday morning.'

'*Dammit!*'

I looked away before she got to see the expression on my face. Don't know why. She deserved to see it, it was her turn. I couldn't stop myself saying it, though.

'I could have gotten there in time, Lian.'

A new flood broke out.

'Yes,' she said. 'You could have, if I hadn't... And you needed back-up. If I hadn't slowed you down you might've got there in time, but you'd have got there alone. They'd still be dead and so would you!'

'I *was* alone and I nearly *did* die, remember?'

Most surprising thing about my outburst was the satisfaction I got seeing the look cross her face. For two years she'd held the moral high ground - I was the fool, the failed cop. Must have hurt her pretty hard finding out I wasn't the only one.

Mephistopheles could have been stopped, could be history by now and those kids, their mom, would still be alive. But because she was angry with me, because she'd lost all respect for me, because she wanted to make me pay, she'd let Harris's family die and nearly got me killed into the bargain.

'I should have let you see Gage's bracer when you first asked. I should have come with you. Matt, I'm so sorry.'

'It's not me you need to apologise to.'

She reacted like she'd just been slapped, but there'd been no way to keep the bitterness from my voice.

Fair or not, I'd be lying if I said I got no pleasure seeing her squirm. Bout time she got to feel it - the same way I'd felt it every time she, or anyone else, had looked at me the day I'd been arrested and every day since. Only difference was, when I'd fucked up, I'd done it trying to save lives.

'Matt, I'm sorry!'

Call me cynical. Call me a hard, unfeeling bastard, but the mystery of the tears suddenly made sense. Her tears weren't for those kids, their mom. They weren't for me. They were for her. Because now she had to live with the knowledge, the guilt, that people had died for the sake of her vengeance. Of all the people I knew, Lian Morrison was least-equipped to deal with that. Guilt and self-disgust had never earned a place in her emotional bag of tools, until today.

'I hate this!' Those tears kept coming and I watched them without speaking, feeling only anger. 'I hate how I always have to make things hard for you. Make you suffer. I hate that I can't forgive you and most of all I hate that I want to hate you and I *can't*! You're the biggest head-fuck I ever met. You screw me up inside until I can't think straight! And now people are dead.'

I wasn't Lian Morrison. I don't spend years wallowing in icy fury. My rage burns hot and it fizzles out as fast as it arrives. But not this time. This time, when she put her arms round my neck breathing 'Please' into my shoulder I reached up, pushed her away.

'Nix!' she cried. 'I need you to–'

'What, Lian? You need me to *what*? Let you manipulate me again? Let you seduce me? Let you worm your way back into my good opinion so I don't think bad of you?'

'I...' Her forehead creased.

Not surprised. That tactic had always worked before. Always. Guessing she wasn't sure what was different this time. I wasn't sure either. I only knew that, somewhere and belatedly, I'd seen it for what it was.

'Come on, Lian! What is it you need me to do? Make it all alright? Tell you it's okay? Forgive you?'

Guess for the first time since it happened, I understood how she'd felt back then. How she couldn't bear to look at me after what I'd done. How the thought of being in the same room with me had filled her with revulsion. Only now, today, the shoe was on the other foot. Don't know which was worse.

'Thanks for returning my stuff,' I said. 'You know the way out.'

*

My bracer told me this was the seventh time I'd had my work license suspended until the Constabulary's Chief Surgeon okayed my fitness for work. So, for the seventh time in my career as a freelance persona expert, I was off sick, without pay. If the financial impact didn't get me pissed enough at the bureaucrats, my being sick or injured in the line of duty didn't earn me any recognition either. And it didn't stop those squirters out there. Didn't stop Mephistopheles.

The Constabulary would bring some asswipe from Bath or Cardiff in to cover me. Someone with no instinct for the local product. Someone half-trained, with a tenth of my experience and no talent for the job. And then, when they fucked up, they'd blame me for being inconsiderate enough to be off sick.

Good job I had other plans or I'd've been a mite frustrated. Speaking of other plans, this one had turned out a lot different than I'd anticipated.

I stared out the window, disappointed.

No one flew these days, solar-powered hang-gliders and micro-lights aside. Nothing bigger. Nothing commercial and definitely nothing private. Not as a general rule. Unless you had money. Money and enough power to flaunt the restrictions, the fiscal constraints, the red tape required each time an aircraft used precious carbon fuels to leave the bosom of Mother Earth. This was, and would probably always be, my only chance to see the ground from four thousand feet. And I couldn't see a thing. Cloud had rolled in that morning - no real surprise given this was Britain in summer. So we flew surrounded by misted windows through a wad of cotton wool.

I glanced at Mr Beck, opposite. Why the hell was I still calling him *Mr* Beck? That was Tyler's thing. Guess he just had that look about him. The look that made you want to call him 'sir' in case he took it into his head to mash your brains. I wondered if *Beck* had been flown over here from the States when he was kicked out. Instead of, like me, shoved onto an overcrowded wreck of a ship and left to fend for myself until I got here. Couldn't see anyone messing with him, if so. Even when he was a kid. Could imagine him being from one of the new Desert States - the first to turn into the wasteland the rest of the US had now become. Growing up in anarchy - tough, angry. Right from day one. Makes for a mean son-of-a-bitch.

Beck caught my look, held it. His eyes were green, apt to stare. Took it as a sign. I hadn't seen many, but I'd come across stone killers from time to time. Ganglanders mainly. They all had that stare. Told it. Beck knew how to kill. He'd done it. It had changed him. I took in the clipped haircut, the build his shake-clean suit couldn't hide. Ex-mil maybe. Marines, Paras, Special Forces even. Something.

Geoff Tyler, beside me, nudged my shoulder and I looked round, reached for the tall glass the steward was offering on a tray. Ice chinked. Seemed there was nothing about these people that didn't cry 'money'.

'Are you enjoying the flight, Mr Nixon?'

Tyler was all politeness. He could afford to be with his pit-bull sitting opposite me.

'View stinks.' I gestured at the window with my glass.

Tyler smiled. 'There are some things even Synapware can't fix.'

The soundproofing in this baby was good. He didn't have to shout. The military still used choppers and they flew over now and again, so I knew they ran loud. I hadn't appreciated just how loud until we'd boarded this one, when the rotors thundering above my head, pressing damp air down like it was trying to flatten me, had prompted me to make use of the ear-buds I'd been given. Once the door closed, though, the sound cut off. All I heard now was a whisper which just covered the air-con.

Once we'd established our 'new understanding', Tyler had invited me to Synapware. Promised me more answers. Yeah. That'd make a refreshing change. Someone actually telling me stuff. Wasn't sure I'd be able to handle it. I accepted anyway. I'd expected a meeting in some windowless office in the Synapware building I'd been warned away from yesterday. Chauffeur ride to the airport hadn't crossed my mind.

I watched the chopper's vibration put ripples on the surface of my drink.

'Where we going?'

Damn. I'd been trying to suppress that question. Wanted to play it cool. Curiosity had gotten the better of me. It always got the better of me.

'To the Island,' Tyler said, touching his drink to his lips and leaning his head back on the seat. 'Creative Acquisitions is based out there. I want you to know what you're up against.'

'Up against?'

'Figure of speech.'

'Sure.' I sipped my own drink. Tasted something bitter with a trace of salt and lime. 'So where's this Island?'

Geoff Tyler pursed his lips. 'If the visibility outside was better, the windows would be opaqued. Does that answer your question?'

I snorted. 'No.' But I took the hint.

The intercom above us spurted to life. 'Five minutes, Mr Tyler.'

Tyler placed his drink on the courtesy table in front of him. 'We're about to land,' he said. 'Drink up. Please.'

Wasn't till he said that - or maybe it was the fact he'd left his barely touched - I started wondering what was in my glass. Ran the idea through my mind of tipping the stuff into his lap. Then Beck sat forward.

'Nothing unpleasant,' he drawled. 'Just a liquid tracker. It's harmless. Eight hours, it'll be gone.'

'Right. So much for our "new understanding".'

'I've read your profile,' Tyler said. 'It's a precaution. In case you stick to form and decide to do some poking around where you don't belong. Drink it or stay aboard. Your choice.'

So I drank. Quite enjoyed it.

*

The island was artificial. Several acres of heavy-duty deck on stilts, landscaped and grassed over. Meant it could be anywhere in the Bristol Channel. Or the Celtic Sea. Or even the goddamn Atlantic. There was no way to tell. And I doubted very much it was anywhere near a shipping lane.

The landscaped 'deck' possessed a jetty and a helipad. Beyond these there was the main building built in the style of an eighteenth century mansion. Its grounds included a swimming pool - looking dejected and abandoned in this weather - a golf-course and a riding stable. Maybe other stuff I couldn't see or didn't recognise as we deplaned on the circle of concrete studded into the biggest, smoothest lawn I'd seen for decades.

As the chopper powered down behind us, I felt the throb beneath me, heard the rush of waves against the steel framework holding the entire platform above the sea. Droplets clinging to the grass silvered the flat expanse and drenched the bottom of my jeans as we headed for the mansion. I noticed, miserably, that the repair lotion I'd lovingly worked into my shoes wasn't keeping the water out of the deep scuff marks they'd acquired being dragged along the magway.

The mansion might be low-tech but the place knew how to impress. Off to my right the lawn ended abruptly and steel-coloured sea began, tens of metres below it. Furthest I could see was a hundred metres, max, where the sea ran into a soft grey wall. Fine drizzle was already dampening my hair. The moisture didn't exactly fall, seemed, instead, to manifest straight from the air. I reached up to brush the damp off my head and my fingers encountered the stitches. Should have been glad they weren't sore, but remembering those stitches might prove to be a problem if I had to do any macho stuff in the near future.

The mansion was built of reclaimed bath stone, embellished to look like it had spent a century surrounded by smog. Gave me some idea how old the thing was - that finish had gone out of date twenty years ago. Still, its columned, buttressed façade looked authentically Georgian. I figured it was just that, though. A façade. Place was probably stuffed to the armpits with enough anti-radar, anti-satellite, anti-neutron resonance shielding to make Whitehall look like they hadn't even bothered.

Took seconds of being inside for me to realise my assessment might be wrong. The house was residential. Not private, more like a hotel. Room and board for the company's hard-working, overpaid researchers. Compensation for being isolated for weeks in the middle of the Bristol Channel. Or wherever the hell we were.

The air con inside was superfluous, cold enough to make me shiver. Obviously no one had told the House Manager the weather had changed out there. Such a blatant misuse of the planet's energy felt vaguely offensive. Didn't realise the propaganda had gotten to me so hard, but it couldn't just be me picking fault. That didn't sound like me at all.

I had to hand my stuff over at a desk tucked away in a recess to one side of the wood-panelled foyer. Sandman, belt, even my bracer. Wasn't any consolation to see Tyler and Beck drop their stuff into a lockable tray, too. I was too busy thinking human liberties and how many the bastards were taking.

Beck followed me into the elevator Tyler picked from the ten or more standing in the mansion foyer. He stood the other side of me to Tyler, so we ended up like Russian dolls. One big, one medium, one small, lined up side-by-side. There were dozens of buttons on the panel next to the doors. I watched to see which one Tyler pushed. He didn't. The lift moved without prompting. Told me Tyler's suit was already deep in conversation with the same House Manager who wouldn't switch off the air con.

The suit would be programmed to keep Tyler fresh and comfortable, whatever the environment. Unlike my faux leather jacket which got clammy at the first sign of a thermostat. Or the first twinge of anxiety, since it definitely wasn't the heat in here making my palms slick.

Being at the nerve-centre of my moral enemy with one of its heavies only inches to my left does that to me. Plus I was beginning to wonder if my long, frosty drink had really contained what Beck said. Seconds after the elevator dropped, I started feeling queasy. The cabin's weird vibration and the fact my stomach kept flipping didn't help.

Wasn't my most brilliant idea, letting them drug me, but Synapware would be stupid to make me disappear - the flight out here had been logged numerous times. If this was a black-bag op, a car trunk would have been better-suited. It took a lot of official clearance to get anyone off the ground these days and my bracer had been flashed at six other devices or more on my way through customs. Powerful or not, even Synapware would have trouble explaining where I'd gone if I didn't make the trip back.

One of my ears popped. I stuck a finger in it, waggled. Tyler glanced at me when I also cleared my throat.

'Any discomfort you're experiencing is due to depth, and because we're no longer going straight down,' he said. 'Let's just say our research teams are accustomed to working under pressure.'

I thought about where we'd started out from and gave a snort. 'We're under the sea. Funny. That crack about the pressure.'

'Our researchers do work very hard, but in terms of psi, there's only a very slight increase. Dealt with in transit by the capsule we're riding in. You just noticed your ears pop?'

I shrugged.

'I assure you, it's perfectly safe down here.'

'Unless it springs a leak.'

'Wherever we sited this facility, we'd have to contend with the sea - tides and so on. Making it part of our environment levels the field somewhat. And being down here makes it easier to monitor all comings and goings. You can appreciate our need to control the transmission of sensitive research, I'm sure.'

Yeah. Like you controlled Samuels and your Mephistopheles Monster.

The doors split open, presenting us with the opposite wall of a clean-lit corridor. Integrated into the wall tiles was a spider-web of red lines making up a map of the facility's layout. The blinking dot halfway along one strand of the 'web' gave me a good idea where this elevator had stopped. I glanced at the writing above the map.

'Life Extension?' My face pulled into a smirk. 'Did we get in the wrong elevator?'

'No,' Tyler said, stepping out and gesturing for me to follow.

The section we stood in contained half a dozen smaller doors set into the walls and was enclosed by tough-looking double doors set twenty yards apart. Solid steel and air-tight, by the look of them. Suddenly my crack about the place springing a leak didn't sound funny anymore.

'So, what does life extension have to do with personas?'

I glanced back as the elevator closed behind me - my single escape route, now blocked. Tyler was already heading down the corridor.

'Very little,' he said over his shoulder. 'Although one vein of research we're excited about incorporates some of the technology we developed for personality overlays. It's a minor crossover. You can't really compare the two.'

I spotted a sign above one of the doors as we passed. '*Nano-technology*'.

Jesus, these guys were good. Nanotech - in a viable format - had only been around for twenty years. And here they were, using it.

'So why are we here? Why'd you hire me?'

'I thought I explained. I need you to retrieve our lost property.'

I sighed. I could see where this was going. This was going to be a case of shut up and let the guy talk, because until I knew what the hell was going on, my questions would just hold things up. But of course, this is me. I had to ask one more.

'And you think you lost it in here?'

Behind me, Beck grunted. Tyler just twitched his lips, indicated the open door in front of him.

'Shall we?'

9

'What's this? A hospital?'

I'd expected an office. Instead it was another corridor. This one was gloomy and lined each side with big windows, each looking into its own private room. Fall-out from the windows splashed rectangles of light on the corridor floor. Just as well, since the corridor itself was unlit. Each of the rooms contained a bed, arranged so the occupant lay facing the window. Equipment was stacked in a semi-circle behind their heads, the readouts visible from the hallway. The corridor was there for observers and, now I was looking, I saw the window glass in each room was tinted - the far side either smart lass or mirrored.

I answered my own question. 'No. It's a lab.'

The corridor was silent, save for the muted hum and beep of equipment coming from the cubicles. Moving past, I got glimpses of each patients' output. I was no expert, but by my reckoning, all these people were either near death or getting there.

Tyler halted to skin-scan the door at the end of the hall.

'Life extension?' I said to Tyler. 'Looks like you got your work cut out.'

The man ushered me through without replying.

This time it was an office. The sterile kind. Everything bio-plastic and vat-grown chitin. There was one occupant. He sat in a visitor's chair, angled towards the desk, hands splayed on his knees.

Maybe it was the time I needed to take in the office layout. Maybe it was just the delay my synapses took to make a connection I'd assigned to my personal trash bin. When recognition hit it was like a bucket of ice water.

I knew the guy. Seen him a hundred times before. But until that moment he was someone I'd never expected to ever see again. Mainly because his execution went ahead four weeks ago.

My fingers headed for the Sandman, remembered it was locked in a tray back in the foyer, decided to get more personal instead. Beck was already between me and the new guy, so he was there when I lunged. I stumbled back, pushed off-balance. Then I remembered. I had no cuffs either. No weapon, no cuffs, no police ID. I wasn't a cop any more.

An ex-cop trying to arrest a dead criminal.

'What the hell?' I thought better of taking Beck head-on a second time. Instead, I jabbed a finger past him, at the man now shrinking back in his chair, agitated as hell.

'That bastard's dead! I saw him *die*!'

The guy was staring at me all this time, eyes wide. I guess most people might do that, seeing a one-eyed, over-stressed idiot lunge at them without warning. But this wasn't most people.

This was Karl Dietrich - the man responsible for the murder of seven schoolgirls. The killer I'd helped hunt down way before ever getting involved in squirts. The killer who'd been on death row for six years - whose execution I'd witnessed a month ago, along with the other detectives responsible for catching him. He blinked, shifted uncomfortably in his chair.

'What *is* this?' he demanded.

What is this? He really just said that?

There he was, right there. Karl Dietrich. Living, breathing. Sitting there while seven girls - girls who should be in their twenties about now and out there building careers, families, lives - were nothing but ashes on a crem site. He was alive, despite my watching his execution, and now he was upset because I'd just tried to arrest him? Fuck! He should be grateful I wasn't tearing his head off! Which, now I came to think of it, was still an option.

Beck was still in the way, though. Guy was beginning to annoy me. This time when I tried dodging past the arm he threw out to block me, he wound said arm round my elbow, locked the joint out straight. He reached over with his prosthetic hand, grabbed the worn lapel of my jacket and propelled me into a second visitor's chair. It rocked back with the force of my entry. Then he stood there, between us, while I fumed and Dietrich cowered.

Tyler had made his way around the desk in the meantime. I switched my attention to him. He had an explanation for this. He damned well better had.

'You think you've met this man,' he said to me, thumping back in the big chair. He turned it slightly on its swivel. Turned it back. 'You haven't. Mr Nixon, let me introduce Mr Faust.'

Dietrich swallowed thickly, frowned. 'N-No. My name's–'

'Let's stick with the pseudonym, shall we?'

'What,' I said. 'The fuck. Is going on?'

'Life extension, Mr Nixon. The next big thing.'

'The hell are you talking about?'

'Mr Faust here was happy to volunteer for our brand new programme following an unfortunate accident.'

My face twisted into a sneer. 'What kind of "accident"? Lethal needle?'

Dietrich cleared his throat. 'A-Actually, it was a car crash. The doctors said I was unlikely to ever–'

'So,' Tyler cut in. 'Faced with the choice of death, paraplegia, or a perfectly normal existence inside a completely different body, Mr Faust chose the latter.'

Dietrich shifted in his chair. 'I wa–I wanted to mention that. It's just. I-I didn't realise–'

'And with facial reconstruction, we'll soon have you looking like your old self again.'

'Y-yes. About that,' he sat forward. 'I'm still not sure why my appearance couldn't have been altered *before* I was uploaded. Surely–'

'Dead bodies don't heal,' Tyler said. 'That should be obvious. We couldn't give you your face back without uploading you first.'

Dietrich shuddered. 'Well, then I'm sure you're right.'

Tyler favoured the man with his non-smile. 'I believe you're scheduled for more physio in eight minutes, Mr Faust. And thank you for your time.'

Dietrich blinked, sat back. 'Oh. Okay. N-no problem.'

Beck's hand gripped my shoulder, kept me in place while the

psychopath rose to his feet. As he left the room I was still trying to work out if my mind was playing tricks. Dietrich had been executed. He was dead. I'd *seen* it. Me and the others who'd stopped him. Along with the families of his victims. We'd all been invited there as a witnesses. We'd all accepted.

It hadn't been easy, no matter what he'd done. Watching a human being choke, try to breathe while his body betrayed him.

Now here I was, watching him walk out the room all but smiling.

It had taken us eighteen months to hunt that bastard down. In the intervening time, Dietrich had added three more to the four bodies we'd already found. His was a case where Lian's profiling skills had paid off. It was because of her, her diligence, we got the possibles narrowed down to five. Cross-checking alibis had given us Dietrich. That was Harris's strength. Plodder, like I said.

As the door slid shut behind Dietrich, Beck's hand lifted off my shoulder. I glowered at him, got his thousand-yard stare back. Grinning obscurely, he found Dietrich's vacated chair, pulled the side of his jacket loose as he sat back, all relaxed.

I shifted my attention to Tyler.

'What the hell's going on? And what's that bastard trying to pull? All innocence and light? Dietrich is a total nut-case - no amount of play acting's going to fool anyone for long.'

'I realise this is confusing,' Tyler said. 'Karl Dietrich is dead, yet you apparently just watched him leave this room.'

'Yeah. You can shove your "apparentlies"! I have fucking *nightmares* about that guy. If you think I'd ever mistake his face for–'

'The man you just saw walk out of here isn't him.'

'The hell he isn't! If I live to bicentennial, I'll still remember that evil bastard! Now you better start explaining what he's doing here, because I'm running out of patience, real fast.'

'On the thirteenth of June, under State medical supervision, Karl Dietrich was injected with a lethal combination of drugs. Forty-five seconds later, he was dead. All this you know. What you don't know is that, upon his death, Synapware gained legal possession of his body, and it was immediately transferred here.'

I shook my head. 'They can't let you do that.'

'Dietrich signed his body over to us prior to his execution. He gave us permission to do with it as we pleased. He had the right. Even criminals are allowed to write wills, Mr Nixon.'

'Hate to break it to you, but that fucker was never the "furthering of medical science" type.'

'No.' Tyler breathed out a sigh. 'We've discovered that for ourselves. Mr Faust, who you just met, is just a desk jockey whose spine was crushed in a stupid car accident. From the sharpest pin in the office to having a machine breathe for him, feed him, deal with his bodily waste. We offered an alternative.'

'What does this have to do with that psycho?'

'Our new life extension programme. We recorded that young man's synaptic and neurological map - his entire mind, not just an overlay - and digitised it. His damaged body was then allowed to die. Once we received Karl Dietrich's cadaver, "Mr Faust's" digital matrix was uploaded into its brain and the corpse itself was then revived.

'That's the criteria, you see? The one I mentioned before. For a Mephistopheles-type upload to successfully integrate with its host, the host body has to be dead. Once the upload is in place we can revive it, restore it to health, and the new personality can make itself at home. With today's cosmetic surgery, we can make the person look identical to their original selves. Or better, if that's what they wish. Mr Faust there has an entire face graft to look forward to. His own face, in fact, taken from his original body. His request. Along with some bone reconstruction, no one will know the difference.'

I gestured at the door. 'That what's going on out there? All those people in the beds? They're all–'

'In the process of revival, yes.'

'They've all got Mephistopheles inside them? Are you insane? You know what just *one* of them out there has done?'

Tyler pursed his lips. 'Don't think you've quite grasped it, Mr Nixon. Mephistopheles is not the name of a persona, it's a code name for that persona *type*.

'The people in the rooms out there, they're just people. For whatever reason - age, injury, disease - their original bodies were no longer capable of letting them lead fulfilling lives, so they've "sold their soul", so to speak, so they can live renewed. Mephistopheles. You get the reference?'

I made a conscious effort to unclench my jaw. Okay, so the guy had had to spell it out, but I still didn't like what I was hearing.

'You're using corpses. You're uploading digitised human minds into corpses and bringing them back to life? Do they know that, before they get handed your nice, expensive pen?'

Tyler shrugged. 'It's not my job to acquire candidates, but I'm sure everything's explained to them beforehand.'

'Yeah. "Mr Faust" seemed really well-informed.'

'It's his responsibility to read all the small print.'

Nice. If I hadn't been one hundred percent sure Beck would have gotten to me first, I'd have been over the desk rearranging Tyler's impeccable features right about then.

I looked from Tyler to Beck, back to Tyler. 'If I understand even a quarter of what you're telling me, what you people are doing here is so fucking dangerous! Set aside the ethical considerations–'

'People want to live, Mr Nixon. They want younger, they want stronger, they want healthier, more beautiful. Anyway, imagine the long-term benefits! Extrapolating how many fresh, salvageable cadavers pass through the morgue on an average week, with these techniques, people could live indefinitely.'

'Except the ones providing those salvageable cadavers, of course,' I pointed out. 'So, as long as you're rich enough, you get to live forever, right? And once the research program's run its course Synapware gets to dictate the price out there. Meanwhile, those guys currently dealing squirts will be dealing corpses instead. To supply the brand new body-swapping trade with black market stock.'

'That's not actually possible. The resources needed to keep a body close to its post-death state, the facilities needed to revive it–'

'Trust me, Tyler. The ganglanders won't care how fresh those bodies are. They won't care how pure the download is, how complete the upload. And, if this ever gets onto the market, they'll find a way to revive a corpse. You're right, people will want it. People will *kill* for it. And it's the nobodies who'll suffer. They'll be the ones who'll die to provide the bodies. Or they'll pay to have themselves downloaded by scumbags, uploaded into a corpse. A mouldy one.'

'The techniques are simply too complex for this to be done outside a laboratory.'

High Tide in the City

'You people said that about overlays.'

Tyler sighed, sat back in his chair again. 'We're not here to discuss the moral side of this research project, Mr Nixon. And at present that's all it is. A promising one, but it's just a project.'

'Oh. You just wanted to freak me out, right? Get me face-to-face with a dead man, see how I'd jump.'

'As I said, the host body should be dead when the upload takes place. It should then be carefully revived. Joseph Samuels was very much alive when he uploaded this "rogue" consciousness into his cerebellum a week ago and walked out of here. Within a matter of hours he was contending with a phalanx of psychophysical issues - nerve conflict, chemical imbalances. Issues he had no hope of dealing with from his subjective position. By the time he reached the mainland he was already very sick and, I would suggest, barely in control of his own decisions.'

'Dietrich.' I closed my eyes, feeling sick to my stomach. '*He's* Mephistopheles.'

Okay. So I'm a slow study. So sue me. Truth is the last thing I wanted to accept was that the thing I'd been chasing out there was Karl Dietrich.

Tyler's hands on the desk folded into fists.

'As you said, he's not the "furthering of medical science" type. But he did need access to our labs. The price for that was his corpse.

'Our internal investigation suggests he paid Samuels somewhere in the sum of two hundred thousand Euros to make the other arrangements. We're not sure how he obtained such amounts whilst on Death Row, but–'

'Angela Bassett,' I said.

When Tyler gave a questioning look, I shrugged.

'Common knowledge. Her parents were wealthy. Paid Dietrich a ransom, against our advice. He didn't give her back. At least not alive. But he took their money anyway. Something in the region of two mil. We never recovered it, so I'm guessing it's stashed somewhere off-shore in some cheap bank. All this time I was celebrating the fact he never got to spend it. Instead he uses it to plan his escape.'

'Anyway. We think initial contact took place months ago, but the download happened, without our knowledge I might add, when he was brought to this lab to be medically assessed as a host for "Mr Faust", three days before his execution. We believe he also gave Samuels the name of a street prostitute - a former paramedic in a hurry to earn some extra cash.'

Tyler saw my reaction, lifted his eyebrow in query.

'Erin Smart,' I said. '*That's* why she was there. Samuels didn't want to screw her, he needed her to revive someone!' I frowned. 'But who? Not Samuels - he was the transporter, still alive and he needed to stay that way or I'm guessing Dietrich's persona would die along with him.'

Tyler nodded. 'Dietrich's new host was meant to be Ray Sands, the courtesy driver, who Samuels asked for specifically that evening, possibly on Dietrich's orders.'

'So Dietrich intended to kill this man, Sands, then upload himself into his body.'

'That was apparently the plan,' Tyler said. 'Things didn't go the way they were meant to, though. Obviously. We can only extrapolate based on Sands' testimony and the VasCard unit and drugs discovered in the boot of the car. How they intended to kill him, I suppose only Dietrich knows. But the kit was there ready to revive him, once Dietrich's consciousness was uploaded into Sands' dead brain.'

'You knew all this,' I said. 'And you didn't pass any of it on to the police?'

'Absolutely not. For one thing, the police wouldn't have a clue how to deal with a situation like this. For another, we have a legal obligation to take care of such matters ourselves. Mop up our own mess, so to speak.'

'*Mop up your*...? Fuck that, Tyler! People have been killed! Innocent people. You can't "mop" that up without involving the law! And what about the victims' human rights? What about closure for whoever else is affected by that "mess" of yours?'

Tyler lifted his hands apologetically. 'There's a lot at stake here. Far more than I'm at liberty to explain at this juncture, either to you or the police.'

'So this is where you throw Special State's Secrets at me. Right?'

'Like it or not, it stands between us and open discourse with the police.'

'So you're telling me extending someone's life beyond death - in this case a complete psycho - is more important than protecting people who have a legitimate claim to it?'

'Some might argue that nobody has a legitimate claim to life. Or that everybody has, even the dead and dying. But I agree with you. These killings are unacceptable. For that reason alone Dietrich must be stopped. But it has to be done without police involvement. They have a mandate to fulfil which would jeopardise a very sensitive issue. For the time being, we do this our way. Without the police.'

I sat back in my chair, dumbfounded. He had a point about that mandate, I had to admit. Being forced by Act of State to tell the public everything they knew was bad enough. If Synapware were to involve them, the police would have to go public on this whole Mephistopheles thing. Imagine what that would do out there. Not just the notion of a body-hopping madman, the whole living again idea.

'This is nuts. Totally fucking nuts! For all your paranoia, your overblown security, you let a madman loose! And how! Murdering people so he gets to live twice? So much for it staying in the lab! This is just the start. This is going to be the future - you realise that, don't you?'

Tyler sighed. 'More melodramatics, Mr Nixon?'

I turned to Beck, stunned. 'Tell me you get what I'm saying.'

The man shrugged. 'Doesn't matter what I think. Our job is to stop Dietrich. That's all.'

'That's all,' I repeated dully. 'You guys really don't give a shit, do you? About anything but protecting your fucking corporation!'

Neither offered an answer to that. Beck leaned to one side, propped his head up on his prosthetic hand. Tyler sat back and flicked invisible lint from the lapels of his jacket.

'Okay,' I said. 'So what about this security guard, Sands. What guarantee do you have that he won't go to the police? Or to the media.'

Tyler re-engaged, sat forward again.

'Ray Sands was scheduled to undergo a two week stint here on the Island. By which time Dietrich will have been dealt with and Sands would be convinced not to take the matter further.'

'Convinced?'

'Financially.'

'Uh-huh. Does he realise how lucky he is? Not about the money. I mean, he could be dead now and no one would even know.'

Beck shifted in his seat. 'Not so very lucky,' he said. 'Your friend Gage took care of him for good two days ago.'

10

It was dark and the rain was heavier when the car dropped me off near my apartment. I knew my cold-box was empty so I got out at the convenience store to grab some items. Told the driver I'd walk from there.

I picked up the usual suspects - milk, bread, beans - then remembered I didn't have a bag. That involved a two-Euro fine and a glower from the shop assistant. The bag he selflessly lavished on me was paper, so I didn't bother thanking him - in this weather, the degradable fibres wouldn't last long enough for the shop door to hit me in the ass.

My hair was dripping before I got ten metres. Rain ran down my scalp, down my neck, into my eyes. I fought a running battle between wiping it away and protecting the bag so it didn't disintegrate. The bottom fell out before I reached the corner, so I discarded the limp remnants and tucked the results of my hunting expedition under my arms.

I did it all without swearing. That's the kind of day I was having.

Set aside learning the most evil son-of-a-bitch I ever met was still alive and running around in someone else's body, I was struggling to believe almost everything else Tyler had said, too. Body swapping? For real? Just when did the world get that insane? Yet I'd seen a dead man walk out the room. And just before the party was over, they'd let me watch some sad sack being uploaded.

It had happened down a different corridor, in a private room. Male lying on a bed, not breathing. No circulation, no brain activity. Dead. We'd stood beside him - Russian dolls again - staring at a corpse. But the readout beside me, drawn from the cap fitted over his head, told me there was someone in there, rattling around a lifeless brain. And then he'd been brought back. The drugs feeding his body had started his heart.

Gentle, like a feather. A moment later, he'd inhaled. A small breath, soft. Each time he breathed, his heart beat harder, his chest lifted higher. At the first spark of electrical activity in the skull, Tyler stirred, turned to me.

'He needs time,' he'd said, tugging my sleeve and pulling me away.

I'd followed, but it had been hard to take my eyes off the bed, that living corpse slowly gaining strength.

'Those drugs...'

'Nanotech.' The door to the ward had closed, shutting off the whisper of medical machinery.

This corridor was cooler, brighter than the first one. Faint whiff of the morgue. As we passed them, I'd locked gazes with one of a pair of security guards standing outside an unmarked door halfway down. I noticed them because they were security but they weren't Wolf Line. These guys wore black. And instead of stun-sticks they packed smokers butch enough to make Mr Beck's look like it shot flowers. The guard met my stare, flicked his gaze off me, focussed on the wall straight ahead. Tyler hurried me past them, but not before I spotted the pin-badge on the guard's collar.

'What the hell?'

'Special States Secrets, Mr Nixon. Best not to ask.'

I'd growled softly, then shrugged. Let him lead me to the exit.

Squirts were bad. I'd always believed they were bad. Bad enough for me to do whatever it took to get them off the streets. But this? The future scenario was so clear, so grim, so terrifying... Global catastrophe looked fun by comparison. And they called it life extension.

Can't be done outside a lab? I snorted into the rain and darkness one more time. 'Fucking morons!'

Within days of it being released as a 'treatment' for whatever ailments rich people suffer from, the ganglanders would be out there kidnapping to order, experimenting with ways to kill without damaging the body, cobbling systems together for downloading...what was it? 'Mephistopheles-type' personas. Within a month the procedure would be available on the streets to whoever had the credit. And God help anyone who fitted the profile they wanted.

It can't be done outside a lab. But Samuels, along with Dietrich, had already tried it. The first victim of the new body-swapping trade was meant to be some security guard detailed to drive an overpaid innovations engineer around for the night.

At some point after he'd been picked up, Samuels had stopped off to load a cap into the trunk of Ray Sands' car - the car he'd been assigned that night. The cap was very like the one sitting in the trunk of *my* car, but presumably more like the one I'd seen in Synapware's Life Extension facility. This one Samuels had built from memory on his kitchen worktop. It was designed to extract Dietrich from his own brain, so he could be uploaded into Ray Sands' corpse through Sands' bracer. That plan fucked up when Sands managed to escape and drive off with the cap and all the other gear they'd needed.

Maybe Dietrich considered using Erin Smart's body instead. Maybe that's why he decided to kill her. Except old habits took over.

I shook my head. Cross-gender body-swapping? Dietrich? Maybe not. More like business as usual.

But Samuels' bracer was a joke and Erin Smart's had somehow ended up at the bottom of the vat of brewers mash ahead of her. He'd had to wait for someone else's. He'd waited for mine. Begged the question as to why he hadn't used Sands' bracer later, while he was inside Gage. Why hadn't he hadn't put himself inside Sands when he had him captive over in Port Town? He could've become Ray Sands then, instead of killing him. Except, I then remembered. No one to revive Sands. Killing Erin Smart right at the start wasn't Dietrich's best move ever. In fact, from Dietrich's point of view the whole thing was a bit of a clusterfuck. Bet he was pissed as hell.

I was so lost in thought I didn't notice anyone behind me.

For a second I couldn't figure out why my stuff had fallen out from under my arms, was rolling and scattering across the pavement under the light of a distant streetlamp. Then it registered.

The dull thud on the back of my skull where something soft and heavy had hit it with force. Hands went under my arms as my knees buckled. I collapsed like a puppet with cut strings. I was dragged backwards, face up so the rain splashed into my eyes.

Someone grabbed my left wrist, wrestled with the catches, tugged hard. I couldn't get my mouth working to object as they slid the bracer off my arm. The finger loops snagged on my knuckles, then the whole thing was gone, leaving nothing but a raw, naked sensation behind it.

Twice. Twice in as many days some bastard had taken my bracer.

But the Sandman... I was beginning to think I should leave it at home, way things were going lately. It went, too. Gone. Before I had time to remember I even had it.

Behind me, a van door rattled open. That's when the fear hit.

These were ganglanders. When they collected you like this, you were a certified dead man.

*

Yeah, I'd pissed him off big time, going to visit him in jail, but I never thought Greg Davies had the balls or the influence to enlist ganglanders. Besides, he'd never been the kind to pay for something he could get a pal to do for free. Fact I was here, kneeling in the dark in ganglander territory told a different story.

I'd dismissed Davies' threat as bullshit. Guess I shouldn't underestimate people.

Feet crunched grit. Their owner was hidden beyond the glow of chem-lights strung between two twisted girders. I heard more than one pair of shoes shuffling around out there. No big surprise. The girders and the surrounding slabs of broken concrete told me where I was - beneath the raised section of the old motorway. The small stretch, anyway, which had survived the earthquake and the ensuing landslides that had wiped half the hill and fifteen hundred drivers and passengers permanently off the map.

Having dug the corpses out, the Brits had abandoned the road. Focused, instead, on raising new infrastructure. The ganglanders had taken over the ruins, using the slabs of rubble and wreckage as low-tech hide-outs or storage for their smuggled goods. It told me one thing, anyway. I was dealing with Brutants.

'Didn't know as he was dirty.'

The voice was resonant and soft. Hard-soled boots crunched broken cement as their owner circled me slowly. Watching me, looking for fear.

'Whatever,' he went on, now on my left. 'I's open to new ideas. One a your friends just paid I big to disappear you. Gave me summik special for the job.'

I closed my eyes and let out a shaky breath. *'Summik special'*. Was not good news. But I'd picked up on something else he'd said.

'Who's dirty?' I tried to keep my voice steady, tried to pitch it low. 'Who paid you?'

Because Greg Davies had never been squeaky. If the Brutant was surprised by who'd hired him, then it hadn't been Davies who'd paid these bastards.

'That don't matter to you, now. Do it? You'm gonna be dead.'

Didn't take a genius to work that out. And now I knew it wasn't Davies, it didn't take one to figure out who else might have hired these thugs.

So. Dietrich was still trying to kill me. For some reason I couldn't fathom, this time he was too busy to do it himself. Went against his MO, but maybe he was on a schedule. Things to do, people to kill. People other than me. If this ganglander called him dirty, then Dietrich had to be inside another cop.

That left a sick feeling in my gut.

I shifted slightly, easing the pressure on my knees. Earned myself a sharp blow on the back of the neck.

'When you say "something special",' I said, shrugging off the blow and letting the same someone straighten me up again. 'I don't suppose you're talking about a handshake and peck on the cheek?'

The speaker finally stepped within the murky glow of chem-lights, dropped to one knee so he was on my level. All I could see of him was a dark outline punctuated by glowing face tattoos, which writhed when he grinned.

'You'm scared a dying, Squirt Man?'

'Wasn't on today's to-do list, I admit.'

'It is now.'

The ganglander stood up again.

'I needs light,' he said to someone on my left.

If I'd been in any doubt, the speed the spot snapped on told me this guy was in charge. When a ganglander prem tells a sub to do something, they do it quick or lose a body part. The light came off a mini-gen, spilled a trembling oval across me so my shadow fell ahead, elongated. The black jeans, etched with grime and standing in front of me, walked round till they ended up behind.

I licked my lips and was instantly annoyed. I didn't want them to see I was scared. They'd like that and that would piss me off. The prem was between me and the light now and his shadow overlaid mine on the floor.

He reached out to the right, took the weapon someone was holding, ready and primed for him.

The gut-deep fear which had slithered inside me while I was bundled into the van reawakened, turned my legs to soup.

Crossed my mind to beg.

I realised as soon as the thought arrived, it would be pointless. These guys had been paid already. They had me. Only reason they'd listen to me plead for my life was for entertainment.

Crossed my mind to ask how much he'd paid. I'd double it.

Yeah, right. Even if I could afford it, they'd take my money and do the job anyway. I was alone out here and untraceable. They could do anything they wanted.

Besides, I then remembered. My bracer was gone. I had no money, no cydentity, no value without it.

Face it, Nix. You're dead.

I willed my voice not to crack. 'Think you'll get away with this?'

I heard a laugh, from several people. The prem deigned to answer. For someone who viewed me as nothing but a payday, I guess I should have felt honoured.

'Course I will. I always does. Hold him still.'

Two people came from the shadows, instantly obedient. Each of my arms was grabbed, just under the armpits, fingers digging in so I couldn't move.

The pistol clicked as the Brutant primed the round inside. Its muzzle tickled the base of my skull, brushed my hair aside so it made contact with skin. As far as something special went, this fell somewhat short. In terms of lethal...

Then the prem's mouth was next to my ear.

'Take a deep breath, Squirt Man.'

I blinked hard, eyes fixed on my shadow where it fell, trembling, ahead of me. I wondered if I'd live long enough to see the starburst of blood and brain splash onto the floor. Or would it be truly instant? So instant I wouldn't even feel it?

The cold spike pricking the back of my neck made me frown. Then a single light blossomed in front of my eyes. It was followed by another.

Two, eight, a dozen. A thousand brilliant lights, bursting across my vision. The spike became a thrill. Sank deeper.

The cut pulled as I opened my eyes wide in shock. It wasn't a pistol jammed against my skull. I'd been so revved up expecting short, sharp violence, it hadn't even occurred to me. I struggled then. Tried to. Hands were still there. So was the squirt gun.

'Get his head! Stop struggling Squirt Man. You doesn't want brain-damage, eh?' The prem gave a laugh. 'I knows you likes this. You likes it a lot. What they goin'a say, Squirt Man? Old Nix made his own exit. Stiffed out on an overlay. He done hisself, they'll say. Stupid cunt couldn't hack it.'

I tried shrugging the hands off again but these guys had done this before. They held me up, kept me still. I got another bruise on my shoulder from the cosh and a dead arm into the bargain. Hands were in my hair now, and someone was in front of me. Gripping, holding my head still as the needle went deeper. My head was full of stars and it kept on filling. So full and bright I was effectively blind. Not just visually. All else - *everything* else - was gone from my mind.

It had always been beautiful. Like looking down on the universe - creating it, unfolding it, embracing it. Like I was God. Then the in-going overlay sparked a flood of endorphins and my legs, my arms, slid loose. My lips relaxed into a smile I couldn't suppress. I sagged, uncaring, against the bastard holding my hair and surrendered to a delicious, long-absent wave of pleasure.

I breathed words. Barely a whisper and incoherent, but I wanted to thank them. Just how the hell had they known? I'd missed it. Every single day. I'd missed it more than I'd've missed my own dick. God knows how I managed to wake up each day without this to look forward to. And now it was back - sweeter, more forgiving than any lover. And this one took me back with no recrimination.

When the needle came out I felt cheated but I was grinning, probably drooling, while the upload crashed through my brain, taking over.

'There he goes.' The prem clicked the squirt gun shut. I got a glimpse as he shoved it in someone's hands. 'Make sure you wipes it properly.' He gestured at the two holding my arms.

'Get him over to Clifton. Let's put opportunity in our boy's way.'

*

'Mind if I sit?'

High Tide in the City

The voice startled me. I glanced up and to my left, hitched my eyebrows up in surprise. Beck was there, artificial fingers looped through the metal lattice running off to either side behind me. Water ran into my eyes. I looked away, blinking, and shrugged.

'Free country.' Even so, I flinched as Beck moved closer. 'Just don't–'

'I won't.'

Beck folded his tree-trunk legs, lowered himself down. Had to admit, he took it slow, careful. Didn't breach my personal space. He perched his butt along from mine on the dilapidated maintenance platform and stared off into the night.

'Great view,' he said.

He was probably just making conversation, but I nodded. He was right.

Port Town was a distant shimmer on the dark expanse of Bristol's drowned lowland. I could see it way ahead, framed by the gorge's rocky sides. Where there had once been rich, commercial dockland the slum had arisen - a tattered phoenix born from those soggy proverbial ashes - and now it shone. All those distant lamps twinkling as the rafts shifted on the swell.

Light pollution and the rain slapping into my face dulled the effect. The rain couldn't be helped and the overspill of light was inevitable - the one thing Bristol had kept up, despite the cost. Matter of pride. We were talking about a symbol of the city here. Thousands of LEDs burning bright in a world turned dark by its own over-consumption.

Beck straightened his legs out ahead of him, flexed his toes. Looked weird - bare feet sticking out the bottom of his designer suit.

'What happened to your shoes?'

'Took 'em off. Had my fingers and toes altered way back. Spider grip. In a situation like this...' He gestured around himself. 'Might come in handy.'

'So. You're one of *those*.' Couldn't help the cynicism. Good news was, at least I could tell it came from me. 'A real live Boy Scout. Should I be bowing in reverence or shaking in fear?'

'Dunno. Keep pissing me off, we'll find out if you can do either.'

That's when I decided I liked Mr Beck.

Here he was at Suicide Central, on the wrong side of the Clifton Suspension Bridge on a narrow platform three hundred feet above a rocky gorge. Add to that the ex-cop whose squirt was telling him to jump and he was making threats.

I shivered, adjusted my slick, aching fingers on the lattice. 'They loan you out or something?'

'Who?'

'Your unit. With that spider grip, you gotta be Special Forces.'

Beck sighed, tilted his chin up so rain splashed onto his face. 'Ex,' he said quietly.

I glanced at the scars on his face, the black hand gripping the edge of the platform.

'Thought so. So you came to join the ex club. Well, there's a lot of ex's around here. Ex-cop, ex-addict, ex-' I couldn't think. 'Whatever.'

'So you gonna do it?' Beck leant forward, letting water drip off his chin into the void. He peered between his knees at the fall below.

The move freaked me out, maybe because I'd spent the last I dunno how long feeling the call of that drop and wondering how much longer I could resist it. I gasped, pressed back against the bridge. My fingers on the railing gripped harder, I think - I couldn't feel them. I started weeping again at the thought. Couldn't help it. Fucking personas!

'They want me to,' I managed, eventually.

'Who?'

I heard the hysteria in it when I laughed. 'Whoever's in here with me. I'm supposed to jump.'

Beck's killer gaze was almost physical when he laid it on me. 'So you're squirting.'

'I was squirted.' Flashed an uneasy look in his direction - humiliated, desperate. 'Brutants.'

If it wasn't for the fact I'd walked so many miles in any kind of overlay, I'd've been unable to tell him that much. I'd've already jumped. Goes to show experience counts.

Beck was nodding. 'Figures. Didn't have you down as the suicide type.'

I wasn't listening.

'I forgot how much I missed it.' My voice was a whisper, but I wasn't really talking to him. 'The upload. Forgot how it... Man, it was so...' I breathed out hard. Sounded more like a sob. Took a moment to get myself under control again while Beck sat there waiting, listening.

'Thing is, they forgot,' I said louder, once the surge of self-pity had been put down. 'I'm an addict. I can handle any shit they throw at me.'

'Is that why we're up here?'

'It's why I'm not down there already.'

'Think you'll end up down there?'

I risked a peek at the darkness below. Faint streak of white where the river, currently at low-tide, churned over something submerged down there. I huddled back against the rail again, closed my eyes. The desire was there. Strong enough to be a legitimate form of ecstasy. My heart banged harder at the prospect of quick, sudden death and how much I wanted it. How easy, how natural, how perfect it would be to let go the rail and tip myself forward. Those precious seconds of screaming helpless, outright terror - the sensation of nothing but air buffeting my body - and then...nothing. Forget addiction to the upload, most people squirt for just this kind of thrill. I caught the sob trying to rip my throat open from the inside. Swallowed it.

'Maybe,' I admitted.

'Is that what you want?'

That had me looking at him again, hard.

'No.' Some part of me, whatever wretched part of me hadn't been shit on as thoroughly as the rest still saw a point in living. Still fought back. 'No, it's not. Hate the fucking scenery down there.'

'Then what we gonna do about it?'

'We?' I almost laughed. Except...chances were I wasn't getting out of this without help. And I didn't really care whose it was. 'If I knew that, I wouldn't be... I can't move. The squirt won't let me climb back up. If you knock me unconscious - I'll fall. If you try to drag me off here - I'll fight you, pull us both down there.'

'Solution?'

'Wait for the squirt to wear off.'

'That could take hours.'

'Two,' I told him. Had enough experience to tell how much more life this squirt had left in it. 'Two more hours.' During which all I would think about was swallow-diving off this ledge.

Beck wriggled his backside, making the platform rattle and shift, and me whimper.

'Another two hours sitting here in the rain while the wind takes your core temperature down one degree every half hour, if not faster. You'll freeze to death before you fall.'

'Freeze?' I gave a choked laugh. It was summer, for Christ's sake! But it was only then I noticed my teeth were chattering.

'Besides, you'd shake yourself off here during the come down.'

I knew it, too, somewhere inside me. 'Any better ideas?'

'You won't like it. And you'll have to let me come a lot closer.'

I flinched, blinked a new gush of tears away. 'Stay back! Don't... Don't grab hold. Don't try to–'

'I won't.'

It felt female, this squirt. This quagmire of emotion, the deep malaise. So deep and dark there was no climbing out. Gender didn't matter, though. A squirt is a squirt. And this one had had enough of life. All it was waiting for right now was death and the excuse to meet it.

I licked my lips. 'If you try to grab me they'll–'

'Make you jump. I know. I won't grab you.'

Beck reached inside the flap of his jacket, into the pocket above his weapon, and drew out a slim, flat tin which gleamed in the LEDs illuminating the bridge behind and above us. Man swung his legs to-and-fro while he did it, like a kid on a park bench. Watching him made my stomach flip but I couldn't take my eyes off the tin. When he opened it, revealing a row of tubes, I shuddered. Needles.

I jutted my chin at them. 'You came prepared.'

'Boy Scout, like you said.'

'Is it–?'

'I don't have Wipe,' Beck said flatly, lifting his gaze to mine. 'But I do have Clean.'

That made me wince. Wipe was the stuff the police gave a squirter once my magic cap finished recording what was inside their head. It eliminated the persona chemicals in seconds, killed the squirt dead.

Clean did the same, only it did a lot more besides. Clean in my system meant eight weeks during which anything I squirted would put me in hospital, in agony or with a brain haemorrhage. Came as a shock to realise I was already planning my next upload. Or the Clean would mean nothing. Here I was, thinking about my next walk and I hadn't survived this one yet.

Hey, once an addict... Letting him put Clean in me, though, meant I would stay clean. Even if I lived, I'd abandon that particular lover all over again. I'd wake up each morning craving her, desperate for her but knowing I daren't touch her. After eight weeks the addiction, the urge to squirt, would be gone. That was Clean's job. But it was the seconds in between which would hurt.

I swallowed hard, met Beck's stare. Nodded.

He was careful. Moved slow. When the needle went in the back of my hand, I didn't move it, but I was weeping again. This time the tears were all mine.

11

The beer was frosty. Two frosty drinks on the same day. My fortunes must have really turned around. Forget that there was a madman out there who'd paid ganglanders to kill me, that I was working for the enemy, that I was going to be strung out solid for the next two months. A *frosty* beer cost three times normal. The bar's payment interface blipped an audible acknowledgement and Beck lifted his bracer off the glass plate, took the barstool next to mine. We stared at the wallscreen in silence.

News was the usual shit. More complaints about the extended absence from public office of King Thomas, our glorious Head of States. Complaints about the stoic silence the previous complaints had been met with. Thirty more container loads of relief for the drought-and-energy-stricken United States. Complaints from them about how it was nowhere near enough; from us about how the European States couldn't afford to bail them out any longer. I watched footage of half a dozen American kids getting themselves carved up by the laser-wire border separating Canada from the rest of mainland North America. Canada was full, the report said - an excuse this time, not a complaint. They couldn't take any more people, legal or otherwise, no matter how desperate said people were.

'Guess we're the lucky ones after all,' I muttered, acknowledging the brotherhood of our origins at last and breaking the long silence. 'How'd you find me out there, anyway?'

Beck pulled his right sleeve back.

'The squirt wasn't the only thing in your system,' Beck said, flicking menus.

He showed me a ghostly image on his screen. The street we were on - each building picked out by transparent walls; floating blobs which were

High Tide in the City

humans moving about; the outline of a vehicle moving south, loaded with boxes. Red icon entitled 'Matthew M Nixon' sat centre-stage.

'The tracker I drank.' I made a face, lifted the bottle to my lips and took a pull. The beer was a good brand - Bosnian - but it didn't take the taste away.

'Just as well you *did* drink it or I doubt I'd have found you. Even a PBC search sent me to the wrong place. If I hadn't kept looking, you'd probably be dead.'

The man laid his forearm on the bar with a steel clunk.

I'd seen images like the one he'd just shown me before. Software-rendered info from an orbiting satellite. Went beyond the old-fashioned spy-in-the-sky stuff. These satellites used neutron resonance imaging to see through solid objects. The software then turned those solid objects into see-through outlines. Meant you could identify and track a specific target, in a crowd, inside a building, or even underground. And Beck had tracked me.

The software screamed Military. Infiltration, remote targeting. With maybe an anti-terrorist or HK application. Then again Beck claimed he was *ex*-mil. A civilian. And besides, as a general rule, satellites belonged to countries and their armies. They couldn't be tuned to a civilian's bracer, especially not with the mundane purpose of locating one fairly unworthy character like me.

I wondered which army the video feed had belonged to and if they knew their targeting hardware was being hi-jacked by some dude, simply to track down another dude. Wondered what they'd do to Beck if said army ever found out. It crossed my mind to also wonder if Beck had access to the other hardware the satellite was attached to - the type that could turn acres of conurbation into slag.

Even the police, whenever they'd requested a similar feed from the MOD, were provided with only a limited link-up to those satellites. So how the hell did Beck get full coverage when the Chief of Police could only get spill-over?

On another note, I lost count of how many privacy laws Beck had infringed just running the PBC search on me. I could get him arrested for just that, forget his screwing over the military to track me down. But the man had saved my life. I wasn't aiming to get him busted for it.

'Why were you looking for me anyhow? Thought you'd've had enough of my company.'

'I wanted a word. Friendly word. In private. When I didn't find you at your apartment, I blipped your bracer's transponder. It told me you were two streets away.'

He'd tried to access my bracer's transponder? More stuff which shouldn't be possible with an off-the-shelf bracer, and more privacy laws trashed.

I sighed. 'Except I wasn't.'

'No.'

He dipped into another pocket, fetched out a folded-down bracer and tossed it onto the bar's varnished surface.

'It was under a car. You weren't.'

'They must have ditched it when they snatched me.'

I picked the device up. I didn't usually bother closing it down to its factory configuration and it took a second to find the button to open it again. The device unpacked itself between my fingers, lobster plates emerging from the more or less solid brick my bracer had become, snicking into their more familiar shape. I unhooked the kinetic bands and wriggled my fingers into the loops then clipped the plates together around my left arm. Whether I liked Beck's methods or not, getting the bracer back was an unexpected bonus to surviving my encounter with the Brutants. Having spent so much time off my arm lately, the device was reluctant to turn on. I worked my wrist and fingers a few times, giving it a charge boost. Watched the 'Welcome' screen blossom into life with a sense of relief.

'I assumed they'd kept it, sold it.'

'Port Towners would have. Ganglanders ain't so stupid. If they'd sold it, or laid it on someone, it would always be traceable back to them and so would your murder. Safer for them to just dump it.'

'Right.' Like a murder charge would worry their misbegotten asses.

But I had my bracer back. A minor miracle. Bigger miracle, my bank account and everything else on it was untouched. My beloved Sandman, however... Its fate was not so rosy. Probably changed hands five times by now. By tomorrow it'd be in some devolved country helping thugs get the better of some sad sack who was just trying to stay alive. That galled me. That was not what my Sandman should be used for.

Beck was right, though. However much I hated admitting it. If he hadn't come looking for me, if I hadn't drunk the chemical tracker, I probably *would* be dead. I wouldn't have lasted much longer up there with that persona telling me to jump every conscious second. Now I was clean, I could see that. It occurred to me I should thank him, but because of him, I was now clean. It was enough to make me hate him.

I sucked on my beer again.

'About what?' I asked, suppressing a belch.

'Huh?' Beck took his eyes off the wallscreen he'd turned back to, laid them on me.

'Friendly word about what?'

'Your visit to the Island didn't go down too well. Someone outside Liaison is calling for you to be put down.'

You know, he could have sugar-coated it, me being a sensitive soul and all.

'The request was denied,' Beck continued. 'You're safe. For now. Just be careful. Don't mention anything you saw out there. To *anyone*. They're seeing you as a loose cannon and for some people there's a lot at stake.'

'So why'd Tyler take me out there if it's gonna cause itchy underwear?'

'Because he knows you're a stubborn bastard and you wouldn't believe it unless you saw it. Remember...' He stood up, tapped his finger under his eye, pointed it at me. Whatever *that* meant. 'Not a word. I haven't touched the beer, by the way. Enjoy.'

I watched him go. When the door closed behind him, I rubbed the back of my hand where a tiny bead of dried blood still sat. Beck might be okay. Hell, he'd just saved my life, that was worth some points, right? But truthfully, I wasn't sure if I was grateful or if I'd like to see him turn up dead.

That last was the addict talking.

The Addict. Me.

The addict was back alright. I'd heard how one squirt was all it took. Now I knew for sure. Didn't matter how many months, how many years without it. After just one upload, I was addicted all over again. Psychologically, at least. Be a while before I could close the door on that particular persona again.

On the bright side, I couldn't remember the last time I'd had so much going for me.

Most bits of me were numb because they hurt so much I couldn't function without the host of painkillers I'd had injected. I had a demented, disembodied psychopath trying to kill me and a multinational conglomerate threatening to do the same thing. And I was clean.

Life, I decided. Was shit.

*

The problem with working nights for too long is that going to bed in the dark feels weird. Waking up at three, sure something apocalyptic was happening because there was nothing but quiet coming from outside meant I was only borderline human.

I waited for the palpitations to stop and rolled onto my stomach, ignoring the numb area telling me I was compressing damaged ribs. I hooked my forearm under my cheek. Tried to think whose code was still good. Danny Brooks was in too tight with Greg Davies - he'd sooner see me dead. Smack the Hack had moved to London a few months back. Laney had been iced a year ago. Jacko was in Chedminster. All the old names came up blank. Truth is, it was an ever-changing scene out there and I'd been on the wrong side of it too long.

I opened my eyes and blinked, slow. What the fuck was I thinking? Even if I still had the contacts, I couldn't take the walk, thanks to Mr Beck and his Clean.

'He had a lot of fucking needles in that kit,' I told the dark. 'Fucker had to have Wipe in there. *Had* to.'

But thanks to Beck and his Clean, there was no way I could make the call my fingers itched for. No way I could take another walk. I threw the sheets off me, letting the muggy air do its best to dry the flush of sweat pricking across my body. I shouldn't be getting them, not after just one hit, and not so soon. The tremors in my limbs and the hot flashes soaking my sheets were imaginary, obviously.

I got up, headed for the bathroom and ran a basin of cold water. Flinched when I caught sight of myself in the mirror. The fluorescent bulb was merciless, picked out details I'd rather not see. The face and its new features weren't much improved on yesterday, even if some of the bruises were yellowing. The sweat wasn't imaginary. A bead of moisture slid down my cheek as I stared, dismayed, at what I'd gone through recently.

Beat up and strung out. Tried to remember if I'd ever felt this sorry for myself.

On the back of the shelf beside the mirror, a brown plastic bottle. My fingers were shaking as I picked it up, rattled it. Still some left. I swallowed one dry. Anti-withdrawal pills. Better than nothing.

I dipped my hands in the basin. The icy shocks to my face took my mind off golf clubs, magtrains and Brutant generosity. Steadied me enough to take me to the kitchen and turn on the kettle. Then I remembered the milk I'd bought had gone rolling into the gutter while ganglanders dragged me into their van. I cancelled the coffee. Went for my bracer instead.

Dietrich - if it really was him out there, not some rogue AI or military weapon like Sitaroo suggested - had tried to kill me a second time in as many days. Time that fucker was history. For real. And if any of this shit was true then at least I knew someone who could help me get ahead of him.

She was probably on duty. My fingers hesitated over her code. After yesterday's fight, Lian wouldn't exactly welcome a call from me. More importantly, I couldn't tell her about Dietrich, even though I needed the files she'd made when she'd profiled him six years ago. Not because she'd think I was crazy, or because I gave a shit what Synapware would do to me if I let their nasty little secret out into the world, but because of what they'd do to her. She'd tell me I was unfit for duty anyway. Off the case. She wouldn't discuss it with me. I finished punching in the number anyway.

Frowned when it came up blocked. Twice.

Okay, so maybe she was more upset than I'd imagined. But I was a police consultant. She had to deal with me in her job. Why block me?

Fine. I'd just go in a different way. She'd told me DI Fox was the Scene of Crime Officer on the Harris murders. I'd go from there. I didn't know Fox. New Boy. Meant he didn't know me either, but in my case that might be a good thing. As SOCO, he might have some news on Harris's missing bracer. That way I could at least find out who Dietrich was now using as a host - who'd paid the ganglanders to upload me with a suicide. And I might even persuade Fox to get Lian to call me.

Since I didn't have his code it meant using Central to route my call. I thumbed the pre-dialled button on my screen, listened to the bracer hunt for a connection. The far end of the signal clicked, but instead of the interactive menu I'd expected, my screen stayed blank. A second later an automated voice thrummed through my aural implant - perfect, polished, polite.

'Matthew Nixon, your license has been revoked by the South West Constabulary. You are no longer at liberty to use police resources, please disconnect.'

'*Whoa*! Wait a sec! Revoked? I'm signed off unfit, not suspended!'

'Your license is revoked, Mr Nixon. Please disconnect.'

'Are you shitting me? I'm fit to do research. You can't stop me making follow ups.'

The AI I was speaking to had a different opinion.

'You no longer have enquiries to continue on behalf of the Constabulary and thus need do no research. You will be required to attend a termination interview within the next twelve hours. Time and location to be advised at six hundred hours.'

A wave of cold travelled along my spine and a stab of disquiet lodged itself in my gut. I began to suspect I hadn't just misheard and the AI hadn't simply glitched.

'What the hell is going on here?'

The AI had almost hung up on me. The exchange clicked again and I was about to send a redial prompt when its voice came back.

'Mitigating circumstances will be taken into consideration following a full medical examination. Due to your valued service to the Constabulary in the past, your arrest will be taken under advisement.'

'My *arrest*? What...?'

Hell! A medical exam? Didn't take a genius to figure out what that was for.

'Check your inbox.'

This time the machine did disconnect. I lost track of how long I sat there, staring at the wall.

I was fired. The fuckers had *fired* me!

So Lian hadn't blocked my call, it was the AI. It had probably blocked every police contact I held, not to mention all the service-related apps I used, the police-tagged information I'd downloaded over the past few months. How the hell was I supposed to operate without resources? How was I supposed to investigate anything with no help? Then I remembered.

'*You no longer have enquiries to continue.*'

I'd heard my former colleagues say much the same in the past. When I was too fired up, or just too stupid to let something go. When I was too obstinate to get out of their way, when I tried to do their job for them. Now the AI had said it and a lot more besides. But was it truly possible? No enquiries? No job? Last time that happened, I'd found myself in Chedminster pumped full of Clean and awaiting trial for squirt abuse. I'd sworn to myself it would never happen again.

Yet here I was. All except for Chedminster.

So far.

I groaned. Lian's password. That's the reason. Had to be. Maybe Greg Davies made a complaint about our little chat the other day. Or maybe I'd tripped something. Used her login while she was logged on somewhere else. Cydentity theft was serious and she was a cop. *Very* serious. Yeah, maybe that was it.

No. That wasn't it. That would be a warning, at least. First time they caught me, leastways. A fine, slap on the wrist.

'*Check your inbox.*' The AI's words still hovered in the back of my brain.

I lowered the bracer and went to the cold box, took a sniff at the dregs of milk left in the refillable bottle it came in these days. Didn't smell too bad. Not bad enough to poison me anyway. And if I'd needed a coffee earlier, now it was a matter of urgency. My hands were shaking again as I poured milk and liquid coffee into a cup.

I kept lifting my wrist, looking at the bracer clinging to it, while the low-capacity kettle took an age to boil.

Check your inbox.

I was thinking clearer now. The déjà vu moment had been and gone and I had a bad feeling I knew what was waiting in my inbox. I just wasn't keen on finding out for sure. How could the police know, anyway? No one had called it in. I was pretty sure Beck hadn't - wouldn't serve his boss's interests. Guy was too much of a brown-noser to fuck up Tyler's plans. Unless he'd told Tyler and Tyler wanted to wash his hands of me. No. Paranoid as I was about anything to do with Synapware, that didn't fit. Although if Beck had told the truth about someone inside Synapware wanting me dead...

I hadn't considered that option.

I ran a hand down my face, slid onto a breakfast stool with the coffee in one hand and leaned my elbow on the bar. I slurped from the cup and winced at the heat while the fingers of my free hand drummed the edge of the counter.

Some hero you are, Nix. Jesus!

I put the coffee cup down. The inbox was flashing when I stopped fiddling and went to 'mail', so I called it up. Found it immediately. It was an image alright, but not what I'd been expecting. I'd expected a video of me scaling my way around West Pier, traversing out along the lit-up rail of the bridge so I could sit on the maintenance platform. How they would ever prove I was squirting from a stream of fuzzy, distant frames taken from a street-cam was debatable and was thus my strongest thread of hope. It crashed to oblivion the second I opened the file.

The image was mostly the grey felt of an evidence table. Resting on it, alongside the optical marker telling everyone where it had been found and where to find it again once it went to Evidence, was a used squirt gun. Finding squirt-guns was rare. Finding used ones... They were so cheap and disposable they usually ended up in the river or on a rubbish brazier seconds after they'd been discharged.

The image and its attached note had been copied to me as an advisory. Its real recipient was the Administrator of Penal Offences over at the Old Corn Exchange. The Constabulary had really gone for it. I was so busted I could see the inside of a Chedminster cell already, smell the stink. Might as well just put on a pair of cuffs and wait for them to knock, because the note attached included the identity of the user - the one uploaded by the gun lying there on the evidence table. An identity ascertained from cells taken from the squirt injector's hollow needle. No guesses who the user had turned out to be. In terms of hard evidence, this was rock solid. Better than a persona report.

12

'Where'd you get the squirt gun?' I wanted to know.

My throat sounded ancient, dusty. Decrepit. I was parched, but refreshments weren't on offer to the disgraced.

Chief Inspector Alexander flicked her desk to a blank page. She sipped her own coffee and sat back.

Would have been nice if the Constabulary had called in person to tell me when and where my termination interview was scheduled for. Instead I got another note in my inbox, which arrived three minutes after six.

Termination interview. Sounded pretty final and I guess it was. The period, the full-stop, the headman's axe signalling the end of my career. I wasn't even part of their organisation, but they were kicking me out anyway.

Before the interview took place, a medical officer had checked the bruising on my shoulders and neck, the bloody mark on the back of my skull where the needle went in. I had to explain the older injuries to her first, so she could dismiss them. When she did, I envied her. Wished I could dismiss them as easily.

Didn't help that the overnight tremors and sweats had continued into the morning, despite the pill. Enough to make it look like I had something to hide. Truthfully, some of those sweats were down to anxiety. Well-founded in my opinion. I knew too much about human error, human prejudice and good, old-fashioned human vengeance to entirely trust the outcome. There was still the fear - the paranoia born of abandonment and deportation - that the doctor would decide I'd submitted to the squirt willingly.

The paranoia proved to be just that. She confirmed the upload had been forcible. I could have kissed her. Bad enough I was about to lose my job but I'd endured prison before, if only for a few weeks, and it had been long and hell enough for me to decide it was the last place I ever wanted to go again.

The outcome was a partial in terms of good news. It didn't get me off the hook. As an ex-addict I was now unreliable. The police couldn't - wouldn't - work with me any longer. I was lucky, the Medical Officer said, that I wasn't on my way to rehab right now. As good as prison, she said, and full of my old magic cap friends, who'd appreciate the opportunity to thank me for my involvement in their past. But she reckoned it would take more than a single squirt to make me dependent. Way I was feeling, I could argue with that, but rehab would be as much fun as prison. So I wasn't about to volunteer.

Twenty minutes later, I found myself in the Chief Inspector's office.

'It was handed into Headquarters at one this morning.' she said, placing her coffee cup, with its newly-acquired crescent of lipstick, into its saucer.

'By who?'

The Chief shrugged. 'A passer-by. He claimed he found it under a car.' She anticipated my next question, jumped to the answer. 'We put the station footage through the face-match files after he left. Nothing came up.'

I nodded. Seemed the Brutants had a liking for disposing of things under cars. First my bracer, then the squirt-gun.

'Prints?' I asked.

Alexander grunted. I think it was a laugh, but I'm not sure she's ever been capable of such a thing.

'A joker, as always, Nixon.'

'Not even from the passer-by?'

She pursed her lips at that, causing a ring of wrinkles to form around her mouth. 'Apparently not.'

'Great. So what, no one questioned that? Some guy without fingerprints just happens to walk in to a police station and hands in a used injector. And no one checks?'

'Don't bother, Nixon. Deflection doesn't work with me.'

'Did you get a name?'

'We got yours.'

So Karl Dietrich had waited around to see if I jumped. When I didn't - when Beck stepped in - he'd had the ganglanders put the squirt gun where someone would find it, knowing the police would wash their hands of me. Or he'd handed it in himself. That would have tickled him for sure. And what better way to make sure I was isolated, vulnerable? Unarmed, too. Nice and ready for when he called on me again.

'You wouldn't consider offering me protection?' I said. 'Given someone's tried to murder me twice in as many days?'

'Murder?' The Chief raked her fingers through chem-blonde hair. 'You said yourself, Harris wasn't responsible for his own actions. And we've only your word for it that the squirt you were given was self-harming - we've no CAP report.'

No, I thought ironically. *It'd be my job to get that.*

'Anyway,' she went on. 'You'd abuse any protection we gave you, Nixon. You know you would.' She sighed. 'You do, of course, still have the right to call Emergency Services. But *only* in an emergency.' She tapped her desk a couple of times, called up some new data. 'All privileges extended to you in the past have been revoked. Monies outstanding for work you've carried out for the Constabulary have been paid in full into your account. I think that just about–'

'There's no chance you'd take me back?'

The Chief levelled her gaze at me. Wasn't exactly friendly.

'Not at present. Try again in a year. If you can prove you've stayed clean in that time, then we'll see. If not–'

'Don't bother. Got you.'

I know I whinge. I know I complain. But this seemed a mite unfair. I'd been kidnapped, forcibly uploaded then dragged to the edge of the Clifton Suspension Bridge and left to the mercy of a death-wish persona. And in response, the Constabulary were dumping me out there without so much as a handshake.

When I didn't take the hint, the Chief's personal assistant, who was *extremely* sorry to interrupt us, called her to another meeting. Wasn't the first time I'd walked out of that office in abject shame, but at least I could tell myself this time I hadn't actually done anything wrong.

*

'C'mon, Plummer. You know you want to.'

'Get out of my face, Nix. I'm busy.'

'You're always busy.'

'Especially where you're involved.'

Sgt Plummer hadn't bothered removing the VR goggles. She sat facing her desk, skeleton gloves clawing the air as she shifted objects around in the virtual kingdom only she could see.

'Someone set me up. All I'm asking–'

'Set you up?'

Beneath the blue-sheened lenses, her lip curled into a sneer which never quite made it. A virtual sneer, I guess.

'Yeah. Set me up,' I said. 'In case you forgot, it means someone planted evidence to make it look–'

'Everyone knows you're a squirt-head. Now you expect me to believe someone forced an upload on you?'

'I have a medical report which proves it.'

She turned in my direction and hooked the goggles off her nose, just for a second, so she could stare at me with blood-shot eyes. She shoved them back.

'Right. And then these, what did you say? Brutants? They tossed the squirt-gun, which was then found by a passer-by.'

'Exactly. A passer-by who just happened to be wearing gloves. In summer. Or who'd had their fingerprints surgically removed, and who felt "compelled" to hand it in. There has to be security footage of that good citizen. I'd really like to see it.'

'That would be a breach of protocol, seeing as you don't work here any more.'

'This guy could be a killer.'

'Oh, please.' Plummer swung her chair so her back was facing me. 'Fuck off. Seriously. Or do I have to call security? If I get time, I'll look for you. No promises.'

*

The street was an ocean of bobbing black mushrooms, all tilted towards the downpour. They parted like the biblical sea as I passed between them.

I don't usually receive so much consideration. Racked my brains as to why I was getting the VIP treatment now and decided it wasn't for my movie-star looks. Unless it was a horror movie. I hadn't glanced in a mirror lately but I knew my eye was still swollen half-shut, livid with the bruising the arnical was supposed to control. Add to that a complexion which hadn't seen sunlight in months and the glower I couldn't get off my face. Plus, no umbrella. In this rain. Equals guy in the grubby faux leather must be bad news.

So arrest me.

No. Actually, don't.

I found a coffee bar and ducked inside, partly to escape the rain, mostly to get away from those hurried glances which made me feel like a freak. There was a knot of unease in my gut I hadn't felt in a long time. Since I was a kid. On top of an empty stomach, it left me feeling queasy, so I ordered coffee and a pastry at the counter, chose a two-seater next to the window.

I stared at the rain dribbling down the glass, struggled with the vague sense of shock gripping my soul until the waitress brought my order. The coffee tasted genuine, not the liquid substitute.

Can't complain about that.

With the introduction of caffeine and carbohydrate to my system, I made an effort to get my brain in gear and forget what had just happened. So the Constabulary had kicked me out. Get over it, Nix. Focus on something else.

I still wasn't a hundred percent sure I hadn't hallucinated about signing either Tyler's contract or those 'Special States Secrets'. Still kind of laughed at the idea the authorities would behead someone when, once upon a time, Britain had no death penalty at all.

And this wasn't one of the devolved countries? Who were they kidding?

Synapware, though. They got to sign people up to the Special States Secrets Act? Since when did they handle information that sensitive? Since forever, probably. MOD contracts and all that. And now I was part of it all. Against my better judgement, but, I realised with something akin to relief, at least I was part of something.

I snorted softly, noting the irony. I'd spent the last year cleaning up the mess Synapware had washed their hands of, now they were paying me to clean up a brand new one.

But, hey! Keeps me out of trouble, right?

I gulped down more coffee.

So Dietrich was Mephistopheles. Still had a problem with that one in the cold light of a new day, no matter what I'd seen beneath Synapware's little island. Body swapping? For real? I caught myself shaking my head and stopped when the waitress gave me a weird look.

Spent a moment trying to pin-point it. The exact moment this world went insane.

Crazy as the whole Mephistopheles thing was, it explained a lot of stuff. Like the look of pure hatred a total stranger had levelled at me when I'd walked into that custody van; like how come Mephistopheles knew my name; like why I'd been summoned to Port Town, just so I could watch John Gage die. I might not like it, might not want to believe it. But it was a starting point.

By now Dietrich would be getting comfortable inside his new host. Getting ready to kill again, if he hadn't done so already. Finding him would normally be a matter of me asking the right questions, a bit of leg work. But with all my contacts, all my resources blocked... I laid my forearm on the dark-stained table and leaned over it, ran my finger in random patterns over the bracer's screen and watched the image distort - the icons drawn to my finger like a gravity-well in a 3D world.

Where the fuck *would* Dietrich go after leaving Harris?

He'd found another cop. That much I'd figured from my date with the ganglanders. But which one?

Didn't know as he was dirty, the prem had said. *He.* A male cop. A contact on Harris's bracer. So who would be on there? I hadn't had much to do with Harris for the past two years and, even if *my* life had ground to an almost stand-still since then, other peoples' hadn't, including Harris. There could be any number of people listed on his bracer. People I knew, as well as people I didn't.

I sighed, called up the search-bot. Maybe something in the public archives would give me a clue? Past collaborations, someone Harris worked with in or outside of his department. I grunted at the top result and gave a wry smile. Might have guessed. Talk about irony. Again. It was old, but it was also the highest-profile case any of us had worked on.

I opened the footage.

The video was of Karl Dietrich, looking a lot younger than I'd seen him yesterday. Handcuffed and dressed in orange coveralls. He emerged from the back of a dark-blue van, looked round at the crowd who'd turned up to see a serial killer with their own eyes. He'd refused to have his head covered that day. He wanted his fifteen minutes in the spotlight. He turned, looked up at the entrance of the Old Corn Exchange, which had hosted the Regional Crown Court back then.

A detective in a black jacket, faded jeans, took hold of Dietrich's bicep while a string of uniformed blocked the bystanders from pushing too close to the murderer. Dietrich was hurried up the steps. The detective in the jacket nodded to one of the blues, gave her a wink the camera didn't pick up. His hair had no grey in it yet and he wore it longer then. The face was thinner, younger. Six years younger. In the pocket of that jacket - where the hell was it these days? - was a black silk hood. It would be placed over Karl Dietrich's head after the sentence was pronounced. Death Hood. The man was about to be condemned to death.

Thanks to the high profile the case had earned itself, it was detectives not prison guards leading him inside the court that day. Public image. Promoting the Constabulary. Showing the world we did our job and did it right. Load of bullshit. God knows why I'd been picked to carry the hood for him, would later hook it over his prison buzz-cut. But if I hadn't been there to lead him up those steps, to watch him being sentenced, I'd've been there anyway. We'd all have been there.

Harris, grey back then rather than white-haired, held the door open for us. John Gage paused while I led the prisoner inside. Seeing him there, I suddenly realised. He hadn't changed in all this time. Looked just the same then as he did the day I last saw him. The day he died. Gage turned round, leaned over to speak to...

The waitress tapped me on the shoulder. I glanced up, startled, and she pointed at the window. It was grim outside - gloomy and miserable. The windows were a little steamed up, but not so much that I couldn't see the figure standing on the other side. I reached over and wiped condensation away with the blade of my hand. The man standing there, still rapping on the pane, paused and grinned.

So I hadn't noticed him hammering on the glass? So what? Hell, I'd been concentrating! I'm focussed, call it a plus. Besides, couldn't the fucker leave me alone for five minutes?

I waved him inside, but Beck shook his head. Beckoned for me to come out. I shoved the last bite of pastry into my mouth. Washed it down with cold coffee and got to my feet. My bracer immediately buzzed, telling me it had just paid for the breakfast. I didn't look to check how much the bill was. Real coffee? I was better off not knowing.

I left the nice dry café with its comforting aromas, joined Beck under the canopy outside. Rain sluiced off the dark-red slats, clattered to the ground beside us. I raised my voice over the whine of fusion engines.

'You know you're not my type, don't you?'

'I'm glad to hear it.'

'So why are you stalking me? Can't I have breakfast in peace?'

'Tyler wants you.'

'I'm freelance,' I said, scowling. 'Not an indentured slave. I don't have to jump every time that bastard clicks his fingers.'

Beck shrugged. 'It's in your interests.'

'Can't, anyway. My car's parked at the University. The space is ticking.'

'License number?'

'Huh?'

The man had lifted his bracer. He looked at me expectantly. 'I'll put an all day ticket on it. What's the licence number?'

I told him. Ungraciously.

13

'This belongs to me,' I said, collapsing the black holster and dropping it into my jacket pocket. For the past year its now-missing occupant had been the only back-up I ever had. 'And the belt's a keepsake. I want it back.'

Now free of the holster, my belt slithered, snake-like, as it abandoned the last loop of my jeans and hit the chair. The worn leather belt was Constabulary issue. Since they'd never asked for it back when they and I originally parted company, I'd kept it. Why not?

Tyler turned, glanced at the belt he'd told me to remove, then measured me from where he stood at a window. We were eight storeys up the art-deco office block - the one I'd visited last Sunday morning looking for Synapware's HQ. Wasn't sure if this was Tyler's office or Beck's but it was a corner one. Four windows - eight panes, counting up and down. All laminated with solar wafers.

'I don't have a problem with the holster.' Tyler jutted his chin at the belt. 'But that's police issue. Our security grid picked up their tag as you walked in. It's an old code, no longer registered. But if anyone's going to keep tabs on my people, it's going to be me.'

My eyes had gone back to the belt. I hadn't guessed. Had no clue my former employers kept such a close eye on their officers. Unless it was just me they'd been watching? Made me mad to think about it, whatever the case - their blithe disregard for basic human freedom. Made me doubly mad once it struck me they'd known for months what I'd been up to while I'd been undercover. They'd known the exact second I'd crossed the line. They'd done nothing. Let me dig myself deeper, let me pull in all the crooks they couldn't get any other way. They'd let me get hooked on the stuff I was trying to abolish then dangled me on the same hook and left me to rot.

Used me.

Bastards!

'That's bullshit,' I said, shaking my head. 'The Constabulary can't infringe human rights like that!'

'Anyway, I want the tag destroyed. Mr Beck?'

Beck rose to his feet and came round the desk. His shiny black fingers slid under his jacket at the hip, came out wrapped round the hilt of the kind of knife that can get you arrested for researching on the net. Before I could stop him, he'd picked up the belt, slit it almost through, smooth as you like, right by the buckle.

'Goddammit...!'

Beck bent the buckle back so it lay flat against the shiny side of the leather, turned it so I could see the silver capsule poking out between the layers. He wormed the tag out with the tip of his blade, dropped it on the floor. There was a squeal as he crushed it under his foot.

To my annoyance, the man then held the belt out to me, as if I might actually want it back again. I ignored it, lowered myself back into the chair.

I made sure I flexed my hand before reaching for the coffee mug they'd put in front of me two minutes earlier - just before Tyler started about the belt. The technique settled the tremors for a couple of seconds, hid the shakes. This much caffeine in one morning couldn't be good for me, but my throat was parched. I sipped quickly, put the cup down again.

Beck had returned to his seat. He glanced over the desk's privacy screen when I clunked the mug down too hard. The desk itself didn't seem to mind. Information windows continued marching under my cup and around the desk's edges - stock market figures, news reports, climate assessments. Enough to give anyone a headache. I winced, looked away.

'I'll order another Sandman,' Beck rumbled. 'Though you might want to consider carrying something a bit more...decisive.'

I shook my head. 'Don't have a license for a smoker.'

'You work for Synapware now.' That was Tyler, talking with his back to us while he continued staring out the window at the rain. 'We can get you a license.'

Bleep from Beck's hidden screen told me he'd called up a new page.

'I doubt you'll need anything punchier than a .38,' he said. 'You want target-assist?'

'I'll stick with the Sandman.'

He looked at me for a second, assessing. Shrugged.

Tyler finally turned away from the window. He crossed the room and snagged a spare chair from against the wall, straddled it backwards so he could lean his smart suit's sleeves on the backrest.

'They took back the Cerebral Anomaly Projector?'

Heck of a mouthful, that. Reminded me why I'd started calling it my magic cap. But Tyler said it so smooth you'd think he'd been practicing all day.

'It was theirs. In fairness, if I was the kind to hold a grudge, which I am, I could do someone I didn't like some serious damage with that thing. So maybe it's just as well.'

Beck paused to stare at me over his monitor. 'You're really gonna to miss all that?'

I opened my mouth to reply, but it was pointless. How could I explain to him, an ex-soldier - a hired thug - why I did what I did? Why it was important. Why I needed to be out there, sorting out the shit, finding those responsible and getting them off the street. Who else would do it, if not me? Who else was going to get in their way every single night? Who else would stop those fuckers from fucking people up like they did to me last night?

'You'll find working for us a lot more varied, Mr Nixon,' Tyler said. 'And a lot more involved. Part of my role as Chief Liaison Officer is ensuring any problems we might have with our products are sorted out before they come to public notice.' He nodded at Beck. 'Mr Beck will tell you, there have been a few interesting moments. A "smoker", as you call it, might not be such a bad idea.'

'I'll stick with the Sandman.'

'Then there's the matter of image.'

'Synapware's image is already fucked. Nothing I can do about that.'

I got one of his cool Nanox smiles for that.

'Your dress code, then. Have you considered wearing a suit?'

'Nope. What? You don't like my smart-casual ensemble?'

'You mean casual, don't you? And I use the term "casual" in a very loose sense.'

'You saying I'm scruffy?' I couldn't help grinning, delighted that he disapproved.

That annoyed him. He rubbed behind his ear, flashed a look towards the windows.

'Listen,' I said. 'I'm just a freelance schmuck. You don't own me and I won't let your organisation swallow me. You got a job for me, fine. I'll do it. I'll especially do this one because it's personal. Dietrich wants me dead, the feeling's mutual. But he's using hosts, innocent people. So there's no way I'm using lethal force, no matter what clothes I'm dressed in. Got that?'

'You actually made it to Detective Inspector?' Tyler said. 'With that attitude?'

'The attitude came later. Now, you said you had something to discuss. Can we do that so I can go?'

Tyler's eyes glittered weirdly as he looked me up and down. Something I couldn't read going on behind them. I stared at him harder - tried to figure out what he was thinking - but the look was already gone.

'Now you're free of other obligations, Mr Nixon, I'd like to offer you a more formal contract. Something with a bit more structure.'

'Not interested.'

'It's well paid.'

'Not interested.'

'You'd have access to state-of-the-art hardware, software. Augmentations, if you want them.'

'Not int... What kind of software?'

Beck snorted from his seat opposite. 'Better than anything the Constabulary let you use.'

I reached for the mug again, forgetting the tremors. Coffee splashed over the sides and I gripped harder.

'That, by the way,' Beck said, 'is the liquid tracker we gave you breaking down in your system. Causes a few sweats, dehydration. The electrolyte imbalance causes glitches to the central nervous system.'

This time the clunk as I put the cup down on the desk was deliberate. 'Thanks for the heads up.'

*

It had to be more than just a tracker they'd put in my drink yesterday. They had to have given me stupid juice, too. Only way to explain why I'd let them put a new and much thicker contract in front of me and let my fingers do the dance with Tyler's pen. Well, in fairness, I do have bills to pay. Running a car takes a lot of mullah and I can't earn mullah without a car.

In my defence, Tyler was a better salesman than I'd given him credit for. Solid paper has the psychological effect of seeming more serious than electronic, plus I liked the numbers it was telling me. Double-plus the pretty secretary, who came in to sign as witness on my employment contract, and who casually placed a brand new belt and a Sandman 790 on the desk in front of me before awarding me a warm and very inviting smile.

I would have blushed like a school kid, but there was a gun between us. *A 790* with its new, lightweight and slim-line shape. Bracer-assisted under-and-over cross-laser targeting. Extended range and delivery speed. .03 second rechamber action with double-ammo combo - tranqs or paralysis darts, take your pick. Didn't even know those babies were on general release yet. And, of course, by general I mean to people authorised to carry anything other than a can of mace.

The numbers, the paper and the beguiling secretary were a powerful combination, but the presence of a brand new top-of-the-range Sandman was a slap of cold water in my face.

Because I'm the kind of guy who never trusts a gift horse, however shiny its teeth.

'Okay, now be honest,' I said to Tyler, eyeing the weapon with its strange new curves and wondering how they'd feel in my palm. 'Are you coming on to me? Because you do seem to be trying, very hard, to get my attention.'

If it wasn't that, it seemed he should at least explain why this organisation - richer than most countries and with the power to mummify its employees even when they'd committed murder - would be interested in me. Because, for the life of me, I couldn't. I hadn't been outstanding, even when I was a detective. Why'd they want me?

To his credit, Tyler ignored the glib comment.

'I go on qualities, Mr Nixon. You're stupidly loyal. You're tenacious. You're willing to get your hands dirty to get results.'

I assumed he meant it as a compliment.

'I'll do what it takes,' I admitted. 'If it gets dangerous people off the streets, I'll do whatever it takes. But I've never used lethal force, I've never taken money to look the other way, I've never let an innocent person suffer because it served the interests of a "worthier" cause. If that's getting my hands dirty, then you might be right. But don't expect me to fuck someone over in favour of Synapware. If this company breaks the law, you can be sure you'll be hearing about it.'

'Yes.' Tyler waved an impatient hand. 'You're a crusader, I know that.'

'Yeah,' I told him, grinning. 'I slam-dunked Synapware's ass enough times.'

The man sighed. 'And as I've explained before, that's precisely why I want you on my team. Your attitude I can tolerate because it's Mr Beck you'll be working with. Try pissing him off, see where it gets you. Aside from administration, you won't be seeing much of me.'

'Administration? You mean like reprimanding me?' I had to grin at that, too. 'You might be seeing a lot more of me than you think.'

As it turned out there was a further sweetener - the clinching one. Beck removed the security screen so I could see what he'd been looking at behind its dull grey uniformity. Showed me the kind of software I'd have access to from the second I signed. As a goodwill gesture, he blipped the first one to my bracer in advance. It was called Sikum and it was the same programme he'd used to track me to the Clifton Bridge. It was exactly the kind of thing anti-stalking laws were made for and, as far as I could tell, highly illegal. But it meant I'd be able to find anyone I wanted to, whenever I wanted to. Whoever they were, wherever they were. And I liked that.

So I signed.

While the pen was in my hand, I'd had a vague idea how it was going to work. Synapware were going to pay me, give me access to all their cool kit. I, in turn, would do whatever the hell I liked. A Squirt Buster without a leash.

Seemed fair to me.

Then, with my signature safely blotted on the last page of the contract, countersigned by Tyler and witnessed by that very pretty secretary, they told me how it was really going to work.

See what I mean? Stupid juice.

14

Parked in my car an hour later, I couldn't resist giving Sikum a try. Put a search out for me. Hell, I was allowed to stalk *me*, wasn't I?

The programme offered several options. Would I like to find my car, my bracer or the chip Synapware had just installed on the inside of my bicep? I chose the 'all' option. Weirdly enough, they all came out at the same location. I put the bracer away, wound up the window of my Ford and got out. Grabbed the shopping off the passenger seat.

This time as I walked the two streets from my designated parking space to my apartment, I was alert for anyone walking up behind me. Another date with Brutants was not high on my agenda for today. I got home without incident. The shopping bag went on the kitchen slide-out and I started unpacking.

I was still asking myself what the hell I was doing signing a full employment contract when working for Synapware as a casual employee was already a step too far.

There were psychological issues there. Had to be. The Constabulary Psyche, when I'd still been on his case list, would probably have told me it was to do with abandonment, the need to belong. I like to think I'm not that needy, but the Constabulary throwing me out had reawakened anxieties I'd thought were long gone. Tyler's offer couldn't have come at a more appropriate moment.

Paperwork. *Dammit*! I forgot to ask. Now that really *was* stupid. Go through all that and end up stuck behind a desk? It brought the inevitable next question and it occurred to me that it might be harder to quit Synapware than it was to join. It was followed up by the notion that they might have a darker alternative to firing me if I fucked up.

I didn't really believe that. A spontaneous and facetious idea typical of yours truly. One born from mistrust of Synapware's vicious PR department - of which, I thought ironically, I am now a part. Then Beck's friendly warning came back to me and suddenly the idea seemed a lot more plausible.

'Working for *Synapware*? Jesus, Nix, what the hell are you playing at?'

Except this wasn't playing.

Tyler had flashed a little money, weapons and software at me and I'd bent over for him, just like he wanted. More than that, I realised, I hadn't read the second contract all the way through.

I'd read the first one. Had to stifle a yawn just thinking back to it. It was a safe, bland and undemanding document - enough to send anyone to sleep and more than enough to get someone's guard down. Had they got me to sign that one for just that reason? I was paranoid enough to think so. Because, thanks to that, I'd just skim-read the acres of legalese contained in the main contract.

Cursing, I lit up my bracer screen, hunted for the copy contract the secretary had blipped to it. All the while, Tyler's glib comment, back at the Island, about reading the small print played through my head. Instead of the contract, I stumbled on something paused in the cache. I went to shut the item down. Stopped.

Shit.

On my screen Gage stood at the top of the steps, frozen by the stalled footage. He was still half-turned, ready to say something to the last member of the team who'd brought Dietrich down and who'd worn her hair loose that day.

Then it struck me, clear as glass, and fear and anger came with it. None of the targets, none of the killings were random. Even Ray Sands, the security guard.

His 'crime' had been to flee for his life, leaving Dietrich stranded inside Samuels. That was plenty for a man like Dietrich to want him dead. So Dietrich had used Gage to track him down, lured him to Port Town, presumably on some bogus police matter, and killed him.

I'd always assumed Dietrich's jumping into Gage, right at the start, was a reflex. Samuels' body had been suffering nerve conflict - breaking down. Dietrich needed someone, anyone, to link to on a bracer and jump clear. The Scene of Crime Officer would be the main person he'd be permitted to speak to so Gage was Dietrich's most logical target.

I'd also assumed it had been Samuels, somehow fighting back, who'd called the cops. I'd been wrong. It was Dietrich. He'd called them on that stupid piece of junk Synapware made Samuels use, then he'd waited. For a bracer and for an opportunity. Both of which I provided.

Thanks to me, Dietrich had gained the means to start his vendetta. Starting with Gage.

Gage and I were Dietrich's arresting officers back when he'd murdered those schoolgirls. We'd been the ones to knock on his door, put the cuffs on him. Could've been me he picked next. Should have been. But he'd picked Harris.

Harris had been the one to question Dietrich after his arrest, worn him down, broken his alibi. Maybe Dietrich had intended to kill Harris like he'd killed John Gage, once he'd finished playing with him. Except I walked in and presented him with another option.

Dietrich was hunting us down. All of us. So far, luck had kept me alive. But he meant to get us all. Everyone involved in the case. Maybe others too. Maybe anyone who'd helped. But he was going for us, first. The ones who'd stopped him.

He'd tried for three of us so far. And the fourth? On my screen Gage was still at the top of the steps, turning to talk to...

'*Lian.*'

*

The bracer was already trying to connect by the time I remembered her number was now blocked. I called Central again, hoping I'd be diverted to the nearest police station, like any normal citizen would be, now that's all I was.

'Matthew Nixon, your licence has been revoked. You have no permission to use this number.'

Could be wrong , but to me the perfect, polite voice sounded a little long-suffering. Okay, so maybe it wasn't Central I'd been dialling all these months.

'Wait. Look, I just need to speak to someone. It's urgent.'

'If you wish to report an incident, you must use the Central Switchboard.'

'Fine! So can you put me through?'

Digital entities can't sigh. At least I don't think so. This one did a good job of emulating it. When it didn't cut me off straight away, I carried on.

'Clifton area. Lian Morrison.'

'Detective Inspector Lian Morrison is off-duty at present. Try again at eighteen hundred.'

'Well can you patch me through to her bracer? This is urgent.'

'I cannot transfer you to a personal data manager. That contravenes Section twelve-one-three of the Persistent Callers Act. If you wish to speak to Detective Inspector Morrison via your bracer, you must request the code from her personally.'

'I *have* her code, dickhead! You fuckers have blocked it!'

I was yelling at a dead connection.

But the call had put enough distance between me and panic for it to occur to me that I shouldn't be using my bracer to contact *anyone* who may have been compromised by Dietrich. Even Lian. Sitaroo's Rooinator couldn't block Dietrich jumping into me if I was the one who did the dialling.

Okay. Plan B. Lian would not like plan B. Plan B meant another six months before she'd speak to me again. But she had to know. God knows how I was ever going to convince her, but she had to know there was a psychopath out there dressed up like one of her friends and looking to snuff her out.

I was halfway to my car before I realised I wasn't even sure if she still lived at the same address.

*

Deep, bass bark when I knocked. Paws scratched on the inside of the door and a warning growl followed. My heart sank when a total stranger opened said door. The stranger pushed her knee out, blocked the golden retriever scrabbling on the slippery floor trying to get past her. I bent down, reached past the leg and ruffled the dog's ears. Got licked enthusiastically in reward. Last time I'd seen him, this savage brute was a puppy. Paws were big, even then.

'Hey, Frisco, how you doing, buddy?'

The dog wagged its tail. Recognition or because it liked its ears scratched, who knew? I looked up at the girl. 'Is Lian home? I need to speak to her.'

The girl looked me over as I straightened up, gave a dubious frown.

She had to be eighteen at most. She'd answered the door in a white skinny vest and baggy shorts. Seemed like she'd just woken up because her hair was stuck out at odd angles and she had sleep wrinkles down one side of her face.

'She went out,' she said, blinking in the dirty light. 'Few hours ago.'

Frisco wandered back inside the flat, having realised he'd got all the attention he was due.

'Did she say where?'

The girl gave an indignant sniff, a shrug. Didn't like being an answering service, obviously. She scratched her head and, just to prove modern shampoos really worked, her hair fell into more-or-less orderly curls around her shoulders.

'It's important,' I said, and tried a grin.

Her reaction reminded me that no matter how charming my behaviour, my present appearance put me in the perv pile.

'I'm just her flat-mate,' she said warily. 'She doesn't tell me where she's going. All I know is she went off with some guy this morning.'

'A guy? What guy? Can you describe him?'

The girl took a step back and I realised I'd advanced on her, invaded her personal space. I cranked my attitude down a notch.

'Sorry, look,' I held my hands up, palms out. 'I didn't mean to scare you, it's just... I think Lian might be in trouble. I need to find her.'

She looked me up and down again.

'You the police?'

In my favour, I didn't say yes. For at least quarter of a second.

'Let's see your ID.'

I sighed.

'Just describe this guy. Please?'

The girl's mouth popped open in outrage. 'You fucking lie to me, then expect me to help you? Get lost, loser!'

The door almost hit me when she slammed it in my face. Force of it made my ears ring. I thumped the wooden panel in frustration, then winced. She was probably calling the real cops by now. Trying to break in would not help my cause.

My car dashboard was dinging when I got back in. Screen told me I had only two minutes left of the ten I was allowed to park in this zone. I shut off the noise, tried to think.

There was a good chance this guy was just some sleaze-bag she'd hooked up with at a bar. Or a colleague she'd gotten friendly with. There was also a chance it was someone I hadn't thought of. Someone from the past who'd had a bearing on the Dietrich case and who was now host to Dietrich himself.

The dashboard started dinging again, while my head was still hearing 'she went off with some guy,' and all I could see in my mind was Jack Nelson, or some equally notorious player, slip his arm round her waist and lead her towards that sleek red number he drove round in.

Asshole!

That was directed at me. Come on, Nix, think!

It was already in my mind. Of course it was. Had been before I'd turned away from the slammed door. Two hours ago I'd been telling myself I'd never use it. Promised myself. The ethical and legal boundaries it crossed were a step beyond comfortable. Even for me. I liked to think I was above that. Above using Synapware sorcery, no matter what the circumstance.

So why had my fingers pulled it up on my bracer? Twice.

Because this was Lian.

I pulled a face, turned my wrist so the screen faced me. Sikum hovered there, still waiting for me to input what it needed. Hell, she never had to know. And if the AI hadn't been blocking all my contacts, I'd have got to her by now, given her a heads up, put my mind at rest.

If I used it and found her and everything was okay, so much the better. I'd just warn her. No harm done.

But if she was in danger... If Dietrich was inside this 'guy she went off with' and I didn't use Sikum. Then not finding her in time would make all my self-righteous morals a fucking joke.

I tapped in Lian's name. When the result came up, it offered just her bracer transponder as a search option. Fair enough. She wasn't bio-chipped like I now was and she didn't own a car. Sikum connected to the satellite a second later, but for some reason it had trouble sorting the image when it came through. Even when the noise finally cleared, I couldn't figure out what I was looking at. Had to ask for more data. Soon as I got it, I knew something was wrong. The gentle motion of the structures had caused the programme to struggle for resolution. Explained why the screen hadn't come up faster. It didn't, though, explain what Lian was doing out in the middle of Port Town when she should, by rights, be tucked up in bed ready for tonight's shift.

*

I drove out over the Avon Barrier - Bristol's biggest contribution to the world crisis. The biggest, but not the only. There were three barriers spanning the New Cut in total, all of them ugly as fuck. Had to learn about it from some lawyer who tried to tell me bodies rot quicker in air than in water.

The smug satisfaction on his face the second he'd guessed my ignorance was enough to make me itch to hit him. Of course, I checked afterwards. More to prove he was wrong than fill in the details. Turned out he was right. About the tide, at least. The New Cut - the seventeenth century river bypass - had once moved Bristol's notorious tide away from the ancient docks, allowing the floating harbours to be built and commerce to flow.

Things had changed since then. Big time. The commercial docks had been moved closer to the sea back in the 20th, and were abandoned altogether after the quake. These days Port Town floated inside the walled harbour, never sinking below the level of the old gates. Meant getting there involved a boat trip, so I cut towards Portbury, hoping to find a ferry waiting.

The Port Town ferry was a small, open-topped vessel with metal grating lined up in rows as seating. Last time I'd come out here I'd been on a police launch, sitting on a padded seat in a heated cabin, drinking coffee.

I missed my old friends.

The middle-aged woman sitting next to me sympathised about the rain, how wet I was getting. Offered to share her umbrella with me. I thanked her, but declined. But it went to show. First kind person I'd met in days. Port Towner. I really shouldn't judge people.

I turned out to be the only passenger who struggled getting off. Blame the conditions. Ferry was yawing and pitching one way - floating jetty was yawing and pitching the other. Plus my leather soles found it slippery. By the time I managed it, and with no shore-bound passengers waiting to get aboard, there was just me and the ferry master left.

I wrinkled my nose at the stench of rubbish festering near the undulating pier.

I'd been to Port Town before, but I'd always had someone from River Division to guide me. This time I was alone and lacking the luxury of time. All I had to follow was Sikum, which presented enough white blobs in the vicinity to saturate the screen. A single red icon nestled among it all, marked 'DI Morrison'. Most of the blobs were motionless - countless people sheltering from the rain inside the jumble of shifting ghost-shapes which were the boats, pontoons and barges of Port Town's superstructure. There was no nice, highlighted route like my bracer's nav page would offer. Not that navigation would work in Port Town. Place was way too ephemeral.

To my unaccustomed senses, Port Town was raw, primal chaos. Rafts and a mish-mash of dilapidated vessels, reclaimed timber and torn-up shoring - all lashed together with rubberised steel cables and sometimes just with rope. Each piece of wreckage was premium real-estate out here. They were homes. People lived in them. Some of the younger ones had been born in them. It was all they knew. Six square feet of squalor. Nice start in life.

Looking around me, I couldn't blame the harder ones for dissing assholes like me, who lived in comparative luxury. Chain of thought reminded me that maybe I should keep my new Sandman a bit handier.

'How does anyone get around out here?' I said.

The ferry master was coiling his mooring rope in loops over his arm, preparing to leave. He lifted an eyebrow when he saw me draw Mr Sandman II from its holster on my brand new belt, watched me slot a clip of tranqs into the casing.

'Use the walkways,' he said.

'Walkways?'

Still staring at the gun, he pointed a brown finger that said he didn't give a shit about UV and I saw what he was talking about. Narrow double rows of floorboards secured by rope between the vessels, lined up to form a winding path ahead of me. The boards were warped, maybe rotted - probably taken from Temple Quay during low tide, dried out and reused.

I nodded my thanks, checked Sikum for direction and headed off.

The rain was a pain in the ass, but it was doing me a favour. It kept people indoors. Including the ones likely to give me trouble. First walkway ran for ten yards, disappeared for two boat-widths then continued. I stepped over the lip of the first of those boats, expecting protests from the residents. But the door next to what had once been a stern remained closed, its occupants staying inside, out of the rain. The second boat had rubberised grip on the lip running round it.

I paused, looked down. Water slurped and sobbed beneath the two erstwhile cruisers, the eight-knot current sucking through, under Port Town's anchored structure. The basin was draining fast but the harbour lock would keep it afloat.

I checked Sikum again. Lian's icon was in the exact same spot I'd first seen it. Hadn't moved in the last hour. Meant she was stationary.

'What the hell are you thinking Lian? What are you doing out here?'

I wanted to believe she was here by choice but evidence was already to the contrary. Stationary for so long wasn't like her, especially not when she was somewhere like this. I no longer had any doubt who 'some guy she'd gone off with' was. Dietrich. In sheep's clothing. He'd got her. Got her out here, alone. Now she was motionless, tied up maybe. Tied up or...

No. This was too public. There were too many people around. Even with her gagged, there was just no space for him to do what he liked to do without it making *some* noise, alerting *someone*.

Then I realised and swore aloud. He'd given her to one of the Port Town gangs. It didn't fit his MO any more than giving me to the Brutants had but he'd done that so why wouldn't he now do this?

Maybe he'd paid them to record what they did to her? He liked recording 'his girls' as he'd called his young victims. Told me that during his confession. I'd seen the recordings, too, once we'd found them. As much as I could stomach of them. Dietrich liked to watch his victims die, over and over. *Sick fuck*!

For whatever reason, he was getting someone else to do this one for him and they'd record it. They'd be brutal too - she was a cop. Hell, I knew she was capable but, cop or not, she would be up against numbers. She had as much chance of resisting what they were going to do to her as I'd had of fighting off that upload.

The thought made me hurry, which was stupid. I found myself flat on my stomach, on muddy planking which had an ominously spongy feel. Two feet below my nose was the outgoing tide, sucking under the lashed-together keels so fast you'd be dead before you came up again. My left wrist complained - first I'd heard from it since the Memorial injected it. I guess slamming my whole weight down on that hinge-joint might have given even the bone-weld a nasty moment. Luckily, the only damage to my right arm was a bruised elbow. The Sandman was still in my grip. I wouldn't have to go fishing.

I lost track of how many wooden paths I followed, how many boats I scrambled over before reaching the one where Lian's transponder was flashing at me. I'd expected to see colours on the outside - Port Towner gangs were arrogant. They didn't hide. On the contrary. Everything they did was a challenge. They'd daub their 'clubhouse' with graffiti - arcane and contrived symbols, obscene words.

The boat I was looking at, though, was neatly-painted, green and yellow, had vegetables growing in pots beside a varnished and stubby wooden door.

I checked my bracer again, made sure this was the right place. Zoomed in on Sikum's ghostly 3-D map. Lian's icon was dead centre - *inside* the cabin I was looking at. I was right on top of her. At this resolution, there was nowhere else for her to be where I wouldn't be able to see her with my own eyes. But she wasn't alone. Four warm bodies in there along with her and for some reason her signature looked weak on the image. I didn't have to wonder too much about that - it just confirmed what I'd already surmised. She was in deep shit, maybe hurt. Maybe dying.

I put my good eye against the door, peered between the slats. They were set at the wrong angle. All I could see was it was gloomy in there. But then it was daytime - it was bound to be darker inside than out. I put my ear to the wood. The murmur I heard over the steady hiss of rain got my heart banging.

Shift off-centre, two-handed grip, left foot up. As the small door splintered under my shoe and flew backwards it suddenly struck me. Maybe Lian was out here on follow up? Taking a statement from someone?

Pity prudence never came to visit me in as timely a manner as impetuosity. Lian wouldn't thank me for this kind of an entrance. Especially not if she was trying to extract information from a reluctant witness.

A woman was screaming. Not Lian. Even so...

'Armed officer!' I yelled. Okay, not strictly true, but they didn't know that. 'Down on the floor!'

The hatch's remains swung slowly back towards me, dangling on their one surviving hinge. When no bullets flew out, I moved in, shoved the splinters aside and took the narrow steps down into the cabin, covering all the time with the Sandman.

Smell hit me first. Raw sewage, rotting waste, stale cooking overlaid by the more immediate stench of urine and ancient sweat. My eyes adjusted to the gloom, discovered a single area, crowded with stuff. Toys, books, piles of folded clothes and bedding. The paraphernalia of an entire family compressed into a single, small living space.

They hadn't taken my warning lightly, although the two year old kid was complaining, trying to get up while her mother tried to hold her down. I heard the woman try to soothe her, heard the terror in her voice.

I lowered the gun.

'Officer?' The voice was muffled, came from my left on the other side of a folded-out table loaded with more stuff. 'What's happened? What are we supposed to have done?'

I brought the Sandman up again.

'Show yourself,' I said, aiming in that direction.

They got up slow, a man and a boy about six. The kid was shaking. Normal reaction to having your door busted in by a nasty-looking bastard with a gun.

'Where is she?' I asked the man.

'W-what? Who?'

I reached across, grabbed the boy and pulled him towards me. He yelped. Fear mainly but maybe a little outrage. What I was doing to him now would help turn him into a Port Town thug of the future. Right now I didn't give a shit. I shoved my fist into the back of his shirt, shook him off-balance.

'Show me!' I said, dragging the kid back to his feet. 'Show me where she is, or you'll be cleaning his brains off the walls of this fucking pig sty!'

In the dim light I saw the man blink. Maybe he knew the topical differences between a tranq gun and a smoker. Maybe he knew everything I'd just said was utter bullshit, but even so, he shook his head.

'I don't... Who are you looking for?'

'Don't give me that shit! Seriously, don't fuck with me. I got a trace on my partner's bracer. It brought me here. Now you bring her out or this kid's fish food.'

I'd always been good at clichés. Sorry to say, they tend to work. The scareder the bunny, the higher they hop.

To be honest, I couldn't see where these people would have room to stash an entire cop-type woman in here without her being immediately obvious to anyone, but stranger things have happened. I wasn't taking chances.

'Dave!' That was the woman. Still face down on the littered floor, fearful, upset. Doubt she could even see me through the dark hair falling into her eyes.

'Ruth, just–'

'*Show* him!'

I couldn't see her face, but I could see the man's in the light coming from the broken hatch behind me. Indecision flickered across it.

I slid my arm round the kid's chest, lifted him off the ground.

'*Dad*!'

'You think I'm fooling around?' I growled.

The man held up one hand, took a hesitant step forward. The rims of his eyes were red.

'Look, please! Don't hurt him. He's just a boy.'

'No kidding. Fetch her out.'

'There's no one *here*! I swear to God! There's no one here but us.'

'Don't make me count.'

'Dave!'

'Ruth, it's...' The guy turned to look at his wife, lowered his voice. Like it made any difference. 'It's our *chance*. To get out of here.'

Ruth raised herself onto her knees, picked up the toddler and cradled her in her arms, weeping.

'We don't have your partner, officer,' she said. 'Just a bracer. Kevvy found it. Please don't shoot him.'

The idea must have turned her brain to mush. Her face crumpled and she dissolved into more weeping.

I stuck my face against the kid's ear. 'You found a bracer?'

Waited for the boy to nod.

'Where?'

The kid wriggled, but the gun almost pointed at his head was enough for even a brat like him to be wary.

'Near the muck barge,' he said, seeing I wasn't going to let him go. 'Someone chucked it from a taxi.'

'Did you see who?'

A head shake. 'Just wanted to see what it was.'

I let him down. 'Wanna fetch it for me?'

He just stood there. 'Dad?'

His dad dashed moisture from under his right eye.

'Do it, Kevvy,' he said shakily. 'It's okay. We'll wait for next time.'

Next time. Kevvy's father knew as well as I did how many chances people got to escape this place. The bracer, on the black market, could get them the deposit for a rented flat on the north side of Bristol. Could get them out of Port Town, give them their lives back. He knew it. I knew it. But Kevvy didn't. The kid squirmed his way across the squalor to what looked like a cot. A baby squalled when he reached under the blankets, disturbing its sleep. The kid brought out a slim black bracer. He waded back to me and handed it over.

'He didn't know it was wrong,' the mother piped up. 'He just–'

'What way was the taxi heading?' I asked Kevvy.

The boy shrugged. 'Old Town.'

15

The tide was on the turn when I stepped off the ferry and back onto dry land. The water couldn't decide, right at that moment, which direction it wanted to go. Not for long though. In a short while Port Town would start to lift, the hydro-turbines on the barriers would turn again and the silted-up floating harbours would sink beneath the surge. In six hours half of Bristol would vanish below water the colour of slate. In some parts of the city, the water level would rise over forty feet.

I turned the car's interior fan to hot, shivered until the blast of air warmed up. I was soaked to the skin but there was no time to head home for a change of clothes. I took my jacket off instead, turned it inside out to dry the lining and tried to think.

Dietrich had Lian and he was going to kill her. I was now positive. Less certain was how he intended to do it and how the hell I would find him before he did.

'*Old Town*,' Kevvy had said.

Old Town meant the oldest part of the city. The part ranging from Brunel Lock to Temple Quay. The part about to be flooded by the rising tide. That fitted. I knew Dietrich's Modus Operandi. How he liked to kill. He liked to put people in situations. Like he'd put Erin Smart feet-first in a vat of simmering brewer's mash, Gage up in the rafters, me on the magrail, Harris's wife and kids... And then he'd watch while they struggled. While they died.

He'd watched Jenny Saunders die. She was the one I remembered most because of what decomposition had done to her by the time she was found.

He'd put her in a smuggling vessel which had run aground trying to get upstream while the tide was on the ebb. Her crew had abandoned her as she keeled over, taking their contraband and scuttling her - leaving the ship half-sunk. Between then and when the reclamation crew took her apart, Dietrich had found his way aboard.

Jenny had been left untied but she'd been locked in a storage cage in the ship's hold while the tide poured in through the gash in its hull. Dietrich had watched from above while the water rose, using his bracer to record every second. Theory was he would masturbate to it later. That and the other footage we'd found once we'd won the right to access his bracer.

He never admitted to the masturbation, but something had made him record Jenny's screams, her pleading. Begging for her mom while she struggled to escape the cold, dark tomb filling up, swallowing her. Fourteen years old. A slow and terrifying way for a kid - for anyone - to die.

When the reclamation team boarded the hulk ready to dismantle it, she'd been dead for six weeks. Forensics think. With that kind of time span, it was difficult to prove or disprove Dietrich's involvement. That was how I'd gotten into the argument with the lawyer. To get Dietrich arrested, we had to prove he'd been around when the girl died and forensics could only give an approximate date. Reason being, half the time inside the hulk her body been submerged, half the time it had been exposed to the air. On that occasion we'd failed to get a narrow-enough window to show Dietrich could have been responsible and, as yet, Harris was still chipping away at the man's alibis.

Dietrich confessed to her murder in the end. He confessed to all of them. But that was later. Dietrich's smile when we'd had to release him that day had made me want to puke. Gage had to be restrained from putting his fist through the smug prick's face and I'd had to ask myself while I was doing it, why? Because we knew. All of us. We knew it was him and we knew he wouldn't stop. Lian had sat down on the steps outside, shaking with rage. Harris had just gone back indoors - back to his calls, his checking.

Dietrich liked to put people in situations. Deadly situations. And then watch. For a man who used the environment as his weapon, 'Old Town' was Dietrich's playground. And he had Lian.

*

'Mr Nixon, if you persist in using this number, you will be fined three hundred Euros for wasting police resources and your access will be permanently blocked.'

The police AI's voice was cool and polite, as ever.

I growled audibly, an expulsion of air which rattled my throat. 'Listen, this is an emergency. I really need–'

'Then please call our Emergency Service.'

'Are you–?'

The signal went dead.

'Are you fucking kidding me?' I said softer. Jesus! What the hell ever happened to police assistance?

Emergency Services were no more helpful.

'If you can't give the location of the emergency, sir,' an identical voice told me. 'Then I cannot despatch assistance.'

'I told you, Old Town.'

'"Old Town" covers two square kilometres of abandoned architecture. I require a more specific location.'

'This is one of your officers I'm talking about. Missing.'

'Since when?'

I had to close my eyes, already beginning to suspect how this was going to play out.

'Since around nine this morning.'

There was no pause while the AI considered. 'Five hours is not sufficient time for someone to be logged as missing.'

'Kidnapped then.'

'Kidnapped?'

'Yes, kidnapped!'

'Your proof of this?'

I groaned, toyed with the notion of flouting Synapware's restriction clauses and telling the goddamned machine everything. Then realised that, even if I did, the AI wouldn't believe me. For all I knew this was the same AI which had declared Dietrich dead a month ago. Even if it wasn't, it read the news. Digested it instead of breakfast. Yeah, Nix. Just try convincing it Dietrich was still out there, kidnapping people.

*

'You hate this, don't you?' Beck's lips on the screen quirked into a sardonic grin.

'Hate what?'

'Asking for help.'

From Synapware? Yeah. I really do.

'She's in trouble,' I said.

She might despise me, insult me, tear me down every chance she got, but it was Lian. We used to be friends. Partners. And more. Briefly. And the world in general would be a poorer place without her in it. Whether she hated me or not.

'You want me to get over there?' Beck asked.

'Over where? I don't even know where she is! The only reference Sikum had was her bracer and Dietrich ditched it two hours ago.'

'And he was headed for Old Town?'

'Yeah.'

I'd filled him in on that much. Not that there was much more to tell. But wiping down a damp Mr Sandman with the rag I used to dust inside my car, the leather on my new belt had creaked. Then I remembered why Tyler had replaced it. It was the only lead I could think of.

Beck was right, I hated asking. But I would.

'You got any software which might let me hook into the police tagging system?'

Beck let out a long, dramatic sigh, but he couldn't keep the brand new smirk off his face.

'That sounds illegal to me, Nixon. You sure your conscience will allow it?'

'Fuck you, Beck! Do you or don't you?'

'Just checking. Making sure you knew the score. I'll send you an update for Sikum. You'll need to enter six-hash-six followed by her police ID. Getting hold of that's up to you.'

No problem. I already had it. Along with most of her passwords. Truth be told, I'd once known Lian so well I could almost *be* Detective Inspector Morrison. Electronically, anyway.

The update was already installing when I finished the call. I entered her ID into the Sikum programme and it went straight to the 3D map.

Four hits. Wasn't expecting that.

Two of them I dismissed because they were both at Lian's home address and I'd already checked there. Flash ID and keys, probably. She wouldn't need the keys on her down time - they'd be the ones all cops get issued so they can use service vehicles, access restricted areas. Flash ID was for crime scenes, so she didn't have to check in and out, like I did, every time she went through a cordon. She wouldn't have carried that off-duty either, unless she was more anal than I remembered.

One of the other signals had to be her belt, because she was like me. She dressed the same whether she was on or off duty. For her sake, I hoped she was still attached to it. Or I was about to head off on a hunt with no quarry and she was about to die. As to the fourth signal... If she'd worn her belt, she'd probably have taken her weapon. Gets to be a habit. It had apparently been ditched because the last two items showed up separately in two very different parts of Old Town. No reason to ditch keys or ID, or a belt, but Dietrich would have ditched a weapon. Safer for him. Man preferred his victims helpless.

I had to find her fast, which meant I had to pick, and pick right. Trouble was, where each of the tags displayed her name, two live bodies showed up on Sikum's display. Two options, equally viable. Both claimed they were Lian, and both companions could be Dietrich.

I made my mind up when one of the red blobs moved - three metres north, two metres up from its first scanned location - Lian going upstairs with a second person in whatever building they were in. As the signal moved higher, Sikum filtered the surroundings and more signals materialised from the ether. More people in the vicinity - fainter, but close enough to the target for the software to include them in its render.

Close enough to a killer and his victim, though, to make the tag less promising. Dietrich wouldn't want an audience and other people had a tendency to stick their butt in at the wrong moment. He wouldn't want that, either. He'd want solitude. He'd want somewhere a girl could scream, maybe for hours, without being heard.

Turned my attention to the second tag. Zoomed in on it. But that didn't make sense either. Black Venice. Most of the old Harbourside was deserted these days, but Black Venice wasn't. So why would Dietrich pick there, rather than somewhere more isolated? Even so, the other signals showing up - local residents - were distant enough for it to look more promising.

The tag was stationary - hadn't moved once since I'd run the search. If it hadn't been for the two signatures right alongside, I'd have assumed it was the gun, discarded, and dismissed it as quickly as I'd dismissed the tags still sitting in Lian's apartment. But this one had a wearer and one other person, standing right next to them. Whichever item was giving off that stationary signal, it hadn't been discarded. It wasn't at the bottom of the river and it wasn't lying on a floating midden.

It had to be her. And Dietrich. I started the car.

Yesterday, I could have put in a call, begged a favour from an ex-colleague, got myself a police launch. Now I was reduced to going by taxi. I took the suspended road, headed into town as far as I could go before the street signs warned me the road ahead would be flooded at high tide. Parking spaces were premium, but I got one, paid for a standard term.

There were two taxis moored beside the lower jetty. At high tide, they would tie up closer to the car park. At the moment they were using the one nearer to the old wharf. I made my way down slick concrete steps, chose the taxi with the lights on inside, ducked under its solar canopy. There were two men in there, huddled around a projector which was running low on power.

'One of you guys want to take me out to Black Venice?'

From their faces I guessed they probably didn't. But a fare is a fare. The younger guy kept his eyes fixed on the game they'd been watching as he stood up. Then, with a resentful glance at me, he tapped his companion on the shoulder and hopped out the boat.

'Get back quick, yeah?'

He unhitched the front moor-rope, looped it up and tossed it onto the bow. The other man, owner of the taxi, pushed a button, starting the electric motor while his buddy set to work unhitching the stern.

'Black Venice is it?' the driver asked me.

'Yeah.' I stepped aboard, pulled the clear plastic sheet down behind me. 'How fast can you get me there?'

I got a sardonic look. 'Depends on traffic.'

I lifted the sheet again, regarded the rain-riddled expanse of water beyond. We'd be the only ones out there.

'I'm in a hurry,' I said, dropping the plastic. 'And you've got an incoming current. How fast?'

'If you cover the extra juice, twenty minutes.'

I swore. 'You're kidding me, right?'

'It costs me to charge this thing up. The faster I go the more juice I use.'

This weather, maybe he did have to pay. Sun wasn't working too hard on the canopy above us right now. But I hadn't been complaining about paying extra. Twenty minutes was a long time. Twenty minutes while the tide rose higher. Twenty minutes while Lian was at the mercy of a maniac. On top of that, once I got to Black Venice, I still had to find her.

I leaned my hand on the boat's dashboard, peered out the small windscreen. 'Are we hurrying yet?'

16

Black Venice was so-named because when the tide dropped, it left dark silt clinging to the sides of the buildings. Some of those buildings had once been warehouses fronting the ancient port. Storage space for the wool, spices, cotton and slaves Bristol had once been famous for handling. Those days had long gone and the warehouses had since become apartments. More recently the lowest of those apartments had been abandoned - casualties of the earthquake and the warmed-up climate. The higher-level ones were still occupied. Those fronting the river were even prestigious. Only adaptation to the new conditions were ladders and chained jetties which rose and fell with the tide, and the addition of new doors higher up.

I guided the taxi driver across what had once been Queen's Square, now kept artificially flooded to provide permanent river access. The signal showed her located straight ahead, on a street beyond the Georgian buildings gliding past to either side. At the junction I pointed out a house standing beside a long-drowned tree and told the driver to let me off there.

'Wait for me.' I blipped him the payment, plus a bit extra.

The driver shrugged, climbed onto his bow and secured his taxi to a rail. He then disappeared back inside his boat and I heard sounds of the match resume on the small projector.

I grasped the iron ladder leading up the building's front and followed it to a platform nailed above the tide line.

Looking at the set-up, I had to wonder how long the people here had used the sash-cord window to get in and out before they thought, '*fuck it*,' and installed a door. If you can call it that. The adapted entrance was as appropriate to its setting as a wart on a beauty queen's nose - nothing like the wharf-front adaptations I'd seen earlier. Truth is it wasn't even a door. A slab of composite an inch thick, black paint peeling and scratched, showing a luminous layer beneath. Looked to be cut from an illegal immigrant container, or at least something where they wanted illumination but no lights.

The slab was fixed to the wall by thick iron hinges and secured shut with a chain. It had no colours daubed over it, but so far this place reeked of ganglanders. I already knew Dietrich dealt with these sad sacks. Maybe they'd let him use their place. For cash, if not something juicier - like footage of what he was doing to Lian.

Ganglander place or not, according to Sikum there was just Dietrich and Lian in a room upstairs. Even so, I shrugged a dribble of rain from under my collar and pretended it wasn't a shudder.

It might be rudimentary, but the entrance was as secure as it was ever likely to get. I wasn't getting through there without a blowtorch or bolt-cutters, and since knocking would have a counter-effect to my intended outcome, I had to find another way in.

First level windows had bars on them. Not an option.

I lowered myself down the ladder again.

The window directly beneath the entrance was below the waterline. Dry for the moment, but at high tide it would be submerged. Most of the window's glass was still intact, opaque and green with algae. The ledge below the frame was slimy. I put one shoe on it, kept the other on the ladder and stooped, tried raising the window. The wood was spongy, so warped there was no way. Even if the sash cord hadn't long-since rotted to slime, there was no way that window was going to move.

I hooked an elbow through a ladder rung. Used the heel of my Sandman to tap out the glass on one of the window's panels. Didn't take much effort. So much for all the security a floor above. The glass fell into the abandoned room without smashing, plopped into a foot of water. The other panes came out the same way. Only one broke and that was cracked to begin with. A couple of good applications with my foot, the rotted window frame folded aside like soggy cardboard.

'Do you really expect me to sit here while you break into someone's house?' My driver obviously considered my activities at least as interesting as the game he was watching and had his head stuck out the side window of his cab.

'Check out that security up there,' I replied, shoving the Sandman away. 'Does that look like someone's front door to you?'

The guy shrugged and ducked back inside.

'If it makes you feel better, call the cops,' I called. 'Wouldn't mind the company.'

'Right.' His voice came back, muffled by the window. 'And get busted as an accomplice? No thanks.'

I'd been about to ask him to look after my shoes but he didn't seem the helpful sort. Besides, although most of the glass I'd knocked through hadn't broken when it came out, there was no guarantee it hadn't shattered beneath the water in the room beyond. Plus there was bound to be other garbage in there. Be fun, stepping on a nail in stockinged feet. Make my day.

'Lian,' I said, lifting one foot onto the sill and grasping the lintel above. 'You owe me a new pair of shoes.'

I lowered one foot into the sludge, felt a crack as my weight came down behind it. Broken glass - probably glass I'd just put there. I ducked through the window, dropped the rest of the way inside.

I hit the button for my bracer light, flashed it around the room. Place was empty. Not just of people, but furniture, fittings. Slime had crept up the walls, and barnacles clung to the dado rail.

Looked like the tide was already up a foot, though it was hard to tell. I sloshed my way towards the opening ahead. The door was missing - reclaimed, no doubt.

The bracer's light reflected the ripples my feet kicked up, shimmered them off the walls, giving the place a dozen ghosts. Sound waves got confused in the confines, echoed and re-echoed until I stopped and stood still. I waited for the ripples to slow, the echoes to fade.

Wouldn't do for Dietrich to hear me coming.

I shielded the bracer's light, checked Sikum. The reading I got came from directly above me. They were up there, Lian and Dietrich. If the signals had moved at all in the last half hour, it was by a matter of feet, closer to each other. So close together it was hard to tell if I was looking at two people or just one.

Realisation spiked through my mind, left me sickened. The people above had to be, literally, on top of one another. The thought ignited something ugly in my guts, set panic loose in my veins. I took a second, steadied myself. Dietrich had never turned to rape, so far as anyone knew. He'd gone straight to killing, to setting up his experiments so he could watch people die from a distance. Like some lab scientist. Didn't mean he couldn't evolve, though.

I passed several abandoned rooms on the drowned level, all missing their doors, all empty except one, which was littered with the floating wreckage of a dozen broken boxes, all new. I gave them a cursory check. The contents had long gone and all the boxes had Siberian stamps. Contraband. Place was being used for smuggling.

I found stairs going up at the end of the corridor. The last two were above the high tide line and, beyond them, I met a closed wooden door. Could have been problematic, except its lock had been forced. Someone, at some time, had obviously forgotten their key.

I twisted the handle, let the door swing open. Fresh air greeted me, reminded me how much the lower floor reeked. Had to wonder how people could live out here while their overpriced palaces rotted beneath them. Stench of decay was bound to drift up while they ate their gourmet dinners.

The air's freshness was relative, though - this particular building contained no hidden palace. I hadn't noticed from the ladder, but the upper floor windows were boarded from inside. My bracer light picked out tattered furniture, more broken boxes. Rotting food, used condoms, needles and other garbage were strewn throughout. If anyone lived here, they were animals. More likely, this place was a den. Forget the smuggling - that was likely a side-line - this was somewhere to bring girls, booze, drugs and squirts, do them all then leave.

Sikum led me up another set of stairs to the third floor. I moved slow, tried to keep the squelch my ruined shoes made to a minimum. There were doors on this level. Most of them were open. I shone my light into each room I passed. Habit. Not much chance I'd get jumped with Sikum watching my back. Made me appreciate why the military favoured this type of software - if there was anyone else around, it would let me know about it. According to the screen, the two people I was tracking were the only ones in the vicinity besides me - both in a room just ahead and to my right. No one else. Even the taxi driver was little more than a ghost on the far edge of the screen.

I reached round, snagged Mr Sandman from my hip. Laid my back against the wall with its rotting paper and abandoned picture hooks, and slid myself along. I reached the door - waited, listened. Took the time to quiet the pounding in my ears which drowned everything else out.

The door to this room was closed. Only one I'd come across so far which was. Light came from under it - a pinkish glow suggesting chemlight. The door had a knob, one of the twist ones they tend not to use now. It squeaked softly when I turned it, making me wince. The door moved free of its catch, fell open into the room.

I turned, filling the opening with my bulk - double grip, wide stance. But instead of announcing myself, my mouth fell open. A dozen thoughts went through my mind, starting with. '*Oh,crap*!' and ending with '*she's blonde*'. Pert cheeks, so involved in what they were doing they hadn't noticed my arrival, were bouncing - rippling - on the hips of a hairy-legged guy wearing nothing but gang-tattoos.

'Sorry to interrupt,' I said, making the girl squeal and leap off while the guy was mid-thrust.

He swore. Understandable. Rolled onto his stomach, reached for something under the bed.

'Don't!'

He must have registered what I was holding before he got there because he froze, hand outstretched. The girl wriggled into a corner and curled herself into a ball on the filthy carpet. The guy turned his head - long, greasy hair falling into his eyes.

'Yeah,' I told him. 'Good idea. Go for that.' I flicked a look at the girl. 'She old enough for you to be doing that to her?'

'It was her idea,' he growled, hand still hovering. He'd been at gunpoint before. Knew better than to move without my say-so.

'Still your fault if she's underage,' I told him.

'You gotta be shitting me.'

I shrugged.

'What you got under there?' I asked him.

'I bought it,' the guy said. 'It's legal.'

'Then you'll have a license.'

'Fuck you!'

I pulled a face. 'No thanks.'

I twitched the Sandman, gestured for him to get off the bed, move to the side of the room. He complied and without the girl's sense of modesty. I went to where he'd been reaching under the bed, found it a second later. Turned it so he could see the scan code etched onto the barrel. Doubt he could make it out in the dim light, but it wasn't like he didn't know it was there.

'You know this weapon belongs to a cop?' I asked him. 'Any idea how big the pile of shit is you're dipped in right now?'

'We just found it,' the girl said. She kept her face turned away from me, hiding a bruised eye under the fall of her hair. 'It was just lying there.'

'Right.'

'It's true!'

I made sure the safety was on, shoved Lian's gun into my jacket pocket.

'You want to leave?' I asked the girl. 'He'll have you working over in Redfield by the weekend. If you're not already. If you want to leave, say now.'

She shook her head, so I turned to go.

'You're not arresting us?' That was the guy. He'd got around to covering himself, maybe because the chill breezing up from downstairs had turned his manliness into an inch of its former self.

'Don't have time. By the way, how'd you get in here?'

When he looked at me stupidly, I asked again.

'The door was chained and padlocked from outside. How'd you get in here?'

The guy pointed up. 'Roof.'

*

Okay, so Lian's gun was back off the street. It was a result, but it was Lian I'd wanted to find. She was still in trouble and I'd just wasted forty minutes. Chasing false leads was a mug's game and I didn't have time for games of any kind.

I went up to the attic, found a skylight. I hoisted myself onto the roof and discovered a ladder which was hidden from the street. That was the other thing I was mad about. My shoes trashed when it could've been avoided.

The last signal left on Sikum lay further upriver, towards Temple Quay. Near to where they used to hold the slaves before shipping them off to the Americas, back in the seventeenth century.

Ironic how the world turns.

Different kind of slave passed through Bristol these days. Same route, opposite direction. The modern slaves weren't captives. At least they hadn't been when they set off. US citizens were willing to sell everything they had for a place on a smuggler vessel which would get them out of the States. Britain was the favoured destination - climate here was still pretty temperate. Of course, slipping under the radar had its risks. Most illegals knew that. But then, stuff like that only happens to other people, right? What choice did they have, anyway? America was suffering a fifty-year famine of the kind seen in Africa eighty years ago. Of those who made it to Europe, the strong ones - now without citizenship of any description - would end up working off some imaginary indenture their new owners had invented for them en route. Sweat shops, prostitution, or worse.

Old story, new resource.

But these days they didn't come through Temple Quay. Temple Quay was abandoned. Truly abandoned. It had none of the historical landmarks which made Black Venice or the Old Wharf desirable. The original earthquake and a flourish of minor tremors had made the buildings unstable - several had collapsed already. Aside from ganglanders and a few illegal parties - so-called powder orgies - people didn't go to Temple Quay any more.

Thirty years ago Bristol had let the river have it back.

Maybe it was why I'd opted to go for the other tag. While the delusion lasted, I'd managed to convince myself it was Lian's belt I was tracking in Black Venice. Until I'd found out different, I was sure it was the gun which had ended up in Temple Quay.

Picture had been clear in my mind. Couple of ganglander kids on their right of passage or some such shit, taking the weapon they'd bought so they could pop someone to prove they had the guts. Now I knew different. Besides, realistically, these hypothetical kids'd use a smoker not a tranq gun.

Realistically, too, there was nobody out on Temple Quay for them to pop in the first place. Which begged another question. What were all those readings? The ones surrounding Lian and the guy standing next to her. They were still there, those unidentified signals, still all-but breathing over my targets.

Wrong time of day for a powder-orgy - wrong time, wrong weather, wrong everything. So who were they, all these people out there where people just don't go? Guess I'd have to find out the old-fashioned way because the satellite had nothing else to show me.

That aside, bringing his victim out to Temple Quay was maybe a sign that Dietrich's host was fighting back. The guy had always been nuts, but this place was way too dangerous, even for him.

On the other hand, maybe he didn't care. What did it matter if he contracted malaria or cholera or liver worms? He could skip to another body whenever he liked. Temple Quay was a haven for such nasties - the tide carried all kinds of flotsam with it, not just debris, when it rose. But the dangers out here could be a lot more immediate and way less treatable - the buildings were rotten and hazardous and there was stuff in the water able to rip someone to shreds if the tide swept them over it.

As the taxi headed upriver, I was pleading with a God I didn't believe in that this wasn't another false lead because my confidence was already shot. If Dietrich had taken her belt, thrown it in the water, it might have been carried up here. Might be nothing but a scrap of leather I was chasing.

To either side the buildings showed evidence of their ulterior existence. Weed, clogged with silt and ensnared rubbish, was draped over the architecture like a khaki veil. The river's mud clung to walls, blackened broken glass, filled the pores of each abandoned dwelling. Filthy water dribbled from cracks, ran in runnels down banks which had grown up since the place was abandoned. Most of all, it stank. Of rot, of ruin. I almost shuddered. This wasn't habitation any longer. The sea had won it. Humans didn't belong here.

We rounded a long bend, one where the river widened, and the taxi headed for a rusting wharf off to the left. The driver didn't hitch up but left his engine turning, nudging the boat against the floats to keep it pushed against the jetty's planking.

'That's it, mate. As far as I go. I'm heading back.'

'You're leaving? You're kidding me!'

The guy pointed through his windscreen at pale ripples on the water ahead. 'D'you see that rubble under the surface? I'm not up for sinking myself out here, thanks all the same.'

'The tide'll be over the lock gates in a few minutes,' I pointed out. 'You'll have loads of clearance.'

'Yeah, and an eight-knot current to contend with. Sorry mate. It's just too dangerous.'

I glanced up at the empty buildings surrounding us.

'How the hell am I supposed to–'

'You can come with me if you want, but I'm turning back.'

Turn back? I shook my head. I'd fucking swim if I had to. Then again... Swimming would not be a clever move, not with the backed-up tide about to pour through this place. Another look outside the taxi's canopy showed me the jetty continued to a ladder which hit a balcony some way above.

'I'll stay,' I said.

Annoyed me, having to pay the driver for abandoning me. But at least he'd gotten me most of the way out here. He gave a half-assed salute then reversed out into the river and let the stern swing upstream. The bow drifted out and he put the boat in drive. I didn't wait for the whine of its engine to fade.

The ladder was iron and coated with slime and, judging by the amount of rust, it had been there since the area was abandoned. It ran up the side of a hotel - now just a shell of stained bricks. Old fashioned concrete leaked from the moorings when I stepped across the gap and put my weight on it.

The balcony was decorative. Low and long and not very practical. Ran past a row of windows that seemed to go on forever. The windows' glass was long gone - shattered or removed for recycling. A glimpse at the rooms inside showed debris, mould and ancient rubbish.

I tested the balcony with a stamp of my foot. Rotten mortar trickled from one of the moorings part-way along, suggesting the brick it was attached to was ready to tear loose. I glanced below, to where rain bounced off the incoming tide. Long way down and the landing would be wet.

I crossed anyway. It ended abruptly at a three foot jump down onto a flat expanse. It was above the silt, above high tide, but the cracked surface was awash with amber-stained puddles - looked to be an exposed concrete floor from a building whose upper levels were gone entirely. It was surrounded on three sides by more ruined buildings. A long-dead fire had burned away the section on my left, leaving a hole. Twisted steel mesh poked through the broken surface.

I looked about, frustrated, until I noticed a catwalk a dozen feet above me. It ran at an angle overhead, crossing the void to one of the other buildings. For a second I saw no way to reach it, then spotted the painted green arrow on the wall ahead, barely visible against the minerals secreted by the brickwork. The arrow pointed to a frameless window. Luminous paint. It was there to be seen at night.

A platform extended across the gap between the buildings. It was braced from beneath and fixed in place with steel bolts. I edged out, keeping my focus on the window ahead, not what was below me, until I was within reach. Leaned across the remaining gap and gave a huff of relief as my fingers met sanctuary.

I stooped and stuck my head inside the opening. The place stank. Of nothing in particular, it just stank. There was another arrow on the room's far side, highlighted by a patch of light coming from a doorway on the right. I hooked a leg over the sill and clambered inside, made a bee-line for the exit.

In the gloom I never saw the missing floor until I was already falling. Got a flash image - bare joists, rotted boards, broken plaster. I grabbed instinctively and my fingers found splintered flooring. I clung on desperately while my legs swung, shedding momentum, threatening to wrench my grip loose. A quick glance at what lay below. Water. Surging through the lower level and churning shards of wreckage into foam.

The board I hung from was already making splintering sounds, bowing under my weight. I hitched my legs to either side, got a better grip.

Using my legs for impulse, I hoisted myself upwards, grabbed for the joist a foot above and to my right. For a second the fingertips of my left hand were the only thing between me and the razor soup below, then my other elbow came up, hooked itself over the beam. I slammed my other arm around it, hugged the damned thing like it was my long-lost papa.

Splinters rained into my face.

'Nix,' I told myself, spitting grit. 'Next time the nice taxi man suggests you turn back, you say *yes*!'

But at least from this position, I could pull my legs up, wrap them around the beam. Done, I scrambled over so I was upright, straddling the narrow perch. Woodworm and rot had already staked their claim on the joist. There was a thump and the whole thing shifted under my weight. I shuffled quickly forwards, anxious to get off onto a more solid surface. The process of doing that got my heart banging again, but I managed it without further mishap. Clambered to my feet with a groan.

Now my eyes were adjusted, I could see someone had been through this room and hammered a haphazard path of corrugated steel across what was left of the floor. Now why hadn't I looked for that in the first place? Knew for sure I'd check for it next time.

The corrugated layers were new. Meant someone had been here recently. The painted arrows and the evidence of recent use flicked a switch in my head. This was bad news. *Nobody* came out here often enough to make such a job worthwhile. Except one type.

I'd just had to hit their turf, hadn't I? Guess I should've expected it, this being me. Small relief no ganglanders actually lived out here. This was a proving ground - one of those the authorities swore didn't exist. They used it for weapons practice, evasion training, testing their street runners. Could've ended up here myself, a couple of nights ago. Instead of Clifton.

I glanced warily through another frameless window, looking for signs of activity out there. Ganglanders didn't appreciate tourists, even the accidental kind.

Better keep an eye out.

From what I'd seen of this place so far, I already had a new respect for the fuckers. No wonder they were so badass if the subs, their soldiers, were sent out here on survival runs against themselves, each other and their own snipers.

Snipers.

I sighed. *Okay, Nix. Update on your last. Keep an eye out for little red dots.*

Whoever put the steel sheets down - probably someone with scars and glowing face-tattoos - should have given a heads up about the hole in the floor, too. I shook my head, complained under my breath about health and safety then followed the path towards the arrow. Found stairs going up.

Back in daylight again, I checked Sikum. Lian's signal was coming from two hundred metres ahead, still stationary. That was a plus. Hard enough to get through this place, I didn't want a chase on my hands. She was lower than me. Hell, I'd already guessed that. She was with Dietrich and the tide was coming in. She'd be near the water.

Two hundred metres didn't sound far but with the city now flooding and these conditions... At least the path looked to be linear. Hazardous for sure, but it could have been more like Port Town - junctions every five yards and each choice looking equally promising.

The walkway was the one I'd seen from below a few minutes earlier.

So much for progress. It was an aluminium grating - tough, rust-free. I had an issue with there being no handrail. Who the hell puts a path this high up but forgets the handrail?

Guess this is about where a Parkour squirt would come in handy.

But that wasn't a welcome thought, even joking. There was already the craving for an overlay nagging at the back of my brain. Bringing it into the light was dangerous, too distracting. On the other hand, if I'd had a street-runner's overlay in me, seeking just this kind of thrill, I'd have been across that gap in seconds. Hell, I'd have likely cart-wheeled over it. I might even have reached Lian by now. Instead, being clean and being me, I would have to do things in a more pedestrian style.

They say don't look down. In theory it's good advice. In practice... How are you supposed to not look down when your feet are the only things keeping you from stepping off the side of a two-foot-wide walkway? So I looked down. Maybe the advice should say, don't look down past your feet. Because the adage turned out to be true.

Took me a good half-minute to unfreeze and carry on and, even then, the urge to sink to my knees and crawl was battling my attempt to man-up. By the time I reached the sanctuary of the next ladder, I hated Temple Quay. Been here five minutes. Never coming back.

17

Didn't take long to get the hang of it. Whenever conditions allowed, the path came inside the buildings, when they didn't it took me outside, to the walkways. I'd just ducked through a frameless window after another hair-raising sky walk when Sikum bleeped, pulling me to a halt.

I brought my bracer up, checked the screen.

For a second I just stared at it. Two stationary signals standing together in a room ahead and off to my left. Neither markers were attached to Lian's tag. She and Dietrich were still two buildings away.

Could only mean trouble.

I reached behind my hip, found Mr Sandman.

There were no intact doors out here and precious few floorboards - all gone, no doubt, to bolster up the encrustation that was Port Town. No doors was a good thing in some ways. Meant I could stick my nose into any room I pleased without the risk involved in cracking the door open. Also meant I couldn't sneak past without being seen by anyone inside.

The room Sikum highlighted was like most of them out here. Floorboards and wiring were stripped and the ceiling from the level below was visible beneath the rotting joists. A group of ancient air-freight pallets were stacked in one corner. Overnight accommodation for transients and/or drug-users. They were also cover for whoever was in this room.

There were no arrows, no metal strips hammered in place to make a path. This room was off-route.

I'd already discovered stepping on the fibre-board between the joists was a bad move. I'd managed three steps in a similar room, before my entire leg went through. With that in mind, I straddled the gap between two of the joists, planted my feet on the beams and lifted the gun.

'Armed officer!' I announced. 'Show yourselves.'

The signals on Sikum didn't respond. Seemed whoever the app was picking up wanted to play this one right to the wire.

'I'm not here to hurt you, I just need directions.'

Plus I wanted to make sure I didn't end up with a slit throat if I turned my back with this unresolved.

Still no response.

I hopped to the next joist. There's a trick to it, keeping your aim steady while your balance teeters. I needed more work on that one.

'Come on,' I said. 'I know you're there. Come out, let me see you.'

A sharp hiss from unseen lips sent a thrill down my spine.

I rested my left hand on the damp wall to steady myself, kept the sandman aimed and hooked the foam pallets aside with my toe. That was enough to spook them.

The yowl was ear-splitting in the small room. One streak of orange fur dashed to the right - used missing plaster to climb the wall and vanish through a gap in the roof above me. The other, black and white, arched its skinny back, claws and teeth angled at me, all spikes and fur. The animal bristled, hissed again.

Cats.

Why had I just assumed every signature on Sikum would be a human being? True, there had to be a limit. A point at which the satellite couldn't register a creature's life signs. It wasn't picking up the seagulls, at least the ones wheeling through the air outside. But it had picked up these cats.

Wondered why I hadn't seen more of them already. They lived in colonies throughout Temple Quay. I'd read about it on the downloads. Complaints from animal welfare workers concerned because, aside from the animals dying in their hundreds of disease and starvation out here, the ganglanders used them for target practice.

Realisation made me groan. The cats were Dietrich's 'audience'. I'd have been here an hour ago if I hadn't been so convinced there were dozens of people surrounding this tag who, I noticed on the bracer's screen, had now dispersed.

*

He'd picked a factory building, twentieth century design. Place must've been cleared out back when the regular people first left. The owners had taken everything worthwhile, so the Port Towners hadn't bothered with it. Hence the doors, and the railings going up the metal stairs, were all still in-situ. I'd gotten a glimpse, as I eased the steel door open, of Lian seated on one of the bottom stairs, holding onto the rail. The level was partway flooded and, as well as rust, I was contending with resistance as water swirled through the widening doorway.

That gap was suddenly filled with his outline.

I recognised his face, but the punch he aimed at my jaw taxed my memory for a second. I dodged the fist, tried to shove my bulk through a gap too small, then found myself wrestling with the door as he tried to close it from his side.

He was up against the same resistance I'd met a second earlier.

Dietrich swore. The hysterical edge to his voice told me he would have to switch bodies soon. He was losing control. Its immune system, or whatever factor triggered the nerve conflict, was fighting him.

I regrouped, lunged forward. Hurled my shoulder against the door. Dietrich had already abandoned that particular battle. I fell through, sending a mini-tsunami surging across the room. The guy was tall and slim, wore a business suit which was wet to his waist - told me he'd fallen in the water or sat down in it because the tide so far was only up to my shins. He was still relatively clean. No moss-stains, no muck. Guess Dietrich had had better luck talking his taxi driver into bringing him upstream - he'd missed the unguided tour. But how much had the driver charged to bring a kidnapped woman along, too?

Dietrich was already pushing past Lian, hauling himself up the stairs, towards another steel door at the top.

Three darts twanged uselessly against metal and the door clanged shut behind him.

'Shit! You fucker!'

Appeared I needed to adjust the sights on the 790.

'Nix!' Lian had a bruise on her cheek and a cut lip.

I waded across to her. 'You okay?'

She was shuddering and her hair was down, tangled as if he'd used it as a handhold more than once.

She nodded. 'Never thought I'd be this glad to see you!'

'Thanks.'

'Tell me you brought keys.' That's when she lifted her hands.

I blinked at her wrists stupidly for a second. 'They're your cuffs.'

I didn't need to inspect them - it was a given. The guy I'd seen slip outside a second ago was no cop. But one part of my theory was right. He *had* worked on the Dietrich case. I'd come up with a name by now. Stephen Morgan, lawyer for the prosecution. He was working in the private sector these days. Helping immigrants fight deportation, naturalising asylum-seekers. A very different lawyer to the one who'd helped convict Dietrich, who'd convinced the jury he was guilty. Harris must have had Morgan's code on his bracer. Or maybe Dietrich had memorised it in prison. Didn't matter. A lawyer had no use for cuffs, so the ones on Lian's wrists - the ones looped round one of those tough steel rails - had to be hers.

'Where's *your* key?'

She gestured with her chin. 'He's got it.'

More reason to go after the guy. When I moved past her to do that, she yelped.

'What are you doing? Fuck it, Nix, get them off me! This water's rising, you know?'

I shook my head. 'We need your key.'

Because the one I'd kept from the old days I tended to keep in the glove box of my car. Only lately it was somewhere beside the magrail, jammed inside the twisted hunk of carbon-steel that used to be Harris's cuffs.

I headed up the stairs. The door at the top was fireproof., solid. Handle wouldn't move - jammed or locked. I tried harder, just to be sure.

'Dammit!'

'He was going to sit up there and watch me drown,' Lian said when I came down the stairs again.

'I know.'

Now wasn't the time to explain about Dietrich.

I switched off Sikum, put an ONA call through to Emergency Services, told the AI the situation.

'Thirty minutes?' I choked on disbelief. 'Listen, this tide rises six feet in one hour. In thirty minutes it'll be too late!'

'Thanks for pointing that out,' Lian muttered.

I gave her an apologetic look, while the AI blathered on.

'The section of river leading to your location is too hazardous for any of our launches.'

'Screw that, send a jet-ski. All we need is a fucking cuff key for God's sake.'

'Police vehicles are prohibited from entering Temple Quay. That's gangland. The use of a jet-ski in that location has a ninety-two percent chance of eliciting wide-scale reprisals. Assistance will have to come on foot.'

Same route as me. Shit!

'You've got to be kidding me! Does the term "Officer Needs Assistance" mean anything to you? *This* is one of your officers. In need of assistance. So get someone out here, *now*!'

'Help has already been dispatched.'

I spent two of the thirty minutes the AI had calculated arguing with the piece of junk, trying to convince it to send someone in by river, by air - *anything* - with no success. Not that I ever believed it would change its mind. The threat of ganglander reprisals was very real and it had to weigh up the prospect of endangering a dozen or more police, and possibly civilian, lives against saving one officer.

I eventually cut the call, disgusted.

'Thirty minutes?'

The water would have risen high enough to cover Lian's head a long time before assistance got here.

I grabbed the cuffs. The bottom rail they were looped round was already low enough to be part-way underwater. I hauled at the joint linking them together.

Lian shook her head. The step she sat on was two above the one her cuffs were linked to, her arms were at full stretch and the tide was already edging towards her hips.

'Asshole! That's printed carbon-steel.'

'Yeah, don't I know it?'

I flexed agonised fingers, shook my hands - sending sprays of water in both our faces.

For the second time since I'd got here, I wished I'd opted for the smoker instead of the Sandman. A genuine firearm could have shot out the lock on the door above me. It might even have let me shoot the hinge linking those cuffs together, blown it apart so Lian could get free. But I'd chosen the tranq gun, the soft option. Guess that says it about me.

The water was coming in through the seals around a fire-exit on the far side of the room. The hinges on those steel doors had long ago surrendered to the weight of water building up behind them twice a day, loosened themselves to ease the pressure. Let the water in - maybe a trickle at first, just to relieve the pressure. Time had done the rest.

Still had a few inches to go before the tide reached the smashed window beside the doors but from the look of this room, it would keep rising until the whole level was submerged. Algae stained the walls, slimed everything, even the ceiling. I spent a couple of minutes wading waist-deep in the pool of muck the tide was bringing in, hoping to find something I could use to tear out the railings. Even as I was doing it, I knew. Those bars were steel embedded in concrete. Nothing short of a circular saw or cutting equipment would shift them.

'Matt, I'm cold!'

I returned to Lian, put my arm around her, rubbed her shoulders. Not much help. I was getting cold myself. Summer or not, the water never got much above ten degrees. The tide was playing tricks with the light coming in from the window. It was already dingy in here, now it was growing dark.

My arm tingled. I lifted the bracer, tapped in the code I'd set for Rooinator and left it poised there, just in case. Then I checked the caller's ID. Decided I trusted it.

'Unless you can get out to me with a pair of handcuff keys in ten minutes, I don't want to talk to you.'

'No cuff keys,' Beck said. 'But I do have an assault kit.'

I sighed. 'This is no time for wanking off. I need–'

'I'm six minutes away.'

I frowned. 'Wait a sec. How can you be out here? Are you *following* me?' More than that, if he knew I was in trouble, he had to be monitoring my calls.

'My assault kit has a blow torch.'

I blinked, turned to look at Lian. She was already as high on the steps as the cuffs would allow. With the water creeping towards her waist, she wasn't interested in my conversation with an unknown caller. She looked up from staring at the water and her eyes were full of dread.

'Hold on,' I told her. 'Beck, the upper door's locked. I got in through the level below.'

'Understood.'

*

Bristol, so I'd heard, had the second-largest tidal range in the world. Thirteen metres. Forty-two feet. When the tide came in it rose by one foot every ten minutes. By the look of it, Lian didn't have ten minutes. She probably didn't have the six Beck had calculated. Assuming he wasn't bullshitting. Assuming he could find us, get through the water which was now more than two thirds up the door I'd come through and cut her free before the waves splashing in through the window drowned her.

He went for the upper door instead. I heard him slam the side of his fist into it, testing its strength, just as a wave hit Lian in the face. She gagged, spat water, then tilted her head again. Strained her neck, her shoulders, so her face was as high as she could get it.

As a cop, I'd learned how brave Lian Morrison was. I'd known her stand there with only her Sandman and a bunch of attitude and bully hard-core Port Towners into surrendering contraband. She'd once tackled a trained attack-dog with only her jacket and a can of hair lacquer. She'd walked up to a bunch of angry protesters and got them to back down with just a quiet word and a joke. Brave woman. The bravest I knew.

But who could blame her for panicking now? As another wave hit her in the face, sloshed over her head, instinct kicked in, made her fight, wrench against the cuffs, shove hard against the steps with her feet. The layer of slime took them, then her backside, out from under her and her head disappeared beneath the murk. I reached under, dragged her back up spluttering.

'Nix!' She coughed water into my face. 'Leave me. Go on, you can't help and I don't want you to watch me die.' She retched on a mouthful of soupy gunk.

'Not a chance. I'm not leaving.'

Reaching under her armpits, I took some of the strain, lifted her higher. But there was no more slack. I lowered her back down, brushed wet hair from her eyes instead.

'Go!' she gasped. 'If you don't get out now, you'll be trapped, too!'

I shook my head, nodded to the top of the steps. The metal below the door handle had an orange pin-point of light pricking through it. Drips of molten steel were dribbling down the inside.

'The cavalry's coming.'

'Well they're going to be too late!'

Lian coughed again. The tide was over her chin now. If she hadn't had it pointing upwards, her head thrown back, it would be over her mouth.

She wriggled hard on her seat. 'Christ, is this it? This can't be it!'

'Keep breathing, Lian.'

Dipped my face to hers. I held her head tighter when she struggled in protest, breathed gently, firmly into her mouth. It took her a moment to get the idea. Then she nodded.

'You're going to have to trust me.'

Little lines of doubt appeared between her eyebrows. I read what that said. It had been gone a while now. The trust I'd killed going behind her back, just to nail some bad guys. Now she needed it back and she wasn't sure she could find it.

It didn't matter any more whether she tilted her face or not. If she hadn't been straining to stay above it, the tide would be covering her mouth, trickling up her nose. Cold and exhaustion were making it hard enough for her to do that much. Another minute and even that wouldn't be enough.

I glared at the door above us. 'Fuck it, Beck! Hurry up!'

Lian blew bubbles, air trickling from her nostrils as the tide finally crept over her face and she had no choice but to accept it.

The room was dark now - the water half-way up the window opposite. Her face was little more than a grey blur picked out by my bracer, fading from sight as she sank onto the step she was resigned to dying on, no longer attempting to stay above the surface. I went under, fed her another lungful of air. Her fingers were like claws round my neck. I had to tear myself free so I could come up, get some oxygen for myself, another lungful for her.

When I came up the second time a hand closed over my shoulder. I squinted at the light spearing into my face - the beam from a torch fixed to Beck's chest. From the look of it, he'd left his nice suit back at the office. He reached for something in the pack he'd dropped two steps above me and the pattern on his sleeve shifted. Even under these circumstances, I couldn't help noticing.

Flageware. He was wearing the latest in a long line of military stealth suits.

'Door handle was missing.' Beck's voice was calm, unflustered. 'She still there?'

Feeling Lian tap urgently against my leg, I nodded, took a lungful of air and went under again.

When I came back up, Beck had set a spotlight up on the steps. Its beam fell on the murky surface, penetrating the water enough to reflect off Lian's pale face. Her hair shifted in the current, a dark cloud swirling round her head. She was staring towards the light, eyes wide, desperate.

Beck pulled a blue mask over the lower part of his face, tightened the rubber strapping round his buzz-cut. Twin gas cylinders protruded either side of the mouthpiece like iron tusks. Mini-lung. That would be his air supply.

'You got another of those in that bag?' I wanted to know, pointing at Lian.

Beck shook his head and lifted a long pistol-looking thing with holes punched through the barrel. He clicked something on the side and a blade of turquoise flame speared from the muzzle.

'Those cuffs are ceramalised steel,' I told him. It'll take ten minutes to cut through them.'

'Just keep breathing for her.'

I frowned. With his mouth full of rubber tubing, there was no way Beck could speak through his throat mike. The voice was his though, and it sounded weird - like it was coming through a drainpipe of gurgling water.

It had to be a voxer - a rare type of wet-ware which took words directly from someone's brain and digitised them. I'd heard of voxers, like everyone else. Had to wonder what esoteric military unit Beck had been with when he'd been on active duty, though, because voxers were still experimental. Made a mental note to ask him about it sometime, but right now I was filling my lungs with air and heading back under.

Lian flinched when she spotted the flame, wriggled as the spear of light approached, passed close by her face. Underwater, the burner gave off bubbles, suggesting the cutting tool had its own oxygen supply. The light brightened and the bubbles churned faster.

Beck ignored the cuffs, started on the rail post they were looped round.

The flame was still visible when I came up again. It flickered and stuttered under the surface, its wash of warm gasses disturbing the surface in a regular stream. Beside me, Lian was tugging harder on my arm. From the look of it she was struggling, wriggling down there. I took a breath.

Beneath the surface I found her kicking, fighting. Her body was bucking so hard I had trouble grabbing her, holding her still. By the time I got my mouth to hers, I was almost out of breath and she was rigid. I clamped my lips over hers, but the air gushed straight out again and back to the surface. I came up for more air, got to her quicker this time. Found her unresponsive, her body limp. I breathed into her anyway, but the same thing happened, her mouth just wouldn't let the air in.

Beck finished cutting through the base of the post, moved higher and started work on the upper section.

I came up, tugged his sleeve and found the flageware slippery, hard to grip.

'She's not breathing!' I yelled.

Beck didn't stop, kept cutting. But somehow he heard me.

'She panicked. Took in water,' the voice came directly through my earpiece again. 'Keep trying.'

Yeah. What else was I going do?

I only knew he'd cut her free when his stubbled head broke the surface. He stood up and strode from the water. Moved so quick, so efficiently, I gaped, shocked that he'd just abandoned her. Then I realised he hadn't. He had her in his arms - a wilted flower. Beck waded the three steps he needed to get her clear of the water, then laid her on the slime-covered steps. By the time I caught up, I'd spotted the waxy pallor, the staring, sightless eyes.

'No! Lian!'

Beck tore the mini-lung off his face. 'Get my kit.'

He rolled her over, got Lian to spit water, but there were no reflexes, no signs of life. He flopped her onto her back again then eased the heel of his clasped palms down on her chest, put his whole weight behind it. More water leaked from her mouth when he compressed her lungs, her heart.

His pack was coated with flageware, too, and hard to pick out in the gloom. I grabbed for a strap. Its photochromic-cells fooled my perception and I missed. Cursing, I grabbed again, tossed it to Beck.

He rummaged inside, found what looked to be an army med-tin. It opened out like a mini tool-kit, unfolding into a series of stacking trays. One tray was a Perspex slab, laser drilled with a network of cavities and conduits and glinting where hair-thin wire and circuits caught in the spotlight's beam. Beck unravelled a tube from the tray below it, sprayed sterigas over the needle at the end. Another squirt of sterigas on Lian's neck and the needle went into her carotid.

'Is that a pulse?' I wanted to know.

If it was a bio-mechanical pulse it was the most compact, and most complex, I'd ever seen.

Beck didn't answer. He was busy entering a sequence via the pin keys on a third tray. He unravelled more tubing, inserted a second needle into the back of Lian's hand. The cavities within the Perspex tray filled with blood and the device lit up, began throbbing softly.

'That'll keep her brain oxygenated till the paramedics get here,' Beck said.

18

The rain had stopped, the sky had turned blue and the sun had begun to blaze. Its light flared off the water below, shimmered on brickwork. Wisps of steam curled from rotten beams and broken walls.

With Beck's help, I manoeuvred Lian onto the roof, three levels above. The steel door at the top opened straight onto it - a flat affair covered with air-con units and ventilation outlets, all rusting in-situ. Lian was breathing on her own now - her heart beating again - but so far she'd shown no sign of waking up.

I propped her against a hollow aluminium cube which bowed as her weight settled against it. Her lips were blue. I shrugged out of my jacket, laid it over her, then examined the sparkle of lights inside the bio-mech pulse in her lap. It was working, but without training what it was telling me was anyone's guess.

The ambulance guys would know. One was already on its way. ETA twenty minutes.

Guess it said something. The paramedics would come, without hesitation, where the police would not. Then again, medics had immunity out here. Even ganglanders needed their expertise from time to time.

I fitted Lian's bracer back onto her wrist so the paramedics could find her. Kept looking over my shoulder, keeping my eye on Beck, while I did it.

He was already out there, hunting, and that left me torn. Part of me was hungry to follow him - I had no intention of losing Dietrich either - but Lian sure as hell wasn't okay.

Problem was, the man Beck was now tracking across the rooftops was as much a victim here as she was - it was the thing inside him we had to stop. But I wouldn't put Beck past using the smoker he was so fond of, rather than try to detain Morgan and get Dietrich out of him.

'Nix, she's fine. Come on!' The drainpipe voice in my head again.

'The paramedics are coming,' I told Lian. 'I'll be back as soon as I can.'

I followed Beck's route across the roof, climbed down a ladder bolted to the side of the crumbling factory. I dropped onto a lower level in time to see him clear a gap ahead that didn't look to be humanly possible.

'Fuck it!' I fumbled for my bracer, put a call through to him.

His real voice answered - slightly breathless and grunting with effort as he climbed over another obstacle.

'Look, the host's called Stephen Morgan - one-time lawyer for the city's prosecution service. Track him on Sikum. Chasing him like that's going to get you both killed.'

Don't know why I bothered, Beck wasn't listening.

'Dietrich has a head start,' he said. 'And we're running out of time. He'll need to find a new host, and soon, or he'll be too sick to do it.'

I skirted the hazards ahead, made a more modest leap across a different gap to a partially-collapsed building. Stairs to my left. I reached the top breathless, stumbled into daylight and caught sight of Beck hopping over a bullet-riddled heating conduit on top of the next building.

'Great,' I muttered. 'Back in ganglander territory and he's armed to the teeth and chasing a psycho.'

When I got to the impossible gap Beck had leapt, I was happy to see jumping wasn't the only option. A narrow, make-shift bridge joined the two buildings. I took it at a half-run, and this time without freezing.

Reached the next flat roof, rolled myself over the heating conduit I'd seen Beck vault. My jeans snagged on torn metal. On the far side there was more evidence of ganglander handiwork. Say this for them, those guys were serious about their combat training. Human-shaped targets were painted on this side of the silver conduit, now reduced to faint outlines due to the number of bullet holes.

'Holy shit!' I said. 'A fucking practice range?'

The next gap was a mere hop compared to the last one but it still put my heart somewhere in the back of my throat. I leapt, limbs paddling air, landed hard on grit and rolled. Wound up on my back, head spinning from the adrenaline rush.

'You okay?' The voice made me start. A real voice I could hear with my actual ears. 'Sure I can't call you an ambulance?'

I ignored the sarcasm, scrambled to my knees. Beck was two metres away, crouched behind an air-con unit.

I goose-walked over until I was tucked in beside him.

'You got him spotted?' I whispered. 'Where is he?'

Beck gestured with his chin.

'Next building over. Seems to be holding up there. Either he's cornered, or he's planning something. Whichever way, we need to move in there and fast.'

'Whoa, slow down. If we move in like an assault team he might do something stupid. And that's an innocent man he's walking around inside.'

'No one's totally innocent, Nix. As an ex-cop you should know that.'

'Yeah, maybe so. But Morgan isn't a criminal. He wasn't responsible for what Dietrich did to Lian.'

Beck shrugged. 'As long as we stop that rogue upload. *That's* our priority. Remember?'

'Yeah,' I said. 'I remember.'

He'd said it clear enough.

You're not a cop now, Nix. You're not even a consultant. Synapware own you. Remember?

*

A pair of orange butterflies danced around each other. Flickered past me like a tongue of flame. The room had lost most of its walls and was open to the sky. Sun slanted in through the missing ceiling, cast bars of shadow from jagged beams onto the weeds growing from the rubble underfoot.

I stayed in the shade, put my shoulder to the wall and slid along the brickwork, quiet as possible.

'Hold it!' Beck's ghost-voice in my head. He'd gone the other way and, wherever he was now, he had a visual on our target. 'He's heading your way.'

I froze, adjusted my grip on the Sandman, moistened my lips. A couple of metres away, on the far side of the wall I was hugging, a shoe crunched grit.

It was him. So close if bricks weren't between us I'd be able to tell his eye colour. I'd been expecting him to switch bodies before we could get to him, but now, even if he went ahead right this second, I was confident. I was so close I'd be able slip round the broken wall, pump him with a tranq before he got the chance to finish his scream.

Around fifteen seconds, or that's how it had seemed the two times I'd witnessed it. A fifteen-second scream at a volume which had near-shattered my eardrums and had burned out both Samuels' and Gage's throat mike and earpiece when they'd each done it. Fifteen seconds. Even if Dietrich made his call right now, I'd be able to stop him before he finished screaming.

'Shit!' Beck again.

I was about to ask, but then I don't have the wetware. Even whispering, at this range Dietrich would hear me ask what the hell Beck was spooked about.

'Move, Nix!'

Not the clearest instructions I ever received. So I made a choice. Could have dodged back the way I'd come, out of sight, but I chose to move in, towards the gap in the wall separating me and my quarry. Two-handed grip, twist to face the gap, feet planted evenly. Dietrich was waiting there. The space between the missing brickwork was occupied by Stephen Morgan's lean frame. I got a flash of manic eyes and a Déjà vu moment reminding me of golf clubs as a length of timber came in from the right.

I blocked the attack with my forearm but the shock travelled to my fingertips, numbing them, and the Sandman clattered to the floor by my feet.

My left hook lifted Dietrich off his feet, sent him two metres in the opposite direction. The weak flooring split as he landed, sending a cloud of splinters upwards as he came down on his back. I lunged after him. The length of timber flew from his hand, courtesy of my right foot. Dietrich tackled my legs, pulled me off balance. I hit the rotten boards next to him. Then we were grappling like a couple of kids in a schoolyard.

No problem, that's exactly where I'd come from. I'd wrestled enough school bullies to know just how to get the upper hand. Dietrich grunted as my fist split his lip. His knee hit me in the gut hard enough to make me loosen the grip I had on his hair. He tried rolling out from under me. Another fist to his face changed his mind, knocked his head sideways. I followed it with another. And another.

Damp grit and splinters flew into my eyes, into my mouth, up my nose. Dietrich chased it up with a punch of his own. I fell back, connected with naked brickwork, staggered clear as part of the wall tilted forward to crash around my feet. I retched, coughing on filth, and kicked out blindly. Luck more than judgement, my foot found something soft. Dietrich yelped and hit the floor again, hands tucked between his legs.

Spitting and rubbing grit from my eyes, I clambered over the rubble, prepared myself to launch at him again. Except the building shuddered, tipped me on my ass. Grit pattered down around me and the air turned hazy as dust filtered from above. Then a chunk of masonry landed two feet from where Dietrich lay, writhing in agony.

Something somewhere had given way.

Beneath me, timbers groaned and a heavy object fell, splashed into water. I swore, got to my feet.

'Dietrich, give it up, you asshole! This whole place is about to come down!'

His eyes stopped rolling, came to rest on me, and their expression changed. I knew that look. No room for negotiation.

The man got into a crouch, gathered himself ready to spring at me. Then he staggered sideways, off balance, as the floor slewed under him. The whole building rumbled, took a step sideways.

I grabbed an edge of broken wall for balance, held up a hand.

'Fuck's sake, don't move!'

He didn't listen.

Of course he didn't listen. He clambered to his feet instead.

Beneath us, the floor was shuddering. From somewhere below came the sound of timbers cracking, nails squealing as they tore loose. Bricks clattered from their rightful places. Within seconds the whole building was vibrating.

Dietrich swayed again, arms flailing. Finally realising the trouble he was in, he looked about, frantic. Then his eyes widened. A bigger, more jagged fissure had appeared in the floor where we'd been fighting. Our eyes locked for a split second, then the crack opened.

Dietrich had no time to leap clear. Just managed a yell as he disappeared into the implosion of splinters and debris draining into the room below.

He wasn't the only one in trouble. What was left of the wall I was clinging to disintegrated and a tide of loosened bricks tumbled towards the gaping hole, carrying me with it. I scrabbled over them, away from the event horizon, while slabs of broken plasterboard crashed from above, exploded around me into fist-sized chunks.

The section of floor beneath me couldn't take the trauma. Broke off in a chunk and dropped nine feet straight down. It slammed into the floor below, and fibreboard shattered on the jumble of torn beams and debris collecting there.

I picked myself up, thankful I'd had something to cushion me when I hit the twisted wreckage, then dived aside as a beam from somewhere above bounced down, quivering. A shitload of broken plasterboard and larger chunks of brick crashed around it. I staggered back, shielding my face. Shafts of daylight poked through the dust as more brickwork crumbled - the outside wall was coming down.

I caught sight of Dietrich through a cloud of powder and mould spores, lurching through a doorway ahead. Tried to gain my feet, but the building shook, knocked me sideways. I connected with crumbling wall, fought inertia as more tremors wrenched the building.

Staggering after Dietrich, my foot connected with something in the rubble that made a familiar clatter. I scanned the debris by my feet, saw it. It was coated in dust but my Sandman had otherwise survived the jumble of falling bricks. Didn't pause to weigh the odds of coming across it just like that, I reached down and grabbed it.

The floor on this level was taking its turn with the weight pouring onto it from above. It wasn't happy. It groaned, shivered under my feet.

'Time you weren't here, Nix.'

Past time, in fact. As I started forward again, the entire room, with its piled-up burden, sagged downwards. This time the outer wall was going with it, plus what was left of the room above. Plus what was left of the roof above that. It all broke apart, came crashing down.

I reeled towards the doorway Dietrich had disappeared through, hit collapsing floor with every stride.

I grabbed the doorpost, thinking earthquakes and sanctuary, but this was no earthquake. The corridor was already sagging, subsiding towards the ruin behind me. The doorway slewed sideways, its supporting brickwork already slithering into the churned up water ten feet below. Dust shook from above as the roof over the remaining building started coming down.

The corridor ahead was dark. Impossible to tell if it led anywhere close to escape, but I didn't like the alternative. I pushed off on collapsing footing and sprinted down the hall, while the floor tilted and sank beneath each step. Behind me the corridor was coming down on itself - sections of ceiling pancaking onto floor already sinking towards the ruin below.

I was running before I'd gotten fully to my feet. The corridor ended with a door on my left, stairs on my right. I skidded to a halt. Snap decision, I took the stairs. Get above the stuff coming down rather than stay in among it. Halfway up, the entire staircase tilted to the right and the wall beside it disintegrated. Fell away like sand, leaving open space and a long drop in its place. I grabbed the rail, clung grimly while momentum slammed me sideways, then hauled myself up stairs that were rapidly steepening as the corridor below collapsed into the growing morass that used to be a house.

By the time I reached the top, the staircase was dangling by its last step and my feet were paddling air. I hooked my elbows onto the floor above, threw my leg over the rail and wriggled to safety, just as the staircase dropped away to shatter on the debris below.

I picked myself up. The building was still coming down in chunks. Only a matter of seconds before the wall supporting this last corner followed the rest into the river. I could already feel things shifting somewhere under my feet.

Options.

A frameless window lay ahead. A surviving doorway to my right. Daylight streamed in through the door, fractured into beams by swirling dust. Beyond it, like behind and below me, was empty space. The window straight ahead was gone in its entirety - had been for decades. The lintel and a rectangular hole in the wall were all that survived. It looked out across an eight-foot gap to another window, three feet lower, in a separate building. The window in the new building was intact, its glass grimy and coated with crud.

The boards I stood on tilted and I teetered sideways. Sharp reminder that time was an issue. Flakes of brick broke loose as I climbed onto the window's naked ledge. I adjusted my footing, already judging the distance, then lifted my forearm to shield my face and leapt. The filthy glass parted, shattered around me as I landed.

I met smooth, solid surface, scraped over floor tiles and rubbish, then my feet slithered over a jagged edge into fresh air.

'Shit!'

I scrabbled for purchase, grabbed wildly at shapes only half-glimpsed, caught something long, smooth and cold. Pipe. Copper pipe from an ancient heating system. It bent, twisted under my weight, but it held, halted my plunge. I hung there, swaying slightly. Listened to the building next door finish its plummet into the river. It didn't take long. Didn't escape my attention, either, that seconds ago I'd been in among it.

I was on the third storey of the new building and the floor, like so many others in Temple Quay, was gone. Tattered paper from the broken ceiling dangled beside my face, limiting my view. Plus it was dingy in here. Christ only knew what was waiting below me. Could be the floor was intact. Could be this whole building was a shell with nothing holding it up but its outside walls. The lip above me was too far to reach without something to brace my feet against and, when I tried climbing the pipe, my dust-caked fingers didn't have enough grip.

I froze, seeing a red line flicker a little way above me. Knew instantly what I was seeing and panic bubbled in my gut. Licking gritty lips, I looked for it again. There! A red beam, thin as spider-silk. It picked out a swirl of dust motes, disappeared again.

Hell! Knew the bastards came out here for target practice. Been a little too busy to think about them since. Came back to mind quick enough, though.

Whoever they were, they'd obviously seen me come through the window. Probably didn't know I was hanging there like some sad sack while my fingers got tireder and number. A sitting duck, waiting to get picked off by a ganglander with a sniper rifle. So there were my choices. Drop into deadly water or wait for a bullet.

I adjusted my hands, convinced my fingers were slipping, and tried again to look down. Couldn't see shit. I weighed the odds of surviving a plunge thirty feet into parasite-infested water with who knew what beneath the surface and decided I wouldn't put money on it.

Footsteps. Movement above my head. Boots planted themselves in the dust. Foreshortened view of a guy standing over me. For a heart-stopping second I thought it was Dietrich. Then I realised his face and boots were practically all I could see of him. Stealth-ware.

'Fuck it! Get down, Beck! Snipers!'

Beck lifted a forearm that was only visible because he moved it, checked his bracer.

'No. There's just us.'

'You sure?'

Beck bent his knees and one of them cracked loudly in the quiet. He braced his false arm on the floor near my head and dropped over the edge. Landed on his feet.

'Stop fucking around, Nix.'

Embarrassed, I loosened my fingers, dropped the remaining two feet to the ground beside him and flexed stiff hands.

'You lost Dietrich,' he muttered.

I choked on disbelief.

'Did you see what happened? That whole building just came down. With me *in* it!'

'And Dietrich?'

'Christ knows.' I gestured in the direction of the demolished building. 'He could be among that lot for all I know.'

19

'This way.'

Beck rose from his haunches and headed for the only doorway in the room.

'I'm glad you're here,' I said. 'I'd've missed that completely.'

Leave it to Dietrich to escape a maelstrom. Hell, he'd survived execution - a collapsing building must have been child's play.

Now we knew who the host was, tracking him was a case of calling up Stephen Morgan's signal on our bracers. Wasn't as easy as it sounds. Sikum could show us where he was but not how he got there. Meant picking our way through the ruins and hoping we got to him before he jumped bodies. The really big surprise was that he hadn't done it already.

The hallway beyond the door ran off in both directions - one way led to a staircase going up, the other ended at a junction intersecting a new corridor.

'I'll take the stairs,' I said.

'Forget it. The stairs must be blocked off - he tried that way and backtracked.' Beck pointed to the junction on our right. 'He went down here.'

Okay. First the blindingly obvious, then the utterly obscure. Beck's tracking skills were pissing me off.

'You know that how, exactly?'

'Enhancements.'

I snorted. *Might have guessed.*

'So they've invented a psychic upgrade now? A little chip in your mind to let you read someone else's?'

Then I recalled a hair-thin beam flickering through dust above me, Beck appearing seconds later.

'Oh, wait! Wait a sec. That was it, wasn't it? There were no ganglanders, the targeting laser was you! You got a retinal implant!'

Beck was already heading down the corridor. 'My right eye's cybernetic,' he said over his shoulder.

I frowned at that.

Assuming he wasn't shitting me - and to be honest, he didn't seem the type - it meant he'd lost his eye entirely. Which, I guess, tied in with the facial scars. That or he'd had it removed just for the purpose, and I wasn't going down *that* mental road. The replacement was good. I'd met Beck's thousand-yard stare more than once. Stared straight into it. If either eye was cybernetic, I should have noticed. High-end job, then. The match was as perfect as it could be. Both eyes moved together, were identical in colour and iris size. Hell, even the pupils dilated in-sync. Had to be connected directly to his optic nerve.

I didn't doubt he could do a lot more with it than see. Targeting laser might even come as standard.

'We need to keep moving,' Beck said, noticing I'd stopped. 'Or his footprints'll cool down too much to track.'

*

The adjacent building - once a shop, judging by the sign poking from the water - was a burned-out shell. Charred brickwork and fire-eaten spars made a series of random hazards jutting from below, creating a lethal gap twenty metres across. The rest of the crumbled remains turned the tide to foam as it sluiced over and between the submerged obstacles. An aluminium bridge spanned the void ahead and, on the far side, Stephen Morgan - Dietrich - was in plain view, down on his knees, grasping a random length of steel and unhurriedly prising up the bolts securing his end.

Too far for a tranq dart to reach. Maybe that was why he was playing it so cool - confident I wouldn't use anything lethal on him. But I wasn't about to let the fucker go. Not after everything he'd done, not when I had him this close.

I stepped onto the walkway, determined to get across there before he could loosen the rest of the bolts. The whole thing dropped two inches. Metal shrieked. I was jerked back by my tee onto solid footing, just as the entire walkway tilted to one side.

'Idiot!' Beck elbowed me back.

The long stretch of grille gave way, its rigid structure juddering as it slid down the far side of the gap, anchor-points gouging furrows in the loose brickwork. Several bricks were plucked free, joined the bridge's far end as it crashed into the water. The section nearest my feet, still attached to the roof, shuddered and twisted under the strain. Two of the six-inch bolts shivered loose, popped free of the concrete.

On the far building, Dietrich rose to his feet, brushed ineffectually at the dirt on his knees then turned and gave a mock salute.

He yelled across the gap and his voice was strained, cracked with hysteria.

'Follow me *now*, Squirt Man!'

'Bastard!'

Beck reached across his stomach. The compartment he clicked open was moulded into the stealth suit, so well-'flaged I hadn't even noticed it. I glimpsed the drilled steel barrel and my eyes widened. I had no idea what make, model, or even calibre the machine-pistol was that Beck slid loose, but I had no doubt whatsoever that the monster in his hand was lethal.

In the time it took me to absorb that much, drag my disbelief into a corner and whip it into submission, Beck had lifted it. A red targeting beam glimmered across the gap as he narrowed his eyes, squinting at Dietrich. His prosthetic arm responded smoothly - eye and hand in perfect sync as the machinery the man used lined up with what he saw.

I yelled, jabbed the heel of my hand into his forearm. Beck's arm remained rigid, solid and unyielding, but Newtonian physics were enough to shove the man himself off balance, and me backwards. A stutter of noise, and brick chips puffed from the wall behind Dietrich.

'Fuck it, Nixon!'

'What the hell are you doing?'

Given what I'd recently found out I had no doubt Beck's aim was flawless and for a second I was worried I'd been too slow. I waited for Morgan's body to crumple, for gravity to get the better of muscles no longer under control. For him to pitch off the drop between us. As it turned out, Dietrich was merely frozen on the far side of the gap - shocked, possibly, by the bullets passing by close enough for him to feel their wind. When the fugitive finally reacted, clearly unharmed, my disbelief bubbled into outrage. I rounded on Beck.

'Are you fucking *insane*? What did I say about no shooting?'

Beck's eyes narrowed but he lowered his pistol. 'You said no killing people. I didn't kill anyone.'

'Yeah, thanks to me.'

'Not necessarily.' The man holstered his weapon. 'I was aiming for his bracer. Take that out, it doesn't matter how far or fast he runs, Dietrich can't switch bodies.'

Yeah. Okay. Good point.

'And if you'd missed?'

'I did. Thanks for that.'

'I mean what if you'd hit *him*? That's an inno–'

'I wouldn't have.' Beck shouldered past me. 'Now we have to find another way over there, and fast.'

Because, big surprise. Dietrich was gone.

*

Never, ever ask me about zip lines. Okay, never ask me again. I despise them. Even in training, when we'd had to practice on them because, in theory, we might one day, under highly unusual circumstances, need to use one. Even then, I hated zip lines.

'You're shitting me.'

Beck didn't take his eyes off his target. Compressed air spat and the sound of chain-fibre rope snaking from its drum buzzed loudly in the stillness. Only when the projectile hit the wall, sunk its teeth deep into a concrete lintel beyond the gap, did Beck lower his sights.

'You're supposed to be the expert,' he said. 'I'm just backing you up. But you can stay here if you want.'

Right. And let him put a bullet through an innocent lawyer's head rather than try to capture him alive? I grabbed the handle he'd just fixed to the rope.

'Make sure you put your feet through the hole before you let go.'

I glared. 'Thanks. I'll try to remember.'

Don't know what kind of kit he was using, but the friction on the damned rope was next to nothing. And the zip ran silent. The wall came up faster than I was expecting and I only just got my feet up in time. I hooked my scratched and dusty shoes over the sill and through the glassless window.

By the time I was on my feet, crunching through grit and debris, Beck had joined me, backpack and all.

'You go up,' he said, heading down the dingy corridor ahead and pointing back at the staircase at the opposite end. 'If we're lucky we can flank him again.'

The stairs ended at a shed-like structure, whose interior was speckled with soot-coloured mould. The small space had once been secure but now its steel door was twisted and broken, held in place by one hinge. The hinge was twisted, too, leaving the door listing to the right. Through the gap, I glimpsed a flat roof littered with ancient antenna, smashed solar panels, and rusting air con units. I heaved the door wider, leaving a gouge in the concrete, and squeezed through. Sunlight flared off puddles, making me squint.

The building must have been an old radio or TV station. The antennas were larger than usual, and there was one old-type satellite dish - more massive than any I'd ever seen before. It had broken from its support and lay on its back, brown with ancient filth. I skirted round it. Darted back again, heart banging, and ducked under the dish's convex side.

'*Stupid*!' I hissed to myself.

Should have been keeping my eye on Sikum - I'd have known he was there, a few yards ahead, pacing through the forest of antennas. I risked a peep over the lip. Dietrich was still there. Didn't take a genius to work out why.

The deterioration to his system was all but crippling him. He was muttering to himself, his fingers agitated, as if they possessed a life of their own. He hit the screen on his bracer, flexed twitching fingers, as I'd seen so many persona addicts on come-down do, then tried again.

I drew the Sandman, held it two-handed and low as I crept round the dish. Movement behind Dietrich made me freeze, hug cover again. Then a blond, close-shaved head appeared over the side of the building. Beck hooked his elbow onto the roof, then his foot appeared. Slow, controlled, he rolled himself onto the bubbled tar surface, came smoothly into a crouch. Hadn't expected Beck to make his entrance quite like that but, as he'd predicted, we'd flanked our target again.

I stepped out from cover.

'Dietrich!'

The man whirled round, hunting the source of my voice. When he spotted me he grinned. There wasn't much in the expression a person could call sane.

'You tenacious little bastard.' He gave a high-pitched laugh. 'So you figured out who you're dealing with, then? Proud of me, Squirt Man? Am I living up to expectations?'

'Give it up, Dietrich.' That was Beck and his voice made the fugitive spin the other way. Dietrich backed up a pace, away from both of us and towards the edge of the building.

'Come on,' I said. 'Do like the man says. There's nowhere else to go.'

Dietrich glanced behind him, to where the edge of the building lay, ten metres away. Beneath his suited sleeve, Morgan's bracer gave a distinctive bleep. *Call accepted.* The killer grinned again.

'That's what you think.'

He turned and, as the call was picked up the other end, the scream I'd been dreading shattered the quiet.

'No!' I was already moving. So was Beck.

So was Dietrich.

Still bellowing his unholy shriek, Dietrich sprinted for the lip of the roof. I increased speed, aware Beck was sprinting, too, and also aware the madman we were chasing had no intention of stopping when he ran out of building. Beck and I converged simultaneously, a metre from the edge. Dietrich had already leapt into empty space. My hand reached out, grasped for the killer's jacket. Beck threw himself forward, his fingers groping for the man's heel as it lifted off and sprang from the roof's surface.

Neither of us connected and Dietrich, still screaming, arced out over the still-rising river, beyond our grasp.

'*No!*'

'Fuck it!'

The scream ended before Morgan's body hit the water. The impact threw him deep beneath the surface. With Dietrich most probably gone and his brain crippled with inflammation, Stephen Morgan was most likely already unconscious. And he had no air left in his lungs. If he reached the surface alive, he still had an eight-knot current, submerged rubble, twisted metal and other debris to contend with down there.

I caught a sight of something dark, a jacket - a brief glimpse as the man rolled over under the slate-coloured surface.

'You go back to the girl. Wait for the medics,' Beck said. 'I'll get the bracer.'

'And Morgan,' I said pointedly. His body, anyway.

Beck shrugged. 'Morgan's attached to the bracer. Amounts to the same thing.'

20

'You're cited as next of kin.'

A female doctor in antiseptic whites was sitting there, watching me, when I opened my eyes. I sat forward, blinking. Used a forefinger to rub grit from the corner of my eye. I hadn't meant to fall asleep, but the waiting room chair was comfortable. Time and inactivity had done the rest.

What she'd said finally permeated through to my brain and I frowned. *Now why the hell would Lian do that?* There had to be *someone* other than me to burden with that? Two years ago, I would have understood it. We'd been close back then. No way she'd consider me worthy enough these days. Could only be because she'd forgotten to update her medical files.

The doctor was flicking through screens on her bracer.

'Do you know of any blood relatives we should contact? Parents? Siblings?'

I rubbed my face. 'Lian's parents are gone. She has a sister but she moved away. Last I heard she was working somewhere out in Siberia.'

'Name?'

'Uh...' My mind was still fuzzy from the nap. 'Jessica. She married a couple of years ago. Can't remember the new surname.'

'Well, if you do remember... In the meantime, we'll see what we can find from Lian's records.'

'So, what's the prognosis?'

So far the only news I'd had was that it was bad. I glanced at my own bracer, checked the time. Four hours. Four hours later they get round to telling me what the bad news even was.

The doctor sat up straighter. Held my gaze for a second, considering.

So it was *that* bad. I knew as much as she did about delivering bad news to friends and relatives. If she had to ask herself how I'd take it, then it had to be a lot worse than I'd imagined.

She clasped her hands together, laid them on her lap.

'Not very hopeful, I'm afraid. Archer's is a new strain. The symptoms show up late, so there's usually less time to tackle it before it becomes untreatable. That's a plus on her side - we've caught it early. Taking in river water today, though. It's put strain she really didn't need onto her respiratory system.' She looked at me in concern. 'Can I get you something to drink?'

Whatever she'd seen on my face, it was nothing to what was going on behind it. Despair and panic had slithered in without warning. They gripped my guts so hard I wasn't sure if I'd lose the breakfast I'd eaten an hour ago, and if so, from which direction.

I cleared my throat but my voice still came out cracked. 'It's TB?'

For the second time in my life, a woman I cared about - God knows why, but I *did* still care about her - was dying from the disease.

The doctor blinked. 'I'm sorry. I thought you'd been told. She's very ill, Mr Nixon.'

'Yeah.' I looked away. 'I know.'

TB kills people. I *know*. I already knew more than I ever wanted to about it. And word was, Archer's was even more aggressive than the strain which had killed Mom.

'Her more immediate problem is what we found in her lungs along with the disease - silt, a whole phalanx of bacteria and several varieties of nematode larvae. She's on antibiotics to kill the Staph and Ebola and we've treated her for the lung and heart worms before they can take hold. The silt is another issue. We might never be able to remove all of it. The river sediment is like talcum powder. It's settled inside her alveoli and a lung-flush hasn't shifted it. In the long term, even without the Tuberculosis... She's not likely to have much quality of life. That's assuming she even pulls through.'

So she was screwed. Dietrich had killed her. Despite everything I'd gone through to stop him. And this would be an even slower death than the one he'd planned for her.

'Mr Nixon?'

I glanced up. Blinked to see the doctor had risen to her feet. Her hand was on the door-handle, ready to leave.

'Sorry, doc. I was just–'

'I wouldn't normally trouble you at a time like this, but your colleague's been waiting downstairs for the last hour. He's been very persistent.'

Yeah. I'd been trying to forget. Been a long time since I'd had colleagues and I wasn't in a hurry to classify him as that, anyway. *Pain in the ass* had a better ring. It took fifteen minutes to walk down two corridors and two flights of stairs. Yeah, it wasn't that far, but my feet weren't in the mood to hurry.

'You're still not my type,' I told Beck when I finally spotted him. 'And right now, whatever you have to say, I don't want to hear.'

Beck was in his suit. The stealth-ninja was back in its box. By the look of it, he hadn't shaved since the last time I'd seen him. When he turned away from the darkened view out the window his stubble glinted in the hospital's artificial light. Reminded me I'd spent a total of six hours here, while they treated Lian and I waited for news.

'You sure?' Beck lifted the thick black wedge he held between his fingers. 'Because I got it.'

Yeah. Okay. Maybe I did want to know.

'And Morgan?'

Beck shook his head.

'Tell me you brought his body back.'

'How do you suppose I was meant to do that?'

I gave an exasperated snort. 'You could have tried.'

'I never said I didn't try. But that tide's a bastard.'

English use of the word. Guess we all adapt, eventually. I pushed fingers through my hair, felt the stitches on my scalp snag and for a moment wondered how much more of this I could take. It lasted long enough for me to hear my own inner voice whimper pathetically, begging for an upload, then I pulled it together again.

'Managed to hack in?' I nodded at the bracer.

'Yeah. I hear you got some sleep while I was doing that. So now you're nice and rested, we're heading over there right now.'

To Dietrich's next host. This time, maybe, we'd get there before he managed to hurt someone.

'So where'd he go? Whose body is he wearing this time?'

*

The stilts were at our backs - concrete tree-trunks on the fringes of an evil forest. Hobgoblins and ogres lurked within. Monsters and self-styled mutants of the cut-your-face-off variety. I tried to ignore the itch on the back of my scalp, focused on why we'd come out here.

I hadn't recognised the name Beck had come up with, and the details were on his device, not mine, so I couldn't cross-reference. Plus, for some reason, Sikum was having trouble locating the new host's bracer signal. So we headed to the man's last known address instead. Meant I didn't know we'd arrived until we were standing by the steps leading down to his front door. Finding myself here confused the hell out of me and I glanced at Beck, frowning.

'You're sure this is the place?'

Beck shrugged. 'That's what it says.'

I turned back to the steps, the warped door with its flaking paint at the bottom. In all the time I'd known him, he'd always called himself Sitaroo Man. I never bothered looking up his real name.

'Why would Dietrich be interested in him?' I wondered aloud.

'More to the point, what's his code doing on a lawyer's bracer?'

I shrugged. 'Sitaroo's not exactly legal. He'd need a lawyer on call, just in case.'

But that didn't fit. Morgan had dropped criminal law years ago. He'd had enough of that game. More sense than me, obviously.

'You know this guy then?' Beck jutted his chin at the door.

I shrugged. 'We've been known to help each other out now and again.'

Beck grinned. 'Well, now we know why Dietrich turned up here.'

I shook my head. 'Dietrich wouldn't know I had connections.'

Beck pulled a face. 'We haven't a clue what Dietrich knows. Still, maybe he picked this guy at random? He looked jittery out there. Maybe he had trouble picking the code he wanted? Maybe he just went for whoever he could reach?'

Yeah. *Maybe.* But I'd told Sitaroo about Mephistopheles. Should have made him wary about answering mystery calls. In fairness, though, he was only a genius about tech stuff. Anything else, he was as fallible as the rest of us. Even so, it wasn't like him to be careless.

Beck gave a sigh of impatience. 'Hey, here's a wild idea. Why don't we ask him?'

It was an old-fashioned door. Took old-fashioned methods to get through it. I held my Sandman ready while Beck took out the lock with his foot. It didn't survive the first kick and the door flew back, hit the inside wall with a rattle and swung forward again more slowly. The corridor was unlit, dark, and we left it that way.

The room at the far end hummed - a soft vibration almost below hearing, but enough to put a person on edge. I recognised it, of course. The only illumination in Sitaroo's living room came from the same source - the Dakka-Hoddern. Its greenish glow lit the cabinet from beneath, seeping out to give the entire room an atmosphere of evil.

Soon as I saw it, I realised why Sitaroo was listed on Morgan's bracer. Nothing to do with his illegal activity. Sitaroo had already told me he wanted his 'baby' declared a living entity. Who better to help with that than a lawyer who now specialised in getting people declared legal?

Beck paused a second before entering, gave a low whistle at the sight of the glowing cabinet. 'Nice rig,' he murmured. Then louder: 'Hello?'

When no answer came, he pursed his lips, moved further inside the apartment.

Sitaroo lived a mean life. Meaner, even, than mine. Living room, bedroom with en-suite, kitchen. While I was still staring at the machine, thinking through about Morgan, Beck checked Sikum again. He disappeared through the only other door, returned seconds later.

'The locator's right. Place is empty.' He helped himself to the moon-chair, hooked a knee over its slanted rim. 'So, any ideas?'

I snorted. *Take your pick.*

Having Sitaroo Man's bracer at his disposal put Dietrich in touch with most of the city's scum, plus a few legit contacts who, like me, liked the man's style of business. He could go anywhere from here. He could be anywhere right now.

'Depends what Dietrich's plans are. He might have chosen Sitaroo because of what he knows about digital stuff.'

Beck shrugged. He was looking round the room, eyes narrowed. Annoyed me in a petty kind of way - if he was going to ask a question, he could at least listen to the answer.

'Lights,' he said. The low-energy bulb above us obeyed, flickered on. Beck scooched further back into the chair. 'How'd you know him, anyway?'

'Former life.' I dropped the peevishness, crossed to the Dakka-Hoddern. Wondered how the hell Sitaroo activated the monstrous manchine interface I'd seen. He'd flicked something towards the back, but when I looked, I couldn't see what.

'That thing's valuable, I assume?' Beck watched as I hunted with my fingertips.

I glanced over. 'Guy would fuck over his own grandmother just to raise the money for juice to keep it running,' I said. 'Don't know how much it would fetch on the street but to Sitaroo... Maybe more than life itself.'

'So why keep it down here?'

'Huh?'

'Why would he keep such a valuable object down here?' Beck pointed. 'In a basement which floods at least once a year.'

I straightened up, followed the man's finger to the tide-mark staining the walls three feet above the floor, the second one higher still - unrepaired water damage from spring tide inundations.

'Because...' I glanced round again. 'I don't know.'

Beck pushed himself out of the chair, sending it backwards, spinning slowly on its balloon wheels.

'It's a relay.'

'A what?'

He crossed the room, rapped his knuckles on the cabinet's surface. The low hum rose in pitch, like I'd heard it do before, and the lights underneath brightened. The man gave a sardonic grin.

'There's nothing in here. Smoke and mirrors. I mean, come on! A light fitting has voice recognition, but a Dakka-Hoddern doesn't? If the machine exists at all, this isn't it.' He tapped his face, next to his right eye. 'According to my infra-red, this is just casing - with maybe a direct link to the actual rig. Face it, no quantum-cascade engineer - even a casual one - would keep a stem-cell array down here. Not somewhere that could flood at any time and short the fucker out permanently.'

'And Sitaroo's more than a casual anything,' I said, feeling stupid.

'So whatever this shell is linked to, there's a good chance Dietrich went there.'

I frowned. 'Why?'

'Because if your Sitaroo Man really does own a rogue Dakka-Hoddern, then we're in bigger trouble than we thought. We're talking about the same kind of quantum-cascade processor Synapware uses to store and process Mephistopheles personas.'

I groaned. 'I've had a bad day. Humour me.'

'You were right, Nix. It wasn't random. He *did* want Sitaroo. He wants Sitaroo's rig. He wants to digitise himself again.'

'No, Beck. Trust me. Dietrich likes killing people. *Likes it*! He can't do all the foul things he likes doing to people if he's inside a machine. Besides, won't he be trapped in there if he's digitised again?'

Beck shook his head. 'The Synapware rig has walls and cages, containment systems built to stop leakage. He *was* trapped - in *there*. In Sitaroo's Dakka-Hoddern he'll be free. He can upload himself to any machine in the world, go anywhere. Even duplicate himself. Once he's inside it, he can hop anywhere he likes instantaneously. We'll never find him and even if we did, we could never be sure we're eliminating the last and only copy of him. And we already know there are people out there ready to help him find a new body whenever he wants one, for the right amount of cash.'

'Jesus!' I perched my rump on the nearest available object, ignored the angry buzz it gave.

'If we thought Dietrich was dangerous hopping from one body to another, Nix, trust me, he can do a lot more damage loose in cyberspace.'

*

I caught Beck's eye. The man shook his head. Twenty minutes going back and forth with variations on the Sikum matrix and we were still no closer to knowing where Dietrich had gone with Sitaroo's skinny Sikh ass.

'Even if he's dumped the bracer,' Beck complained. 'Which I doubt, *it* should still show up. Somewhere.'

'Yeah, but this is Sitaroo's stealth stuff we're talking about.'

I'd quickly gained a new level of respect for the eccentric geek. Hell, we both had. Despite Beck's faith in what Sikum could do, Sitaroo's software had blocked it. Beck's frustration at that matched my own.

I squatted down in front of the machine.

'Why'd he pick up the call?' I said again.

Hell, he'd provided *me* with protection against a call from Mephistopheles - the Rooinator. He'd put a copy on my bracer. So why hadn't he used it to protect himself?

Beck shrugged, tired of the question he'd answered at least three times already in as many different ways.

'He trusted his caller. He was hoping Morgan had some news for him.'

Yeah. Smacked of desperation, too. For all I knew the Turing Regulation Authority were breathing down the man's neck, trying to find his rig and shut it down. Dietrich's call had looked to be from Morgan, and Sitaroo was getting antsy.

He would have answered.

I straightened up. 'So, if Sikum can't help, how we going to find him?'

Beck stroked his jaw, stare fixed on his bracer's screen. All this time he'd been talking to Tyler through his implants, getting new uploads, adjustments to the app we were using. Now he paused, listening. Gave a nod.

'Tyler says there's something else we can try.'

'Try it.'

'It won't find Dietrich, it'll just find the rig, but—'

'*Try it!*'

Because, if Beck was right - I wasn't wholly convinced he was, but I didn't have any better suggestions - then assuming Dietrich wanted to redigitise himself, he'd need to be physically linked to the machine. Find the rig, find Dietrich. Obvious.

Beck was already fiddling with the heavy-duty bracer he wore. A second later the screen lit his face and a synthetic voice said, 'Ready.'

The steel gauntlet clicked as he laid it on the Dakka-Hoddern casing.

'This dummy rig is linked to something,' he said. 'I'm guessing it's the real thing. Doesn't matter how many times Sitaroo's programming sends me round the world, this new programme will find it, eventually.'

*

Lian's hair was shorter and she'd lost weight in the intervening time. That old *Brantia* was clamped to her wrist like a black-and-silver growth. I'd forgotten how bulky those things were. Bulkier, even, than Samuels' dinosaur, even though it was way smarter. Now, three years on, the technology they'd had to cram inside that over-sized gauntlet could fit into the nib of a stylus. Back then the *Brantia* was the latest thing. Six months later it had been junk.

The figure on screen tucked a strand of hair behind her ear, cleared her throat.

'This is my living will,' Lian said. 'I make it in the event that injury or sickness prevents me from forming sound and reasoned decisions on my own behalf. I name Matthew Marcus Nixon as my next of kin and my sole executor. I hereby authorise him to...'

I pushed my chair back and stood up, causing the playback to pause.

'What is this? Where'd you dig this up?'

We were in the corner office again. The one in the Synapware building. This time I was the one behind the desk and Beck was elsewhere, his bracer still tracking the trails Sitaroo had laid to throw just this kind of trace off his scent. Tyler sat in the chair I'd occupied last time I'd been here, playing with his infernal pen. If I hadn't been so pissed off right then, I might have paused to wonder what damage he intended doing with it this time.

'Once they learned there was a living will, the hospital contacted Synapware,' Tyler said. 'We have priority on such cases. When your name came up as Executor so did the fact that you're my subordinate - the matter was thus passed to me. Mr Nixon, I need your signature.'

'My signature. On what?'

The man gestured at the display in front of me. 'Take a seat. Pay attention. You'll find out.'

I thumped back into the chair, rolled it forward onto the pressure plate, so the desk activated again. Already knew what the will was going to tell me. She'd talked about it more than once.

She didn't want to stay a vegetable. She didn't want to be kept alive if she had no quality of life. *What was the point?* she'd asked me. *Why keep someone going if they're in pain or so unaware that there's no life left to speak of?* Back then, when we were still partners, I'd agreed with her. Today, it was a different story.

When the file finished playing, I sat back in the chair and stared at the screen, where the final frame had stayed, frozen. Lian was still-framed, touching the bracer's pad with her forefinger, switching off the recording.

Tyler leant to one side, snagged a corner of his jacket loose from where it was caught between the chair and his hip.

'These are new regulations. Current National Health Service policy stipulates that in a case such as this, where there's a living will requesting termination, they should maintain life for a seventy-two hour period. After that, they'll switch off life-support and allow the patient to pass away with dignity.'

'Jesus.' I let my breath out slow but it was still shaky. 'Seventy-two hours? That gives her barely any chance to recover.'

'The window's not there for the benefit of the patient, Mr Nixon. The seventy-two hours is to give loved ones a chance to reach the hospital and say their goodbyes. It's a controversial policy, but these are rather desperate times. The system's been in place for eighteen months now. They need the beds. Too many sick people, not enough hospitals.'

I sat back in the chair, studied Tyler's face.

'I never heard of any such "new policies",' I said. 'Plus, even if they exist, she made that will before they were brought in. Surely that nullifies it? I doubt she seriously thought her will would ever get activated. And this seventy-two hour bullshit? She wouldn't have gone along with that, I guarantee it!'

'No one knows what she would and wouldn't have gone along with. Since nobody can ask her, we have to take the will as it stands. It was her responsibility to make sure it's up-to-date, Mr Nixon, as much as it's *not* yours to interpret her wishes according to *your* views. But none of this is the issue. If the hospital believed there was any chance she'd recover, they wouldn't have even looked for a will. Since they did, it means they believe she'll have no quality of life whatever treatment she receives, however long she's given to get better.'

I stood up again, turned away from her face on the screen and began to pace the room.

Lian had put my name on a document that was as good as her death warrant. Now the hospital aimed to carry it out. She'd been in ITU less than twelve hours, how could they even make that call, that fast? Hell, how could that kind of policy be legal in the first place? It was barbaric. Then again, this was the UK. It was the UK in the 2070s, which meant anything was possible. But didn't she, anyone, deserve more than three days before the blue-jackets pulled the plug?

Anyway, if they were waiting for me, as Executor, to go ahead and approve their psychotic plan of action...

I leaned my palms on the desk, met Tyler's gaze. 'What happens if I don't agree to it? If I contest the will, whatever? What can the hospital do?'

Tyler ran his eyes over me - regarded the clothes I knew he considered scruffy, even though I'd just showered and changed.

'They have a legal obligation to fulfil the terms of the will and an even bigger obligation to provide care for the patients they *can* save. Remember also, you'd be going against Miss Morrison's wishes. You have a legal obligation in that respect, to see those wishes carried out to the best of your ability.'

I shook my head. 'This is insane. This is *fucking insane*! Why the hell didn't she change her will? And the hospital has no right. They're talking about someone's life. A policewoman, for God's sake!'

'There is an option you may not have considered.'

The sound of Tyler's pen-lid clicking quenched the outrage and froze my blood in a heartbeat. *That fucking pen*! I returned my attention to the man's face.

I swallowed thickly. 'What option?'

'You have to admit, she's a good candidate.'

'What are you talking about?'

'And the signature is for Synapware, not the hospital.'

I glowered at him over the news articles marching around the edges of the desk, vomit warming the core of my gut.

Tyler held my stare. Said simply, 'Mephistopheles.'

'You gotta be kidding me.' Though I knew he wasn't. And I'd known what he was after the second he'd talked about options.

Tyler provided me with his crimped smile. 'It would solve your dilemma. You'd be carrying out her wishes according to her will, but you'd also be saving her life. She'd get a second chance. A longer, healthier life, free of the TB which would shorten hers considerably, even if this hadn't happened. With us she'll have the highest level of ongoing medical care, at no charge. Even you must see - the benefits, compared to the alternative, are immeasurable.'

'You're a sick man,' I said. 'The fact you'd even think–'

'Sick? That's ironic, don't you think? Mr Nixon, I'm offering for free what any number of people would pay millions for. How is that sick?'

'You're offering it for free because it's still experimental. You don't know whether Mephistopheles even works, what the long-term effects are. She'd be a lab rat, that's why it's free!'

'Actually, the success rate so far is astonishing. All the subjects are doing excellently - Dietrich aside, and he's an exception, as you know.'

The man's expression grew frank. 'I should warn you, Miss Morrison is not the only candidate on our list. More to the point, suitable bodies are at a higher premium than suitable candidates. Just so you know, there are several other women out there as much in need of a second chance as Lian. Women whose loved ones, I imagine, are prepared to do *anything* to keep their sick relative around.'

First time I'd heard Tyler use anyone's first name. I grinned sourly.

'What was that, the hard sell? They know where these "candidates" end up, right? All these so-called "loved ones". They're told where you get the shiny new bodies for their nearly-departed?'

'I gather most people would rather not know. Interestingly, those who do often go somewhat further. I understand one husband was quite adamant about which body his wife should receive when she was selected for the procedure.'

I grinned coldly. 'Corpses to order. Told you, didn't I?'

'This offer will not be on the table for long. You can comply with the will here, Mr Nixon, and still get to keep your friend. What more could you ask for?'

21

I never liked Tyler, or his pen. Now I liked them both a lot less.

I was still wondering what the hell made the suited exec tick, when I met up with Beck in the lobby downstairs. I fell in beside him as he turned towards the exit.

'We're heading out to the Island,' he told me. 'We'll keep the Dakka-Hoddern trace going, but there's another option for finding Dietrich. We both gotta go out there and get something installed.'

'When you say installed,' I said, rubbing my good eye to ward off an avalanche of fatigue. 'We're not talking wetware, are we?'

Beck grinned. 'You worried Synapware might put something useful in your head or something?'

'Yeah, something.'

'Well, this is bracer hardware. Custom made, just for you and me. Happy?'

'At the prospect of having my bracer altered? What do you think?'

Beck didn't reply. Guess he'd figured out the kind of mood I was in. I followed him into an evening which hissed and sparkled with the rain coming in on a new weather front.

*

Two hours later, Beck ushered me inside the downways-sideways box waiting in the foyer of the island mansion. The doors whispered shut behind us.

'So why didn't we use this upgrade earlier?' I wanted to know. 'Instead of trying to ping the Dakka-Hoddern. Would've saved me looking for Dietrich in the wrong place, letting people die.'

'They just finished building it. Took the best part of three days and it's untested. But they think it's gonna work.'

'They?'

'The nerds. Don't worry, they're house-trained. Say please and thank you and everything.'

'It's not the nerds I'm worried about down here. It's the walking corpses.'

Beck muttered something under his breath and gave a shake of his head.

'That's a prejudice you're gonna have to lose pretty soon,' he said more audibly. 'They've scheduled the preliminary launch for eight weeks time.'

'Well, you can guess what I think about that. And that prejudice you just saw? Out in the real world...trust me, I'm just the start.'

Beck grunted, gave me a sour look.

'I just wish they'd had this stuff around when my wife was still alive. Hell, I'd have sold myself to the nearest slave ring if it meant she'd survive.'

Yeah. Like Tyler said, some people will do pretty much anything to save someone they care enough about. Yet they didn't seem to see it as a problem, him or Beck. Way I saw it, 'anything' covered a whole range of shit, starting with the voluntary slavery Beck just suggested and ending with murder. Beck had just confirmed it and I could see it happening wholesale the second that launch happened. That and a whole lot more.

'You know they can alter schemas, don't you?' I said. 'It's how they cleaned up personas before releasing them onto the market. Put aside any residual trace of whoever the second-hand brain first belonged to, there's no guarantee Synapware's gonna give you back the same person you lost.'

'Man. You're so paranoid.'

'This is messing with dangerous stuff, Beck. God stuff.'

'So you're religious all of a sudden?'

'This shit weirds me out, that's all.'

'This shit,' he said, as the elevator pulled to a halt. 'Saves lives.'

I had a retort all ready for him about exactly how that was utter bullshit, but he stepped out before I could use it. By the time I'd caught up with him, the moment had passed. Already figured this was a touchy subject for him, anyway, so I let it slide.

Beck halted at a door with a window in it, palm-scanned himself on the plate beside it. The door opened, leading us down another corridor. Identical to all the other corridors I'd seen down here save one thing, which told me I'd been here before. Two thirds of the way down, two black-uniformed guards flanked a door on the right. This was the same corridor Tyler had brought me down to watch someone being brought back from the dead.

The guards wore black utility suits, black webbing belts, and the weapons they carried said 'Military'. The clipped hair, lean muscle and solid, straight-ahead stare said the men were, too. Only insignia anywhere on them was the button-badge on each collar. Same badge as last time but Household these guys weren't. Just looking at them told me they were bodyguards of a much more personal calibre. Beck prodded me in the back, moving me on. One of the guards, the blond one to the left of the door they guarded, gave Beck a crisp nod, took his hand off the weapon he'd slid it onto.

We didn't go down as far as the resurrection room this time. Three doors past the one with the guards, Beck palm-scanned himself again and it opened into a low-lit lab occupied by three men and a woman, who all looked up, uncomfortable, as we entered.

'So who *are* those guys,' I asked Beck, tilting my head back the way we'd come as the door shut behind us.

Beck gave me a warning look. 'We're here to see *these* guys.'

I grinned sardonically, glancing back at the closed door. 'They're Synapware Special Forces,' I decided.

'These guys? No, they're nerds.'

'Actually,' the shortest of the three technicians hopped off a stool and approached, lifting the eyepieces he wore up onto his forehead. 'We *are* special forces. Of a type. And if you don't mind, you can leave your stereotypes at the door.' He extended his hand to me. 'Welcome to Nerd Central,' he said.

*

I hate people touching my bracer. I especially hate people I don't know - and therefore don't trust - not only touching, but inserting needle-like hardware into, the chips and circuits hidden inside my bracer's chrome housing. I was told the new processor could sift satellite data three hundred times faster than the onboard Omni Canverse 3. Guess I was supposed to be impressed because the things it could apparently then do with that data was the reason we'd trekked all the way out here.

Beck had handed his bracer over without flinching and the new processor was already installed on it. Now it was my bracer's turn. I took it off and slid the plates together, so it was little more than a concave wedge of chrome, held it clenched in my fist, just out of reach of the woman with the plate-release. She lowered her outstretched hand, glanced from me to Beck and back again.

'Isn't one upgraded bracer enough?' I wanted to know.

To be fair, Beck's wasn't yet a fireball or spewing sparks.

'No,' Beck said. 'What the hell's the problem?'

'This is my *bracer*. I don't like people messing with my bracer.'

'Don't be a pussy, Nix. Hand it over and quit whining.'

When I still procrastinated he shook his head in disgust.

'I can't believe you're making a fuss! This is custom-made, quantum-generation hardware. People like your buddy, Sitaroo, would fall over themselves to get hold of it.'

'Yeah, but these guys haven't even tested it yet! What if it deep-fries my architecture? Did you think of that? Will it short out? Set up a feedback loop?'

The woman reached for the bracer again, without success. 'This chip has a gamma-level core running eight synthaptic nano processors. It *can't* fail.'

'Yeah. They said that about the Atlantic tunnel.'

Beck gave a snort. 'We both need this upgrade, Nix. Now hand it over before I bounce you off the nearest wall.'

Subtlety always works with me. I sighed, handed it over. Couldn't help noticing the woman's hands had a distinct tremor, though, and had to look away while she took my bracer apart.

'So how does it work?' I asked Beck softly, anxious not to disturb her concentration.

'In layman's terms, it throws what it expects to find away, keeps everything else.'

'It takes an entire chip to do just that?'

'Yes it does.'

'How does that help us, anyway?'

'Dietrich's an anomaly. Two personalities in one body. He should show up as the only thing out there, once the new chip filters out everything else.'

The woman handed my bracer back. I clipped it on, started it up. It took a few seconds longer than usual to initialise, while the screen advised me it was installing the new device. I only relaxed once I got my home screen back but then I wasn't convinced it looked the same as usual.

*

'Nerd Central' was one of those places it's good to leave. The stuff inside it was weird, the people weirder. It was obvious they were happy to be rid of us, too, although their sighs of relief were muted by the door closing behind us.

Back up the same corridor, past the same black-uniformed guards, who stood outside the same door.

As we drew abreast, the door opened from the inside, causing the blond guard to turn towards it. A youngish woman sidled out, beckoned him closer. Twin-set and classic pearls spoke of a much older woman and might have indicated a lot of surgical intervention, but for the eyes. The eyes matched the face. Youngish. Not middle aged. Besides, I knew her face. Everyone knew her face.

The woman didn't notice me. She leant closer to the guard, murmured quietly in his ear.

'Yes ma'am.'

He said it the English way, making it sound like 'mum'.

The guard turned towards the wall, hiding his lips while he made a call. I sneaked a look past the woman into the room behind. Inside was a bed much like the ones I'd seen the first time I'd come out here. Ranks of machines surrounding the headboard.

An emaciated guy with greying temples lay on it, covered with just a sheet. Couldn't read the machines, but I heard a slow beeping - he was either just about dead or just about alive.

Beck grabbed my jacket and propelled me ahead of him.

'Keep walking!'

I hadn't realised I'd stopped - too busy slotting pieces into place.

In the main corridor, Beck let the doors shut behind us before he grabbed me again, rammed me against the far wall.

'Hey!' I shoved him in the chest, hard. 'What the fuck?'

He backed off a pace, but the grip on my jacket didn't ease up.

'Listen,' he said. 'What you just saw back there. That was your imagination. Got it?'

'Yeah. I'm not fucking stupid.'

He nodded, let go. 'Special States Secrets, remember?'

Fuck Special States Secrets. What I'd just seen back there could get me taken out by guys a lot tougher than Beck.

Beck kept staring at me, until I threw my hands up, exasperated.

'I *know*! Jesus!'

I followed as he started towards the elevator - couldn't resist a last glance over my shoulder.

'One question though.'

'Don't bother.'

I shrugged. 'I just wanted to know if *he* gets more than seventy-two hours before they pull the plug.'

'I haven't the faintest idea what you're talking about.'

'Yeah, that's what I figured.'

22

The energy farm's array spanned both sides of the Rhondda's glacial valley, running several kilometres, north and south. The towers were circular, like lighthouses. Fifty metres high and encrusted with glittering blisters - ranks of photo-voltaic cells. Each tower was connected to its twin on the opposite side of the valley by half-a-dozen thick, horizontal turbines. Fitted to these, like giant prayer flags, were spirals of off-set fins - double-sided solar panels that whirred at deadly speeds in the gusting wind.

On a sunny day the thousands of panes glinting and flashing as they turned must have been an awesome sight. Didn't look too inspiring today. Today, while the turbines rotated like giant screw-threads, the fins reflected only the dull grey of the sky and threw arcs of water down into the valley.

I wiped rain off my bracer and checked the solitary signal showing up on Sikum. I didn't like the new version. It didn't approximate the territory like the old one did. It didn't show structures or features, it just gave me a red blob and a series of numbers scrolling down one side of the screen - altitude, bearing, distance. Uninspiring, and less intuitive than the old Sikum.

'How the hell am I going to find Dietrich among this lot?' I complained, looking from the bracer to the long line of towers my side of the valley.

'Same way you found Lian. You follow the signal.' Beck was using his throat mike and his voice sounded normal, not the drainpipe gurgle I'd heard out on Temple Quay.

I scowled at his reply and hunched my shoulders. I felt exposed, visible to the entire array, standing alone in a parking lot reserved, the sign said, for maintenance staff only. There was just me and my car parked here, so at a guess this power station was mainly automated. That much, at least, was in our favour. No innocents to get in the way.

'You really think the Dakka-Hoddern's up here?' I asked Beck.

'Maybe. Don't you?'

'Dietrich doesn't do sightseeing,' I admitted. 'He didn't come up here for his health, either. So, yeah. Maybe he's looking for a new home, just like you said.'

Except the idea of him jumping back into a computer still didn't fit, not for me. Computers don't get adrenaline rushes, they don't feel pleasure watching little girls struggle and scream for their moms while they die. Dietrich wouldn't want an existence, even temporary, which gave him no physical sensation. He just wouldn't. And duplicate himself? Why the hell would he do that? He wouldn't want the competition. Besides, being a digital entity made him vulnerable - he could be wiped in a heartbeat. Evil fucker though he was, he wasn't stupid.

He wasn't out here for the Dakka-Hoddern, if it was even here at all.

Beck believed it, though. He liked things neat.

And, face it, Sikum had brought us here.

'Plenty of juice for that rig up here,' Beck was saying. 'And no...*flooding*.'

The last word crackled in my ear as he grunted through his throat mike. He was out there somewhere, among the array, seeking a vantage point. Climbing one of those towers, I'd bet. Most probably the hard way - from the outside.

I looked around again.

The area was too barren to leave a vehicle anywhere without it being visible from where I stood. Couldn't imagine Dietrich using Sitaroo Man's slender geek body to walk the long way up either, or climb those cliffs. Unless I'd passed a parked car back on the gravel road, which I knew I hadn't, then he must have got up on the Rhondda by a way I hadn't thought of.

'Beck, you sure this thing's working right?' I shook my wrist.

A sigh whistled through my implant.

'What now?'

'I kind of liked the old Sikum - being able to see everything. No surprises. Right now we can only see Dietrich. If that's really him showing up.'

'It is. Your point being?'

'Maybe he brought friends.' Even so, I finally slammed the door of the Ford shut, let my bracer set the security.

I put the pause I got down to Beck being too busy hanging on to something for dear life to answer. But when he spoke, his voice was calm.

'You're being paranoid again. He works alone. *You* told *me*.'

I'd taken a step towards the nearest tower. Beck's comment stopped me dead.

Yeah. I'd told him, on the way over here. Dietrich always works alone.

Hearing it from someone else brought it home. He works alone yet he'd hired Brutants to take me down. The uneasy feeling I already had got uneasier. Maybe if I hadn't been strung out on Clean, I might have questioned it more at the time. Might have asked myself if that was really something Karl Dietrich would have done. I already knew it wasn't. It didn't fit, any more than the Dakka-Hoddern being all the way out here didn't fit. Any more than Dietrich wanting to digitise himself.

Or maybe Beck was right and I was just paranoid.

Hell, what the fuck did I know? Maybe being inside another guy's brain made Dietrich think different?

I puffed out my cheeks, looked up at the rain and the fins scattering water down on me from on high.

'Sitaroo Man's my friend,' I said. 'So no heroics. And no smokers this time.'

Beck let out an exasperated breath.

'I'm just saying!'

'Get moving, for Christ's sake! I'm freezing my nuts off up here.'

I cut the connection and shuffled screens on my bracer, entered the five-digit code I'd allocated to the Rooinator - a precaution which was fast becoming a habit - then craned my neck at the towers lined up on the valley's crest. Wondered if he could see me yet.

Yeah, he could probably see me. Doubted he'd see Beck, though.

I'd watched as Beck had slunk off, his stealth-suit making my eyes ache as its patterning cells shifted format. A moment's distraction and I'd lost sight of him. Now he could be anywhere and, with the new upgrade tuned to Dietrich, even Sikum couldn't see him. Or me. Or any other living creature. It could only see Dietrich.

Gravel crunched under my feet when I started forward again. The small stones had migrated into dips and mounds over the years, making footing across the entire site uneven. I cursed as my shoe slithered into a puddle and filled with water.

My face and hair were dripping, and water was sluicing off my jacket cuffs by the time I got to the first pylon. That's what they were called, these towers. I knew because the sign above the door at the base of this one announced that it was 'Pylon three-alpha.' Three-beta, I supposed, was its Siamese-twin, way across on the other side of the valley and linked to it by those cork-screw turbines.

Three-alpha wasn't my destination, although I was pretty sure Dietrich was inside one of the towers. The information scrolling down my bracer-screen showed the target was elevated more than twenty metres above me and two hundred metres north, on a bearing of 145.

I crunched and stumbled over the gravel, no longer caring what the mud did to shoes already ruined beyond salvation, until I reached 'Pylon Seven-Beta.'

Fifteen metres up from me, Sikum said. Thirty to my left. Up there, right among the solar fins.

I backed up, took another look at the whirring turbines and spotted a narrow bridge running between two rows, half-way up. In reality the 'bridge' was a lightweight series of gratings spanning a thousand-foot drop, stabilised by suspension wires strung along the turbines, above and below it. Its only protection from the elements appeared to be waist-high alu panels fixed to either side, all the way along. There was just enough overhead clearance for a person to pass along it, but from where I stood, it looked like they'd need to duck. According to Sikum, Sitaroo Man - Dietrich - was currently walking along it.

I shielded my eyes from the rain and scanned the bridge's length, where it reached out across the steep valley. Failed to spot any movement.

I sighed. Time this whole fucking thing was over.

More conventional than Beck might have done it, Dietrich had accessed the pylon through the control booth at the base. I discovered that by trying the door, only to find the lock had been shot out.

Okay, maybe not so conventional.

More importantly, it looked like Dietrich had found himself a weapon.

I examined the broken lock a second more, let out a long, slow breath. Presence of a smoker put the stakes higher. Didn't escape me that the bastard could've put a hole in me while I was making the walk to the foot of this tower. The fact he hadn't was maybe just luck. That, or he had something else in mind.

I drew the Sandman and tapped the door sharply with my left hand, let it swing open.

The room beyond was empty. No one around. Even so, I stayed cautious. No way to know how imaginative Dietrich might get with all the volts flying around upstairs. I gave the place a once-over. No sign of tampering.

The reprieve from the rain and wind was welcome. I blinked water from my eyes and swiped it off my face, shook it from my jacket while I took in the relative calm and quiet of the small room.

The warm-electronics smell in here reminded me of school and the only light came from a single LED cluster set high in one corner. Twin rows of servers ran down the middle. They created sharp blocks of shadow big enough to hide any number of nasty interludes. I checked the darkened areas with my bracer's lamp, found nothing. Meanwhile the servers continued humming to themselves. I played the torch over them. None had the distinctive look of a Dakka-Hoddern, but suddenly Beck's notion was starting to look more likely. Easy to hide something like that up here, in an automated installation where people rarely ever set foot.

In fact, judging by the dust, the place looked to have seen no human activity for years.

There was one inner door, beyond the servers, whose mangled lock glinted in the LED glow - fresh metal torn by gunfire. That, I could guarantee, was a sign of recent human activity.

Past the equipment to the door, which led to stairs winding up the tower's insides. Unearthly moaning filtered down from the top. I peered upwards. No movement.

The stairs were a spiral of wedge-shaped grilles on a steel carcass, fitted so they narrowed towards the middle, forcing users to stick to the wall. The stairs were shallow. I made the mistake of taking two at a time and was breathless and wheezing by the time I reached a door halfway up.

The stairs continued - up to the higher reaches of the pylon. I wondered what the hell could be up there, but a glance at my wrist told me I wouldn't need to find out. I was now at the same elevation as my target, though he was now a hundred and thirty metres away and to the west.

The wind had strengthened with the altitude and the fins outside produced a howling drone, which varied in pitch along with the gale, like a set of ghostly, giant bagpipes. I cracked the door, waggled my finger in my ear to combat the change in air-pressure. Wrestling with suction, I opened it further, peeked out. The spinning solar panels were higher above the catwalk than I'd imagined - gave a couple of metres clearance.

Satisfied the top of my head wouldn't start resembling a boiled egg the second I stepped outside, I scanned the bridge ahead. Deserted, just like Sikum said. But it was a long way from here to the next tower and the bridge vibrated so hard in the wind in places it appeared to blur, just for a second, before re-materialising into rain-slick metal. It was also narrow enough to vanish to infinity over the distance.

If I was reading the data right, Dietrich was already across it and inside the far tower.

A gust of wind shunted me aside when I stepped out. I grabbed the handrail as my shoes slid on wet metal, throwing me off-balance and against the safety-rail. I found a wider stance, risked a glance over the side. More sets of fins whirred below, like the shimmering teeth of a giant meat-grinder. Perfect view of the Rhondda beyond them. Given my current circumstances, it went utterly unappreciated. The valley's only relevance right now involved how high I was above it and how far below me the road was.

I pushed rain-slick hair out my eyes and turned towards the far end of the bridge. It was a long way across and the wind and rain would only make the crossing longer. I kept my hands on the rail, planted my feet square each time so the shoes didn't slide. By the time I was close enough to make out the door to the new tower I was soaked to the skin and shivering.

The sight was not as welcome as I'd imagined, either.

The door stood wide open. Beyond it was the darkness of another low-lit stairwell. If Dietrich had spotted me crossing the site earlier, he could easily be waiting there ready to take pot shots with that weapon he'd found himself. With him in shadow I'd never see him and, even if I did, I had no cover up here. Returning fire was out of the question - my non-lethal darts wouldn't reach that far, let alone hit their mark before getting blown off-course by the wind.

With these thoughts and others like them running though my mind, and all the time expecting a gunshot to be the last thing I ever heard, I kept my grip on the rail and hauled myself through the gusts and squalling rain. The shot didn't come, but I was jittery by the time I finally reached the second tower.

I stumbled inside, darted right, clear of the wedged-open door - whose frame would silhouette me against the sodden sky - and immediately checked around, covering with the Sandman. This tower was clearly the lesser of the pair. Its door had no lock and there were no steps leading down. Only up. Plus, there was no lighting. I flicked my bracer's torch on and ran it around the space above me. Nothing. Empty. No sign of anyone. But I knew he was in here. Somewhere.

A slam echoing from above made me flinch, draw back against the wall, aiming upwards into the gloom. When nothing else happened, I leaned out again, pointed my bracer beam up there, Sandman resting on its casing. Saw only the light from a door at the top as it swung wide, banged shut again in the wind.

A glance at my screen confirmed it. Dietrich was up there, above me. If what I'd just experienced of the elements was anything to go by, I seriously doubted Sitaroo Man would have put his prized Dakka Hoddern up there. Made Dietrich's reasons for coming here a bigger mystery.

Unless he'd brought a victim. Sikum couldn't tell me one way or the other, and the top of a power pylon was exactly the sort of place Dietrich would appreciate. Great for bringing someone's life to a terrifying and painful end.

At least the pylon had only one exit, and I had that covered. If he tried to leave, he'd have to come through me. Having him cornered was one thing. Tackling him while he possessed a firearm, of course, was another.

Crossed my mind it would have been nice to have Beck around right now, watching my ass, instead of out there doing his ninja stuff. I considered calling him, find out what he was up to. If he'd found the high spot he'd been looking for. But it meant cancelling the Rooinator and I didn't want to miss the moment.

Assuming there'd be one.

That was my big plan. Confront Dietrich, convince him he wanted to be inside me more than he wanted to be inside Sitaroo. I'd offer him whatever he wanted. If nothing else, the fact I'd been the other officer to arrest him way back might make him interested in seeing me betray myself - make me kill and torture someone like he'd made Gage do to Ray Sands, like he'd made Harris do to his family.

I shoved the door closed, shutting off the wind and the drone from the turbines. Now there was no daylight coming in, I spotted the light seeds. There was one fixed under the lip of each step - just enough to see its outline so you could tell where to put your feet. Far as I could tell it was the only job the tiny LED clusters did. They for sure weren't there to light the place.

I used my bracer instead, followed its narrow beam as it ran ahead of me, up the twisting stairs. The pylon's interior narrowed as it went up, and the drone of the fins slowly shifted to below me. The tower's apex didn't have the door I was expecting - just a hatch in the ceiling, at the top of a short steel ladder. A peeling sticker on the hatch's underside warned of danger of death beyond. With no wind gusting through since I'd shut the lower door, the hatch had now stopped banging. Like the door below, it had no lock. Just a handle to secure it from inside - and that had been left in the 'open' position.

Pretty obvious who'd left it like that.

I paused at the foot of the ladder to wipe water off the Sandman with the corner of my T-shirt. Then I switched the active clip to paralysers. Never used the blue-coloured darts before, but I knew they acted faster than tranqs. Fast enough, maybe, to stop Dietrich shooting me if he wasn't in the mood to negotiate.

23

The solar elements lining the pylon's roof were sandwiched between glass and ceramic and laid like tiles. The ceramic made the tiles tough enough to walk on but I stayed on my knees - less visible while I clambered off the ladder and lowered the hatch into place behind me.

The wind up here had teeth, spat rain at me hard enough to sting. I shielded my face, scanned the area. The roof was convex - down-curving towards the rim. There was no guard-rail and the wind was strong enough to shove someone over if they didn't watch their step.

A forest of glass transformers was planted across the shallow dome, each raised six feet off the tiles by a skeletal pyramid of insulated aluminium. Strung above the pyramids on tall poles were webs of inch-thick cabling designed, at a guess, to channel all that power across the country. It sang in the wind, while flickers of raw lightning arced between the transformers and their couplings.

Seeing Sitaroo standing between the glass spires, his back to me and staring out across the Rhondda, made me pause a second. I'd forgotten. Still had Morgan in my head when I thought of Dietrich. It was tough keeping up with who the bastard was wearing - adjusting my expectations each time so I remembered who it was I was chasing, regardless of how he looked. Christ knows what it was doing to Dietrich. Identity crisis didn't come close.

Sitaroo was missing his turban and his hair was bound into a top-knot by a strip of white cloth. Escaped strands writhed in the wind like pale medusa-snakes. The man seemed to sense me there, turned slowly and found himself face-to-face with my Sandman. He grinned a welcome broad enough to show the missing incisor. It was a twisted smile. One which didn't belong on Sitaroo's face.

'Thanks for coming,' Dietrich said, raising his voice over the gale.

'I'd hate for you to miss your own exit.'

I blinked but didn't ask. Guy was a nut-case. Wouldn't be the first time I'd heard him spout bullshit. I gestured with the Sandman.

'Move away from the edge.'

Dietrich spread his arms, letting the wind wrestle with the white, embroidered kurta he wore, making him fight for balance on the roof's curved lip. The slit opening at the tunic's neck flapped aside, exposing a thin, pale collar bone.

'Or what?' he called.

'Or you'll fall off and die, asshole.'

'*So will your friend.*'

That voice came from a newcomer. Okay, so it had crossed my mind Dietrich would like this place for its recreational value. Even that he'd bring someone to play with, too. When he stepped from between two spires on my left, though, it was clear the second man wasn't the captive I'd immediately assumed when I heard his voice. His smart-suit was protected from the elements by a woollen, camel-coloured overcoat which reached his calves. Gold satin lining flared at his knee as the coat gaped in the wind. He stood with his hands in his pockets caressing, at a guess, the pen he always carried with him.

'What are you doing, Tyler? Get the hell away, that asshole has a gun!'

Tyler tilted his head. 'Actually, no he doesn't.'

I shifted my glance back to Dietrich, realised belatedly that he was bare-handed. The killer grinned again, shrugged. I blinked rainwater from my eyes, adjusted my grip on the Sandman.

When I looked back at Tyler he'd taken his hands from his pockets but the pen was nowhere in sight. Instead, his right hand was wrapped round a snub-barrelled pistol whose muzzle was thicker around than its short, stubby handgrip. Row of lights running down the barrel's length told me it was a smart weapon. Not great news. Didn't matter if the man was a bad shot, if its target was marked, the weapon would hit it. The bleep as Tyler marked me was barely audible over the wires singing above our heads.

'Let's not make things complicated,' Tyler said, jutting his chin at my Sandman.

I didn't feel surprise. Just a cold, soggy churning in my guts. I flicked my hand, let the weapon clatter across the slick tiles.

'Careful,' the exec said, twitching his pistol. 'This is programmed to fire if you move unexpectedly.'

I had no reason to disbelieve him.

'Tyler, what exactly are you–?'

'I'm sorry, Mr Nixon. The collateral damage on this one is already too high. I'd love to take him in *"nice an' quiet"*, just like you want, but you had your opportunity and you missed it.'

I looked from Tyler to Dietrich, back again. 'I still don't–'

The smart-gun's muzzle lifted, pointed at my chest. I raised my hands.

'I want a body,' Dietrich shouted from where he stood. 'One I can have all to myself. One I don't have to fight, or keep replacing.'

I had my attention on Tyler, but I didn't miss it. Dietrich wasn't complaining. He was explaining.

'You made a deal with him,' I said. 'Are you insane?'

Tyler shrugged. 'I'm doing my job.'

I tipped my head towards Dietrich. 'I was talking to him.'

Tyler gave a humourless laugh. 'Droll, as ever, Nixon.'

'To be honest,' Dietrich said, ignoring the exchange. 'I'd have preferred not to have to see your face every time I looked in a mirror, but I can always get surgery. And at least I know the corpse I'm taking will be fresh.'

As his words sank in, my heart, and everything else inside me, sank with them. So that was the deal.

'You trust him?' I asked Dietrich. 'He's fucking over one of his own colleagues and you think he'll let you live?'

It was Dietrich who shrugged this time. He was shivering in the rain-laden wind, but he was still grinning.

'I've made it worth his while. He can retire, move to Russia, China, wherever he wants. And I get a new body, new identity, new bracer, new life.'

While I get dead. Yeah. That about says it all.

Movement out the corner of my left eye.

I resisted turning my head. Kept Beck in my peripheral as he rolled himself, backpack and all, over the edge of the roof. Seemed he'd scaled the entire pylon from the outside.

I kept my gaze fixed on Tyler, praying he hadn't noticed my expression freeze. I needed to keep his and Dietrich's attention on me while Beck got into position.

'You honestly think you'll get away with this?' I asked.

Tyler raised his eyebrows and that tight smile touched his lips.

'Get away with what? There'll be no blood, no apparent victim. There won't be anything for the police to investigate because no one will be missing. There won't even be a body to call attention to itself.'

Beck had risen to his feet. He slid smoothly between the maze of transformers, bare feet silent even in the puddles, until he stood directly behind Tyler. The exec's attention, and his gun, stayed on me the whole while.

I couldn't help grinning. 'Aren't you forgetting something, Tyler?'

'I don't think so, no. I usually take everything into consideration.' Then a look of understanding crossed his face and he smiled again. 'And Mr Beck always follows my orders like the good soldier he is.'

And he was right. Instead of taking Tyler down, backing me up like a partner should, Beck stepped past him into the open, came forward until he was face to face with me.

'Sorry, Nix.'

I blinked disbelief off my face, replaced it with a sneer.

'What, you needed the exercise? You couldn't come up the stairs like everyone else? Why not just hit me over the head when we were back there and be done with it?'

'Had to arrange a small malfunction first. The cameras out here are EM shielded. Took a bit of finesse, but I'm adaptable. There'll be no record of what happens out here today and, no, they won't spot my tampering.'

'So you knew this was coming. All the time, you knew.'

Tyler interrupted before Beck could reply.

'Do you have that revival equipment, Mr Beck?'

Beck's eyes stayed locked on my face, no trace of guilt, no remorse -

not a flicker.

'Yes, sir.'

His matter-of-fact reply sent fear slithering through my guts, turned them liquid. *Revival equipment.* For reviving my body after I was dead. Only the person coming back wouldn't be me.

'Best if you get on your knees,' he said.

'You aren't serious?' I nodded at Tyler. 'He's going to kill me!'

'No. As a matter of fact, *I'm* going to kill you. Now get on your knees.'

I shook my head. 'I have a thing about kneeling. Reminds me of church.'

'Just relax, Nix,' Beck said, gaze fixed hard on my face. 'You're in good hands.'

I opened my mouth to deliver something sardonic, but the man was already stepping sideways. His foot hit the back of my knee so it folded under me. A black hand grabbed my wrist, twisted, collapsing me the rest of the way down. Beck held me there, my arm jammed against my back, just long enough to let me know I wasn't getting up again, then let go and stepped back a pace. I straightened upright, worked the shoulder joint with a wince, and switched my attention to Tyler, to the smart-gun in his hand.

'You dress nice and civilised,' I said, flexing my wrist. 'But I've seen more humanity in an artificial.'

'Make this easy on yourself, Nix,' Beck warned. 'No need to make it worse than it has to be.'

I gave a bark of disbelief. 'Worse?'

'I know it's scary. Dying always is. Doesn't have to be unpleasant though.'

Dietrich had edged forward, intrigued. It still hurt to see him wearing Sitaroo's face. Sitaroo had been my friend for years - since he was a spotty kid and I was still in uniform. Now his bearded face was contorted with a lust for my death that left me sick to my stomach. Dietrich wanted to watch. Hell, of course he did. Watching people die was what he lived for.

'How long will it take?' he wanted to know.

Tyler waved him back. 'Have some respect,' he said. 'We're not doing this for your *pleasure*, Mr Dietrich.'

Dietrich scowled at that. 'Just don't damage him! He's in a bad enough state already.'

'My Sandman,' I muttered to Beck while they bickered. 'Dietrich's right there. Fuck's sake, just take him down!'

'Shush. Be quiet. I got my instructions, and I'm sorry. This is damage limitation. No more bodies.'

No more bodies. They wouldn't let Sitaroo die but they were going to kill me in cold blood. He was right, though. There'd be no body. And no one would know there'd ever been a victim.

'Besides,' Beck went on. 'In this wind, even I couldn't hit him with that stupid pop gun.'

'So you're just going to do it? Kill me and let Dietrich live.'

'Looks that way.'

'Dietrich's a psychopath. He won't stop killing. And he has a penchant for schoolgirls.'

'Not my problem.'

'Jesus!' I twisted round to look at him. 'What the hell are you?'

'Enough!' Tyler had his hand up, warning Dietrich not to approach any further, but he waggled his weapon at me. 'Just get on with it.'

I was still in denial as Beck unslung the pack from his shoulders, flipped it open. Couldn't help thinking while I watched him. We were supposed to be working together. He was meant to be my partner. Just how the fuck could he *do* this?

I watched him extract a wedge-shaped device and peel two wireless sensors from its surface. He fixed one on my neck. The other he reached inside my tee for, stuck it next to my breastbone, over my heart. The device in his hand began making rhythmic bleeping sounds.

Beck gave a grunt. 'Heart-rate's up, Nixon.'

'No kidding.'

He crouched next to my left shoulder, slid the device across the tiles to Dietrich, who stopped it with a sandaled foot, picked it up and waggled it in curiosity.

'A goodwill gesture,' Tyler told him. 'So you know when his heart stops beating.'

Guess the denial fizzled out about then. I shook my head, stunned that I'd ever trusted either of them. I gave a snarl of disgust as Beck settled the jacket back on my shoulders.

'Tyler...' I'd finished trying to reason with Beck - man had to be a fucking robot, the way he took orders.

I wanted to growl at Tyler that he wouldn't get away with it, he'd get caught. But I already knew it wasn't true. He wouldn't get caught. Beck - the one about to do the actual dirty work - wouldn't get caught either. To the world Matt Nixon would still be alive, would no doubt soon retire from everything, move to another part of the country, the world, and start a new life. Who would question it? Who would care?

Dietrich - a madman and a psychopath - would have carte blanche to start a brand new life, a brand new killing spree. Synapware would stay clean, protected, because no one would know Dietrich had ever got loose, that the government-monitored system had failed. Even Sitaroo would be saved.

Everyone would win. Except me.

Beck leaned forward, his upper body pausing between me and Tyler, and grabbed my left wrist, examined the screen glowing on my forearm. He cancelled the Sikum programme, flicked through my screens until he found what he was looking for.

'Rooinator,' he said. 'What idiot thought up that name for it?'

I was too sick to my stomach to give an answer and he didn't really expect one. He was looking where I'd left the programme active and waiting. So much for that little plan.

Beck's fingers blocked my view while he tapped the screen, pinched out on something. When I next saw it, my bracer was back on the home page. An icon was flashing there, blurry with rain behind the plexi sheet - mail, no doubt, which I'd never now answer.

Except... Beck was still in Tyler's line of fire. And, hell with it, what did I have to lose?

My elbow came up, and connected with his chin. Tyler hadn't lied about the auto-fire function. The smart-gun roared and belched blue smoke. Beck's bicep erupted and his blood splashed into my face. The weapon's report would rumble for miles and back again across the valleys, but the chance of anyone else being there to hear it were close to zero. Besides, I wasn't waiting around for the echo.

I went for Beck's stomach compartment, thumbed it open while he was still reeling from the impact. I reached inside. The handgrip felt solid and practical. The machine pistol came up, unfamiliar in my grip. Its drilled barrel swung past Beck, drew level with Tyler. I had to cut him down, and fast, before he could mark me again, or send a random rain of bullets in my direction.

I let off a burst, chest height.

At least I meant to. But my hand was tingling, my finger numb on the trigger. My first thought - weapon security. It was tuned to Beck and when it didn't recognise me, I'd gotten a jolt. But that wasn't right. This was more than just a jolt. The weapon was now a dead weight in my hand, pulling my arm towards the floor. My arms, my legs, felt disconnected, distant.

Beck was rolling in pain, his artificial hand clamped over the blood spurting from the wound on his left arm.

For the second time, I watched a weapon fall from my fingers and clatter onto the rain-soaked solar tiles.

I hadn't felt the dart hit me - too pumped. Too focused on Beck, on Tyler. I'd forgotten Dietrich, forgotten my Sandman and the paralysing darts I'd loaded. Dietrich lowered it. He wasn't grinning any more. Instead, Sitaroo's face was snarling.

'That's my body,' he told me, waving the Sandman. 'Hand it over.'

Beck rolled to his knees, rummaged one-handed into his pack and pulled out a spray. Gelled the wound on his bicep. He then opened the rip-tab on his sleeve and pulled out a grey syringe. Stabbed it into his leg.

Meanwhile I slid sprawling onto the wet tiles, my limbs no longer a part of me but vague, alien phenomena I had no control over.

Tyler hadn't moved but the smart gun was out of sight, back in his pocket.

'Very stupid, Mr Nixon,' he told me. 'If Beck's arm hadn't stopped it, that round would have gone between your eyes.' He gestured at Beck. 'Can you still use the revival kit?'

Beck grunted in relief as the painkillers kicked in. He nodded in reply.

'Very well. In that case, get on with it. Before this idiot tries something else.'

Beck caught my eye, pulled a face. He knew as well as I did I wouldn't be trying anything. Not with that paralyser blocking every conscious signal I gave my body. What small amount of movement I still had was barely enough to lift my head - and that was restricted, thanks to me lying prone on the wet ground.

The silver tin I'd first seen on the Clifton Suspension Bridge appeared in Beck's hand. He flipped the lid, ran his finger across the contents. Could've been picking chocolates from a tray. The syringe he chose was purple. Long, slender and mean-looking.

'Nothing to worry about,' he told me. 'It'll be just like going to sleep.'

Dietrich gave a convulsive giggle, the tone high with excitement.

'Ironic, isn't it?' he sniggered. 'A needle killed me. Another one's bringing me back.'

He'd already backed up again, out of my view, but I knew he'd be watching the heart monitor, waiting for my vital signs to drop. Waiting for the moment he could - safely now Beck had disabled Rooinator - dial my code and give his long, ululating scream.

I couldn't stop it happening. I couldn't even swear. I couldn't tell Tyler, or Beck, or Dietrich they'd be sorry for this. Besides, they wouldn't be. In the next couple of minutes I was going to be dead.

Pissed me off big time.

Thing about paralysers I didn't realise, you still feel stuff. Yeah, sure, my extremities were numb, but most of my nerves were still awake. I felt the needle go in. Second one Beck had given me and I hated him twice as much for it this time.

He was right, though.

It was just like going to sleep.

24

'You know you were dead for less than a minute, don't you?'

I didn't turn. I didn't need to - I knew the voice well enough by now. He'd come to stand behind me while I'd been staring through the observation window, looking at what meagre signs of life the figure on the bed could manage.

'Yeah. They told me.'

We were God knows how many feet underwater, maybe a mile away from the island whose name I still didn't know, in a corridor I'd never visited before. It was pretty much like the one I'd first seen what seemed a dozen years ago, but this one didn't deal with bringing back the dead. This one dealt with the sick.

Beck moved forward, took up the space next to me so he could stare through the window too.

I shifted position, unfolded my arms. There was no creak of faux leather, reminding me my jacket was missing. Had a feeling they'd already told me why and where it was, but I'd forgotten.

It wasn't the only thing I'd lost.

'Where's my bracer?'

Breath whistled through Beck's nose. Guess my tone said more about how I was feeling than my words.

'Nerd Central,' he replied. He tilted his chin at the man in the bed. 'They're pretty impressed with your friend.'

I'd stopped seeing the patient lying there unconscious. Now he'd been mentioned, I focused on him again. Until yesterday I'd ignored the fact he had a real name. I hadn't known what it was till now. Charles Mayhew. Sitaroo Man.

'The Dakka-Hoddern was never out at the solar wind farm, was it?'

Beck's reflection in the window shrugged. I felt cheated that he could manage it without wincing - the sling on his left arm was a reminder I'd deliberately got him shot. Fucker should at least be in pain, after what he'd done.

I shook my head. 'Man, I must be stupid. Fact I ever trusted you makes me stupid.'

'I was just following orders.'

'Like a good little soldier, just like Tyler said.'

'You're taking it personally, aren't you?'

'Personally? Me? Why in the world would I do that?'

Beck sighed, didn't answer.

'So was it you who came up with that genius idea?'

He shook his head. 'Tyler.'

Had to admit, the whole Rhondda thing had Tyler's stink. Didn't mean I forgave Beck.

'When? When did he decide my life was worth shit?'

'That's not how it was, Nix.'

'When?'

'Does it matter?'

'I want to know when he had me pegged as a vic. Was it all along? Before I signed that fucking paper?'

Beck snorted. 'Don't flatter yourself. It was Dietrich who asked for you, once he'd agreed to a deal. Tyler just put it together.'

'Remind me I need some alone time with Geoff Tyler.'

Beck turned away from my reflection, looked at me directly. 'I wouldn't recommend it.'

'So, the Dakka-Hoddern being a relay. That was Tyler's invention?'

'You think it was mine?' Beck shook his head. 'My mind doesn't work like Tyler's, never will. I had no idea what he was up to, Nix. Swear to you. Not till we came out here for the upgrade.'

'For the upgrade? So you knew early enough. Thanks for the head's up.'

Beck said nothing. I guess there was nothing he could say.

I sighed. 'So the rig in Sitaroo's basement is the real Dakka-Hoddern?'

'I guess so. Though why he'd put it down there is beyond me. Then again, the man's a genius. They tend to be stupid like that.'

'And the upgrade? The one which stopped me seeing anything but Dietrich out there? Was that all part of the plan?'

'That's genuine. You being blind to Tyler was a bonus. Would have made you suspicious if Sikum had shown him up there on that pylon with Dietrich.'

'Yeah.' That was for sure. 'So why the farce? You had to play me? Let me run round like an idiot all that time?'

'Told you why. Besides, I had to let you enter the code for Rooinator. The nerds like that one, by the way. They'll be wanting to talk to your friend once he wakes up. I suspect they'll be offering him a job.'

'Yeah. Good luck with that one.'

But hey, at least they believed Sitaroo would wake up, and his mind would be okay when he did.

'So what happened? Why am I still here? You cancelled Rooinator. How come it's me you're talking to right now, not Dietrich?'

'I didn't cancel it,' Beck said. 'I told it to accept the next incoming call. Didn't you even look at your bracer?'

All I remembered was an icon flashing behind a rain-blurred screen.

'Had a few things on my mind.'

I gave a sigh, turned to look at Beck at last. 'So, this plan of Tyler's. Dietrich bought it?'

Beck grinned. 'Yeah,' he said. 'Completely.'

*

The lab was cosy enough with only the technicians in there, working elbow-to-elbow on their single, long workbench. Geoff Tyler was already there when we arrived - along with another guy I'd never met before - making the place feel crowded. Beck and I turning up as well made it distinctly cramped. Plus the nerds were itchy, their tension ripe as a boxer's armpits. Like Sitaroo Man, they didn't do people and in this situation they had no choice but to stand back, wringing their hands, while the guy I didn't recognise - their chief, I figured - tried explaining to Tyler in a language other than jargon.

The object under discussion sat on a chrome cradle, suspended above the bench and lit from overhead by a ring of LEDs. It didn't need highlighting like that to reveal just how humble a piece of hardware it was - nowhere near as flash as the bracer John Gage had worn. Its metal plates, which usually clung to my arm like a steel lobster, were scuffed. One of them was dangling. One of them was bent. The non-scratch touch-screen was scored and pitted with wear. It was a wreck of a thing, but it was my soul-mate.

'That's my property,' I told Tyler.

The man's dark eyes glinted oddly as his gaze swung in my direction.

'I'm well aware of that, Mr Nixon,' he said. 'Good to see you back, by the way.'

Good to see me back? Yeah, the hell it was.

My lip curled and I looked away before I could say something to tempt Beck to put me back in their hospital wing.

Good to see me back. Wasn't that long ago Tyler had stood watching, while I'd been forced to my knees and murdered. Hell, it had been his idea! Yeah, they'd revived me. Me, not Dietrich. But it's not a good feeling, being in that moment. Might be something Geoff Tyler could forget in a heartbeat. My memory's not so selective.

Tyler had already turned away, focussed on the bracer again.

'Now you're here,' he said over his shoulder. 'We have Karl Dietrich locked inside your bracer and your friend's bespoke application won't let him out again. I'm assuming he's told you how to access it?'

I shook my head, not as a negative, but in disbelief.

'Why the hell would you want to access it? Why would you want to access *him*? Man's a serial killer, a psychopath. He killed seven schoolgirls while he was alive. He killed another six people and tried to kill more while he was dead. He's fucking dangerous! Leave him in there to rot!'

'Hmmm. Not possible, I'm afraid. We rather need him.'

'You *what*? Why?'

It was the chief technician who answered. 'It's invaluable research,' he said. 'What Dietrich can tell us about existing as a digitised entity could save billions of Euros, years of study. It could kick off a whole new branch of investigation.'

I stared at him until he blanched. Until Geoff Tyler stirred himself from where he'd been studying my bracer and turned away from the bench.

'Mr Nixon your co-operation–'

'You're going to give him what he wants,' I realised. 'A body. Oh, you've let me keep mine. Thanks *so* much for that. But you're going to put that butcher in someone else's cadaver, just like he wanted.'

I took a step towards him. Give him his due, he didn't back away.

'How much did he pay you?' I wanted to know. 'He said he did. So what the hell did he offer you to make that prospect even remotely attractive? Or are you just so blinded by your own, or this company's, ambition you'd risk letting that monster out? What kind of man are you, anyway? What kind of slimy son-of-a bitch would even consider–?'

'Nix.' Beck's shiny hand was on my shoulder, warning.

I considered turning and punching the mindless goon's lights out, right there, but I didn't have room. No space for my fist to get up a good swing, and Beck deserved more than just a tickle. I shook free of his grip.

'Um...' The chief technician was holding his hand up like a school kid. He waited for me to look at him. 'I can assure you, we've no intention of using this particular Mephistopheles pattern to animate one of the volunteers.'

'Volunteers?' I sneered. 'Corpses, you mean. Just say it. You're animating the *dead*!'

The man flinched at my vehemence, cleared his throat.

'One of the corpses, as you say. You have my guarantee - throughout this research Karl Dietrich's persona pattern will remain digitised, contained in our data banks. We can access him via a virtual reality, we don't need him in person. He won't know the difference and he won't be able to do anything about it even if he does. We know he's too dangerous - he won't be used for animating anyone. Trust me, we'll keep him secure.'

'Right. Until someone else like Joseph Samuels comes along and decides he'd quite like a new yacht.'

The man shook his head. 'We'll be stepping up security on the storage facility. No one will be able to steal Dietrich, or any other persona, ever again. And now we're aware of the bracer signal problem, we can fix it. There'll be no more body switching. I guarantee it.'

'Mr Nixon,' Tyler could barely contain his sigh. 'We can't release your bracer to you while a valuable and, as you point out, dangerous entity is contained inside it. If you want it back, you'll have to let us have him.'

I laughed. 'You're holding my bracer to ransom?'

Tyler shot me his cool smile. 'Not ransom, security. How would you feel if it was *me* walking around with Dietrich stored on my bracer?'

'More to the point,' Beck said from where he stood behind me. 'How would you feel walking around with him stuck to your arm?'

'And can you guarantee Sitaroo Man's programme won't leak?' Tyler added. 'Do you really want him corrupting your bracer?'

It was my turn to sigh. The bastards were right. For all those reasons, and more, I didn't want to keep Dietrich on my bracer a second longer than I had to.

'Okay. Hand it here, I'll unlock Rooinator.'

I pointed at my bracer, waggled my fingers until someone unhooked it from the workbench. I wriggled the kinetic loops down to the base of my fingers, turned my wrist and clicked the plates together.

One of the nerds was already waiting with a cable. No sending this one over the ether, Dietrich would go down the tube, directly into their data bank where, presumably, there was a nice, warm, digital cell waiting for him. The technician plugged the cable into the port on my bracer and stood back, looked at me expectantly.

'Ready when you are,' Tyler said.

The code to unlock Rooinator was the same as the one used to prime it. I tapped it in, pinched the window shut, opened a new one and tapped again. In the bottom right corner an icon was glimmering - the progress wedge - showing Dietrich draining away, off my bracer.

The process was almost half-way done, when one of the techies tapped the smart-glass plate in front of him, shuffled through a few screens.

'Excuse me, sir?'

Tyler turned, but the man had been talking to his own boss.

'What?'

'Something's not right.'

'What's going on?' Tyler demanded. 'What's not right?'

The technician gestured at his screen. 'I can't find him.'

Tyler bumped my shoulder in his haste to brush past. He leaned his hand on the console behind the desk, bent over the man's screen.

'The file's not coming through. That's an old bracer, but the download should be showing up by now.'

The guy's chief had gone to the man's other shoulder. He was already flicking screens, tapping the input box, interrogating the data bank - searching with rising panic to discover where Dietrich's Mephistopheles was being sent.

I glanced at my wrist, still trailing its white cable. The Rooinator was three-quarters empty.

'You've lost him?' Tyler demanded. 'It's a hard download! How can you lose him?'

The technician shrugged helplessly. He pointed at his screen. 'He should be there. The system's working perfectly. He should be *there*! I don't understand it.'

Tyler blinked, turned to stare at me. His dark eyes narrowed and he shoved the chief tech aside, headed in my direction. I let him grab my wrist. Let him turn it over to look at my bracer screen. What was left of Dietrich was a tiny nibble in the corner of an empty cheese wedge.

'Where?' he wanted to know. 'Where did you send him?'

See, it goes to show. Tyler was so fixated on getting Dietrich, it never occurred to him, even then. But I'd had my fill of trusting these guys. And I'd had more than enough of Dietrich.

Pity he'd never know. Dietrich. He'd never know who finally killed him. Deleted him. The last thing he'd remember was uploading himself through Sitaroo's bracer and into mine. But Rooinator intercepted him. *Tyler's* plan, I knew that now. And there I was, thinking it was mine. Should've kept quiet about Rooinator. Shouldn't have trusted Beck. Of course, Tyler had very different ideas about what would happen to Dietrich once he was captured than I'd had.

Fuck knows how he imagined he was going to interrogate him once he'd been stored inside the Synapware data bank, but he obviously had ideas about that, too. Maybe he intended to keep him - a bunch of ones and zeros trying to make sense of themselves - forever more. I had no problem with that, aside from hating the idea that Dietrich still existed.

But there was always the risk. Someone, one day, would try to bring him back. As a programme, as a zombie, maybe even as a weapon. Well, I wasn't having it.

'Shouldn't have fucked me over,' I said. 'Do that to me, I get all petty.'

25

Whatever I expected Tyler to do once he realised I'd deleted Dietrich, he didn't do it. In fact, he didn't do much at all. He stared at me some. Which got to be creepy. Then he just sighed.

'You're right,' he said. 'I shouldn't have fucked you over. I'll remember next time.'

Next time.

He really thought there'd be a next time? Another Dietrich? Another of Synapware's research projects gone rogue? Another opportunity for me and him to work anything resembling together? I didn't think so.

Beck pulled me out of there by my arm - away from Tyler and the stunned-looking nerds.

Back in the corridor I noticed something I'd missed on the way here.

'Where'd the creeps go?'

Twice I'd seen them, down here in Life Extension. Two guards with royal insignia collar-buttons and humourectomy scars. Now they were gone. Patches of tarry scuff-marks on the corridor floor showed where their combat boots had stood. Now, aside from that, the door was identifiable only by skin scan.

Beck gave me another impatient shove with his prosthetic arm. 'You're already in the shit, stop sticking your nose where it doesn't belong.'

Anyone who's ever known a detective, even a former one, would know that's like telling ice not to melt in a desert. Wasn't so much the guards I was wondering about. It was the room's occupant. He'd been in Switzerland for two years. In seclusion, so the news said. Well, I knew one thing. This was seclusion all right, but it sure as hell wasn't

Switzerland.

'What happened to him, anyway?' I said.

Because if the king was being treated down here, hooked up to all those machines, he had to be terminally ill, if not already dead.

'Really,' Beck told me. 'Shut up.'

'Hey, I signed that special secret stuff, too. How come you get to know, but I don't?'

'What makes you think I know?'

'You know everything,' I said. 'You're Tyler's pet.'

'What makes you think *he* knows?'

I left it there.

*

Beck didn't speak again until we were aboard the company chopper and heading back to civilisation. He sat in his plush leather seat - the one opposite me - and stared out the window while we tilted off the helipad and headed out over pewter waves I couldn't see through the blacked-out glass.

I stretched my legs out, wriggled my butt in the seat, settled back further.

'I reckon he thought about killing you,' Beck said the second I closed my eyes.

I didn't need to ask who he was talking about. I sighed, peeled my eyelids open again.

'Well, he needn't hurry about making his mind up. I intend to carry on living, regardless of what Geoff Tyler does or doesn't want.'

'He already made his mind up. You get to live. Or I'd be pushing your body out the door about now.'

Or uploading some digitally stored 'volunteer' into it, I could have said.

Instead, I laughed. 'I love that about you guys. Really. I'm touched.'

'Well, don't go buying chocolates. If you pull any shit like that again, *ever*, you won't get to live. I'm not kidding, Nix. Tyler's not what you think he is. He belongs to Synapware, body and...' he waved a hand. '...whatever. He doesn't go home at night and worry about this shit like we do. Trust me.'

'Another friendly warning?'

'Exactly.'

'Why bother? Why work for him, if "this shit" plays so much on your conscience? What button did he push to make you sign *your* body and soul over to him? Because that's what you're like. You do everything he says. Anything he says. If he'd told you to cancel Rooinator up on the Rhondda, you would have, wouldn't you? You're like his dog. Barking to order.'

Beck didn't like that. He stiffened in his chair, flicked his gaze to the chopper's blank window then back to me again.

'My "buttons" have nothing to do with it,' he said. 'Just remember. You don't get to leave Synapware just because you don't like the smell of their poop. You signed triple S. That means they have to keep you close, or make sure you're not in a position to tell anyone anything you've learned in their employ.'

Great. I'd forgotten that. Breaching Tyler's contract might be enough to get me fired, but the first thing I'd ever done where Synapware was concerned was sign the Special States Secrets Act. Forget what I knew about Synapware itself. Those two patches of scuff marks on the corridor floor reminded me I already knew more than the entire European States wanted me to. I wasn't getting out of this shit in a hurry.

*

In Britain, in summer, sunrise comes early. Four in the morning, give or take a few minutes. The tide was full and the thinnest shred of moon hung in the orange sky like an angel feather about to drift to earth. Its bright curve was poised high above the Synapware building as I entered, this time unimpeded by either the security turret or the Wolf Line guard seated at the desk. My entry came courtesy of an unseen, unheard conversation between my bracer and the building, which opened the central pair of double doors for me as I approached.

I tried not to look surprised.

You work for them now, Nix. You're authorised.

Employees arriving at any time of the day or night must have been routine here because, aside from a brief glance up from her bracer, the guard ignored me.

I had on an old pair of sneakers - my Italian shoes would never walk again. The sense of trauma I'd always expected to feel when those shoes went the way of the recycle cart was still pending. Guess I was already too traumatised.

The trauma might still be there, but it was currently in the background - I had other issues right now. Issues which put so much tension in my jaw my teeth felt ready to crumble under the pressure. I opened my mouth, worked the knot loose for the dozenth time.

The guard had already forgotten me and the sneakers were quiet on the foyer's shiny floor. She didn't hear me approach the desk, didn't see me reach round to my hip for the Sandman. She only looked up when I was standing right over her and the dart was in her neck before she had time to move. I went round her side of the desk, caught her before she slid to the floor. I settled her back in the chair so she wouldn't flop forward and hit something that might activate the security system.

I made a visual sweep - automatic reflex. Confirmed it with my bracer's original version of Sikum. Nothing. No one but me and the guard on this level and no one but the building to see what I'd just done. And those AIs were never that smart. Knock out its human security, the building wouldn't notice. Deface one of those nice marble tiles it would arm all its systems, call the police.

The elevator was at the back of the foyer, past some shrubbery and a pair of ornate columns. It was whisper-quiet and fast. Two seconds later the door opened on the floor I wanted.

I took some long breaths, blew the adrenaline rush away.

I'd tried. Tried to sleep, put a little distance between finding out and acting. Fact I was here now was testament to how that had gone.

Beck had mentioned somewhere along the line - the guy always left work late, started again at stupid O'clock. That was why I was here now, before the rest of the world was even yawning. Wanted to get here before him, compose myself. Be seated at that glass desk. Maybe have my feet up on it, leaning back in the chair, all nonchalant, when he arrived.

But Geoff Tyler was already there.

Figures.

Man had a knack for changing the game.

The desk's glass interface was a shimmer of light at this angle, the images passing around its edge so oblique they were just moving patterns. The colours they gave off glimmered on his face as he flicked files aside, opened folders, pinched them closed. His fingers moved

High Tide in the City

faster and more expertly than even Ginnie Plummer's down at Parson Street. Faster, maybe, than I'd ever seen anyone work on a desktop.

I was mildly impressed.

The man paused mid file-flick, looked up.

'Mr Nixon.' The smooth features crinkled only the slightest amount - Nanoxed muscles unwilling to accommodate his frown. 'I wasn't expecting you this morning.'

'I know you weren't. I wanted to make sure your hound was still in his kennel before I did this.'

Tyler pursed his lips, took his eyes off the Sandman pointed in his direction and shook his head. 'I don't follow.'

I waggled my left wrist, indicating my bracer. 'Interesting, what you can do with one of these.'

For a second Tyler's eyes widened and I took it for hopeful.

'No,' I said. 'Dietrich's really gone. I erased his ass, just like I said.'

The man tapped his desk, shut down whatever he was looking at and sat back in his chair, laced his fingers together across his stomach. I had to admire his cool. No Sandman's lethal, but they can sure as hell make you helpless and, as I'd recently found out, that's no fun at all. Right now he had one pissed-off bastard in front of him, ready for some payback.

'Are we in any danger of your getting to the point?' he wanted to know. 'I *am* rather busy.'

I glanced from the desk, to him, to over my shoulder. I'd been slow there. Chances were Tyler had just alerted the building. The AI might be able to ignore a human act which didn't affect it - being told about one was a different story. I shrugged inwardly. Tyler's suit would have already warned it something was up anyway, since the smart fabric was bound to register his heightened anxiety - sweat, pulse, muscle-tension. He was hiding the symptoms well, though. Guess he was confident someone would come save him.

Fact is, what I was doing right now was one of those impulse things I'm sometimes afflicted by. Meant I hadn't done much research before getting here. Going off 'half-cocked', Lian used to say. Someone with more forward planning would have checked how this building ran outside office hours. I hadn't. If it wasn't for Sikum telling me otherwise, there could be a whole army of Wolf Line guards sitting somewhere nearby - drinking coffee, playing dice - while they waited for the chance to do some ass-kicking. They had to be somewhere, though. Probably on their way right now.

Yeah. Time I got to the point.

'I was aiming to be waiting for you when you got to work this morning. Wasn't expecting you to be here already, but, hey. All that does is tell me a man like you doesn't have a life. Or friends.' *Great getting to the point, Nix.* 'Okay. Maybe I don't have many friends, either. But I have people who watch my back some. Do me favours. That's why when Chief Inspector Alexander told me I was fired because some good citizen had handed in a used squirt gun, I had one of my friends check out the security footage for me.'

Tyler remained unflustered. I'd already noticed that about him. In the face of what he knew I was about to say, he didn't bat an eyelid. So, hell with it. No point boring myself, or him.

'Why?' I said. 'That's all I want to know. Why get me fired?'

Didn't know as he was dirty.

The Brutant prem's words had come back to me a dozen times since I'd accessed the file Plummer had finally sent me. The one I'd received while I'd been getting ready to die on top of the pylon. I'd seen the flashing icon waiting there, blurry beneath the rain-soaked screen. Wasn't till I got my bracer back and had the solitude to access it at my apartment that I'd seen the footage and figured out who the Brutant had really been talking about all those days ago.

Didn't know as he was dirty. I'd assumed he meant a cop - Dietrich inside a cop and acting dirty. I'd known something hadn't smelt right - Dietrich always worked alone. But who else would have had the balls, and the money, to pay Brutants to squirt me? Then look who hands in the very same injector they did it with?

'As we agreed when I recruited you, Mr Nixon, the police would consider your working for both them and Synapware a conflict of interests. I said I'd take care of the situation and I did.'

'*Took care of it?*' A rush of anger took me further into the room, the Sandman aimed at his skull. I halted directly in front of the desk, hand shaking with fury.

'Did you care that I was an ex-addict? Were you bothered what being squirted would do to me? Hell, fuck that! Fuck what it left the police to think! What it did to my career! I was ready to leap off the Clifton Bridge! I could easily be dead right now.'

'Nonsense. I sent Beck to retrieve you. I wouldn't have let anything happen to you, any more than I let anything happen at the solar farm, despite your best efforts to get yourself shot.'

My jaw dropped at that one.

'I need your expertise, Mr Nixon. You're an asset. I don't waste assets.'

I somehow found my voice. 'Would have been easier if I'd never found out about this, though, right?'

'Okay, Mr Nixon. Fine. You got me. Guilty as charged. You've had your opportunity to vent, now put your gun away and let me get on with my work.'

I was over the desk before he could react, jeans sliding on the slick glass, feet thudding down right next to him. I grabbed the lapel of his expensive suit and hauled him out of his chair, shoved the business end of the Sandman under his chin. Annoyed me that he just let me do it. Like he didn't mind.

Such fucking arrogance! Even so I threw a quick glance at the door. How long did it take Wolf Line security to get their act together, anyway?

'Do you think I'm worried what that thing can do to me?' Tyler wanted to know.

'No. But you should be worried what *I'm* going to do to you once I've pulled the trigger.'

I shoved him hard enough to make him stagger back. His left foot caught on a leg of the desk and he stumbled further. Even so, he didn't take his eyes off me. Even when the tall solar-glass window he fell against developed a web-like crack as he collided with it, he kept eye contact, stayed unruffled.

Infuriating as hell.

'Trust me,' I said. 'Paralysed isn't unconscious. You'll know everything that's happening to you. And you'll feel it.'

Tyler gave his tight little smile. Yeah. He actually *smiled*.

'So this isn't about the Brutants. It's about me selling you to Dietrich. Or maybe it's about your being kept out of the loop?'

I charged forward, rammed my forearm against his throat so his head went back and hit the glass, making a second, smaller web.

'It's about *all* of it you piece of shit!'

Tyler stayed unfazed. Worse, he didn't seem to get my point at all. As if, in his mind, the fact someone could stack one outrage on top of another and use it as motive was impossible.

'If I'd told you my plan, you'd have behaved differently on the pylon,' he said. 'Dietrich's not stupid. He wouldn't have believed it. He wouldn't have voluntarily uploaded himself to your bracer.'

I snorted. 'Thanks for explaining. Makes me feel much better.'

'Mr Nixon. We both know you're no murderer. You might be prepared to kill to save another life, but to extinguish one from vengeance?'

'You believe that?' I asked him. 'Do you? Really? What, you think my deleting Dietrich instead of handing him over to you was a mistake? A typo?'

'At the very least, that act puts us even. You made me look extremely stupid back there. The huge resources channelled into finding him were my responsibility, and one of my employees just wipes him? Lost. All that potential research. How do you think that made me look?'

I stared at him, dumbstruck. Not sure he even noticed. He was still talking.

'So, put the gun away now. Let's stop this stupidi–'

He might have said more, I guess. Except the butt of my Sandman smashed him in the mouth. I adjusted my grip on his jacket, waiting for him to sag. Instead he just stood there, head twisted oddly towards the window. Then he turned to face me.

'Under normal circumstances,' he said. 'That would require a level seven response. But I'm making allowances for the fact that you don't actually know what you're dealing with. To ensure something like that doesn't ever happen again, I'll now educate you.'

Tyler's hands came up between mine with such blinding speed my arms flew outwards. Then he grabbed me. The world tilted and the wall ten feet behind came forward and slammed me in the back. I collapsed to the floor, winded. Rolled over, struggling to get my knees under me. Had to use the wall for balance as I clambered to my feet. I shook my head, desperate to clear my vision while my mind was still trying to figure out what had just happened.

I straightened up in time to see Tyler, still standing by the spider-web cracks in the window, shrug his jacket back onto his shoulders. He straightened his tie, used his fingers to comb a dislodged lock of hair back in place.

His eyes showed nothing when they fixed back on me but they had that odd glint in them I'd noticed a couple of times. Something not quite right about that glint. The instant he stepped towards me I raised the Sandman so it was aimed at his face again. The man slid his gaze to it, shook his head.

'You still haven't worked it out?' he said.

There were at least fifteen feet between him and where I stood. He leapt across them so fast I barely had time to snap off the paralyser dart before he barrelled into me. I struck the wall with at least as much force as last time and fell, winded, onto plush carpet, plaster sprinkling onto my back. Tyler was there before I could muster the strength to raise my head. His left hand, cold and unexpectedly solid, snaked around my throat. He lifted me off my feet one-handed, slammed me back against the damaged wall and held me there.

I kicked out, found shin. Tyler tightened his fingers. Hard pads pressed against my carotid, making the world darken. Desperate, I slammed my forearm against his, did it again when I failed to break his grip.

'Stop that, Mr Nixon. You're being rather silly.'

Instead of tightening further Tyler's fingers relaxed, though he kept them wrapped round my neck as he lowered my feet to the floor.

He reached up with his free hand, plucked the paralyser dart from his cheek. He turned it between his fingers for a second then tossed it aside.

'That made a hole,' he said peevishly. 'Rather annoying.'

He finally let go of my neck, leaving me to collapse, gagging, turned his back on me and returned to his desk. 'I'm impressed by your reaction speed, though,' he said, sitting down. 'I calculated a three percent chance you'd hit me in the time you had to aim and fire.'

I wasn't paying attention. I was still on my knees, the dart he'd just discarded lying inches from my nose.

'You issued me with dud rounds?' Another indignity.

Tyler grunted. 'They seemed to work all right on *you*, as I recall.'

Okay, so he was right about that. And I was using the same clip I'd loaded before Dietrich got hold of the Sandman and shot me with it. Not empty darts, then. But what the hell kind of ammo would work on me but not Tyler?

I clambered to my feet, swayed a moment, then followed him over to the desk.

Tyler was still prodding the injury to his cheek with the manicured fingers he'd nearly snuffed my life with. The wound was like he said. A hole. There was no blood, and it opened and closed as he moved the skin around, like it was a tear. Watching him sit there, fascinated by it, I had the unnerving feeling there was more to Tyler than I'd ever suspected.

'Exactly what the hell *are* you?'

He finally stopped tampering, turned his attention to me, and his smile was back.

'I'm rather flattered you haven't worked it out,' he said. 'Officially I rank an eight on the Turing scale. The fact you've taken this long to realise I'm not human pushes that towards a nine, if not higher.'

An avalanche of clues dumped themselves unceremoniously into my forebrain and pieced themselves together, albeit at tad late.

'You're an artificial,' I said.

'I prefer the term synthetic. Artificial has connotations of prosthetics. And I'm much more than that.'

I cleared my throat, massaged my neck. The fight had gone out of me and it had nothing to do with realising I was up against an artificial - way more sophisticated than Constable Jasper or the Constabulary's other robot policeman, but still an artificial. Faster, stronger, smarter than me.

I found a chair, dropped into it and let the Sandman fall into my lap.

Tyler was good. Whatever generation he was, he was way beyond anything I thought they could make. The skin could almost be real. So I'd assumed that Nanoxed look was just that and dismissed it. Easy enough mistake. Body language emulator was premium, too - yeah, he smiled too often, and not genuinely enough and inappropriately, but there were plenty of geeks out there with a lot worse social skills. Beyond that, he had to be one of the most capable artificial sentients I'd ever come across. Aside from the skin and that odd glint in his eyes he'd pretty much fooled me, and I had a lot of experience sizing people up.

'What way *do* you view yourself, then?' I wanted to know.

'I'm Geoff Tyler. I work as Liaison Manager for Synapware Labs. I consider myself mid-thirties. Unmarried, no children.'

I had to grin. 'No kids? You planning any in the future?'

He smiled back. 'Oh, I'm pretty sure there'll be offspring. My specifications aren't on general release as yet, mainly because of my evolution mode. I learn on my own, you see, and Synapware are anxious to monitor how that goes. But so far, I'm doing admirably. Still a bit to learn, as I'm sure you'll attest to, but I'll get there. And when I do, there'll be offspring. Lots of them.'

'*Jesus*!'

'That worries you, does it? Don't. My purpose - at least, my progenies' purpose - will be deep space exploration. It's cheaper to create synthetics like me, who can withstand the rigours of vacuum and high-G acceleration, than build ships constrained in design to accommodate a human's more limited specifications. Once they've got the EM shielding sorted, we'll be ideal explorers. Robust, impartial, able to think and decide for ourselves under the most extreme conditions. We'll be the ones, Mr Nixon, who explore these new worlds people seem so keen on finding. We'll be the ones who tame them, adapt them for human habitation.'

'So you're superior to us?'

Tyler emulated a sigh and shook his head. 'I'll say the same thing to you that I said to Mr Beck. I may be stronger, faster, more resilient to physical danger, but I struggle to understand why that should make me superior.'

With your IQ? Yeah. Course you do.

'Really? How come?'

'I will never love. I'll never have sex, never taste anything, never feel sensations or recognise beauty. I'll never experience joy or pain, happiness or grief. Yet I know these are things of extraordinary value. I've witnessed human reactions to emotions and sensations, so I know their power and yet I will never experience or understand them. They've been denied to me. Not deliberately, but because of what I am. In every way possible that tells me I'm inferior to any human you care to point at.'

'Good answer.' Rehearsed, of course.

Tyler leant his elbows on the glass desk. 'Now, as I said. I have work to do. I'll be in touch about your next assignment. Good day, Mr Nixon.'

EPILOGUE

It was the same pub as last time and the nearest order-plate, fitted into the polished wooden bar I leant on, was beside my right elbow. So I couldn't help but notice the badly-scuffed combat bracer thump down onto it. If I didn't recognise that, the shiny black arm it was attached to identified its owner. The display lit up, glaring the menu and payment options into my face. The bracer's owner selected a chilled beer, winced as he lowered his left arm back into the sling it was cradled in.

I almost said sorry. Sorry for getting him shot. Then realised I wasn't sorry at all.

Beck waited till his order was accepted and paid for then swivelled the barstool he'd somehow acquired - despite their scarcity in the busy pub - and turned to look at me.

The room was loud and I wasn't inclined to yell over the noise, so I called him through my bracer. Took two attempts, since my fingers weren't in a co-operative mood. Beck watched, a sardonic expression on his face. I knew what he was thinking. The bleary squint and the head-wobble as I hit 'send' must have confirmed it for him.

'You drunk?' he wanted to know when the call went through.

I held up the fourth - or maybe fifth - scotch I was drinking, pulled a sour grin from somewhere.

'What else is there to do? I can't get squirted, can I?'

He twitched an eyebrow. 'I guess not.'

'What the hell do you want, anyway?'

Beck lifted the beer that had risen from the bar's delivery system, tilted it to his mouth. He sucked foam off his lips.

'Just looking out for my buddy, that's all.'

'Right,' I snorted and lifted my hand, waved it to indicate the room in general. 'Well. Only person in here you might have a remote connection to is the guy you killed not so long ago. And he's not your buddy.'

Beck sighed. 'We did this already, didn't we?'

'I want to do it again.'

'Let it go, Nix.'

I winced as another gulp of fiery liquid seared the back of my throat.

'Why are you really here?' I growled. 'And cut the bullshit about my health and well being. We both know that for the crap it is.'

Beck shrugged, dropped the pretence. 'I guess I got something on my mind.'

'Really? You? You have a conscience?'

He pulled a face at the sarcasm. 'Not especially. I don't do guilt either, so knock it off.'

He stopped there. Ran his thumbnail over the smart label on the bottle in his hand, lost in thought.

I had nothing to add, so I focused blearily on the screen across the bar from us. News report. Some pubs feature sports, this one always ran the news. Meant you got a different clientele in here. Business types - smart suits, expensive shoes. Right now the screen was running a live report.

Tall, slim guy. Greying at the temples. He stood on a balcony next to his wife and waved to a thousand cheering people gathered in the square below him. I wondered how they'd got the face on his new body looking like him so quick.

Dead bodies don't heal.

Meant His Majesty's new body might not have been dead while they did the surgery. Didn't like where that line of thought took me. I skipped past it, grateful my capacity for denial was still in working order.

The TV was silenced out, but the flashing number in the bottom right corner told you where you could tune in through your bracer to get the audio.

Well, Beck could pray over his beer forever if he wanted. If he had something to tell me, I wasn't in any mood to sit here and pull it out of him. Besides, until he'd arrived I'd been enjoying the warm buzz of alcohol in my system. Now it felt uncomfortable.

I hit the number for the audio, just as Beck started speaking.

I wasn't interested in the news report. I already knew what it was going to say. Even so, I waited a few heartbeats before muting the sound again.

'Hell, why am I even asking?' Beck was saying. 'I doubt you'll tell me anyway. Forget it.'

'Forget what?'

Beck took another pull on the bottle, smacked his lips. 'Told you I lost my wife, didn't I?'

I gave a sigh.

'You did. And I used to be a detective. We're trained to remember stuff like that.'

He leaned towards me.

'I have to know,' he said. 'Tyler offered you the choice. You had the chance to save her.'

I glanced away quicker than I meant to. Beck might not do guilt, but I did. 'We're talking about Lian, right?'

'Who else?'

I was annoyed. Not just at the direction this conversation had gone, but annoyed Beck knew. He knew I'd had to make a choice. But, clearly, he didn't know everything.

'You mean there's something Tyler didn't share with you? Man, that must be frustrating.'

'Don't be a dick. I need to know what you decided. And why.'

'You *need* to know? Since when was it even your business? Why the hell should I–?'

'If my wife was in that situation today, I might have begged Tyler for the chance to save her. Instead, I had to stand there and watch her die. I would have swapped places with her in a second, but I couldn't. Mephistopheles came five years too late!'

'Or she died five years too early,' I pointed out. 'And, face it, would she really want to wake up looking like you?'

Have to hand it to Beck, he took that without flinching. Just rolled his eyes a little, curled his lip. I always read that as contempt. I should know. I've come across it enough times.

I shoved my empty glass away. I hadn't missed it, the slip he'd made. And now I understood what he was really asking.

'You said might.'

'What?'

'You said you *might* have begged Tyler. So you're not sure, are you? Not sure if it's the right thing to do. Put someone you love inside a corpse and expect them to thank you? It's one thing for them to make the choice for themselves, but for someone else to make the choice for them? You tell me, Beck. Would you really have sold her to Synapware?'

He sat back on the stool, face solemn, eyes thoughtful.

'Way I see it,' I went on. 'The real choice is this: Do what they would have wanted you to do, or do what *you* want to do. Be selfless or be selfish. So, since we're such close "buddies", what choice do you think I made for Lian?'

Beck's eyes searched my face, sized me up for a good ten seconds then, 'You let her die.'

I just smiled at that.

Guess he had nothing more to say. Same as me. We left the bracer connection open between us, but we fell quiet, alone with our own thoughts, and watched the news.

There was a dead king on the throne. In less than a year there'd be many more dead people walking the streets. In bodies which had also once been dead. What that world would be like, I could only guess. For my part, I'd be meeting it taking orders from a robot human and partnered to a human robot. With a deceased ex-girlfriend who would probably be looking for some payback.

There's this ancient Chinese curse.

May you live an interesting life.

Had to wonder. Just when had I gone and pissed off a Chinese witch doctor?

Enjoy a taste of a further title from this author.

Blightspawn

By

Martine Lillycrop

THE END

Mum always said I came into this world kicking and screaming. She said I'd go out the same way. *Old Grim will have to grab you by the collar, Bethany Sweet,* she'd say, *and drag you off hissing and spitting.* I believed her - I was too selfish, too curious about life, too downright pig-headed to go out any other way. But in the end it wasn't like that. In the end I went without a fuss.

I've never been religious but I've always believed in an afterlife. I mean, mostly I've always taken things at face value - we're born, we live, we die. But if I ever stopped to think about it, it was always there. An afterlife of some kind. Heaven. Hell. Coming back as a slug. So when I died, maybe I shouldn't have been so surprised to wake up again.

But that wasn't my biggest surprise.

Waking up - my Awakening - was just the start. I had no idea, when I opened my eyes after thinking I'd closed them for the very last time, how much expectation can differ from reality. Well, experience is a bitch. Likes to kick you in the bum, just when you least expect it.

So now, here I am, about to die all over again. Only this time it's going to be a lot easier. And a lot harder.

Easier because it'll mean something this time.

My death will save lives. It'll save an entire world. This time, too, I make the choice. I have that opportunity. I can sacrifice myself willingly.

The problem is, my life isn't the most valuable thing I have to lose this time.

But I'll sacrifice even that. I'll do it.

Because dying here, right now, is the right thing to do.

Chapter 1

Something warm pulsed against my throat. It was uncomfortable, in the way wet socks are uncomfortable when they squelch inside your shoes. Then an ugly sound, like bubble-wrap popping, erupted next to my ears. Something fell away from my neck and warmth seeped down, dampened my hair.

'There go the tubes!' The voice was male, nervous.

I cracked my eyes open, blinked them clear of sleep-grit and found myself in a dim-lit room - leather and wood with tarnished brass fittings. It smelled of dust and flowers. No windows, so I had no sense of day or night, but hazy lights above me - made hazier by gum-ridden eyes - gave just enough light to see by.

At first the room looked circular. The illusion was partly down to the lighting, partly the vitreous material the walls were built from. Another couple of eye-blinks and an effort to focus harder showed me the room had corners. Six of them. And the bricks were shiny, run through with exotic colours, like oil on water. I was surrounded by banks of equipment straight from a Jules Verne novel. It pumped and clicked quietly to itself while I lay on a hard leather table trying to work out which hospital this was.

I'd heard the voice, but it hadn't registered. When I tried sitting up, though, I discovered strong hands were clasping my shoulders. They shifted, gripped harder, held me still.

It took a total stranger holding me down to finally produce the reaction my mum would have expected. I screamed and bucked hard, tried to throw myself off the narrow table. But the man was stronger and he had the advantage. He was standing over me.

One of my thrashing heels found something yielding and I heard an angry yell.

'Gish!' The man above me said. 'She's awake.'

A second man used the equipment positioned near my feet to prise himself off his knees while working the jaw I'd just kicked. He glared angrily. First at his companion. Then at me.

'I *know*,' he said.

He leaned across to thumb a row of switches, cranked a lever, checked a rank of dials set into walnut veneer, then paused. He peered at me through a fringe of hair the colour of steel and drew the back of his hand across his mouth. It came away streaked with blood. Something unpleasant flickered across his features and then he looked away, nodded to his companion.

'Start the timer, Salic.'

The second man, Salic, released my shoulders and picked his way around the clutter of wires and tubing strewn across the floor. His attention was already on the door straight ahead. As he moved, he fumbled under the hair at his collar, feeling for a chain around his neck.

A tug and what he was after slid through his shirt opening. It was a sphere, golf-ball-sized, and it swung on its blackened, rusting chain until he snatched it into his fist. He shook it, squeezed it - did something - and the sphere came to life - glowed yellow, started clicking.

Gish reached over and grabbed my wrist.

'Don't talk, girl. Don't struggle. Just do as you're told. Got it?'

He didn't wait for me to answer. He hauled me off the table and dragged me, stumbling, through the doorway, yanking so hard my shoulder-joint clunked. I caught a brief flash of hairy thigh as the sudden movement caused his leather kilt to fly upwards.

Weird, isn't it, how it's the little stones which start the avalanche? It took something that stupid to get my mind working. I mean, since when did men wear leather kilts? And, let's be clear, I'm not talking designer-style gay avant-garde, I'm talking about a worn, grubby, greasy, ineptly-stitched and badly-cut flap of leather.

Since when did men wear kilts like that? Never. That's when.

It took seeing it for me to come to my senses. This was too bizarre, too weird. Not just the kilt, everything. Weird as in seriously, totally, insanely weird. Okay, granted this whole situation was odd, but the sense of disorientation was more profound than that. There was something wrong - deeply wrong - about me.

'Wait!' *My voice. Wrong.* 'What are you doing? Where am...ow!'

'Shut up!' Salic had taken up position behind me. He shoved me in the back, knocking me into Gish, who cursed.

As my head lurched forward, a curtain of pale hair fell over my face. I twisted in Gish's grip, managed to grab a strand before he could yank me again.

See, that's what I mean about something being wrong with me. I mean really wrong. Completely. The hair couldn't be mine. I mean, blonde? I wasn't blonde - never had been. And I couldn't stand long hair. Yet I now possessed a head of long, creamy waves. Gish tugged my wrist again, making the hair snag between my fingers, proving it was attached to me by the roots.

The staircase outside - hexagonal rather than spiral - was one of those which turns forever out of sight, the end always lost beyond the next corner. It appeared we were at the top, because the stairs ended at the room we'd just left. What I took for dim, rounded light bulbs were positioned on the exterior walls at regular intervals. The steps ran around a thick post occupying the central well. Gurgling pipes, cables and power supplies coiled and pulsed around the post like fat worms.

'What is this place?' I tried clearing my throat, but my voice still sounded wrong. 'Where are you taking me?'

They didn't answer. Neither did they let up - tugging and prodding me downwards until I had no time for more questions. Or even for thought. My lungs were soon raw and the soles of my bare feet burned from having nothing but grit between them and cold stone.

Goaded into too much haste, I slipped and fell face-first onto the gap between the pipes and the stairs, glimpsed a dizzying view of what lay below and cried out. Countless turns, an endless spiral and no sign of the ground. The gap was too small for me to fall through, though, and I was pulled back, shaken by the arm and snarled at so fiercely I nearly slipped again.

'Gish!'

The younger man pushed the sphere under the other's nose. It had stopped glowing yellow, was flickering orange. While they stared at it - and I gasped for breath - the flickering stopped and the ball became solid orange.

Gish said nothing. Instead, he yanked my arm again, pulling me onwards. 'Keep going, Salic. We can do this!'

To my disbelief, they increased their pace, their bullying, prodding, pulling becoming more frantic. When the globe turned from orange to red it stopped clicking and started beeping. Gish rummaged into a fold in his shirt, retrieved a dense wad of cotton and stuffed it into my hand.

'If the gas comes, breathe through that,' he said.

The globe died completely at a point just past where my eyes were rolling and my thighs had seized into painful knots.

'Here it comes,' Gish said grimly.

Hissing sounded from under the lip of each stair and yellow mist turned the air hazy. Call it instinct. Whatever the mist was, I knew I didn't want to breathe it. I pushed the cotton wad against my face with my free hand then yelped in surprise as I was hustled through a doorway into sunlight and fresh air.

'We did it!'

Salic punched the air in triumph, then ducked as a deep, visceral sound passed over our heads. I looked up, wondering what the next bewildering thing would be.

The sky above was luminous blue, tufts of brilliant cloud scattered across it. I staggered, trying to follow the tower's straight line upwards and winced at the hexagonal walls - built of the same oil-on-water brick as the room upstairs - shining like a rainbow pillar in the sunlight.

I was grateful when Gish let go, let me sink to my knees on the warm grass. My mind was still confused, dawdling behind events, leaving me unable to think straight. Well, ignorance is bliss, they say. At least until it kills you.

The overhead sound came again. Its vibrations churned my stomach, sent a wave of dread washing along my spine. Looking at the men, though, I think of the three of us I was the least unsettled by it.

That would be the ignorance again.

Salic gave a cry of dismay.

'That's the alarm. They'll be here in a few minutes and we've got to get through the thorns yet!'

'Just keep calm, we'll be fine.'

Still agitated, Salic stooped to grasp my upper arm. He yanked me to my feet, hard fingers digging into my flesh. I twisted, which made him grip harder. The man thrust his face closer to mine.

'Just behave!'

His expression was a little too unhinged for me to hold his gaze, so I let him haul me on shaking legs across the expanse of grass separating the tower's base from the tall hedge surrounding it.

Close up, though, I saw it wasn't a hedge but a wall of twisting, slithering steel blades. The entire thing was in constant motion - its tangled, creeper-like wires coiling and writhing like sharp little maggots. The barbs covering every inch of the 'branches' crunched and squealed against each other as they rotated, forming grotesque and deadly-looking blossoms.

'We have to get through there?' I asked.

In answer, Gish tugged a thong on his leather shirt, wormed his fingers into a pocket. He assumed the air of a side-show conjuror as he produced a small glass ball - something like a marble. He balanced the object on his palm and held it up for me to take a look, clearly impressed by his own resourcefulness. I frowned, noticing phantoms of darkness squirming inside the marble and the man's face creased into a grin.

'The Caul ent the only ones able to conjure theotic powers.' He gestured at it elaborately. 'This is a death sentence anywhere in Splyne. *If* they catches me using it.' He winked.

I glanced at the tower again - the hedge surrounding it and the forest surrounding that.

'Splyne? Is that here? This place?'

Gish's self-satisfaction dissolved as the siren sounded again. Turning, he hurled the marble at the hedge. It smashed against a branch and black powder scattered, sifting down through the barbs to the barren soil beneath. Where it touched, wisps of steam trailed off and the deadly thorns stopped turning. A white bloom appeared on them. Gish stepped forward and used his boot. Where they'd turned white, the barbs shattered, crumbled to dust. Before long, a small, irregular gap had appeared in the fence, revealing open forest beyond.

Gish nodded at Salic, who shoved his fist into my hair and dragged me after him through the hole. The man cursed when I didn't move fast enough for him and his consequent yanking caused me to trip and stub my toe against his boot. Once we were through he let go and shook a snarl of ashen strands from his fingers - hair wrenched from my scalp in his eagerness to get through the gap. It drifted like gossamer on a waft of air, until the soft tangle snagged on a rotating thorn and stuck fast.

As soon as Gish had followed us through the barrier, the two set off, forcing me to run between them. I didn't argue - by now I didn't dare. They moved fast, glancing over their shoulders from time to time, presumably looking for signs of pursuit. I yelped and hopped frantically when a sharp twig dug into my already-tender sole, but Salic didn't let me slow, dragged me onwards.

'There are soldiers coming!' Gish growled from my right. 'They won't ask questions. If they catches us, they'll kill us, get it? So keep moving!'

Dappled sunlight strobed across my face as we ran, filtering through the leafy canopy above us. Creepers snagged my ankles, trying to slow me down while my kidnappers bullied me to hurry.

Finally, unknown minutes - possibly hours - later, my legs collapsed from under me and I sprawled onto the damp forest floor with a cry. Gasping for breath, I rolled onto my back, ribs heaving.

As I raised my knees to make it easier to suck in air, the hem of the satin shift I'd woken up wearing slid up my thigh. I tugged it down again quickly, but Salic had already noticed.

'Get up, girl!' He looked away, flustered. 'You... Don't you care that... if they find us?'

Gish laid a steadying hand on Salic's arm as he stepped past him. 'Easy. There's no sign of pursuit.'

The older man's eyes were fixed on me and his expression stirred a cold, uncomfortable feeling in my belly. I was already forcing my weary body to sit upright. Now I straightened the dress, feeling vulnerable.

'Why don't you check?' Salic was scanning the surrounding area, anxious to confirm what Gish had told him.

Gish turned to him, taking his eyes off me at last.

'Give her some water.'

Salic had a leather flask attached to his hip. He unhooked it with shaking hands, twisted the stopper free and thrust the flask against my mouth hard enough to bang my lips painfully against my teeth. Nevertheless, I grabbed it and eagerly sucked water down my throat.

Gish, meanwhile, had stuffed his hand into his pocket again and produced another glass orb. It was much bigger than the one he'd used on the hedge and had a metal band around its middle. Like Salic's timer, it glowed when he touched it, but this ball shone white. Gish dropped to his haunches in the centre of the clearing.

Apparently underwear round here was optional. I hastily lifted my gaze to his face while he braced himself on both elbows and cupped the sphere in his palms. Squatting there, he stared into it, the orb's glow lighting his features from below.

This apparently meaningless activity at least gave my head time to stop spinning, gave me time to catch my breath. Plus it kept their attention off me. Even so, I watched, puzzled.

Several minutes passed while Gish stared intently at the glowing object, muttering from time to time. Finally, he raised his eyes to Salic.

'We're clear,' he said.

'No pursuit?'

'None.'

The two men stared at each other as if they couldn't believe it. The underlying air of tension they'd carried with them until now dissolved.

'We did it, then!' Salic was grinning. 'We got the Flower Maiden! I can't believe it!'

He returned the flask to his hip then regarded me intently - possessively.

'Told you, didn't I?' Gish stood up, slid the orb back in his pocket and beckoned to me. 'Up.'

He wasn't expecting protests and he wouldn't get any. Not from me. Not right now. Under his renewed interest, I felt exposed again and wondered why I hadn't tried to run while they were staring, transfixed, at their stupid glass ball. As I climbed to my feet, I remembered one good reason for not running and winced.

Gish nodded. 'I know as you're hurting, lass,' he said. 'And scared. Likely you'll find it hard to believe, but we're trying to help you.'

I'd stopped listening. Salic, the more nervous but also more physically powerful man had sidled closer - positioning himself behind me so he could lean forward and inhale the scent of my hair.

'She smells of flowers.'

Gish grinned. 'Of course she does, idiot!'

'I was just checking.' Salic sniffed at me again, this time letting his face linger in my hair a moment longer. I stepped away from him. His attitude gave me the distinct impression that, whatever Gish claimed, I was far from safe.

Salic closed the gap again. This time he slid his arms around my waist, pulling me firmly back against him.

'Let go!'

Caught between outrage and terror, I tugged at Salic's wrists, trying to prise them away, without success. His companion moved to stand in front of me, studied my face.

'Calm, girl. I needs you to listen,' he said.

'I don't... Just tell me what's going on!'

'You're in grave danger. That's what's going on.'

'Oh God, what are you going to do?'

Gish's fingers trembled as he reached out, captivated, to brush a wisp of hair from my cheek.

I knocked his hand aside. Okay, pure bravado, but it was all I had.

'I knew as the Flower Maiden would be beautiful,' Gish said, as if he hadn't noticed me hit him. 'But not as you'd be so truly...'

The man paused, frowning, and lifted his head. For a moment he studied the line of shrubbery over my shoulder then shrugged.

'I got a weird feeling,' he said, then shook his head. 'We're not going to be doing anything to you, lass. Aside from get you away from here. Long as you behave, you'll come through unharmed.'

'Where are you taking me?'

'Behaving means listening when I say. *So shut up!*'

I blinked. If I needed reminding I was at the mercy of this pair, the man's tone did the job.

'The problem is,' he said. 'Everyone knows your face. By nightfall all Splyne'll be hunting you - and us - counting those Maidgard as we outsmarted at the tower among the top of them.'

'Hunting me?'

'Shut *up*!' It was Salic this time, his voice harsh and hot in my ear. His grip around my waist tightened.

'Not too rough, boy.' Gish looked back at me. 'You was meant to stay in the tower till it's time. But there's those we know as'd like to put a snake in the Cauls' bed, know what I mean? And they got a much better use for you.' He squinted past me again. 'I keep thinking there's something - '

Salic growled, irritated, his chest vibrating against my back. 'You always got to wind me up, don't you?' he said to Gish. 'The charm gave the all-clear. Even I could see.'

Tearing twigs and leaves sounded from behind me and I heard a grunt. Something solid and heavy dropped to the floor, brushed my ankle. I glanced down, more puzzled than alarmed. And shrieked. Under the momentum of its fall, Salic's head continued rolling, blood dribbling from the severed neck. The grisly object came to rest under the hem of dark leaves surrounding the clearing. I flinched, sensing wind and a dark blur move smoothly past my left shoulder. The arms around my waist had already gone slack. Salic's corpse went limp and toppled backwards. Its feet slid from under it, slamming into my heels, knocking me aside.

Gish had grabbed my wrist. He yanked me towards him, and gathered me up ready to flee, then paused, frowning. I registered his look of agonised horror a moment before I saw the bloody sword-tip protruding from his torso. The blade had entered his back, travelled through him until its point burst clear of his chest. The lethal tip had halted inches from my throat.

I lifted my eyes to the dying man's face, saw his lips were trembling, his eyes wide with disbelief.

'We was just trying to save you,' he said, his teeth coated in blood. 'The Flower Maiden is created to be—'

The blade twisted inside him as its owner turned the hilt and the light in Gish's eyes died. The man's body collapsed and I stumbled back, toppled over Salic's leg where it lay behind me. The ground hit me, knocked my breath away. Horrified, I scrambled backwards, away from the black figures closing in, until I was pressing hard against a moss-covered tree-trunk with nowhere left to go.